Friday 10 May [illegible] a devastating attack that within days will overrun France, Holland and Belgium, and bring Britain to its knees at Dunkirk. It is also the day Winston Churchill becomes Prime Minister. He is the one man capable of standing in Hitler's way—yet Churchill is still deeply mistrusted within his own Cabinet and haunted by the memory of his tortured father. *Never Surrender* is a novel about the courage and defiance that were displayed in abundance—not just by Churchill, but by ordinary men and women over three of the most momentous weeks in British history. At the end, Hitler stood at the gates of Paris and was master of all he surveyed. But Churchill had already broken him on the most crucial battlefield of all, the battlefield of the mind.

# NEVER SURRENDER

Michael Dobbs

WINDSOR
PARAGON

First published 2003
by
HarperCollins *Publishers*
This Large Print edition published 2004
by
BBC Audiobooks Ltd by arrangement with
HarperCollins *Publishers* Ltd.

ISBN 1 4056 1011 5 (Windsor Hardcover)
ISBN 1 4056 2007 2 (Paragon Softcover)



This is a work of fiction. Apart from well-known historical figures and events, the names, characters and incidents portrayed in it are the work of the author's imagination. Any resemblance to actual persons, living or dead, events or localities is entirely coincidental.



**British Library Cataloguing in Publication Data available**

Printed and bound in Great Britain by
Antony Rowe Ltd., Chippenham, Wiltshire

FOR RACHEL.

*Winston Churchill's literary life was extraordinary. It encompassed histories, biographies, his own memoirs, speeches, many hundreds of articles, short stories and even a novel. In 1956 he was awarded the Nobel Prize for Literature. Yet amongst all this prodigious outpouring, one of the most inspiring pieces is also one of the least known—a private article he wrote for his family and which wasn't published until after his death. It is entitled 'The Dream'.*

*It concerns a conversation with his father's ghost, which he conducted while copying an oil portrait of his father that had been damaged.*

# PROLOGUE

*Ascot, 1883.*

The boy was small, only eight, the youngest in the school. Red-haired, blue-eyed, round in face, and nervous. He had been at the school only a term and was not popular. One of the older pupils had written home that this new boy was 'irksome'; the headmaster already found him intolerable. 'A constant trouble to everybody and is always in some scrape or other,' the headmaster wrote to his parents. 'He cannot be trusted to behave himself anywhere.'

The boy didn't fit in. And he was about to discover that failing to conform carried with it a heavy price, even for an eight-year-old.

St George's School was a private educational establishment of four teachers and forty pupils, set in woodlands that had once been the ancient hunting forests of Windsor. It couldn't claim much of a tradition since it was only six years old, so it sought to make up for that by charging outrageously high fees. It made the place instantly exclusive. Perhaps that was why the boy's father, a man habitually committed to over-extending himself, had found the place so attractive. Anyway, it was time for his son to move on; up to that point he'd been educated by private tutors and seemed ill at ease amongst other boys—he'd developed both a nervous stammer and foul temper. But that, as his father had written to the headmaster, was what he had been sent to St George's to cure.

He was almost a year younger than any of the

others, but within days of his arrival, perhaps seeking the approval of the older boys, he had leapt onto a desk and begun to recite a bawdy song he'd learnt from some of his grandfather's stable lads. Only his recent arrival saved him from a punishment harsher than being sent to bed without his supper.

Yet the boy carried with him his own sense of justice, and the following day he felt not only hungry but also poorly treated. After all, St George's was one of the most expensive schools in the country: he felt sure his father hadn't sent him here to starve. So, in order to balance the scales of elementary justice, he had sneaked into the basement kitchens and stolen a pocketful of sugar. Inevitably he'd left considerable evidence of his crime spilled upon the counter, so the kitchen staff had reported the loss to the headmaster, the Reverend Herbert William Sneyd-Kynnersley.

'Mr K', as he was known to the pupils, was tall, almost gangling, mutton-chopped and sandy-haired, a graduate of Cambridge with very distinctive ideas about education. To some he was a man of impeccable standards and something of a reformer, a schoolmaster who liked nothing more than to join in with his pupils while they swam naked in the pond or pursued him on a paper chase through woodlands they called the Wilderness. For others, however, he was nothing less than a ruthless brute, who punished pupils so savagely that he would not stop beating them until they bled. It was also remarked upon that, for some reason no one either could or wished to explain, Mr K seemed to pay particular attention to those with hair of a colour even more red than his own. His childless and overwrought wife had red hair, and pupils with similar colouring seemed to be summoned frequently to the headmaster's study. The young boy had been dubbed 'the red dwarf' the day he arrived, and he seemed to spend more time in the study than most.

For Kynnersley, chivalry, posture and truthfulness were the highest virtues attributable to an English gentleman. The boy's relationship to these virtues was, in Mr K's opinion, 'like a rainbow in the night'. His habits and language belonged more to the stable yard than the schoolyard, he disliked sports, was constantly late, had few friends and was rebellious with the teachers. There seemed no one in any part of the school who seemed capable of exerting a positive influence on him, with the possible exception, it was noticed, of the gardener. He was a child doomed to failure.

There was also the matter of the stolen sugar. When, at morning assembly, the miscreant was instructed to do his duty and to own up, the entire school had remained silent. But Kynnersley knew there would be tell-tale traces, and there were. In the boy's pockets. Both of them. In such circumstances, the Reverend Kynnersley found his duty clear.

The boy stood in the entrance hall outside the headmaster's study and considered what lay ahead. He knew of the punishments, had heard the cries of others even as he sat at his desk, had seen the welts at bedtime and knew of the desperate sobbing beneath the covers from boys much older than he. Now it was his turn.

He gazed at the clock, ticking so slowly, then up

at the leering faces of the stuffed fox heads on the wall. He paced quietly in an attempt to compose himself, then fiddled with the ornate carvings of the mock Tudor fireplace, trying to find something for his fingers to do other than to tremble. On one side of the mantel stood the figure of a husband, on the other side stood his wife, separated by the fire. Just like home.

Suddenly the door to the study opened. Towering in it stood the headmaster. The boy wanted to run, every ounce of common sense screamed at him to flee. He strode forward.

The study was not large. It was dominated by two French windows that looked out onto the lawn and to the woodlands of the Wilderness beyond. Near the fireplace was a wooden block. It was upon this block that the Reverend Kynnersley had sat and toasted teacakes for Churchill's mother when she had first brought him to this place. Neither of his parents had been back since.

On the back of the door hung a straw boater. It was a favourite item of the headmaster, one he wore throughout the summer and would raise in greeting to all visitors. Beneath the boater, hanging from the same hook, was a length of hazel cane. That, too, judging by the splayed end, had been raised with equal frequency.

The boy was ordered to take down his trousers and underwear, and to raise his shirt. He did as he was told. The Reverend Kynnersley, cane in hand, adjusted his gold-framed spectacles.

'You're a thief, and you will have your nasty little habits beaten out of you. Do you have anything to say?'

What was there to say? Sorry wouldn't save him,

and anyway he didn't feel in the least sorry. Only scared. And thankful that they hadn't noticed the apple he had stolen at the same time.

Kynnersley nodded towards the wooden block. The beating block. It was whispered about between the boys, and no one ever came back bragging. The boy shuffled forward, his trousers around his ankles, like a prisoner in chains.

Eight is such a tender age to deal with adversity, but perhaps lessons learned so young are those that endure. Certainly the Reverend Kynnersley thought so, which is why he persisted in trying to flog the qualities of an English gentleman into his pupils. Break them while they are young, the younger the better, and rebuild them in a better mould. It's what had made an empire.

The boy's thoughts didn't reach so elevated a plane. He was putting all his concentration into controlling his bladder and denying the flood of tears that demanded to burst forth. He knew he would cry, and scream, as they all did, but not yet. Sunlight flooded in through the French windows and he struggled to look out at the woods beyond, trying to imagine himself romping through the Wilderness, a million miles from this block.

Suddenly, he thought he saw a shadow at the window, a silhouette that looked remarkably like his father. But it couldn't be, his father had never come to the school, not once. He was always at a distance, somehow untouchable, elevated. The boy adored his father—no, worshipped him rather than adored, as one might worship a god. And feared him, too. Yet the greater the distance that stood between him and his father, the more eager he grew to bridge it. The less he knew about his father, the more the son invested him with almost heroic powers; the less he heard from his father, the more ferociously the young boy clung to his every word.

Never cry, never complain, his father had instructed, for they will only take advantage of your weakness.

So throughout that thrashing, he refused either to cry or to complain. The only sound to be heard was the swishing of the hazel branch, which fell with ever greater force as Kynnersley insisted that the boy submit. Again, and again. But the boy's fear of Kynnersley was as nothing compared to the fear and adulation he felt for his own father, standing there in the doorway. And when the pain became extreme, unbearable, he cried out for his father, but only inside.

They had to get two of the older boys to help him back to his room.

'You are a thief,' Kynnersley shouted after him from the doorway of his study, struggling to smooth the creases in his self-control. 'You'll never come to any good. You hear me? Never!'

Once alone, Winston Churchill sobbed into his pillow until there were no more tears left to shed. In later years he would cry many times, but never in fear.

* * *

Some days later, Churchill slipped away from the swimming pond where Kynnersley and the other boys were cavorting. He ran quickly back to the school buildings, being careful not to leave any trace of wet footprints on the polished floor. He tried the door to the headmaster's study, but it was locked, so he slipped out to the garden and rattled the French windows. They were also locked, but loose. A twig thrust between the doors enabled him to slip the catch.

It was the work of only moments to snatch the beloved straw boater from its place upon the door, and it became the pleasure of an endless afternoon, alone in the Wilderness, to kick it to a thousand pieces.

# CHAPTER ONE

*Flanders, 1940.*
In Private Donald Chichester's view, the war in France had been little short of sublime. Month after endless month of—well, nothing. No shelling, no air attacks, scarcely a shot fired in anger since they'd arrived the previous September. *La drôle de guerre*, as the locals called it. No war at all.

That suited Donald Chichester. He was not yet twenty, with dark hair and deep-set, earnest eyes that seemed to be in constant search of something he had lost. He was tall, well sculpted, but on the lean side, like a plant that had been forced to grow too quickly. There was an air of vulnerability about him that set him apart from the other men who had gone to war brimming with extravagant if superficial claims of confidence. Yet he was always bound to be set apart from the others, for he wasn't any proper sort of soldier.

Don Chichester was a nursing orderly serving with the 6th Field Ambulance Unit. Woman's work, as the fighting men suggested, a soldier who had taken up bucket and mop rather than arms, who made other men's beds and who cleaned up after the sick. There were many ways to fight this war, but being a nursing orderly wasn't any of them.

He had arrived in France eight months earlier after a crossing from Southampton to Cherbourg that had been a misery. He'd reacted badly to the typhus and typhoid vaccinations, which had made his arm swell like a bloated pig and given him a raging temperature, but there had been no point in complaining. Sympathy was as short in supply as everything else. The 6th had arrived in France with old equipment and slack-geared vehicles, only to discover that their food supplies, spares and half their officers had been sent to an entirely different destination. The confusion of disembarkation had grown worse when the only new ambulance the unit possessed was hoisted on a rope cradle from the deck of the transport ship and swivelled over the side of the dock. As Don watched helplessly, the cradle had begun to unravel like a Christmas pullover, sending the ambulance thumping to earth. It bounced almost a foot in the air, then promptly collapsed into every one of its component parts.

The fate of the ambulance had reminded Don of the last time he had seen his father. Their last row. Not too many words, they'd never gone in for words much, only periods of cold silence that seemed to say it all. His father had been standing in front of the old Victorian fireplace, beside the photograph of Don's mother, the mother he had never known. But how he had grown into her looks, and more so with every passing year until there was no mistaking the resemblance. The only attributes he seemed to have inherited from his father were a stubborn chin and an ability to harbour silent fury.

They lived in his father's vicarage—a house of peace and goodwill, according to the tapestry on the wall, but not on that day. Don had tried to explain himself yet again, but the father wouldn't listen. He never had. He was a bloody vicar, for pity's sake, he preached eternity to the entire world, yet never seemed to have any time left for his only son. Perhaps it would have been different if there had been a mother to rise between them, but instead they were like strands of badly knotted rope that twisted ever tighter. The Reverend Chichester had stood in front of the fireplace shaking with anger—the only emotion Don could ever remember him displaying—and called him Absalom.

The son who betrayed his father.

Then he had used that one final word.

Coward.

Any further exchange seemed superfluous.

So Donald Chichester had gone off to be trained for his war, watching at a distance as the others wrote letters to their loved ones or bargained feverishly for two-day passes home. When the training was over and their war was about to begin, they had hung despairingly out of the windows of their embarkation train until distance and smoke had finally smothered all sight of the families they were leaving behind. Through it all, Don sat back, gently mocking the overflowing affection, and twisting deep inside.

The 6th had left England in emotion and arrived at Cherbourg in chaos. They had then driven to their billet three hundred miles away in Flines-les-Râches on the Belgian border. It was raining. The British Expeditionary Force had arrived.

It continued to rain. In fact, the weather proved to be abominable, the autumn one of the wettest on record followed by a winter where the snow lay thick and everything froze solid, including the radiator in every ambulance. But so long as German radiators froze too, Don was happy. Even when they attempted to dig sanitation pits and



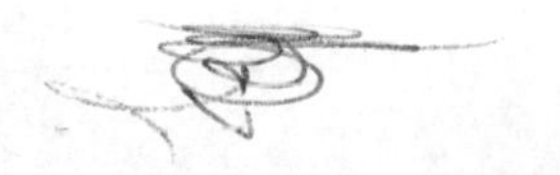

discovered that the water table lay beneath their feet, turning their main dressing station into a quagmire, Don was content. The war was worthless, and every step he took in the fetid mud served only to confirm it.

The conditions caused disease, of course. All drinking water had to be treated with sterilizing powder, a process which usually left the water tasting so disgusting that many Tommies decided to drink the foul French water instead, with predictable results. There were many other ailments. Training accidents. Traffic accidents. Afflictions of the feet. Bronchial troubles brought on by the fact that most of the soldiers had only one uniform, which had to be dried out while being worn. And venereal disease, as the British soldiers grew tired of their phoney war and succumbed in ever-growing numbers to boredom, drink and the local doxies. The follies of Flanders. Just like their fathers before them.

As the dismal months of phoney war stumbled on, there was an ever-increasing number of men who complained about the uselessness of it all, how it was a mindless war and not worth fighting. Wrong place, wrong time, and an awful bloody idea. Just what Don had argued.

That was, until the early hours of 10 May. Things changed. Dawn broke through a cloudless sky, and breakfast at the field dressing station where Don was posted found the officers squinting into the rising sun. They were muttering about reports of air activity. A church bell began ringing insistently in the distance. Something was up.

A sense of anticipation crept amongst those around him, a nervous excitement he was unable to share. The distance he had always known stood between him and the other soldiers once more began to assert itself.

'There's going to be a shooting war after all, Chichester,' the sergeant snapped. 'Not that you bloody care.'

An hour later, the sergeant was back with new orders. They were moving out. Two hours' time. Into Belgium. Problem was, none of their training had had anything to do with Belgium. They'd been preparing themselves for a war just like the last one, a steady, solid, stay-where-you-were war. A war fought from behind those tank trenches and pillboxes they'd spent their months in France building. They hadn't even been allowed to recce inside Belgium, it was off limits to everyone, they'd been told, and particularly the Germans.

So it was with renewed confusion that the unit prepared to get under way. Don packed the surgical kit, checked his medical bag, counted the field dressings and knocked down the casualty tents until he thought he was ready, but then he was instructed to help load additional supplies from the officers' quarters into one of the ambulances. A desk, several filing cabinets, a typewriter, a small library of Michelin guides, two tea chests of crockery, a fishing rod, a case of sherry, three new uniforms and a pair of highly polished dancing shoes: all were piled on board. Only then did Private 14417977 Donald Chichester, Nursing Orderly Grade 3 and noncombatant Conscientious Objector, drive off to war.

* * *

The three men gathered at the tall window to mourn, their cheeks fired by the setting sun as they sipped at glasses of champagne. The wine was warm. It always was in the Foreign Office.

'A day for our diaries, eh?' suggested the Minister in whose elegant office they had gathered.

'The darkest day in English history,' the second man suggested, practising a line for the entry he would make that night. Henry Channon was known by all as 'Chips'. He was the Minister's parliamentary aide, an envied and potentially influential position, but it would be for his keen-eyed diaries rather than for his notoriously blunted political wits that his reputation would endure.

'Will any of us survive?' the third and youngest of the companions enquired. 'Jock' Colville was only twenty-five yet for seven months had been a private secretary to the Prime Minister, Neville Chamberlain. It had given him a ringside seat at the bonfire of hopes, conceits and monstrous complacencies that a few hours earlier had finally consumed his master. Chamberlain was no more, his resignation handed to a reluctant monarch, and now many more sacrifices would be required.

'Has it come to that? A struggle to survive? Oh, I do so love being part of all this. I should miss it so,' Chips muttered wistfully.

'I was rather thinking of the war,' Colville countered.

'Ah, but we seem destined to fight on so many fronts,' the Minister added, his eyes wandering northward across the gravel stretches of Horse Guards Parade to the white sandstone of the Admiralty building beyond. 'Rab' Butler was the second most senior Minister in the Foreign Office, a man of considerable intellectual powers whose career had embraced both ambition and Neville Chamberlain. He was talked about as a future leader. Inevitably it made him enemies, and perhaps the most significant of all his enemies was the man across the way in the Admiralty—a man who, less than an hour ago, had taken the King's commission to become the new Prime Minister.

'They say he cannot last. That he will soon be gone. Even that Neville may be back,' Channon suggested.

'To save us all from disaster,' Butler intoned.

'From the Luftwaffe.'

'From Mr Churchill,' Butler corrected.

'Such a vulgar man,' Channon muttered, replenishing their glasses.

Butler's lips drooped in distaste. He had extraordinary lips, weak, as though constructed of wax that had strayed too near the flame and been melted. His eyes also drooped. It gave him an air of ingrained disapproval.

'But Churchill's a man with experience of war,' Colville reminded them.

'There is nothing to be gained either from war or from Winston Churchill,' the Minister all but spat. 'The fate of our country has been placed in the hands of the greatest political adventurer of modern times. A half-breed American whose entire life has been littered with failures for which other people have paid.'

'And now poor Neville.'

A pause.

'What will you do, Jock?' Channon asked the younger man.

'I think I might apply for a transfer to the armed

services. The RAF, perhaps.' He seemed unaware of his implied rebuke to Butler. If war was not an answer, what was to be the point of fighting it? But the Minister had more advice to offer.

'No. Wait, Jock. Don't draw stumps just yet. This game isn't over. Let Winston have his day dabbling at war. And when he falters, and then fails, as he always has, the country will need men like us. More than ever.'

'And after Winston?'

'Pray that it will be an Englishman. Perhaps Neville once more. And if not him, then Halifax. But better Neville.'

The sun was almost set, its embers sprinkled wide across the spires and cupolas around them. The end of more than just another day. Chips raised his glass.

'Then, to the King over the Water.'

'To Neville,' Butler agreed.

'And may God send us victorious,' Colville whispered, finishing the last of his warm champagne.

* * *

'So how was he?'

Winston Churchill looked up from the letter he was writing to inspect the man who had just burst in upon him. A pall of cigar smoke hovered across the room in the Admiralty.

'His Majesty was as ever charming. A little awkward, perhaps. Dressed in his uniform as Admiral of the Fleet.'

Unbidden, his visitor helped himself to a large whisky from the tray that sat beside the Prime

Minister. The splash of soda was brief, no more than a gesture.

'You know,' Churchill continued, 'I do believe His Majesty would willingly give up all the splendours and circumstances of his role in order to return to the duties of his career in the navy.'

'He's out of his depth.'

'No, I think more out of his experience,' Churchill growled. 'Rather like us all at this moment.' He thrust his own empty glass in the direction of his visitor, silently demanding it be refilled. As on almost every occasion in the seventeen years since they had met, Brendan Bracken complied with his older friend's wishes. Bracken was a man often derided as an outrageous fantasist by those who knew him slightly, and no one could claim to know him well, not even Churchill. But for all his faults and legendary confrontations with the truth, he had remained loyal to Churchill when more respectable political colleagues had deserted him. All his life Churchill had been a man of few friends, and this friend he valued more than most.

'Still, must have been awkward for you. For both of you, given the past,' Bracken continued.

Ah, the past . . . Churchill wanted to believe that all his past life had been but a preparation for the trial that lay ahead, yet in truth it had been a lifetime of uneasy adventures thrown together with outright failures. During the last war, for instance, he had been hurled from office—not simply resigned as his father had done before him, but thrown out by those who thought him inadequate for the job. Many of them had still not changed their minds, the King included. No, it wasn't success that had brought him here, only the still more monumental failures of others. Churchill looked up once more from his blotter. 'He covered it with a little joke. Asked me if I knew why he had summoned me. I replied that I simply couldn't imagine. So he offered me a cigar and asked me to form a government. Of which, I suppose, you expect to be a member. Along with many others.'

'The joy of it!' Bracken threw his arms around in excitement. 'After all these years, the chance to even the score. To do unto others . . .' He clapped his hands. 'You know, I've just been over to Downing Street. Thought I'd take a look. Went by the back gate into the secretaries' rooms. Rushing around bundling everything into sacks and waste-paper baskets, they were, even had a fire roaring in one of the grates. Several in tears. It was as though the enemy had arrived.'

'You don't understand, Brendan: in their eyes, he has.'

Bracken lit himself a cigar using a petrol lighter that threw an immense flame, adding to the aerial confusion. 'So—who is to be in this government of ours?'

'My War Cabinet,' Churchill responded, 'will consist of four men, apart from myself.' He cleared his throat as if making an official proclamation. 'There will be Mr Attlee and Mr Greenwood from the Labour Party.'

Bracken shifted uneasily in his chair.

'Lord Halifax.'

An eyebrow arched in disapproval.

'And Mr Neville Chamberlain.'

Bracken gasped, momentarily brought to silence. 'You cannot be serious.'

'In most deadly earnest. Our lives may depend upon it.'

'But . . .' Suddenly the energy was upon him once more, his body contorting in exasperation. 'They're the four most bloody-minded men in the country. Two socialists with whom you've got nothing in common, the former Prime Minister who's devoted most of his limited talents to keeping you at the outer edge of the universe, and . . .' He wondered for a moment how best to sum up Edward Halifax, Churchill's chief rival for the post. 'And an Old Etonian.'

'You're right.' Churchill smiled. Throughout all the years of drought Bracken had had an unquenchable talent for making him smile. 'You are absolutely right. We need more Harrovians.'

'Seriously, Winston, how can you include Chamberlain after everything that's happened?'

'Can't you see, Brendan, it's because of everything that has happened that I must embrace him? He is still the leader of the majority party in the House of Commons, and if I am to build a truly national government I must include him as well as the socialists.' He picked up his pen and resumed his work. 'That is what I have had to insist to Mr Attlee, who, I'm afraid, rather shares your opinion about Mr Chamberlain.'

'But you've nothing in common with any of them.'

'I can count on the claws of a chicken's foot the number of men you and I can trust. It's not enough. We need more.' He finished off the letter with a flourish. 'Which is why I have just written to the Kaiser enquiring whether, before the Wehrmacht arrives, he would wish to exchange his exile in

Holland for a suitable small establishment in this country.'

Bracken choked on his drink, spluttering, when at last he could, 'You expect the old Kaiser, the man who started the last bloody war, to help you in this one?'

'No, I don't expect that. But I would like it. I know him, of course. Attended manoeuvres with him in 1909. An odious and ill-formed man. But useful. If by any chance he would agree, oh, how it would distract Hitler. Take his eye off the ball. Kaiser versus the Fuehrer, German against German.' He sealed the envelope he had been addressing and rang a hand bell. 'I would do a deal with the Devil if only he would part company with Hitler for a moment. We do so desperately need some distraction. We have enemies enough without creating more. Which is why we must have Neville, and Edward Halifax, too. And all the rest.'

He rang the bell again, more impatiently.

'And for me?'

'For you, Brendan? Minister of Information, I thought. My own private Goebbels. Waging war with words. You're good at that. And we have so little else with which to wage war.'

'Thank you, Winston. With all my heart. But—no. I think I should be here, by your side. At least until you have the show up and running.'

'You would refuse your own ministry?'

'There are so few who know you, understand your ways.'

Suddenly Churchill rose to his feet and flung open the door behind his desk. It led to a corridor, and at its end, deep in conversation, stood two male secretaries. Churchill's shoulders heaved in irritation.

'Have you both been deafened by the blast of some enemy bomb?' he shouted at them. 'Can there be any other reason why you have failed to respond to my bell?'

Bemused, they looked towards him and started to approach.

'Fly! Fly! Or shall I call the guard to encourage you at the point of a fixed bayonet?'

The first man broke into a hurried shuffle; the second, seeking salvation, ducked into an open office door. It was Colville who arrived, his face a cauldron of embarrassment and anger.

'I'm sorry, Prime Minister. A little confusion in responsibilities. We were rather expecting you to arrive at Downing Street this evening.'

'Downing Street is still the home of Mr Chamberlain. I have offered it to him and Mrs Chamberlain until they can make suitable alternative arrangements. In the meantime you are to attend upon me here.'

'I'm sorry, sir. As I said, a matter of confusion.'

'And you are to run, do you hear me? Every time you hear that bell, you run, not walk, for so long as this war is in progress. I will not have walkers.'

Colville swallowed, his mouth suddenly dry with resentment. Never in his public service had he been spoken to like this. Still, it made his decision all the easier. He wouldn't put up with it for a moment longer than would be necessary to get himself a transfer. Submarines, for all he cared, after this.

'Tell me, where did you go to school?' Churchill demanded.

What? What had his wretched school to do with it? 'Why, Harrow, sir. But a while after you.'

'Ah, another Harrovian. We make good runners at Harrow. You'll do.'

And so, through the accident of his education, Colville stood condemned.

'Now, get me Lord Halifax on the phone. I have an urgent letter for him to deliver.'

'It's gone midnight. His Lordship will be asleep in bed, I'm afraid, sir.'

'You know that for a fact?'

'I know His Lordship, sir.'

'Nevertheless, get him on the phone for me.'

'It will be a most exceptional pleasure for him,' Colville responded, tripping over his own sarcasm.

Churchill thrust his head forward. It made him look like a cannonball in flight. 'No, it will not be a pleasure for him at this hour. And in future it will not be exceptional, either. Pray inform His Lordship of that, and anyone else that matters.'

Without another word, Churchill went back to his work and began writing a fresh letter. Colville, his face ashen, backed slowly out of the door.

Bracken hooked his leg over the arm of his chair and began to chuckle. 'As I said, Winston, there are so few who understand your ways. I think I'd better stay.'

Churchill's head fell towards the notepaper. 'Thank God there's one person in this room who knows what to do.'

* * *

It had been like a triumphal progress from ancient times. Slowly the British army moved forward across the frontier into what, until that morning, had been the green fields and gentle canals of neutral Belgium. At every village and crossroads they were greeted like heroes. Old men shuffled forward in carpet slippers to offer them bottles of beer, with womenfolk at their side bearing baskets of cheeses and oranges, and daughters who climbed up on the vehicles with their snatches of schoolgirl English to hand out an abundance of flowers and kisses. The BEF advanced upon the enemy with lilac on their helmets and dictionaries in their pockets, and soon the songs of old could be heard encouraging them on their way—'Tipperary', 'Pack Up Your Troubles', and a new one, a tune about how they were going to hang out their washing on the Siegfried Line.

The column was closely packed, a confusion of every sort of vehicle grinding along at the pace of the slowest, but they were all heading in the same direction. North, towards the enemy. Belgian bicycle troops meandered beside the convoy, frantically ringing their bells. It was spring, hawthorn blossom blew across their path, and the British army sweated gently in the sun.

By early evening they had passed through Brussels and were making camp in an old deserted brewery outside Mechelen. They unloaded the chairs, filing cabinets and the bottles of sherry while tea was brewed. This site was to be the Casualty Clearing Station, for the time when there were casualties. But of the enemy there was no sign. Perhaps this one was going to be easy, after all.

In the evening, the padre came round with a billycan of corned-beef stew accompanied by cigarettes and a homily about the morality of their cause. Strange, Don thought, how morality had become such a moveable feast. Why, it was less than two years ago when vicars throughout the land had climbed into their pulpits to denounce aggression and offer prayers for the triumph of appeasement and Neville Chamberlain. Yet today, from those same pulpits and plundering phrases from the same scriptures, they prayed to the Almighty that they might remember their gas masks and gain rapid victory. Whichever way you read it, kneeling down or standing on your head, it simply made you giddy.

That's not what he had explained to the Tribunal for the Registration of Conscientious Objectors, of course. For them he had displayed a morality that was clear, principled and utterly inflexible—he'd copied that much from his father. And it was his father's God-fearing morality that he offered them, everything taken from the Book, every argument backed up by scripture and psalm. They quoted the Book back at him, all the bits about eyes for eyes and the righteousness of vengeance, but he'd spent so much more time in church and Bible classes than they had that putting down their counter-case had proved to be, quite literally, child's play.

It troubled him that he couldn't be entirely honest with the Tribunal. He would have liked to tell them that reasons why the world shouldn't set out to slaughter itself were so bloody obvious you didn't need the Bible, but that wasn't the way the Tribunal game was played.

Don had played, and he had won. Noncombatant service. No weapons, no killing. But it troubled him more than he cared to admit that he had won only by leaning on his father's beliefs, and that his father knew it. There was a little of

Absalom in everyone.

As he tossed in distraction upon the floor of the abandoned brewery, other thoughts began to chisel away at his sense of well-being. If God moved in mysterious ways, so, it seemed, did the generals. The men of the British Expeditionary Force had spent half a year working flat out to build a defensive line of tank traps and pillboxes. They'd been assured it would be all but impregnable.

So why, at the first sign of trouble, had the generals ordered them to come out from behind its cover and move forward into a field of fire that was totally unprepared?

And let's not turn our back on good fortune but why, during all that long first day of advance, had there been no sign of the enemy? There hadn't been a single air attack.

As Don struggled to find some comfort on the cold concrete, one thought kept nagging at him. It was almost as though the Germans wanted them there.

* * *

At last Churchill was alone. Letters written, appointments made, officials dismissed, Bracken on his way home. The path begun.

He felt exhausted. Keeping up the spirits of others had sapped his own, and a mood of darkness clung around him. It had been a day he had dreamed of for so long, yet the reality had proved so very distant from the dream. There had been no cheering crowds at the Palace to greet him, not even curious onlookers, no one but soldiers in war garb who had stood in front of a palace that had retreated behind sandbags and shuttered windows. Then the King's little flash of humour to cover his unease. Faces long, brimming with concerns. No victorious arrival at Downing Street. Only Bracken to lift the gloom.

How he had longed for this day! A Churchill as His Majesty's First Minister, his destiny achieved, his father's memory vindicated. Yet all around he found nothing but sorrows and unspoken fear. Instead of triumph, he had found his way into a tragedy.

He sat slumped in his chair, an old man, clutching his glass of whisky in both hands as if he were afraid it might fall. No one there to see him, to help guide him through the depression that emerged like a mist from a swamp to surround him. He had such a way with words, brave and magnificent outbursts that stirred hearts, but words were for others, while he was left with nothing but his own dark thoughts.

These thoughts carried him to the oil painting that hung in a corner near the bookcase. It was a portrait of his father—not a particularly magnificent piece, one that had been painted long ago in Belfast. It showed Lord Randolph small and slim, with delicate ears and a twirling moustache, his neck surrounded with a huge moleskin collar and a polka-dot bow-tie that Winston himself had adopted. The painting followed the son everywhere, almost haunting him, for it had been completed in 1886, the year of his father's brief triumph, which had turned so quickly to endless disaster. Lord Randolph was a rising star, one of the most powerful men in the country—some said *the* most powerful, and he believed it. He had quit the Government in the expectation of being recalled with ever greater honours, only to find his resignation greeted with ridicule. His reputation had crumbled. So had his mind, relentlessly. Winston had been still a schoolboy, not yet twelve. So long ago, yet the pain still so fresh.

He stared at the portrait. What had his father been thinking when it was painted? Had those bright protruding eyes been able to see any of the misery that lay so close ahead? Had he felt any symptoms—had he guessed in any way that he had already set out upon a path that would lead to a slow and wretched death?

No, he could not have known. No man ever knew what lay ahead.

Tiredness gnawed away at the old man and his head sank towards the glass, still clutched tightly in his two hands. Yet as the head fell forward he was once more jerked awake. He opened his eyes to find himself staring at his father. Lord Randolph was sitting in the chair opposite—not an oil painting, not an hallucination, but body and blood, so far as Winston could tell. It wasn't possible, of course, but . . .

'Papa?'

'What are you doing, Winston? Where are we?'

'In my office. At the Admiralty.'

'So, you've become a clerk in the navy, have you?'

'I followed you, Papa. Into politics.'

'Brutal game. Surprised you had the stomach for it. You were such a weakly child, always sickening for something.'

'Politics have been my life. I entered Parliament at the same age as you, Papa. Twenty-five.'

'Ah, all those years, but to what end?' The father managed to sound both envious and dismissive. He began filling his amber cigarette-holder with a little pad of cotton wool to soak up the nicotine. The process seemed to absorb him, to the annoyance of his son. Instinctively the son decided not to reveal all of his hand, to keep something in reserve.

'I have been Home Secretary and, as you were, Chancellor of the Exchequer. For five years.'

The father, who had been Chancellor for a mere five months, seemed not to hear, his attention focused on the search for a match from deep within his pockets.

'I used your old robes, Papa, the ones you wore.'

Randolph scowled impatiently as his search continued fruitlessly.

'And until this morning I was First Lord of the Admiralty,' the son added.

'Under whose authority? Who as Prime Minister?'

'Neville Chamberlain—Joe's younger son.'

'What? A Chamberlain as Prime Minister?' The eyes of the father bulged in displeasure. 'Praise be that I never lived to see the day. Nothing but ironmongers. Why, in my day you could buy a dozen Chamberlains for a single Churchill and still get change.' He stared at Winston as though he were directly responsible for the devaluation of the currency. 'So how did this young Chamberlain do?'

'Not well.' The son chose the words with care, speaking them slowly. 'We are engaged in a horrible war with Germany, Papa, for the second time in my life. With flying machines and other terrible weapons that slaughter millions of men.'

'Millions, you say?'

'Tens of millions.'

'My God, is it possible? Then I'm glad not to have lived to see such terrible days. But we will prevail, of course.'

Again the words were chosen with care. 'Not necessarily. We may not prevail. And if we don't, we shall lose not only our armies but also our empire, even our independence.'

'Takes my breath away to hear it. Not the place it once was, eh, our England? But something always turns up. Like fresh cavalry riding out of the afternoon sun.'

'The British cavalry hasn't charged in anger in more than forty years.'

The father shook his head in consternation. 'So, who is to lead us from the jaws of such adversity?'

'I hope it will be me, Papa.'

'You, Winston? My God, but you only just sneaked into Sandhurst by the skin of your breeches. And at the third attempt. With your school record I couldn't even consider you for a career in the law. You, of all people?' He tugged at his moustache in puzzlement. 'You are an admiral? Or a general?'

'No, Papa. But I was once a major in the Yeomanry.'

The father wrinkled his nose. 'You were always getting yourself into scrapes. Getting beyond yourself. Like that time you fell off the bridge in Dorset.'

'I didn't fall. I jumped, Papa. To evade capture by my friends. I jumped onto the higher branches of a tree, but they gave way.'

'Seem to remember you were in bed for months. And for what? It was a childish game, nothing more. No judgement, that's the thing.'

'There are those who would agree with you, I fear.'

'Always sickening in bed. Caused your mother no end of inconvenience.' The voice trailed away, diverted down a new, more gentle path. 'So . . . what of Mama?'

'She lived a long life.'

'There were . . . other men?'

(Did he truly want to hear? But he knew there would have been other men. There were always other men.) 'She married twice more.' The son pondered telling him that they had been young enough to be her sons, the last even younger than he. But somehow it didn't seem to matter any longer. 'Neither of them matched up to you, Papa.'

'Two, you say. Always a little careless with her men, your mama.' The voice now seemed strained; Winston put it down to his father's need for a smoke. He had still not lit his cigarette.

'But, in the end, loyal enough,' the father continued. 'Can't fault her loyalty, not through the last years, at least.'

The painful years of his father's decline came flooding back to the son, when his brain disease had got hold of him and he had died by fractions in public. Winston himself had died a little as he watched his father being led stumbling and incoherent from the Chamber. Decay of the brain, and of the character. The Churchill legacy.

'You have sons?'

'One. And three daughters.'

'Is he up to carrying the Churchill name?'

'A father should never give up hope for his son,' Winston responded. It was both reproach to his father and injunction to himself. His son had been named after the grandfather, Randolph, and had inherited so many of his characteristics. Rudeness, inconstancy, infidelity, lack of judgement—that's what they said about the younger Randolph, and they had said no less in the grandfather's time.

'And Jack? What of him?'

'My brother is happy. Married. A stockbroker.'

'A stock—' Randolph bit off the thought, but there was no hiding the disappointment. 'Went too soon, I did. Before my time. Always wanted more sons, but your mama . . . There was so much more still to do, to make the Churchill name stand out above the crowd. So, you have a role to play in this war.'

'I was with the King this evening.'

'Which King is that?'

'George. The Sixth.'

'What? Two more Georges?'

'And two Edwards.'

'Hah! I knew the first, of course, royal rogue that he was. Once challenged me to a duel, he did. Couldn't accept, of course, not a contest with the Prince of Wales. A pickle over some damned woman. Can't remember her name.'

The name had been Edith, Countess of Aylesford, a woman to whom passion spoke more loudly than discretion. It had caused her to become entangled not only with the Prince of Wales but also with the Churchill family in an affair that grew into one of the most sensational *causes de scandale* of the time. It had pushed Randolph's legendary lack of judgement to new and intolerable extremes, and he threatened the heir to the throne with public exposure. As a result, Randolph and his young family had been condemned to exile in Ireland and many years of royal ostracism. Winston's first memories had been not of his beloved England, but of Dublin.

'In my life there was but one monarch, Victoria. It gave us all a sense of continuity, of stability. But four since then?' the father muttered in astonishment.

'In less than forty years. And scarcely any great kings left. No Habsburgs, no Romanovs, not even a Kaiser.'

The father's jaw sagged in disbelief.

'There has been war and revolution in every corner of Europe.'

'And in England?'

'We still live as a democracy.'

'Then there is hope,' the father concluded. 'I always said: "Trust the people." Built my reputation on it. It's only a democracy that can weather the storms of political fortune, link the past with the future.'

'Tempests have struck with remarkable ferocity since democracy took charge, Papa. We may yet be swept away.'

'But still a kingdom, you say? And you are friendly, are you, with the King?'

'No, not friends. In truth, I don't think he cares for me very much. I was too close to his elder brother, the second Edward. He abdicated.'

'Oh, misery. A realm in which kings abdicate and enemies prevail? My poor, wretched England . . .'

'Papa, these times are harder than any I have known. But perhaps you can help me.'

The sharp eyes bulged in alarm. 'What? Not money again, Winston? Always begging for money.'

If it were so, it was another trait inherited directly from the father, but there seemed little point in saying so.

'No, Papa, not money. Advice. I fear our country faces nothing but disaster for a very long time. What would you do, in such hard times?'

The father's head was raised again, his impatience washing away in satisfaction that the son had acknowledged the greater wisdom of the father. 'Well, only one thing for it, Winston. Know your enemies. I didn't, you see, underestimated them, and so . . . Know your enemy. In that way you will discover how to beat him. That's it, and all of it. So if you have the ear of the government . . .' He had at last discovered a match and bent his head to light it.

'Papa, I should tell you—'

But it was too late. As the match was struck there was a flash of considerable brilliance, and Lord Randolph was gone, the chair empty. The son was once more alone.

'Know mine enemies, Papa? But all I ever truly wanted to know was you . . .'

## CHAPTER TWO

Whit Sunday. The first Sunday of the real war.

The Reverend Henry Chichester climbed into the pulpit of his ancient parish church of St Ignatius-without-the-Walls, which stood above the port of Dover, and confronted pews that were crowded with parishioners. There was no denying it: war had been good for business. The flock grew larger with every passing month. What did it matter that these people had grabbed their gas masks and ration books before they'd given a thought to embracing religion, so long as they had ended up here?

*I will have mercy, and not sacrifice: for I am not come to call the righteous, but sinners to repentance . . .*

Time, he thought, was man's greatest enemy. Time passes, and time destroys. There was a time when he had been a young man brimming with self-belief and optimism, before the trenches of Flanders. There was, too, a later time when he had gathered the pieces of that lost happiness through his love for Jennie, yet God seemed unshakable in His plan that Henry Chichester's days were not to be spent in a state of contentment. Jennie had died giving birth, and had taken with her the last flakes of colour in his life. He had found many other things to fill the void—duty, obligation, ritual, the son—yet still it was a void. And it felt timeless, without end, a life surrounded by so many people, yet spent so much alone.

Behind his back they called him Bishop Brimstone in recognition of the strength of his faith. Henry Chichester was a good man, a strong and awe-inspiring preacher for these hard times, which is why they crowded into his pews, placed money upon the plate, filled the churchyard with flowers and left his surplice whiter than any summer cloud. All for faith. Yet none of the eager faces now raised in front of him could comprehend how, alongside his faith, sat failure. His life had been a litany of failure. He had failed in the trenches, simply by surviving. He had failed Jennie, too, by letting her die, and then failed as a father by letting Don go. He had even failed his God. The Reverend Chichester was not a wicked man but he knew he was a dishonest man, for while he preached duty as being the way to salvation he was aware that the only thing duty had delivered unto him these past years was unhappiness and a feeling that his soul had been placed on a bed of ice, where it had somehow become frozen, unable to move.

'Today—Whit Sunday—we celebrate a time of accomplishment,' he began from the pulpit. 'When men shall go forth and do great deeds.'

It wasn't the standard Whit Sunday sermon, but present circumstances called for something a little different. Many years ago his college principal had told him that while the Word may be eternal, a congregation's attention span never was, so Henry Chichester had developed a reputation for his vivid sermons. But how could he inspire others when his words had long ago ceased to inspire him? He raised his eyes heavenward, but all he saw was a large patch of damp above his head that was growing steadily worse in the salt-wind storms. The roof was long overdue for repair, but what was the point when the entire building might be blown away by a single bomb? Dear God, what was the point?

'The Whit Sunday story began a little while after Our Lord's ascension into heaven, when the Apostles had come together to celebrate the day of Pentecost. They were alone, uncertain, worried about what the future held in store for them. And as they assembled in their small room, from the sky came a noise like that of a whirlwind and they were surrounded on all sides by leaping tongues of fire.

Imagine that. Imagine how those men must have felt. In just a few weeks their Lord had been crucified, then resurrected, after which he had disappeared. And now this. Fire and chaos on all sides. Those poor Apostles must have been terrified.' He cast his arms wide to gather in all the concerns his congregation were wearing so openly. 'O Lord, how many of our young men in France must share that fear today.'

They wouldn't fall asleep today. Nowhere in the country was closer to the war than this place and not a family in the town could escape it. The town was the port, and the port was the highway to a battlefield that was being fought over for the third time in seventy years. Like it or not, it was Dover's war. All the newspapers carried large maps of Flanders, and the Reverend Chichester had cut out the map from *The Times* and pinned it on the noticeboard in the porch alongside the brass-cleaning roster. Something to help focus their prayers.

'Before his ascension Jesus had told the Apostles, "I leave behind with you—peace. I give you my own peace, but my gift is nothing like the peace of this world."' The vicar stared over his reading glasses and repeated the words for emphasis. '*Nothing like the peace of this world*. Our Lord knew that peace didn't come naturally to this world; his message was that it would have to be laboured for—yes, even fought for. He was telling us that the crusade for Christ might involve much hardship.'

Eyes gazed up at him, the majority female, anxious, all desperate for reassurance.

'And he told us this. In his own words, Jesus said:

"Let not your heart be troubled, neither let it be afraid." That's what he told the Apostles. And that is what he is telling us today.'

Mrs Parnell had seen him post up the map as she arrived for flower duty. There seemed to be more flowers this year than ever. Her eyes had brimmed as she saw what he was doing. 'My youngest, Harry,' she said, fighting her tears. 'Just got his call-up papers this morning.' She had made no complaint, simply grabbed her flowers and began cutting and arranging them with even more care than usual. It was only later he had found her sobbing in a rear pew. 'I know, I know'—she waved away his awkward attempt to comfort her—'he's got to do his bit. But as a mother it's so . . . well, you understand, of course. With your Donald.'

Reverend Chichester had smiled grimly and nodded. When his son had left, his parishioners assumed that he had gone off to fight like all the rest. It was an impression his father had done nothing to dispel. It wasn't a lie, not at first, but it had taken root and grown to the point where his silence screamed of falsehood. But what was he to do? Admit the truth and lose the respect of all the Mrs Parnells in his congregation, just at the time they needed him most?

Or lose his self-respect, by admitting that every time he looked at his son he was reminded of Jennie and everything he had lost, and acknowledging that, in spite of a lifetime of faith and duty, he still couldn't cope? He'd spent three years in a tunic constantly spattered with blood and he'd survived, yet inside he felt . . . a coward. Which is why the word had sprung so easily to his lips and been hurled at his only son.

'Our young men are like the Apostles,' he told them. 'Sent out to follow in the footsteps of Our Lord and to cleanse the world from sin. May the Holy Spirit be with them, too.'

A chorus of 'amens' rippled through the congregation. The sun shone through the south windows into the nave, filling the church with warmth and comfort. He hoped it was an omen.

'And let us take the words of Our Lord as our message today, when he said: "I am going away and I am coming back to you." *Coming back to you.* Jesus passed through many trials and tribulations, but he came back to us—as we pray with all our hearts that our loved ones shall. May the Holy Spirit be with them, to bring them courage in all they do and victory in their task. May the Lord comfort them, keep them in His care and deliver them from evil, for thine is the kingdom, the power and the glory . . .'

As he offered the sign of the cross and bade his flock to stand for the next hymn, his mind went back to the map on the board. He'd noticed there were no battle fronts or lines of trenches marked on it, not like last time, just the outline of a chunk of northern France and Belgium. But that was understandable, he decided. The Reverend Chichester, like so many others, concluded that the BEF was probably advancing too fast for the cartographers to keep up.

* * *

The morning had burst forth most gloriously, filled with birdsong and with the aroma of fresh spring grass still carried on the breeze. The clouds stood high and like gauze—an excellent day for cricket, Don thought, or some other game the Germans were no good at.

The old brewery in which the 6th had landed turned out to be rancid, full of pigeons and other pestilence. The task of transforming it into a Casualty Clearing Station was Herculean, and to be finished by the end of the day, they were instructed. They set about their labours with hoses and mops, encouraged by both the barks of their NCOs and the strengthening sun, while around them the local inhabitants carried on with their lives as they had always done: the milk was delivered, post collected, the children sent off to school as if war were no more than a distant rumour. And so it seemed. As the day drew on the men in Don's unit began to relax; there had still been no sign of the enemy. Perhaps Hitler had thought better of the whole idea.

The news was brought to them while they paused for their first brew of the afternoon.

'Right, then,' the sergeant announced. 'Pack it all up again. We're moving.'

'Where?'

'Back.'

'But, Sarge, I don't understand, we only just got here . . .'

'If you had been meant to understand, matey, God would have made you a general instead of a bleedin' nursing orderly. So let's just agree in this instance that the Almighty knows a half-sight more than you and jump to it. We move out. In an hour.'

'We haven't had a single casualty,' Don complained, bemused.

'And you'll be the first, Private, if you don't get

off your backside . . .'

A wasted day. Grand Old Duke of York stuff. Yet Don found consolation. The fresh orders suggested there was an alternative plan. They were moving back towards the defensive positions they'd spent so long constructing. That had to make sense, so Don told the others. Only problem was, it seemed to involve so many filing cabinets once again.

* * *

The two men met in the middle of the huge walled garden. One bowed, they shook hands.

'I must confess that I have been lying in wait for you, Edward.'

'Then it is my turn to confess, sir, and tell you that I fear I've been avoiding you.'

They walked on, casting long evening shadows on the lawn, taking in the false sweetness of that spring. They were the two most respected men in the country, yet both victims of their birth. One was King, the other the most influential of aristocrats, and between them they represented all the powers and privileges that had kept the kingdom undiminished for a thousand years. Now it might not see out the summer.

'Why have you been avoiding me, Edward?'

'Because I fear I have let you down.'

'Perhaps you have let yourself down.'

'I fear that, too.'

King George VI walked on in silence with Edward, the Third Viscount Halifax, at his side. The two men were far more than monarch and Foreign Minister. There was an intimacy between them, a deep friendship that extended far beyond their formal roles. They and their families dined together, went to the theatre together, sometimes prayed together, down on their knees, side by side, and Halifax had been given a key to the gardens of Buckingham Palace for his own private recreation. Two days earlier he'd also been given the opportunity of becoming Prime Minister, and only because of his own overwhelming reluctance had the office been handed to Winston Churchill. Now, as they walked, Halifax's tall, angular frame was bent low, like a penitent. A flight of ducks flew noisily above their heads, wheeling sharply in formation before crashing into the lake, where they began a noisy confrontation with the birds they had disturbed.

'The ducks rather remind me,' Halifax began tentatively, anxious to avoid the King's questions, 'of those poor Dutch ministers.'

'The Dutch? Tell me, I've heard nothing,' the King insisted anxiously. He was always concerned about keeping up with information; he found his job wretched enough without having to do it in the dark.

'They were flying from Holland yesterday when they were intercepted by German fighters. They made it through, but badly damaged. Forced to ditch in the sea off Brighton. And that's where the most dangerous part of their enterprise began. They managed to swim and stumble ashore and had just fallen exhausted upon the sand, when they were surrounded by a suspicious mob and arrested by the constabulary on suspicion of being enemy spies.'

'Are you serious?'

'Desperately so. By the time they arrived in my office they were in a terrible state. I told them they had set a splendid example, and were clearly invincible.'

'What did they want?'

'Oh, an army.'

'Pity. Brave souls.'

'I've just seen their ambassador—you know him I think, van Verduynen. Assured me that the Dutch will resist with the same stubbornness and perseverance they have always shown.'

'Without an army,' the King added softly.

'The Belgian ambassador assures me of victory. Says they are ten times stronger than in 1914.'

'And they have our prayers.'

'Not forgetting our own Expeditionary Force,' Halifax added a trifle too quickly, missing the irony.

The conversation was proving difficult, and at first Halifax was relieved when they were diverted by the arrival of the Queen, Elizabeth. Halifax responded to her warm smile by kissing her hand and enquiring after the children, but he was to find no relaxation on this occasion.

'Edward,' the Queen began, 'we are so disappointed.'

The Minister stooped once more. 'I'm a little mystified myself. It's not easy to explain but . . . I thought—I think—that Winston's temperament, however unreliable and impetuous, may be better suited for this particular moment than perhaps is mine.'

'You don't sound terribly certain of it,' the King commented.

'I'm not. Certainty is a luxury at times like these.

But think of it this way, if I were Prime Minister I would have Winston prowling up and down outside Downing Street. You know how much damage he can cause when things go to his head. So better the tiger inside the cage.'

'With you holding the key.'

'Yes, something like that.'

'Until he has been either tamed or trampled by events,' the Queen added. 'Nothing lasts for ever in this chaotic world, Edward. Your turn will come.'

Halifax nodded diffidently in the manner of all Englishmen confronted by their own ambition.

'Oh, Winston!' Elizabeth uttered the name in exasperation, and without affection. 'He will cause problems, you know he will. Always has.'

'And already is,' Halifax responded. 'Wants Beaverbrook back.'

'What?' Elizabeth exclaimed. She neither liked nor trusted Max Beaverbrook, a Canadian émigré who had spent a long life charting a career through some exceptionally murky waters. He had been a Cabinet Minister during the last war, was now a peer and the immensely powerful owner of the *Express* newspaper group, and would for ever be an incorrigible conspirator. In his time he had schemed against both Churchill and the present Royal Family; it appeared that Churchill was far more ready to forgive him than was the Queen.

'Wants to put him in charge of aircraft production,' Halifax added for detail.

'He must be stopped,' Elizabeth insisted. 'Beaverbrook is incapable of responsibility. Remember . . .' She waved her hand in exasperation. There was so much to remember from Beaverbrook's long career, not least his unflagging public support for her despicable brother-in-law, the abdicated Edward.

The King, less voluble, was nevertheless shaking his head. 'No, no, it won't do. I must write to Winston immediately.'

'Yes, hobble his horse,' the Queen insisted.

Halifax swallowed deep, calculating. Should he mention the other matter? But he was exhausted by the events of the last few days and no longer trusted his own judgement. Instead he allowed base instinct to rule and to stir the Prime Minister's pot.

'He also wants Bracken as a Privy Councillor.'

'No!' Elizabeth once more led the objections, more vehement than ever. 'Bracken as part of the King's own private council? That we cannot have.' Membership of the Council was an exceptional honour reserved for the most senior in the land, not a jumped-up Irish adventurer. She hooked her arm through her husband's and clasped him tightly, as if they both required an extra measure of support. 'Those men around Mr Churchill,' she exclaimed, 'are not gentlemen.'

'I fear the government is being given over to gangsters,' Halifax muttered miserably. He knew that both the King and Queen believed it to be largely his fault.

They wandered on in silence, skirting the lake, passing beyond rhododendrons that were raising flower-drenched branches in seasonal triumph, until Elizabeth turned to her husband, as always wishing to share his burden when he appeared distressed. 'A penny for those thoughts of yours, my dear.'

The King seemed startled for a moment, dragged back from distant troubles. 'I was thinking, well . . . like you, how very much I had wanted Edward for the job. And then worrying—just a little—how can I put it? About us and the Germans. That our gangsters may not be as good as theirs.'

*    *    *

It was beyond midnight when Churchill's private detective, Inspector Thompson, ushered the woman into Churchill's study. Churchill was busy writing a letter and didn't look up. Without being asked, Thompson refilled his master's glass, then offered a drink to the woman. With a curt shake of the head, she declined. Thompson left, closing the door quietly behind him.

Only then did Churchill raise his eyes.

'Didn't know if you would come.'

'Didn't want to. But your private policeman waved his warrant card. You know we Germans are helpless in the face of authority.'

Ruth Mueller was around fifty with a thin, elegant face that had worn well and fading blonde hair trimmed severely at the neck. She had probably cut it herself. There were other signs of self-reliance about her, apart from defiant eyes—her tweed suit was frayed at the cuffs and clearly designed for someone several pounds heavier, her shoes were old, her fingers unadorned by any jewellery. She held an ancient handbag protectively in her lap.

'You look well,' he offered clumsily.

'No thanks to you.' Her vocabulary was precise, her accent stiff.

He cleared his throat in irritation. He could still

remember his surprise at their first encounter. He had received a letter from an R. Mueller explaining that the writer was a refugee from Germany, had an academic background as an historian, and wondering whether Churchill might be in need of any researchers for his forthcoming writings. The letter had added in impassioned terms that the threat of events in Europe were so imminent and the lack of understanding about them so immense in everyone but Churchill that he was the only man in Europe the writer wished to work for.

It had been a timely letter, arriving at Chartwell at the moment when Churchill, under severe pressure from both his publishers and his multiple creditors, had turned once more to his *History of the English-Speaking Peoples*, a book commissioned many years previously and repeatedly pushed aside for the distractions of politics. Yet as interested as Churchill was in politics, for the past decade politics had displayed precious little interest in him. He had been a political outcast, lost in the wilderness, out of office and largely ignored. So he had picked up his pen once more, believing that his *History* would in all likelihood be his last endeavour on this earth, and in a typically impetuous moment had written offering R. Mueller a position on his team of research assistants.

He was shaken when, on the appointed day, a woman had turned up. Churchill was not good with women, not in a professional sense. For him they were creatures of romance, to be admired when the moment was right, then left in their drawing rooms while the menfolk got on with business. He'd had severe doubts about giving them the vote and was aggravated beyond endurance by most of those who had found their way into Parliament. When, with some awkwardness, he had sat R. Mueller down and suggested there had been some confusion but he might have a vacancy on his staff for an additional typist, she had not taken it well. She was a qualified historian, she told him, one who had spent several years researching an authoritative biography of the Fuehrer. Her abilities had been recognized even by the Gestapo. They had visited her several times and suggested several other professional avenues for her to pursue, ranging from a teaching position in almost any other subject than Hitler studies, which she had declined, to a librarianship in Dachau, which she had avoided only by fleeing. But even the Gestapo hadn't suggested she be a typist. She had waved Churchill's letter of appointment and insisted that she be given the proper job on his staff.

The engagement had lasted three weeks. She was brilliant, incisive, immensely hard-working, and impossible. When she had discovered that he was spending most of his time working on a history of the English-speaking world, she had asked why he wasn't writing about the contemporary threat in Europe. He had offered many reasons: he was under considerable contractual obligation to his publishers, he had told her, and people were fed up with him going on about impending war. Anyway, it was necessary for him to think about his financial survival. She had looked him in the eye and told him that survival was about much more than his silk underwear and champagne. It had been the last time they had spoken. Until tonight.

'Many circumstances have changed since we last met, Frau Mueller,' he began, smiling.

If he was expecting congratulation, there was no sign of it.

'I have a war to fight. Against your Herr Hitler. I was wondering if you would like to help.'

'Help you?' she enquired, startled.

'Help Britain. I know it is a lot to ask.'

'Help? How?' She stared at him fiercely, across a desk that was cluttered with piles of papers weighed down by gold medals and surrounded by bottles of pills, potions, a magnifying glass, two spectacle cases and a small pot of toothpicks. There were also two cuffs made of card to prevent his sleeves getting dirty.

He was examining her, weighing her up. 'I take a risk even in having you here. But it is a time when risk arrives with my breakfast and lingers on to tuck me in at night. We face a formidable opponent in Germany and its formidable armies. We also face Hitler.' He began jabbing his chest with his finger. '*I* face Hitler. I, Winston Churchill. And yet I don't know him. One of the few significant men in Europe I have never met.' The room was dark except for the light of his desk lamp, yet she could see the exhaustion that hovered behind his eyes. 'He refused to meet me, you know. In 1932 when I was motoring in Europe, inspecting the old battlefields. All the rest, Chamberlain, Halifax, Lloyd George, they met him. But not me. He simply refused. Mistook me for a man with no future, apparently.'

'He may yet be right.'

'Indeed he may,' Churchill muttered, refusing to rise to the bait. 'My father was a great English statesman, Frau Mueller. It's partly due to him that you are here.'

'But he's . . . ?'

'He gave me an excellent piece of advice. My father instructed me, never underestimate your enemy. Know your enemy if you want to beat him. Words of wisdom. So I was wondering . . . if you would be willing to help me thrash Hitler.'

'Help? You?'

'I am sure if an apology is owed for any misunderstandings we may have had in the past, it is freely offered on my part.' For a man who had such an easy way with words, the apology sounded contrived to the point of insincerity.

'You also owe me a week's wages. You never paid.'

'I . . . I . . .' The old man began to splutter helplessly. This was leading nowhere. 'Frau Mueller, you know Hitler better than any man in Britain. I need to understand him in order to crush him. I thought you might want to help in that enterprise, but if I am mistaken then I—'

'You make it sound terribly personal.'

'In some respects, it is.'

'Hurt pride? Because he refused to meet you?'

'It has nothing to do with pride!'

'Then what are you fighting for? The British are fighting for no better reason than that you are too proud to admit that at almost every step of the way you got it wrong. Versailles. The Rhineland. Austria. Czechoslovakia—'

'We are fighting for principle, not pride!' he snapped, with an undertone of anger.

'Poland? Poland's not a principle, it's a miserable afterthought from the last war that's been pulled to pieces while you sat back and watched.'

He was beginning to breathe heavily, his teeth clamped fiercely around the butt of his cigar. 'Well, now we are fighting because Hitler insists upon it, whether we like it or not. You said this was personal. It is. Both he and I have been recalled from obscurity to guide our nations through this hour. I am a Churchill, for all the strengths and faults which that has bred in me. Now I need to know what a Hitler is. And you can help me, if you will.'

'You are a lot like him.'

'Like That Man?' He spat the words out, as though his face had been slapped.

'Unruly, bad-tempered rabble-rousers, propagandists, nationalists, outsiders.' She began ticking characteristics off on her fingers. 'Why, you are both even painters—although in my view you show rather more talent than Hitler. And you both love war.'

'I do not *love* war, as you put it.' They both knew he was lying. 'And perhaps I have made a mistake in thinking you could help—'

'There is one difference which I think is very important, Mr Churchill.'

'And what, pray, is that?'

'I do not know you well, Mr Churchill, but I have my instincts. As a woman. And I believe you are capable of compassion—love, even. I see it in your eyes, in your words. But Hitler knows only one thing. Hatred. From his earliest days he was conditioned to hate—even to hate his father. Perhaps he hated his father most of all. He was an Austrian, a customs official on the Austro-German frontier, you see, and there is part of me which thinks that the Fuehrer's first great coup, when he marched his army into Austria, was driven as much as anything by a desire to sweep away his father's entire life work, to smash down his border posts and erase all traces of him. You think that ridiculous, of course, to suggest that the political ambitions of a man like Hitler could be driven by the memory of a long-dead father.'

Churchill paused before replying. 'No, I do not think it ridiculous.'

'Hitler has always needed someone to hate. When he was young it was his father, and now it is the Jews. Never forget how much he hates. But also never forget—never dare forget—Hitler's extraordinary achievements. He took a nation as broken and decayed as Weimar Germany, where old women and babies starved to death in the streets, and he rebuilt it.' Her mood had changed; it was no longer a lecture, her words carried growing passion. 'While you English were clinging to your old ways, he built something new—not just the autobahns and barracks but a new people. He ripped out their sadness and restored their hope. He has raised them high and made them feel all but invincible. Germany is a land where no one starves any more. And what does it matter if a few Jews or Social Democrats don't join in the general joy? What do a few cracked heads matter when an entire people who had been denied any sort of future have been lifted up and made proud once more? For the happiness of the whole, aren't a few whispered sacrifices acceptable?'

He suspected she was goading him, but that was what he required, for his mind to be bent into focus.

'So why did you not accept his bold new world?'

'To my shame I did. For several years. I was one of those young mothers of Weimar who had starved like all the rest. Do you know how we survived in those years after the war, Mr Churchill, do you have any conception of what it was like? Once a month, every pay day, we hired a taxi to take us to the market—a taxi, not because we were rich but because every moment that passed could be measured in gold. With every breath we took, the money in our pockets grew more worthless, like butter on a hot stove. If we were lucky what had been worth a king's ransom the previous week would now buy a few essentials, and if we weren't lucky, if we were delayed, if the taxi was late, perhaps not even that. We stood in line, and prayed that by the time we reached the head of the queue there would still be something left, and that the price wouldn't have shot out of sight even while we looked on. So in the end you stopped queuing and started pushing, and those that couldn't push got trampled. We would spend everything we had, everything! Every last pfennig in our pockets. Then we would climb back into the taxi with whatever we had been able to buy and go home. Sometimes we might have meat, sometimes it would be off a cheese stall, other times just vegetables. But whatever it was would have to last us an entire month, until the next pay day, because we had nothing left. Nothing. All my jewellery gone, all our best clothes pawned. Can you understand that? I'm not talking about money for champagne but money for a little sugar and milk and bread.' Her voice suddenly softened and began to break. 'Nothing left for school. For medical bills. For heating in winter. And eventually, Mr Churchill, it wasn't enough even for bread. One day I woke up and discovered I had no more milk for my baby. A week later she was dead.'

'My heart breaks for you,' he whispered.

'No one starves under Hitler. And as long as we ate we gave thanks. We gave money when the Brown Shirts came round with their begging buckets, we gave salutes as their parades passed in the streets and we closed our ears to those noises in the night. When we woke up we might hear whispers that one neighbour or another had disappeared. It seemed a small price to pay for the food on our plates.'

'So why did you eventually . . . ?'

She looked into her lap, her fingers running distractedly along the frayed edges of her cuffs.

'If only I had a simple answer. There was a madness about our lives that infected us all. How mad can you get, driving into starvation in the back of a taxi? You know, Mr Churchill, in the whole of the last war when I was a young woman, I never heard a single shot fired. But under Weimar, shots were being fired all the time—at each other. Our leaders, our opponents, eventually even at the bread queues. Our streets became a battleground, our schools the headquarters. Children grew more used to the sound of gunfire than they were to their teachers' voices. Instead of carrying around schoolbooks they began carrying around knives and hammers; their sports teams became nothing more than gangs of thugs. Can you imagine how much I and every other mother in the land begged for it to end? Then Hitler came along and made it all seem so simple. It was the fault of the Jews and the democrats. And we asked ourselves, what good was democracy if the water didn't run and the lamps went dark? Better that we see by the light of burning torches. Our political leaders had been so weak, so false, but Hitler seemed above all that. Different. Exciting. Almost—what is the word?—spiritual.'

'And we had Stanley Baldwin,' Churchill muttered in contempt. 'So tell me, pray, why you put it all behind you. Why did you choose to resist when so many went along with it?'

'It crept up on you so slowly, what was really happening. Made it so easy to accept. Of course, there were those that had to be punished, the guilty men. The Marxists, the Social Democrats, the Jews. They almost seemed to prove their guilt when so many of them were shot trying to escape. But slowly it crept closer to us all. Everyone became a suspect. We had to give up our friends, our lovers, our beliefs—even renounce Belief itself. You could trust no one. And suddenly there was no private life at all, no space even to think.' Her head fell to hide the pain. 'After my baby died I went back to work—as a teacher in the *Grundschule*, the primary school, where my other child, my son, was a pupil. One day I was supervising in the library when the Brown Shirts came in. Very polite, apologized for the disturbance. But they had come for the Jews, they announced, and started leading the Jewish children out, one by one. I asked what the children had done, and the Brown Shirt leader just looked at me curiously. "Done? They are Jews." But they were my pupils, my son's classmates, *my* Jews, and I demanded to know why they were being taken. The Brown Shirt's attitude changed; a rage came over his face. "Are you a

Jew?" he asked. And I almost fell over in my rush to deny the charge—of course I wasn't a Jew. I was furious with him, how dare he accuse . . . ?'

She was silent for a moment, needing to recover herself. When her head came up once more the eyes were filled with tears. 'After he had gone I realized what had already become of me. I watched as they dragged them all away. I looked at the empty spaces in the library, the schoolbooks still open on the tables, the satchels on the backs of the chairs, and wondered when the Brown Shirts would be coming back for more.' She leant forward, bent with feeling. 'No, I can't pretend I saw it all at that moment, that I became an opponent. I am not a hero, Mr Churchill, and I had no idea where they were taking them. But I knew the Brown Shirts would be back, and eventually they would come for my son, and either he would join them, or be taken by them. This was the new Germany, my son's Germany, and I wanted to find out more about the man who had made it. That is when I started reading about Hitler, talking about him, studying him. In the end I decided to write about him. A biography.'

'You were seeking to know your enemy . . .'

'My enemy?' She shook her head. 'No, he wasn't my enemy, not at first. The book wasn't intended to be an attack upon him, I was doing no more than trying to understand. So I started asking questions about him, but that meant that very soon they began asking questions about me. I had become *their* enemy without my realizing it.'

'I am so sorry.'

But she had no desire for his pity. Already she had shared with him far more than she had intended. Once again her life was being invaded. It was time to push him back. 'Did your father know his enemies?'

'No, I think not,' Churchill replied, startled at the sudden change of subject. 'Why do you ask?'

'Because I've noticed that when you talk about him you seem . . . stiff. Formal. Almost anxious.'

'I loved my father.'

'No. You were afraid of him, I think.'

Churchill bridled. 'My whole life has been dedicated to his memory.'

'Dominated by his memory, perhaps. A bit like Hitler.'

His hand slapped down on the desktop to demand her silence. It landed with such force that the toothpicks jumped in their pot. 'I asked you here to talk about the Fuehrer, not to offer crass remarks about my father, a man whom you never met.'

'I've never met Hitler.'

And they were back where they had always been.

'I have no time for cheap comparisons, Frau Mueller. I thought you might help. Will you?'

Her cheeks flushed. 'Help you? Why should I? I don't like you, Mr Churchill. I don't like any politicians. They've done nothing but ruin my life.' She sprang from her chair, not wishing to be near him any longer. 'What reason could I have for wanting to help you?'

'Not me personally. Our crusade.'

'In which millions will die. To save your old man's pride.'

'To save both our countries.'

'I have no country any more.'

'Then do it for the simple pleasure of proving

yourself right—and for the satisfaction of proving That Man wrong!' He was shouting, although he hadn't intended to.

'You and your ridiculous male vanity. You two men will destroy the world with your war. You are so much alike.'

She was already at the door.

'You will come again,' he barked, the intonation halfway between question and command.

She had opened the door and was almost out.

'Please!' he called after her. 'I need you.'

She turned, startled. Then she was gone.

## CHAPTER THREE

Monday 13 May. Winston Churchill had been Prime Minister for just three days. And on that third day it all began to unravel.

Churchill was striding down Parliament Street, Bracken at his side, distractedly acknowledging the waves and shouted greetings of passers-by as he walked to the House of Commons. His mind was ablaze with doubt. So many thoughts crowded in upon him, so many concerns; in less than an hour he had to address the House of Commons like Brutus in the marketplace with Caesar's blood still fresh upon the floor. Yet less than four years earlier those same men, in that same place, had inflicted upon him the most profound humiliation any Member could imagine. They had jeered him into silence. It had not been a good speech by any standard; it had been an inappropriate and, if truth be admitted, a slightly inebriated intervention on the delicate matter of the abdication. A foolish speech, but not exceptional for that. Yet it wasn't the speech so much as the speaker they couldn't stomach. They didn't care for Winston Churchill, didn't trust him, thought that even in the egotistical world of Westminster he rose above all others in being outrageous, unprincipled, unreliable and supremely bloody ungrateful. So they had relished their opportunity to jeer, to wave their papers at him in distraction, to screw up their faces and cause so much noise that he couldn't go on. He had been forced to leave, head bowed in shame, his speech unfinished. Just like his father before him.

Now he would be facing them as Prime Minister—a Prime Minister that many, and perhaps most, did not want.

'They will render me their bloody hands, and swear unto me their loyalty, assure me of their constancy, even as they march to the fields of Philippi . . .'

'What?' Bracken spluttered in surprise beside him.

'Shakespeare, you ill-educated louse. They cheered Caesar, then watched him die at the hands of Brutus. After which they cheered Brutus, before watching him die at the hands of Mark Antony.'

'Thought he committed suicide.'

'Don't quibble, man!'

They passed the sandstone obelisk of the Cenotaph, the memorial to the fallen. Churchill raised his hat in respect then clamped it forcefully back on his head. 'They want Neville back,' he growled. 'Even those who voted against him declare they never wanted Neville out; they intended only to shake him up a little, not to shake him right out of Downing Street. He's not even Caesar's ghost; he'll be sitting right beside me this afternoon, watching, waiting.'

'For what?'

'For calamity, which may not be far away. For all his faults, Neville is an excellent party man and he still holds the majority in Parliament in the palm of his hands. One wink from him and the House will fall down upon me more certainly than if Goering had sent over every last one of his bombers.'

Churchill strode on, his cane flying out in front of him, revealing remarkable energy. Although Bracken was more than a quarter of a century younger, he was having trouble keeping the pace.

'Can it be that bad, Winston?'

'You yourself reminded me of the doleful circumstance that I have not a single friend in my own War Cabinet and precious few in the Government as a whole.'

'There have been a few mutters, of course. Some of the old sods saying that if they're forced to share power with socialists then the war's already been lost, that sort of nonsense. But—'

'I know, I've heard. But I thought you were supposed to keep me informed of such things,' Churchill accused.

'I thought you had more important matters on your mind. Where did you hear?'

'It is not widely known—and it must not become widely known—that Mr Chamberlain had a most suspicious mind. Didn't trust his colleagues, not a bit. So he had their phones tapped.'

'Bastard,' Bracken exclaimed in appreciation.

'It is, of course, illegal, unethical and entirely inappropriate. It is also unfortunate that he left office in such a hurry that he forgot to cancel the phone taps. As a result, yesterday evening I, as his successor, received a large file of transcripts.'

'Must have made entertaining reading.'

'They made most depressing reading,' Churchill snapped. 'Most of my Ministers appear to have the loyalty of maggots. It appears I run a Government worthy of little more than being fed to the fishes. Incidentally, I have withdrawn the tap on your own phone—'

'What?'

'And instructed that your substantial file be condemned to the fire.'

Bracken's face grew ashen. He was perhaps the most private of politicians, an enthusiastically unmarried man who revelled in the intrigue surrounding others' private lives while using his considerable personal fortune to protect his own. But phone taps? For how long? And how much did they know? In a pace he had resolved never to trust his life to the telephone again.

'You look as though you've seen a ghost,' Churchill growled, amused at his friend's discomfort.

'Have to say I feel a little like Brutus.'

'Ah, but it is I who must go to the marketplace and address the mob.'

'What will you say?'

'I have never been more uncertain. I pray for inspiration . . .'

They stood on the edge of Parliament Square waiting for the traffic to clear. The edges of the pavement were daubed with thick white paint to make them visible in the blackout, and the traffic lights stood obscured, showing nothing but faint crosses on their lenses. Three elderly women were waiting with them and they turned to wish him well; automatically he raised his hat once more.

'We're with you, Winnie,' a passing taxi driver yelled through his window.

'Ah, the people, the people,' he muttered mournfully to Bracken.

The traffic thinned and they set off toward the Parliament building until, in the middle of the road, Churchill came to an abrupt halt, smacking the silver top of his cane into the palm of his hand.

'But perhaps that is it, Brendan. The people. The marketplace. And ghosts . . .'

It meant nothing to Bracken who, mystified, shuffled his companion beyond the reach of the advancing traffic.

'They are the answer, Brendan, the people.' The cane smacked down once more. 'Forget Brutus, think of Mark Antony. An appeal over the heads of the conspirators. Trust the people. Just as my father always insisted. That was the rock on which stood his entire career.'

Bracken knew this was balderdash. For all the father's wild protestations about democracy, at the first opportunity Lord Randolph had cast aside his radical ideas and grabbed hungrily at Ministerial office. It was another of Winston's romantic myths and Bracken considered telling him so, but thought better of it. The old man had been in such a fragile mood.

'But . . .' Churchill seemed somehow to deflate. 'How can I expect their loyalty when I have nothing to offer them but calamity?'

'Why not surprise them? Tell them the truth.'

'The truth is too painful.'

'Not half as painful as all the lies they've been fed and all the easy victories they've been promised.'

'I'm not sure I can offer them victory of any kind.'

'You must. Otherwise they won't follow and they won't fight. But offer them the scent of hope and they will give you everything.'

They were at the gateway to the Palace of Westminster; a duty policeman saluted. Bracken's mind raced. He was no intellectual but he had an unfailing capacity for borrowing arguments and detecting what others—and particularly Winston Churchill—needed to hear. Frequently the old man wanted to argue, to engage in a shouting match that would see them through dinner and well into a bottle of brandy. But this was a different Churchill, a hurt, mistrustful Churchill, a man who needed bolstering, not beating.

'Winston, I've never fought in a war, while you've fought in several. Always thought you were a mad bugger, to be honest, risking your neck like that. But this I do know. War has changed. It's no longer a matter of a few officers and a handful of men charging thousands of fuzzy-wuzzies. It involves every man in the country, women and children, too. Modern war is people's war, and the people are as likely to die in their own homes as they are on the front line. They have a right to be told the truth. You've got to trust them.'

They had reached the threshold of the Parliament building.

'Anyway,' Bracken added, 'you've got no other bloody choice but to trust the people. Nobody else trusts you.'

Churchill forged ahead once more, the cane beating time, his eyes fixed upon an idea that was beginning to rotate in his mind and spin aside so many of the doubts that had been plaguing him. His concentration was total and he offered his friend no word of thanks or farewell. His colleague was left staring at his disappearing back.

'Remember—like Mark Antony,' Bracken called after him.

'Like my father,' he thought he heard the old man reply.

* * *

When, later that day, Churchill entered the Chamber of the House of Commons from behind the Speaker's Chair, it was packed. For two days and nights of the previous week this same place had heard protestations and denunciations of Neville Chamberlain so terrible it had caused his Government to fall. Now, like a wicked child caught in the act, it protested its innocence.

As they spotted Churchill making his way towards his place, there were those on the opposite side of the House who cheered and waved their papers in the traditional form of greeting. It scratched at their socialist hearts to show goodwill towards a man such as this, but there were the common courtesies to be observed. Yet from his own party, which was more than two-thirds of the House, there came nothing but embarrassment. No one stood to cheer, few hailed him, most had suddenly found something of captivating interest amongst their papers or in the conversation of their neighbours.

Moments later, it was Neville Chamberlain's turn to enter and walk the same path, squeezing past the outstretched legs of others until he had found his place on the green leather bench beside Churchill. And as they saw him, his colleagues offered an outpouring of sympathy so vehement that they hoped it might wash away any mark of their guilt. He had last left this Chamber as a condemned man, and already he was a saint.

The House was like an excitable and over-bred greyhound; at every mention of Chamberlain they leapt up and barked their loyalty, while as Churchill spoke they crouched in anxiety, their tails between their legs, as he treated them to one of the most brutal and honest expositions ever offered by a Prime Minister at a time of great crisis. Many, it seemed, simply did not understand.

'Can you believe it?' Channon was still protesting some hours later as he stood on the lawn at the rear of the Travellers' Club. It was early evening; the weather was still glorious. 'What on earth did all that mean? "I have nothing to offer but blood, toil, tears and sweat",' he growled in mock imitation.

'Not the sort of stuff to get the common man jumping for joy, that's for sure,' Butler agreed across a glass of sherry.

'Extraordinary performance,' Colville added.

'D'you think he was drunk?'

'Always so difficult to tell.'

'Not something you drafted then, Jock?' Channon enquired. The stare he received in response was so stony he felt forced to leave in search of the bar steward.

'Truly, Jock, I fear for us all,' Butler muttered.

'Winston will say anything if the words take his fancy. We shall be swept away on a flood of oral incontinence.'

The words still rang in his ears. He was a diplomat by trade and an intellectual by training, a man who took pleasure in toying with every side of an argument in the manner that a cat plays with a ball of wool. Yet Churchill was a man stripped of any trace of either sophistication or the values Butler held so dear in public life; his speech had been nothing short of vulgar.

'You ask, What is our policy?' Churchill had declared. 'I will say: It is to wage war, by sea, land and air, with all our might and with all the strength that God can give us: to wage war against a monstrous tyranny, never surpassed in the dark, lamentable catalogue of human crime. That is our policy,' he had told them. 'You ask, What is our aim? I can answer in one word: Victory—victory at all costs, victory in spite of all terror; victory, however long and hard the road may be; for without victory there is no survival . . .'

Butler was far from certain that he would want to survive in a world of crude simplicities of the sort embraced by Churchill. 'I feel violated,' he muttered, his lips wobbling.

His misery was interrupted as Channon returned in the company of the American ambassador, Joseph Kennedy. They were followed by a club steward carrying a tray with three small sherries and an enormous glass of bourbon.

'So, what are you Three Musketeers up to?' the American demanded.

If diplomacy was seen by many as a carefully orchestrated minuet, Joe Kennedy could always be relied upon to arrive wearing hobnail boots. He had worn them throughout a career that had carried him through the boardrooms of major banks and into the bedrooms of Hollywood starlets, and he had kept them ever more tightly laced as he had kicked his way into the smoke-filled back rooms of the US Democratic Party where he showed as little loyalty to his President as he did to his wife. He was a man with a roving eye and a slipping tie, and in the two years since his arrival at the Court of St James's he had come to hate Winston Churchill.

'Not drinking to Winston and his war, I hope,' Kennedy continued, waving his bourbon. 'On the other hand, if all you've got is Winston, then I'm not surprised you drink.' He smiled from behind round tortoiseshell glasses. 'I'm sure I'm not telling tales out of school with you three when I tell you that even Halifax is complaining,' he added. 'Ridiculous working hours, sometimes up till two or three in the morning. This toil and sweat nonsense may sound fine, but what the hell can you achieve in the middle of the night with a man who's been drinking whisky since breakfast?'

'Joe, how did you get to be a diplomat?' Butler enquired provocatively.

'Funny thing, heard that Winston's been asking how the hell you got to be a Minister.'

The response brought a flush to Butler's cheek. He expected to be sacked—his views about Winston and his policies were far from a private indulgence—but he still hadn't heard, and he found the uncertainty offensive.

'We live to play another day, Joe.'

'Not if Winston gets going, you won't.'

'You may well be right. But the game isn't over yet.'

'So I hear. Fact is, one of the Whips told me that two-thirds of the party would have Neville back like a shot, given half an excuse.'

'And most of them think that Winston is just the sort of person to provide it,' Colville added.

'Not won over by his charms, then, Jock?' Kennedy enquired.

'May I put it this way, Mr Ambassador? I've never known a Prime Minister to come into office with so many people expecting him to fail—even wanting him to fail.'

'They don't want this war. It's what I've been saying all along!' Kennedy exclaimed. 'Gentlemen, you go ahead with this fight and you're gonna get beat. Look what happened in Poland. Look what's happening in the Low Countries. Just heard from our embassy in Holland that the Luftwaffe is turning Rotterdam into the back side of hell. It's chaos over there.'

'Do we have a choice but to go ahead, Joe? I fear Herr Hitler might insist,' Butler prodded.

'What are you fighting for, Rab?' Kennedy barked back. 'Hitler doesn't want to touch England, he doesn't want your empire. Leave him alone in Europe and by Christmas he'll be sipping tea and chomping through cream cakes with your King, all friends together. Why you ever got involved in this damned war I'll never understand.'

It was a view that was also close to Butler's heart. 'But we are involved, whether we like it or not. What can we do?'

'Play the Italian card. Hitler listens to Mussolini. Wrap up a couple of your Mediterranean islands as a gift for Il Duce and he'll whisper whatever you want into Uncle Adolf's ear. Otherwise you're gonna end up at war with them both.'

The three Englishmen stood mournfully.

Kennedy finished off his drink in one huge swallow. 'Still, can't stand around here all evening. Got other diplomatic duties to perform, strengthening the Entente Cordiale with the assistance of a little French lady I know.' He smiled and tried to straighten his tie. 'Musketeers, it's been a pleasure.' He waved and was gone.

'I know I'm a bit of a snob,' Channon began, 'but I can't help feeling he's right.'

'Of course he's right,' Butler snapped irritably.

'And what do you think, Jock?'

'You see this suit I'm wearing?' It was offensively blue and exceptionally bright. 'From the fifty-shilling department of Monty Burton's. Rather cheap and sensational, I'm afraid, but entirely suitable for this administration.' He plucked a loose thread from his lapel. 'I don't expect it will prove to be much of an investment.'

* * *

The public library in Pimlico was open until seven that evening. It had a ground-in, sweet-and-sour aroma of beeswax and half-burnt coke, but it suited Ruth Mueller. She did not want to get back to her rented room before eight. By that time the family who lived below would have finished their dinner; it was bad enough having to go hungry without smelling the rest of the world at the trough.

Unlike her room, the Pimlico library was warm and quiet, but it was the books, of course, that had first drawn her here, particularly the Hitler books. Sadly, they had long since been banished from the shelves, and none of them had been very good, either Marxist tracts or hagiography. So she was left to wonder and to grapple with her half-formed impressions of the man. What about his childhood? What about his early days as a vagrant on the streets of Vienna? What about his early friendships with Jews, his devotion to his mother, his inability to form any other close relationship with a woman, his vegetarianism and his fondness for cream cakes? Who was he, why was he? He was physically brave, a man of courage. Like Churchill, so she had been told, and perhaps more so, for the young Hitler had received many wounds and war decorations. Yet he was childish. In 1918, Hitler had been invalided to a military hospital. When he heard that an armistice had been signed and that Germany had surrendered, he'd put his head beneath his pillow and sobbed. Bawled like a baby. And he'd been shouting like a petulant child ever since. Some said that was like Churchill, too . . .

She'd been trying to forget about Churchill but he had an irritating habit of wheedling his way back into her thoughts. She picked up a newspaper and tried to shake him away once more.

Hah! Civil servants, *The Times* announced, were to get a war bonus. The guilty men cosseting themselves at the very moment they were putting up the price of coal yet again. Outside the library the sun was shining brightly, but she couldn't prevent a shiver of apprehension running through her body. She had frozen in her garret through the last winter, and dreaded what the next one might bring. On the following page there were tips for 'cooking through the war without fear of rationing'. Dishes such as eggs with anchovy, bean and liver casserole, coconut rounds (a concoction based on bread soaked in evaporated milk) and macaroni and rabbit pie. She imagined every rabbit in the country dashing for cover.

Not that *he* would be eating anchovies or rabbit pie. At Chartwell it had been salmon, venison, pheasant and beef, washed down with the finest wines. The cost of a single bottle would have got her through an entire week, rent and all, yet he had the impertinence to lecture her about his sacrifices! What did he know about sacrifice?

Her mind wandered back to that summer of 1914, August, the last time she could remember being happy. There was sun, and the sound of children's laughter. Then the summons had come. War. And the men had left with the horses, leaving behind the women with their young ones and their unspoken fears. So it had begun. The war was fought a million worlds away in France and Russia, but it had come rapping at their doors, gently at first. Strange shortages appeared. Suddenly there was no paper. She had begun to write letters not only across the page but up its length, too, in writing so minuscule her husband had required a glass to find his way through the kaleidoscope of scribbles. Worn-out shoes had to be repaired with card or resoled in wood; the children were asked to bring all their old bones and even cherry stones to school, to be turned into fertilizer. And they brought illness with them, everyone got sick, not least in their souls. Children were taught to hate, to kill even before they had become men, and were told by their teachers and priests that this was good and right. Hatred and intolerance were taught alongside geography and the Lord's Prayer, and was so much simpler to learn. Hatred had become a great patriotic game, honed by hunger, and it had been played so long that it would never be stopped, not while Germany, this Germany, survived.

Ruth Mueller was a German. But she was also an intellectual, a free thinker with a mind of her own, for what it was worth. And above all, she was a mother with memories of a starving child whose cries still woke her in the darkest moments of the night. She had fled, but she had not escaped, and whatever she did now, in the end some part of her soul would be shredded. She was a German in a foreign land, an intellectual reduced to scraping through on scraps of translation and proofreading, a mother with no child. But doing nothing would not be an option, not in this war.

Then she remembered that Winston Churchill had said *please*. It was a cry of vulnerability, like a child's plea for help. It had been a long time since anyone had said please.

She put aside the newspaper and went to the enquiries desk.

'May I help you?' The assistant was formal, unfriendly—she disapproved of Ruth Mueller's strange reading habits, and of Ruth Mueller even more.

'I would like some books. Something written by Mr Churchill, please. Perhaps something he has written about his father?'

* * *

They had expressed their collective concerns and

reservations about the new Prime Minister, after which, politics being politics, they had trooped through the Division Lobby to give him a unanimous vote of confidence. Afterwards it had taken Churchill some while to leave the Chamber for, politicians being politicians, many had paused to congratulate him—but not for too long. Even Chips Channon had joined the throng.

'Not one of us,' Bracken had warned, whispering in Churchill's ear.

'Chips? Of course he is. Chips is everyone's,' Churchill had replied gaily. 'Don't worry about him. It's the other buggers we have to watch out for.' And Churchill had forced his way through to the side of Neville Chamberlain, taking his arm, smiling, ensuring that they were seen together and offering him an ostentatious display of gratitude and warmth.

Afterwards he had noted Bracken's quizzical eye. 'That's the way it shall be, Brendan, both publicly and in private, for as long as is required. I'm haunted by enough damned ghosts, I've no need of more.'

They strode away, out of earshot and hidden behind a fog of cigar smoke. 'Brendan, I have a task of some delicacy for you. I am being forced to fight on too many fronts. I have nominated the most senior Ministers in my Government, now I want your help in selecting the great mass of the remainder. I need to get on with the other war.'

'Magnificent. I always enjoy a little vengeance.'

'You will start this evening. You will do it with David Margesson.'

'Margesson? Winston, you've gone mad . . .'

David Margesson was a name no one took

lightly. He had been Neville Chamberlain's Chief Whip, his immensely powerful organizer of the parliamentary party. He had known the details of every plot and piece of parliamentary wickedness during the last decade, largely because he had initiated most of them, and none of his plots had been more vicious than that against Churchill himself.

'Winston, barely twelve months ago Margesson was on the point of getting you deselected. Thrown out of the party. He tried to destroy your whole life—he hates you! The only reason you're here today is because the Nazis invaded Czechoslovakia the night before the deselection meeting. God knows, but Adolf Hitler's done more for your career than bloody Margesson! He's a comprehensive bastard!'

'Ah, but a most effective one. Which is why you will sit down with him and reshuffle the rest of my government, allowing as many as possible of the other bastards to remain.'

'I am lost,' Bracken gasped, his mind exhausted.

'Come on, Brendan, it's your own idea: Mark Antony, embracing the conspirators in order to give himself enough time.'

'For what?'

Churchill stopped, grabbed the other man's sleeve and spun him round until he was staring directly into his eyes.

'To survive! If we rock this boat too violently, it will sink. It may be overloaded with men not to our hearts, but if we are to let them go, slip them over the side, it had best be done as quietly as possible and at night. So mark out the troublemakers. Give them new jobs, different jobs, impossible jobs, but always some job; never forget that their love of office—any office—is stronger than their loathing for me. Keep them busy with the war against Hitler; give them not a moment for their war against me.' Churchill was panting with emotion, struggling to keep his breath. 'And if we are to go down in flames, then they too shall shed tears, share the toil, be drowned in sweat. But if we are to survive, it can only be together.'

So they had gathered in the Admiralty later that evening, Bracken and Margesson in one room while Churchill buried himself with his papers and maps in the inner sanctum. Bracken and the Chief Whip had bickered and debated, weighing dubious merits against more certain sins, moving from one to the next, pricking a few names, moving others to more minor posts, getting Colville to telephone the news through to the victims while they themselves congratulated the victors. In the end two-thirds of the existing members of the Government were reappointed, only twelve senior offices went to newcomers. Chamberlain remained prominent on the poop deck while Margesson continued in service as the master-at-arms.

But even as they worked, the boat was to be rocked far more brutally than ever they imagined.

Churchill heard it first, on the radio, from an American, a respected CBS correspondent named William Shirer who was based in Berlin. His broadcasts were inevitably filtered through the coarse gauze of the German Propaganda Ministry, but what squeezed past the censors was often useful, helping to know the enemy.

*Good evening. This is Berlin . . .*

The voice was flat, reedy, its tones stripped of emotional emphasis as it wowed and fluttered its way through the ether. Churchill tapped a dial; it made little difference. But the message did.

*Liège fallen! German land forces break through and establish contact with air-force troops near Rotterdam! Those were the astounding headlines in extra editions of the Berlin papers that came out about five, our time, this afternoon.*

'Colville. Mr Colville!' Churchill first muttered, then roared. There was a sudden scrabbling in the outer office.

*Today was a holiday in the capital—Whit Monday—and there were large crowds strolling in the streets. They bought up the extras like hot cakes. The announcement by the German High Command on the fourth day of the big drive that the citadel of Liège had been captured, and that German—well, the Germans call them "speed troops"—had broken through the whole southern part of Holland and made contact with the air-force troops who've been fighting since the first day in and around Rotterdam on the west coast, caught almost everyone by surprise. Even German military circles seemed a bit surprised. They admitted that the breakthrough to Rotterdam, as one put it, came somewhat sooner than expected . . .*

Colville was standing aghast on the other side of the desk. None of this had been mentioned in the night's situation briefing. To be sure, the Dutch had been talking of 'modifications' and 'confusion' in the military position, but this . . .

'Get the Chiefs of Staff back here. Every man jack of 'em. And find out whether m'Lord Halifax is in the land of the living. If he's not, drag him out of bed. Tell him there's a war on!'

## CHAPTER FOUR

Tuesday 14 May. The Reverend Chichester rose before dawn, turning his back on his bed. Sleep had been elusive and, when at last it had come, a river of troubles had run through his dreams, destroying his peace and reminding him of so many unanswered prayers. It had been his birthday on the previous day, his fifty-second, a time for reflection, although it had passed unnoticed by anybody else, apart from a card from his sister. Nothing from Donald.

Everything in his mind kept moving in circles and coming back to the same point. Donald. Even Jennie stared back at him in reproach from the mantelpiece, as if to say there should have been another photograph of their son alongside her. But he hadn't any recent photos of Don.

The vicarage seemed empty, the hallway too tidy; the kitchen had an unaccustomed echo; even the driveway taunted him. Not so long ago Don's motorbike, an AJS, had stood there on the gravel, leaning drunkenly and leaking oil. It was an ancient machine and Don had spent many hours repairing it, not always successfully. The Reverend Chichester hated motorbikes. As a young man he'd almost killed himself on one and he was afraid that Don would do the same. So he had objected to the bike. He was trying to protect his son, but instead of a discussion about caring it had been reduced to a shouting match about filthy sinks and oily clothes. Ridiculous. Pointless. Splinters in the eye, for in spite of Don's offensive language, he knew it was his fault. It seemed he would say anything rather than admit to his son that he loved him.

The previous evening he had returned to the vicarage to discover that his occasional gardener had cleaned up the soiled gravel. It was in pristine condition, no trace of the bike. Every fragment of Don's memory was being leached from his life, leaving them to stumble around his dreams.

He began to prepare another solitary breakfast, his newspaper propped up above the sink. Across the Channel that lay beyond his kitchen window, a new war was raging. He could see and hear nothing of it, there was little to witness apart from the calm of the sea and the outline of Calais beginning to emerge from its morning veil, but the headlines gave him the story of a 'Total War' in which the 'RAF had triumphed'. One hundred and fifty enemy machines shot down. Good news, great news, God's work. Set out in *The Times*.

Yet, as seemed increasingly to be His habit, God moved in ways that left mysteries in their wake. As the vicar pushed aside his breakfast plate, the same newspaper announced that the Belgian army was falling back, the Dutch, too. Yet only yesterday it had announced that the BEF was sweeping forward. Backwards, forwards—this was unlike any war the Reverend Chichester knew.

*The Times* assured him that the Belgians and

Dutch were withdrawing 'without heavy casualties'.

Which puzzled the Reverend Chichester. For why, in God's name, if they had suffered no heavy casualties, were they moving back?

* * *

Where had they gone, those people who only days before had been smiling, blowing kisses and shouting their encouragement as the 6th had made its way to the front? Now, on the way back, there was no greeting, no warmth, nothing but tired eyes that spoke of concern and even contempt.

Don's unit were withdrawing to a suburb of Brussels called Boitsfort in a tight convoy consisting of fifty ambulances, water trucks, troop-carriers and other vehicles. A few refugees had begun to appear on the road in front of them with their cars and overladen carts. Progress began to slow, and a sense of fading order crept up on them. The 6th had seen no direct combat yet, but planes had begun to appear overhead, high in the clear sky, and they came from the east. They must have seen the convoy; you couldn't hide an entire field unit, not with all their bright red crosses painted on the roofs.

They passed a single bomb crater at the side of the road. A dead horse lay beside it, the carcass still smouldering, its stench sweet: the first casualty of Don's war. And moments later there were others, Belgian soldiers, a group of them at the side of the road, abandoned and bleeding. Some were badly injured from shrapnel wounds. They kept gesticulating towards the sky, but otherwise there was little sense to be had from them in their strange language, and no one seemed inclined to delay in order to discover more. The wounded were loaded into the back of the ambulances and other vehicles. First blood. Belgian blood.

Yet, that evening, Boitsfort displayed the air of a prosperous suburb whose mind was fixed on moving gently into the embrace of nothing more threatening than a glorious summer. The gardens were full of flowers, the restaurants and cafés crowded, the young women gay, even while in the back of Don's vehicle a soldier was bleeding silently upon the floor. Someone mentioned they were passing near the battlefield of Waterloo.

The 6th drew up in front of an imposing building, the Hôtel Haute Maison. Inside the hotel a dinner-dance was in progress. Most of the male dancers were Belgian officers in freshly pressed uniforms, with women on their arms and champagne at their tables. As the British marched in bearing the bloodied casualties, a woman screamed, but in a moment the surprise was overtaken by a hurried calm. A Belgian officer began issuing orders to the hotel staff, the tables were cleared, the women ushered out, the band dismissed. The maître d' passed calmly from table to table, extinguishing candles, removing bottles, everything else being swept up in the starched linen tablecloths so that it took only moments for the tables to be laid bare. The two largest of these were then positioned beneath the chandeliers, their tops scrubbed with disinfectant and transformed into operating tables. The walking wounded slumped into the dining chairs to wait their turn, while those who were beyond helping themselves were carried in on stretchers that were already stained beyond cleansing. The maître d' brought in armfuls of clean towels and napkins to use as bandages, tears pouring silently down his cheeks. A priest arrived.

There was little time, often not enough time for the anaesthetic to take effect. More casualties arrived throughout the night, some civilian, all Belgian. The surgeons did whatever they could; often it was not enough. The dead were laid out in the ballroom.

War had at last caught up with Don.

Then, as the sun rose, the 6th were given fresh instructions. New orders. Fall back. Again.

* * *

'How is it possible? How can it be that three armies have fallen back because of the approach of a mere handful of Nar-zi tanks?'

Churchill hunched over the map spread before him on the Cabinet table and held it down with his clenched fists. For many long moments he stood like stone as he studied what lay before him, refusing to believe. All day long he had been pacing up and down as reports flooded in of ever-spreading disaster, his head bent forward as though he intended to butt his way towards victory, but no matter how furiously he paced he couldn't prevent disaster from catching up with him. The Dutch had surrendered, laid down their arms, given up. The Maginot Line was broken: the French were falling back, the Belgians with them, while the Germans had pushed beyond Sedan and were now halfway to the Channel. Luftwaffe bombers were now at airfields no more than thirty minutes' flying time from the English coast. That morning he had been shaken awake by a telephone call from the French Prime Minister Reynaud. 'All is lost,' he had said in English. 'The road to Paris is open. We have been defeated.'

And all through the day the calamities had continued.

'Impossible!' Churchill's fists pounded the table and he exploded back into life. He turned to his right, to where Newall, Chief of the Air Staff, was sitting. 'How many planes? How many planes do we have in France?'

'Prime Minister, we had four hundred and seventy-four. I regret to tell you that as of this morning we had barely two hundred left still operational.'

'In five days? We have lost more than half our strength in five days?' Churchill gasped.

'The Germans have lost a great many more machines,' the Air Marshal responded sharply. 'But we are outnumbered. I've heard of three Hurricanes taking on flights of thirty or forty enemy planes. They fight magnificently, but the French fuel is poor, their landing fields a disgrace and their radio communications nonexistent. This morning we attacked the pontoon bridges around Sedan. We sent in nearly eighty planes. Thirty-seven of them failed to return.' He glared defiantly at Churchill through exhausted eyes. 'If the RAF is in peril it is not through want of courage. Or of sacrifice, Prime Minister.'

'The French want more. They want us to send over more squadrons.'

'To what purpose, Prime Minister?' Newall countered. 'If the French are already beaten it would be like cutting out the heart of the RAF and offering it on a plate to Goering. There's no point in sacrificing our aircraft simply to help the French improve their terms of surrender.'

'We must keep them in the fight! No surrender. If France were to fall . . .'

The thought was so terrible as to be inexpressible. He left it hanging half-formed before them. A military aide came in, offered a smart salute and with lowered eyes placed another map before the Prime Minister. An update from the front. It showed an arrow through the place where the heart of the French Ninth Army should have been.

'Dear God,' Halifax whispered from his seat opposite Churchill. 'I despair.'

'Despair does not appear on the agenda of this Cabinet, my lord,' Churchill growled. 'Why, there is opportunity in such chaos!'

'Then it eludes me, Prime Minister,' Halifax responded calmly. 'Opportunity for what?'

'For counterattack! To mobilize our forces and take advantage of their tired and overstretched panzers before they can recover. I remember the twenty-first of March 1918. All experience shows that after five or six days they must halt for supplies—I learnt this from the lips of Marshal Foch himself. Look, look!' His finger stabbed at the enemy salient protruding into France. 'Once more they have exposed their neck like a wretch stretched out on a guillotine. So let us grab the moment to cut it off!'

'This time, I fear, the French are fighting with a decidedly blunt axe.'

'Then what do you propose as an alternative?' Churchill all but spat, his frustration bubbling over.

'Prime Minister, I have neither your abilities nor experience in the military field. I leave the art of fighting to you and the late marshal.' His artificial hand moved awkwardly across the papers set out before him on the table. 'But I am a diplomat. That is a different game and perhaps we might play it with rather better fortune.' He looked around the room, bringing the other Ministers and military men into the discussion. 'At this point the impetus appears to be with Herr Hitler, but he is isolated, alone. If we can prevent other nations from siding with him we can perhaps help stem his progress. We all know that Italy is threatening to come into the war on his side. That would be a disaster which would threaten our Mediterranean possessions and make the situation of the French impossible. I suggest, with all the powers of persuasion I command'—they all noted the implicit words of warning—'that the Prime Minister write immediately to Signor Mussolini and make it clear to him that we bear Italy no ill will, that the dialogue between us remains open, and that if the Italians have any cause for grievance with us it can be settled without turning the Mediterranean red with each other's blood.'

'Ah, play the Roman card,' Attlee muttered.

'You think it a sensible suggestion, Lord Privy Seal?' Churchill enquired.

'I do,' Attlee replied. 'Nothing to be lost from it.'

'But what if he says he wants Gibraltar, or Malta, as prizes for his co-operation?' Which he would, damn him, like any jackal.

'Better that such issues be resolved across the table than across a battlefield,' Halifax insisted.

Churchill stared at him; Halifax stared straight

back. He had given his advice 'with all the powers of persuasion I command'. In the muted language of Halifax's world, the Foreign Secretary was announcing that he would not tolerate rejection. And Churchill could not withstand rebellion. He had no choice. Anyway, it was only a bloody letter.

'An excellent idea,' Churchill announced. 'You have a draft for my consideration, Foreign Secretary?'

'Of course.'

'Then it shall be done.'

Halifax nodded his gratitude. For a moment he tried to convince himself that perhaps it would work after all, this ill-conceived administration led by the charging bull that was Churchill, with himself to guard the gate of the corral. And suddenly Anthony Eden, the Secretary of State for War, was speaking. A fragile man, in Halifax's view, and his predecessor as Foreign Secretary until he had fallen out with Chamberlain over appeasement and flounced out of the Cabinet. Now they were all back together around the Cabinet table, as uneasy as ever. Halifax sat back as Eden reported on his attempts to raise an army of local volunteers to defend the homeland.

'From all corners they have come forward,' he said in his precise, over-trimmed voice. 'In every town and every village, bands of determined men are gathering together for duties on the home front, arming themselves with shotguns, sporting rifles, clubs and spears . . .'

Dear God, thought Halifax, is this what it has come to? The greatest empire in the world defended with clubs and spears? And by fools?

He looked around the table, from man to man,

from failed politicians to failing military commanders, and knew he had been wrong. This ill-conceived and misconstructed machine could not be made to work. It was written on all their brows. Britain had already lost the war.

*   *   *

Don was confused. The BBC announcer had told them that Allied forces were counterattacking all along the front. Germans were being repelled at the Sedan salient, he claimed defiantly. So why were the 6th moving back once more?

A few hours earlier there had been a trickle of refugees on the road in front of them, but now it had swelled to a stream that meandered as far as his eye could see, like a tangle of fishing net caught at the edge of the surf. It slowed the 6th's progress to a crawl. The radiators that had frozen throughout winter began to overheat, and just after noon the convoy pulled into a farmyard for water and a little rest. Don hadn't slept in thirty hours.

They were only miles from the border, almost back where they had started. Bizarrely, as they drew into the farmyard, they found a huge tent festooned with coloured banners in the neighbouring field. The circus was in town. Around the tent, the people of the circus were practising their arts, balancing on tightropes, juggling, tumbling, even washing down an elephant.

'What am I to do?' the circus owner explained. He was short, like a Toby jug, sad, with a huge moustache. 'I have three elephants, several lions, my wife's mother and eighteen other relatives. Where could we possibly go?'

No one else had an answer, either. As they rested, Don noticed a young girl, the owner's daughter, riding around a makeshift ring balancing on the backs of two white horses. She waved. He waved back. The show must go on.

And so did the 6th, more slowly than ever as they approached the border. A mile beyond the farmhouse they had to manoeuvre around two British Matilda tanks that had broken down. Don had heard there was a lot of that. He'd heard many things about the BEF—that equipment was in short supply, badly packed and often sent to the wrong units; that the tanks had no wireless sets, that they were no match for the German panzers; that the twenty-five-pounders had arrived in France untested and unfired; that . . . well, there came a point when you didn't want to hear any more.

He didn't hear the Luftwaffe, either. He was aching from lack of sleep and the constant grinding of low gears had left his ears ringing. Up ahead he could see that the column had come to a complete halt. Civilians were looking up into the sky and pointing; a few soldiers began firing their rifles. Then, from behind, came the dull crump of explosions, and suddenly the refugees were on the move again, scattering to the sides of the road and throwing themselves behind every available tree and piece of cover. When he saw tracer fire ripping the trees to shreds, Don decided to join them, head down in a ditch.

And so the 6th survived their first encounter with hostile fire. Little damage was done on that occasion; most of the attention of the Luftwaffe appeared to be back down the road, from where

Don could see a column of smoke rising, the only mark upon a cloudless sky. The circus tent must have seemed like a military bivouac from the air.

As Don and the others began to emerge from their hiding places, they became aware of the sounds of a commotion. Screams. Shouts of dismay. Hooves clattering on the metalled road. Drawing ever nearer. Suddenly two white horses, their eyes red with fear, flew past. They were dragging something behind them, tangled in the reins, bouncing off the tarmac.

Don ducked behind a tree and was sick.

*    *    *

In Joe Kennedy's view, it had been a splendid evening. Dinner at the Italian embassy, theatre, a new flirtation, then back to Beaverbrook's for a drink. Beaverbrook's door just along from the Ritz Hotel was always open and awash with good company and gossip. The two men were excellent companions and Kennedy was a frequent house guest at Beaverbrook's country home at Cherkley, where he had fallen into the most pleasurable habit of sleeping with one of Beaverbrook's research assistants. All in the line of business, of course; she would whisper in his ear all through the night, then write him a weekly letter full of her own endearments and the press man's private news. Keeping abreast, as the ambassador put it.

What he couldn't know was that the research assistant sent her letters through the *Express* office, where the manager would steam them open and copy the contents before posting them on. So everything got back to Beaverbrook—keeping the

American ambassador on his back, where he belonged, as His Lordship put it. No hard feelings. They were both businessmen, and information was a commodity from which they both made a handsome profit.

It was around midnight. Kennedy was just tucking into a fresh bottle of the Beaverbrook bourbon when the telephone rang. A summons. The Prime Minister wanted to see him. He made a point of asking for another drink before he left.

He found Churchill in his Admiralty workrooms. He had transformed the ground-floor dining room into an office, where he was pacing up and down, waving a glass, dictating to a female typist who was tapping out the words on a special silent machine. Churchill seemed not to notice his visitor, lost in concentration, and Colville scurried forward to guide the ambassador into the next room.

'It's a message to the President,' Colville whispered, pouring Kennedy a drink and settling him into an armchair crafted in the form of two hideously ugly dolphins.

Kennedy smirked. 'Let you into a secret, Jock,' he replied, assuming that any friend of Rab Butler's could be entrusted with a little gossip. 'The President doesn't like him. Ever since they met, back in '18, right here in London. Says Churchill treated him like an unpleasant smell, then forgot they'd ever met.' Kennedy shook his head dismissively. 'But Roosevelt hasn't.'

Colville started. Could it be true? There had been rumours, but Churchill placed such faith in the American connection. Could he be so appallingly wrong?

Of course he could.

And now he was at their side, dragging Kennedy into his inner sanctum, checking the draft of the message as he continued to stride up and down. Then he thrust it at Kennedy. Through eyes that had grown bleary, the American tried to take it in.

*As you are no doubt aware, the scene has darkened swiftly. The enemy have a marked preponderance in the air . . . Hitler is working with specialized units in tanks and air. The small countries are simply smashed up, one by one, like matchwood . . . We expect to be attacked here ourselves, both from the air and by parachute and airborne troops, in the near future . . .*

Kennedy wiped his brow, trying to clear his mind.

*But I trust you realize, Mr President, that the voice and force of the United States may count for nothing if they are withheld too long. You may have a completely subjugated, Nazified Europe established with astonishing swiftness, and the weight may be more than we can bear.*

Kennedy smiled to himself. He'd been warning about catastrophe all along, but it was breathtaking to hear it from Churchill, too. The bastard knew he was going to lose.

*All I ask now is that you should proclaim non-belligerency, which would mean that you would help us with everything short of actually engaging armed forces. Immediate needs are, first of all, the loan of forty or fifty of your older destroyers . . .*

There followed a long begging list that pleaded for old ships and new aircraft, financial credits and diplomatic support. When at last he looked up, he found Churchill staring at him.

'Joe, we haven't always seen eye to eye,' Churchill began, 'but I know your heart stands true.' This was nonsense, they both knew it, and his words couldn't wash away the antipathy they felt for each other, but such deceits were all part of the game. 'This is a message of the greatest importance. In the last few months your President and I have exchanged numerous messages, but none has been as fateful and urgent as this. I ask you to ensure that it is forwarded to the President immediately. Tonight. There is not an hour to waste.'

'Sure, Prime Minister.' It was the first time he had addressed Churchill by that title. It stuck in his throat. 'Then I'd better get out of here.' He rose and was almost through the door when Churchill called after him.

'Never forget one thing, Joe,' Churchill cried. 'We shall fight on, alone if necessary. And we shall win.'

'Sure, Prime Minister.'

Colville saw him to the door. As they walked out into a clear and starlit night, Kennedy paused and waved the paper in his hand. 'Jock, you heard it here first. There's just no way that Roosevelt can come out to play on this one. He's got a nominating convention in July, an election in November and a bunch of voters who'll go to hell before they watch American kids die in France once more. You understand me?'

Colville nodded gloomily.

'And one more piece of advice, Jock, friend to friend. Stop the old man drinking.' And Kennedy was gone.

Later he was to write, less than eloquently:

*I couldn't help but think as I sat there talking to Churchill how ill-conditioned he looked and the fact that there was a tray with plenty of liquor on it alongside him and he was drinking a Scotch highball, which I felt was indeed not the first one he had drunk that night, that, after all, the affairs of Great Britain might be in the hands of the most dynamic individual in Great Britain but certainly not in the hands of the best judgement in Great Britain. He was frankly worried about the situation but, as usual, he was clinging to the theory that, regardless of anything, we will never be beaten . . . I would say that a very definite shadow of defeat was hanging over them all last night.*

* * *

Henry Chichester was in his early forties. Secure job, steady income, and extremely well turned out for a man who'd been without a wife for so long. He took pride in his appearance and in the tidiness of the life around him; it was his way of showing that he could survive perfectly well on his own. Sadly for him, he failed to understand that it was precisely these qualities that attracted so many women to his congregation.

They brought their troubles to him, believing he would understand. Some of their difficulties were philosophical—was it a sin to instruct children to lie if strangers asked them for directions? Some were purely theological—should they pray for the souls of German dead? But mostly they were intensely personal. A young parishioner had turned up at his door that morning, sobbing in distress and wanting to know whether she would be condemned if she gave herself to her boyfriend before he went off to war. The vicar had offered her a cup of tea, a clean handkerchief and a homily about how it would be wrong to put aside personal morality simply because of the war. It seemed to help.

Later that morning, a sad-eyed pensioner had taken the wedding ring from her finger and pressed it into his hand, begging him to make sure it would be used for the war effort. She'd heard that German women were giving up their wedding bands, and she wanted to do her bit. He had pressed it back upon her. If that was the practice in Germany, he told her, it was the best reason he could think for an Englishwoman not to do anything of the sort. That, too, had helped.

With every word of comfort, the reputation of the Reverend Chichester rose in the eyes of his parishioners. It left him feeling a fraud. He made most of it up. God knew what the answers were to their questions, but he didn't. How could he talk to others about the wickedness of lies, when he wouldn't own up to the truth about his own son? He praised others for maintaining their moral codes, yet that was precisely what he had condemned Don for. The certainties in his life had gone, and what was left was obscured in clouds of spiritual dust.

He couldn't find sanctuary even in his church. He'd had another visitor that morning, a man from the War Office with a large paper file and a considerably smaller map of Dover, who had announced that he was requisitioning the tower of St Ignatius for use as an observatory. They were going to watch for enemy parachutists. Chichester had enquired whether this was wise since St Ignatius was the only tall building in the area that didn't have a telephone, but the man from the ministry was adamant, warning that he could have Chichester arrested if he caused difficulties, vicar or no vicar. Chichester responded that the lack of a telephone would be more likely to cause the difficulties, and left it at that. Perhaps he'd ask for a good peal of the bells at the weekend, just to ensure that those above the belfry were awake.

Even those wretched maps of the battlefield in *The Times* had begun causing trouble. He'd pinned the latest one up in the porch that morning. Still no fronts marked on it; in fact, it contained very little information at all. To the untrained eye they all looked the same. Except the Reverend Chichester noticed that the map, day by day, was moving ever farther westward.

* * *

Convoy. The dictionary talked about an escort designed for honour, guidance or protection. If that were so, the 6th no longer seemed to merit the term. They had moved back, even beyond the defensive works the BEF had spent so many months constructing, but it had done nothing to halt the tide of withdrawal. They had begun the day based at a chateau, had moved back to a small brewery at Laventie and were now on the move for the third time that day. The order and discipline that Don had associated with a life in the army had broken down with astonishing speed—they had lost all contact with the Casualty Clearing Station and had no idea where it had been moved. The station was supposed to assess the injured and hand them on for treatment, but now the 6th had to carry the wounded with them, crammed into the back of the ambulances. Many were too badly injured to make it. They were left behind with large red crosses pinned on their uniforms.

The number of casualties had begun to grow. Belgians, French, a few British, many civilians. The Luftwaffe was attacking indiscriminately, firing at ambulances, women, children, farm stock—anything to increase the mayhem and slow down the retreat. There could only be one point to this: the panzers weren't far behind.

The BBC announced that Brussels was not threatened—news that would have come as a shock to the grieving owner of the circus. And if Brussels wasn't being threatened, how was it that Don could hear the din of battle around Tournai, thirty miles further west?

The Medical Corps manual he'd trained with was no bloody use. It had nothing about how to deal with confusion and chaos. Don found himself doing whatever was required—tearing up sheets for bandages, boiling tools for the surgeons, disposing of the waste bits of war. He even had to start foraging for food—a NAAFI truck had driven past shortly after dawn, throwing out a little food and some cartons of cigarettes, but it hadn't stopped and they'd had nothing since.

While they were at the brewery there had been a

shout for medical tubing, something to keep airways open; he'd found some rubber tubing that was being used as a drip hose from one of the vats. It had done the job, *in extremis*. Most things seemed to be *in extremis*.

And so they moved on, but always back, until they arrived in Le Doulieu, a hamlet that consisted of no more than two farms and some outbuildings. It was getting late, too dark and too dangerous to go on, and they were all exhausted. It would have to do.

The stench as he opened the doors of the ambulance was indescribable. Twelve injured men strapped inside a vehicle designed for four. Something trickled onto Don's boots. The men were carried to the outhouses.

Don was astonished at how primitive French farms could be, yet it would have to do, and within minutes the kitchen had been turned into an operating theatre with water being brought to the boil and the table scrubbed and ready for surgery.

A patient was brought in, a young French soldier. Two orderlies held him down on the table as the surgeon cut away his uniform and began working on his legs.

Most of these patients, Don knew, would have to be left behind, spoils of war for the advancing Wehrmacht. And then what would happen to them? For the thousandth time he wondered what it would be like to face an enemy with a loaded rifle; for the thousandth time he heard his father calling him a coward. Inside, part of him wanted it to happen, for the Germans to catch up with them, so that at last he might know who was right.

He had sworn to the Tribunal that he was not a

coward, that he would do his duty, that he would not run. He wasn't certain of it, of course, couldn't be, not until the time came. Yet all around him the British army was running.

He was shaken from his thoughts by the cry of impotence that came from the surgeon as he threw his scalpel into the kitchen sink. For a moment his head bent wearily over his patient, as if accepting defeat, then he turned upon Don, his eyes filled with anger and awe at the mess God could make of His Creation.

'Hurry. Go out to the woodshed. There's got to be one. While there's time, fetch me a saw.'

* * *

'We always seem to have a drink in our hands,' Butler commented, greeting his friend.

'I, for one, need it,' Channon responded. His cheeks were flushed. He was in full evening dress, as was his colleague. 'Felt like death most of the day. Temperature of a hundred and three.'

'You should be in bed,' Butler replied.

'My dear Rab, we may all be going to die very soon. Personally I'd rather go down beneath a streptococcal virus with a glass of champagne in my paw than at the end of a German bayonet.'

The bar of the Savoy was beginning to fill with the evening crush. 'Cometh the crisis, cometh the crowd,' the barman had intoned as he'd polished fresh glasses. Money was being spent while it still had some value. The dining room was already overflowing and Channon had needed to part with a substantial tip in order to reserve a table.

'Pity you were laid low,' Butler muttered, his

eyes scanning the evening tide. 'You missed the fun.'

'Where?'

'At Downing Street. My summons came today.'

'Oh, dear. Had to happen, I suppose.' Channon's face fell. He was an exceedingly rich and inexhaustible socialite, yet he treasured his role as Butler's parliamentary aide; they were fastened together by ambition and would sink together, too.

Butler picked up the tale. 'It was brief. To the point. He sat there with a wet cigar between his lips, relighting it with the aid of something that resembled a Bunsen burner. Terrible eyes—I remember the eyes. Old. Worn out. I had to say I was feeling rather privileged that he'd brought me all the way over there to do it personally—Jock tells me most of the others have been sacked by telephone.'

'Damned rude.'

'What else do you expect from this gang? Anyway, he started by telling me how much he appreciated the subtlety and skill with which I handled difficult questions in the House.' Butler paused to raise an eyebrow in greeting at a passing acquaintance; it really was growing uncomfortably crowded. 'Said much the same thing during the India debates when we first clashed all those years ago. Accused me of being able to take any position on any matter and hold it in all sincerity for so long as I was expressing it. Suggested I should be a lawyer.'

'*He* accused *you* of insincerity?' Chips was incredulous. 'I hope you put him in his place.'

'Well, I was about to, prepared to hit him straight back over the boundary, when he bowled me something of a googly. Said he wanted me to continue at the Foreign Office.'

'What?'

'Yes. Took me aback for a moment, too. But the fact is, dear Chips, you and I are still in business.'

Chips struggled to compose himself as delight squeezed alongside his confusion.

'So I asked him. Why? Point blank. In all honesty I was too startled to be subtle. And d'you know what he said? *Because, although we have had our differences—*'

'I should say so!'

'—*I had once asked him to my private residence.*'

'I never have.'

'And that is why, dear Chips, I am His Majesty's Minister for Foreign Affairs and you . . . are not.' The lips wobbled; it looked like the slightest of smirks.

'Is that the price of a position in this new Government: a lamb cutlet and a bottle of claret?'

'Apparently. Must admit, I feel as though I've been accosted by a passing bank robber and had a ten-pound note thrust into my hand.'

'I don't know whether to laugh or burst with misery.'

'Neither do I. But I suppose we shall potter along for a while longer.' At this point his attentions were drawn to the other side of the bar. 'Ah, there's Jock. Inexcusably late. And not dressed for dinner.'

Colville was forcing his way through to where they were standing, launching hurried apologies both for his unpunctuality and for the fact that he would be unable to join them for the evening.

'Won't Winston let you come out to play?'

'It's . . . it's just awful,' Colville spluttered through the champagne that Channon thrust towards him. He appeared greatly distracted. 'It all started happening just after you'd left.'

'What started happening?' Butler enquired gently, trying to hide his irritation that he wasn't fully in the picture. It wasn't the first time; Churchill never entirely trusted the Foreign Office.

Colville took a conspiratorial breath, trying to ensure they couldn't be overheard. 'Panic. Or something close to it. It seems that Brussels has gone. Antwerp is about to fall. And the panzers are only a hundred miles from Paris.'

'Oh, my poor Paris,' Chips cried, his face once again growing fevered. He'd spent much of his peripatetic youth in the French capital, an education that had left him with a taste for most French vices, except those relating to women.

'Winston's flown there this afternoon,' Colville added.

'Searching for excuses.'

'I don't think we can blame Winston,' Colville countered.

'But fault has to find its home, Jock. He will be blamed—blamed for what is beginning to look like the greatest military disaster of all time.' Suddenly Butler stiffened. 'Which is why he reappointed me—and the others. So that we can all share in the responsibility. Had nothing to do with lamb cutlets, after all.'

'Lamb cutlets?' Colville muttered, but Butler swept his question aside.

'Tell me, Jock, has Winston heard back from Mr Roosevelt?'

Colville's eyes fell. 'Usual story. All support

short of actual help, I'm afraid.'

'Of course. Joe Kennedy had said it would be—what was his phrase?—"all smiles but no sausage".'

'So what are we to do?' Channon demanded, an anxious hand on Butler's sleeve.

'Have you ever read *Mein Kampf*?' the Minister enquired.

'You're kidding.'

'Terrible tome, but . . . Hates the Jews, of course, and the Russians. French, too, because of the humiliations they inflicted after the last war. Yet he seems almost to have a soft spot for the English. He talks about a division of the spoils. To us the Empire, and for him the rest of Europe. Something along those lines.'

'Why would he do that?'

'A sense of Aryan togetherness, perhaps. A desire for a new world order, with us controlling the seas and keeping the natives quiet while he does'—the most fractional of pauses—'whatever it is he wishes to do on the continent. It's all set out in his book.'

'Judging by the last few days he seems rather to have changed his mind,' Colville interjected.

'Really? I'm not sure, Jock. It's just that we haven't tried. And never will, so long as Winston's in charge.'

'But what do we do?' Chips demanded yet again.

'Do, my dear Chips?' Butler muttered, his lips quivering in surprise. 'Isn't it obvious? We do a deal.'

# CHAPTER FIVE

Don hadn't thought it possible to fall asleep standing up. But he had, in broad sunlight, against the wall of the barn with a cigarette between his lips. He hadn't woken until his legs had collapsed beneath him.

The first thing he noticed was that the casualties were still coming in. Hundreds of them. Soldiers, civilians, French and British, even a few German troops. They'd all found their way to this farmhouse in the middle of nowhere. It was as if the rest of the world had ceased to exist, and the survivors had struggled to this last and most remote place on earth.

The BBC had announced that the French forces had the situation under control, but not here they didn't. The outhouses of the farms were overflowing with casualties; newcomers were being left outside in the sun; and it seemed to Don that their injuries were growing ever more terrifying. His physical and emotional strength was almost overwhelmed, and he didn't think he could take much more. As he relit the cigarette that had remained stuck to his lips, he noticed that his hand was trembling uncontrollably. And all for two shillings a day.

Yet there could be no escape. The screams of those injured mixed with the cries of instruction from the doctors, and Don found himself running to help with another of the wounded, brought in on the shoulder of a fellow soldier, his head wrapped in a red tablecloth.

They laid him on the kitchen floor—the table was occupied—and a doctor slowly unwrapped the sodden cloth. Two terrified eyes stared out, but of the rest of the face there was almost nothing. No lower jaw, no tongue, no cheek, only those two staring eyes which understood it all. Fingers clutched at Don's sleeve with the force of a man under siege from pain he was incapable of resisting.

Don's stomach heaved in revulsion, and perhaps it was only his exhaustion that prevented him from throwing up. He'd never encountered such horror. But the eyes understood it all, staring at him, pleading. Gently the doctor replaced the cloth over those parts where the lower face should have been. He paused in prayer.

'God help him,' he whispered, 'for we can't.' He heaved himself back to his feet—it seemed to consume most of his remaining energy—and returned to his patient on the table. 'Give him morphine,' he instructed.

As he lay there the wounded soldier began to foul himself. He was no longer in control, carried away down a path of unbearable distress and darkness. He knew what was happening, for nothing had dulled either his mind or his pain. The eyes had taken on a new sharpness, and were screaming silently at Don.

With great tenderness, Don prised himself free from the clenched fingers and did as he was instructed. He gave the soldier morphine. Unscrewed the cap, squeezed the capsule. Marked an 'M' on his forehead. Then he gave him another dose. Two syringes. Too much. But still it seemed to have no effect, so ten minutes later Don gave him yet another. And slowly the eyes began to change, to lose that edge of fear, to go gently into his night. And to smile, Don thought. Don stayed with him, holding his hand, feeling him slip away.

Don did not stir until it was done.

'You did your best,' the surgeon offered, trying to console.

'I might have given him too much,' Don blurted back in shock. 'I didn't know how much to give him.'

'Do you think I do?' the man at the table spat, bent over yet another patient. There was bitterness in his voice.

'But you're a doctor . . .'

'Me? Not now, and not ever, not after this. I'm nothing but a dental surgeon,' the man replied, turning back to his work.

* * *

'I wasn't sure if you would come,' the old man muttered as he clambered into the back of the Humber.

'Neither was I,' she replied bluntly.

They said no more. Inspector Thompson sat up front alongside the driver as their journey unwound across the river and through the jumbled suburbs of south London until they had left behind the respectable brick fronts of Norwood and were into the open hills of Surrey. Churchill was hunched, bound inside an overcoat in spite of the sunshine, his hands resting on his silver-topped walking stick. His cheeks were grey. Ruth Mueller wore the same frayed suit, although he wouldn't have noticed.

'I have been Prime Minister for a week, and every day of that week I have woken with dread in my heart.' He sounded bitter, as if it were her fault. 'We are facing disaster.'

She considered this outburst for a moment. 'I'm puzzled, Mr Churchill. I am, by the definition of your own Government, an enemy alien. A security threat. Why are you telling me this?'

'Because That Bloody Man Hitler already knows,' he growled. He took a large handkerchief from his pocket and blew his nose fiercely. 'I was in Paris. Went to see for myself. Everyone had gathered together at the Quai d'Orsay—Reynaud, Daladier, General Gamelin—their top men, dripping dejection across every thread of carpet. They were standing; no one sat. It was as if at any moment they expected to start running.' He wiped his eyes, but she could sense that his sorrow was beginning to give way to anger. He sat up, more alert.

'The panzers push on, they told me, scattering the French armies in front of them. They had a large map set up on a student's easel. It had a battle front marked on it in a thick black line, but as they talked their fingers were always pointing to places behind that line. As if the line meant nothing any more. So I asked them: where is their strategic reserve? No one answered. I thought they had misunderstood, so I tried it in French. "*Où est la masse de manoeuvre?*" I demanded.'

He rapped his stick sharply on the floor.

'D'you know what Gamelin told me? Know what he said? Simply shrugged his shoulders and said, "*Aucune.*" None. They haven't got a bloody strategic reserve! Five hundred miles of front and they haven't got a single man, goat or mattress to plug the gaps!'

The grey cheeks had grown crimson with fresh life.

'And while we were talking, outside in the garden I could see bonfires. They were trundling out papers in wheelbarrows, and all for burning. The Third Republic disappearing in cinders and ash. They say Paris may fall in days. You can see it written on the faces of the people. Last time I was there they applauded as my car passed, but now there are no cheers, no salutes, no waving arms, nothing but the ripe stench of fear. They know their country is dying.'

And suddenly his whole body sagged, the anger giving way to exhaustion, as though all the sinews and strands that held his body together had been cut. It seemed that only the buttons on his overcoat kept him from collapsing completely.

'We have been fooled, duped, Frau Mueller. Hitler has shown us not only daring but also great wisdom. This has all been to his plan. He *wanted* us to advance into Belgium, encouraged us to move out from behind our defences. That's why he didn't bomb us during our headlong rush to adversity. We were blind, jumped to do his bidding. And now he has swept behind us and we are in danger of being cut in two. It seems barely credible, but we have been overwhelmed by a handful of tanks. Holland has gone, Brussels has been surrendered without a shot being fired, and his troops will soon be on the outskirts of Paris. Our great alliance with the French lies in ruins.'

He was weeping quietly now, the handkerchief to his eyes, the dark smudges beneath them like dead ash scattered over a hearth. 'It is said that the French troops are surrendering in entire companies with their officers at their head. They are throwing their weapons into the road to be crushed by the passing panzers. But the panzers don't even stop to take the surrender, they roll onwards, thirty and forty miles a day. Nothing like it has ever been seen before in the history of warfare.'

Suddenly he was staring at her, eyes still flooded but waving his hand in passion. 'He is beating me, Frau Mueller. Not only out there upon the field of battle, but up here'—he began jabbing a finger to his massive forehead—'in the battle of the mind. Out-thinking me, outsmarting me at every turn.'

He fell to brooding once more until they had rolled into Kent. A little more than twenty miles from their starting point, they drew into the driveway of an old brick-fronted house. The windows on the ground floor were shuttered and weeds were beginning to peer through the gravel of the driveway. In front of the house a bank of rhododendron bushes was in full and violent flower, but to her mind it only served to make the old house look more forlorn.

'Welcome back to Chartwell,' he announced as the car drew to a halt. In normal times his arrival would have lifted his heart. She remembered how he would leap out, scattering dogs and papers before him as he revelled in the joy of returning home. But these were not normal times. The house had been shut since the start of the war and an air of melancholy had settled around it. He made no attempt to go inside but led her around by a path that brought them to the rear of the house, and there his spirits seemed to lift, for Chartwell was set upon the side of a great Kentish hill that looked out upon endless miles of misty countryside. Nature had chosen this spot as a great stage with half of England as its audience. While Thompson and the driver disappeared inside the house, Churchill led her down towards the lakes in the valley below, and with every step his energies slowly returned. The back straightened, the gaze lifted, the walking stick became a weapon rather than a prop, slashing angrily at nettles that had begun to grow in corners, digging at young bramble shoots that would soon burst into a jungle of thorns. Yet the beauty of spring could not be turned by a few weeds; this was much as the Tudors would have seen England from this spot, and much as it might appear in another thousand years, if England still lived.

'Ah!' he exclaimed, poking with his stick amongst a scattering of feathers on the grass. 'Old Reynard's taken one of the ducks. But look, my black beauties are still here, every one of them. Remember?' He waved at the small flock of black swans that cruised on the larger of the two lakes. 'Survivors,' he whispered in awe.

Butter-dipped primroses were still in bloom along the banks of the lakes, and a carpet of bluebells had been rolled out for inspection beneath the beeches and great oaks. Squirrels rustled, ewes grazed, moorhens and coots protested at the intrusion and scampered into the reeds. Overhead a pair of buzzards wheeled and turned like dancers in the sky.

'Oh, how I love this place! One day, one glorious day, we shall return.'

'One day I would like to return home, too,' she responded dryly.

'Then it is agreed. We shall help each other.'

Instinctively she wanted to argue, to push against his presumption, but why else had she come if not to help?

He sat down on a stone cairn overlooking the lake, one of his favourite spots for easel and paints. Almost reluctantly, she settled beside him.

'You have a beautiful home, Mr Churchill.'

'A family home. So important, is family. You must miss yours.'

'I have no family to miss any more.'

He carried on; she wasn't sure whether he had heard her. 'I only wish my mother might have seen this place. She died shortly before I bought it. My father, of course . . . he died long before that. He was very young.'

'Hitler expects to die young.'

'I always thought that I would, too.'

'Perhaps that's why you—and he—have always been in so much of a hurry.'

He refused to rise to the bait she seemed constantly to dangle before him. 'I sometimes wonder whether my father knew that he would die young; if that was the reason why he seemed always to be so preoccupied, so precipitate. Tilting at every windmill. I must admit it was sometimes a struggle for a young boy to keep up with him.' He squinted into the sun, pretending that it caused the new moistness in his eyes.

If the young Winston hadn't been able to keep up, it was largely because he'd never been asked to. Lord Randolph had been a careless man, jealous of others, even his own sons, and Winston had spent his adult life trying to show his father how it might have been. That was what Chartwell had always been about. Family. Together. Not Christmases spent apart or summers spent adrift, and a child's letters from school left unanswered.

*Family!*

Suddenly he'd had enough of introspection. He sprang to his feet, setting off at a furious pace up the slope towards the house, head forward, cigar ablaze, his stick flying before him like a dueller's sword.

'The French,' he shouted over his shoulder, 'will want to make peace with Hitler.'

'They can't,' she insisted, already breathless in pursuit.

'They will, I fear. And not just the French. There are people in this country, even in my own Cabinet . . .' He slashed with his stick at some more rising weeds. Yes, it seemed that everyone wanted to bloody well talk.

'No, you do not understand.' She grabbed his sleeve, forcing him to stop. 'They *cannot* make peace with Hitler. Peace is not possible. You must understand . . .'

He could see desperation in her eyes, a haunted look as if a terrible tragedy that had once overtaken her was about to catch up with her again.

'Hitler is a man who is defined by war—and only by war. Without war he is nothing. He failed at everything—as a son, as a schoolboy, as an art student, as a friend. He finished up as a penniless vagrant on the streets of Vienna. He had no home other than a shelter for tramps, one step above the gutter. Then came war and suddenly he was no longer half formed but a complete man, with a sense of purpose and the respect of his fellows, a war hero with the Iron Cross. He couldn't let it go.

It was war that gave his life some sort of meaning. And only with war will Hitler's life retain any meaning. Don't you see? He can never stop.'

'Some of my colleagues argue that he will leave us alone. That he doesn't hate the English in the way he hates others.'

'That is true, he does not hate the English, but that will not save you. Look at Germany. He doesn't hate his own *Volk*, yet what has he done to us?'

'Given you victory after victory.'

'You think we are victorious? Open your eyes, Mr Churchill! We Germans were his first victims, long before Austria and Czechoslovakia and the rest.'

Abject incomprehension crept across his face.

'In Germany today there is no hiding place from him,' she continued, her words tumbling over each other in their determination to escape. 'No private life, no corner that you can claim as your own. You think you can see and understand what is going on, that your eyes are wide open, but then you blink and someone has disappeared. A public figure, perhaps, a writer, an actor, yet no one knows where. You shrug, you do not know them personally, they must have done something wrong, else why would they disappear? There has to be a reason for such things. Then you blink again and someone else has disappeared, but this time someone close to you, a neighbour, a friend, even family. For why? You ask what has happened, you demand to know, but then you discover that it has become an offence even to ask, and you realize that soon it may be your turn to disappear. And that is the reason it happens. Everything is broken down, every friendship, every loyalty. You still greet your neighbours, but *Wie geht's* and *Guten Tag* has suddenly been replaced by *Heil Hitler* and *Perish the Jews*. You want to keep breathing, but there is no air left any more, you are suffocating, and the only place you can get oxygen is from the Party. So you do as you are told. You stop asking questions. You think only what you are allowed to think, you admire only what you are authorized to admire and you love only with permission.' Some memory had brought her close to tears. 'Mr Churchill, you say we Germans are victorious but we have become less than slaves, for even slaves can live in hope that one day they will be given their freedom. Under Hitler, there is no hope.'

'Nevertheless, there are those who will insist that we talk with him.'

'You said the other day that your purpose was nothing less than victory. At all costs, in spite of all terror, because without victory there is no survival. Were they just words, Mr Churchill?'

'I also asked that we should go forward together with our united strength. Yet we are not united. Better a poor peace than a terrible war, perhaps.'

'You are being ridiculous. You cannot have peace!'

Churchill bristled.

'Do you think you can get away with inviting Hitler over for a ride up the Mall alongside the King?' she continued. 'That's not what this war is about. It's about'—her arms flew wide—'all this. Your island. England. What makes you different. And if you are willing to give that up then you don't understand the privilege of being English.'

'But if I try to fight on, I might end up destroying

everything—England, the Empire, all I have ever loved. Is that what you would have?'

'You stupid Englishman! You don't have any choice!'

That was enough—too much, in fact. Churchill was fond of both women and strong argument, but he had always found their combination irritating and Frau Mueller exceptionally so. German tanks were slashing their way across Europe; somehow he simply couldn't conceive of the Germans inside them as helpless victims and frankly he didn't care to try. If that was getting to know his enemy, he might as well call a halt here and now. And he felt suddenly exhausted. Nine days into the job; it hadn't been a lot of fun being Prime Minister so far.

'I understand your passion, Frau Mueller, and your personal experience commands all my sympathies,'—the words echoed with disdain—'but I think it has rather coloured your conclusions. You will have to allow we Englishmen to make up our own minds.'

She stood close to him, clenched her fists. 'Tell me, Mr Churchill, what would your father have done?'

Churchill winced, lost in momentary confusion at this unexpected alliance between Frau Mueller and his father.

She answered her own question with contempt in her tone. 'He would have fought, of course. But then they said he was mad.'

They stood glaring at each other, neither willing to give ground, her slim frame lost against Churchill's awesome shadow, until the moment was broken for them by an approaching figure.

Thompson was running down the slope towards them.

'Telephone,' they heard him cry. 'They want you back, sir. They say it's very urgent.'

* * *

It was part of Don's duties to clear up, even the bodies. He helped bury the dead soldier, along with several others, in the field behind the farmhouse. It turned out he had been an officer, a lieutenant in the Royal Artillery, and some idiot had even started an argument that he should be buried apart from the other ranks. The padre had suggested that as they had died together there couldn't be too much harm in burying them together. If it was good enough for God, it should satisfy the War Office. And so it had been done.

There had also been a discussion about two dead Germans. In the end, with the agreement of the handful of other German wounded, it was agreed that they should be buried with a few prayers in their own language. So the German dead were given their own ceremony, which, with seemingly comic irony, had been interrupted by the arrival of the Luftwaffe, two Me-109s that strafed the farmhouse and began turning for a second pass. Don found himself dragging a Wehrmacht soldier with a badly lacerated leg into a ditch, landing on top of him and instinctively trying to protect him from the attack. When it was over, Don was shaking, but despite his pain the German began to laugh. 'Too many bullets, eh, Tommy? Yesterday English bullets, today German. War is bloody dangerous, eh?'

When he clambered out of the ditch, Don found a new body by the graveside. It was the dental surgeon.

Suddenly Don began screaming at the disappearing Messerschmitts, hurling after them all his anger and frustration at a war that was so unjust, until the German limped over and stood in front of him.

'No point, Tommy. No one listens.'

Artillery shells began to fall, very close. Time to move on once more. But there were too many casualties to transport in the few ambulances that had survived the attack. There was nothing else for it—the most seriously wounded would have to be left behind, along with all the Germans. And some of the medical staff.

'So, some of us are going to have to stay, lad,' the sergeant explained. 'Your war might be over even before it's got going.'

They cut cards, everyone, right up to the lieutenant colonel. Don's was a jack, but the sergeant drew a deuce. As he turned the card over, he forced a grim smile. 'It's an honour, that's what it is. A bleedin' honour. Just pray for me that it's all over by Christmas, eh?'

But if prayers got answered, this would never have started . . .

Don carried the German on a stretcher to lay him in the open outside one of the outhouses. It had been decided that the advancing Wehrmacht should meet the German casualties first. They could report on their good treatment. And if by chance the Luftwaffe came back and started shooting the place up once again—well, it seemed only fair they should have a German target rather than a British one. The hazards of war.

Don laid his patient down in the sun and offered him a cigarette. The German nodded his thanks.

'We win this one, eh, Tommy?'

'Don't be bloody stupid,' Don snapped, suddenly and surprisingly angry. 'This is just the away match. You wait till the return game. We'll have home advantage then, just you see.'

As the remnants of the 6th Field Ambulance Unit drove off into the gathering dusk, Don knew more clearly than ever that war was unjust and evil. The trouble was, he knew that running from it didn't work any more.

* * *

Bracken rushed in as soon as he heard raised voices—or, in truth, one raised voice. There was rarely more than one raised voice in this room.

Churchill was behind his desk, surrounded by a snowdrift of papers that had been swept aside. In front of him stood Colville. The civil servant was writhing in discomfort. Bracken had an appetite for blood sports, particularly when it involved over-elevated bureaucrats and placelings, but there was nothing sporting in this. Churchill had lost control. His temples were swollen and purple with rage, his knuckles showed white, and he had hurled his reading glasses into one corner. As Bracken approached, he hurled a cigar into another.

'Am I to fight this war single-handed, denied help from any quarter?' Churchill stormed.

'Winston, you're making enough noise for an entire army. Calm down. And give me a clue.' Bracken was calling on almost twenty years of friendship and shared adversity, but the flash of temper in the old man's eye suggested that even Bracken had overdrawn his credit.

Churchill struggled to respond with anything less than volcanic intensity. 'The French,' he spat, 'have dissolved. The slightest rumble of mechanical thunder and they have disappeared into the night like bats driven from their belfry.'

'Paris has fallen?'

'No!' Churchill pounded the table. 'The panzers have swung north. North! North! They are no longer heading for Paris but for the Channel ports. That Bloody Man means to encircle the entire British Expeditionary Force and strangle it to death.'

'Damn. That's not what we expected.'

'Who knows what to expect any more? And while the French generals disappear, our own generals dicker and disobey. I have given them orders to strike south. South! So that we may join up once more with the French and cut the panzers off. But instead of doing as he's told, Gort has demanded that he be allowed to withdraw. Retreat. We've suffered fewer than five hundred casualties in the entire campaign and yet our leading commander wants us to run away with our tails between our legs. And those bloody Yankees . . . !' He slumped back into his chair and reached for another cigar. 'We asked for destroyers. Only old destroyers they did not want and would've scrapped. But for us, they might be a lifeline. Yet they put us off—and why? Tell him, Mr Colville.'

Colville stood silent.

'Tell him!'

'Prime Minister, I am not a squaddie. If I am to

be yelled at like one, then I request permission for a transfer to armed service.'

'What? You want to fight?' Churchill growled from behind a huge flame. Bracken began silently laughing.

'Yes, sir.'

A hesitation; a pall of blue smoke. 'Excellent!' Churchill snapped, but both the tone and volume had softened. 'At last, someone who wants to fight this wretched war with me. But for the moment, Mr Colville, carry on.' Churchill spat out a fleck of tobacco. 'Please.'

Colville stiffened to attention. He understood that he had come as close to an apology as he was ever likely to get with this man. For the moment, it had to be enough. In his blue suit with toecaps polished to perfection, he turned smartly towards Bracken. 'Mr Kennedy has advised the President that it would be unwise to offer us any assistance at this point. He says that in his opinion either England will fall, or some new government will be installed which will conclude a peace treaty. Either way, anything that America sends is likely to end up in the hands of the Germans.'

'Bastard.'

'So Joe ensures we get no help and does his damnedest to make sure his own dire prediction comes true,' Churchill seethed. 'Meanwhile I'm left to pretend to the world that I am at one with America, that I believe in the French and that my generals are doing what I bloody well tell them. And piled upon that there's the most monstrous pretence of all, that my government is united behind me. Makes you wonder who the hell the real enemy is.'

'Winston, stop being so stinkingly miserable. You're not fighting this war on your own. There's me, and Jock here.'

'If only your undoubted martial enthusiasm were matched with any shred of experience.'

'Not to mention millions of ordinary Englishmen.'

It was offered, and taken, as justified rebuke. The old man's tempers were thunderous, yet could disappear as quickly as a flash of lightning. He began to collect himself. It wasn't Colville's fault that he was so young, or Bracken's fault that the only military experience in his family was traceable to his father, an ardent Irish republican who had been in the habit of blowing up buildings owned by Englishmen.

'And, come to think of it, there's a peculiarly irritating German woman, too,' Churchill mused, sucking at the cigar. 'She wants me to fight. In fact, insists upon it, says I've got no option.'

'But what shall we fight with if Roosevelt won't give us the destroyers?' Colville enquired.

The passion was back, but this time channelled and sustained. 'Why, we shall fight them from rowing boats and paddle steamers if necessary. We can't give in, never, never! At least, I shan't. So this is what we'll do. We shall confirm our order to General Gort to advance south towards the French. We shall offer the French more aircraft and encourage them to advance north. And we shall telegram to President Roosevelt yet again. If he cannot give us old destroyers, then let us ask for some new fighters. I won't let him sleep with an easy conscience. So summon them all, Mr Colville, the Chiefs of Staff and my War Cabinet. Instruct them to bring their fighting boots, and inform them that if any of those boots arrive without the mud of Flanders clinging to their welts, there will be hell to pay!'

As Colville bent to retrieve the old man's reading glasses, Bracken smiled, content that the master was restored.

'Tell me, Winston, how the hell did you find out about what Kennedy was telling the President?'

'Ah!' Churchill looked up, a gleam of mischief in his eye. 'For that I must thank Providence. And Mr Chamberlain. Do you remember me telling you about the phone taps he had forgotten to cancel? Well, by some extraordinary oversight, I appear to have forgotten to cancel his tap on Mr Kennedy's phone.'

'We are bugging the American ambassador?'

'I shall do more than bug him! You know, if ever I had any doubts about this war, Brendan, the fact that he's such an unquenchable defeatist makes me sweep aside all hesitation. I have no idea how our cause will progress, but I vow on my father's grave that if I am to be dragged down to the gates of hell, I shall take Joe Kennedy with me. Then I can die a happy man.'

Churchill was to live. Yet he was still to be pushed to the gates of hell, with Joe Kennedy lighting fires all the way.

## CHAPTER SIX

At around ten o'clock on the morning of Monday 20 May, four men gathered outside the door of a bedsit at 47 Gloucester Place in London's Marylebone. It was the home of a young American, Tyler Kent.

Kent was twenty-nine, a clean-cut American with excellent academic credentials. He spoke several languages, had been born in Manchuria, had spent several years in Moscow and claimed to be related to Davy Crockett. He was also a cipher clerk at the US embassy.

Two of the men who stood outside his door were detectives from Scotland Yard, another was from MI5, and the fourth a senior official from the embassy. When they knocked, they heard scuffling, and were told by a male voice that they couldn't come in. They broke down the door and found Kent in a state of undress with a young woman, his mistress.

They also found the most extraordinary hoard of diplomatic papers. Stuffed inside a cupboard and a large leather suitcase they found 1500 embassy cables, two photographic plates and a pair of duplicate keys to the embassy's code room. The cables contained some of the most sensitive messages to have passed through the embassy in recent months, including what was known as 'Naval Person' correspondence—the private messages Churchill had sent to Roosevelt. It was believed that within days of being sent they had all found their way into German hands.

Kent's arrest was the most extraordinary affair. It was the first (and only) time in American history that an embassy official's diplomatic immunity from arrest had been waived. Permission for this had been granted two days beforehand by the ambassador himself.

When Kennedy had first been told about the spy in his embassy, it had placed him in a quandary. Any scandal would reflect badly on him, particularly since he himself was often accused of reckless chatter. He was always being quoted by the Nazi-controlled German News Agency. Then there was the added complication of the mistress, which would inevitably draw further unhelpful comparisons. And although Kennedy couldn't recall ever meeting Kent, there were only two hundred employees at the embassy and nobody would believe there wasn't a close personal connection. Kent and Kennedy would be wrapped up in it together.

Yet, as he listened to the story, Kennedy began to find comfort. There was even an attraction in allowing Kent to be arrested. In the first place it would disseminate the papers found in his cupboard ever more widely, which would make it clear to even the slowest of wits that America had no intention of becoming embroiled in yet another of Europe's monstrous screw-ups. But there was more. Amongst those papers were internal embassy notes recording American opinion about Churchill himself. Like Roosevelt's reflections, shared with Kennedy a few months beforehand, that 'I have always disliked him since the time I went to England in 1918' when Churchill had, in the words of the American President, 'acted like a stinker'. Or the views of the senior diplomat Sumner Wells, who after a tour of European capitals had concluded that Churchill talked too much and drank even more. These were personal opinions, private treasures, not intended for public display, but if Scotland Yard insisted on breaking open the vaults there was little that could be done to stem the resulting gossip. And Kennedy knew about gossip. His own conduct had so often been the subject of gossip, which was difficult for a man whose wife was a pious Irish immigrant wedded to the idea of fidelity and interminable prayer. On a petty level it seemed like an opportunity to spread the load a little, while on an altogether higher plane it would provide ammunition for those who wanted to cut Churchill out of the picture and bring the war to a swift conclusion. Hell, the more the ambassador thought about it, the better it got.

There was also the consideration that Scotland Yard was investigating a couple of matters involving clumsy investments in which Kennedy's name had an infuriating habit of cropping up. Nothing illegal, of course, but . . . well, distracting. It wouldn't do to upset the men from the Yard.

So, at their request, he made a little history and permitted Tyler Kent to be arrested.

* * *

The flat landscape of the Pas de Calais just north of Béthune allowed you to see for miles. And to be seen. The convoy had been attacked twice that day, despite the vivid red crosses on the tops of the ambulances. They'd lost their commanding officer and many others, dead or left behind wounded. The 6th was down to eleven crowded vehicles and its last second lieutenant, with Don driving the only remaining jeep after it had turned over and rolled upon its driver in the raid an hour ago. It was still possible to see the wreckage of the convoy burning several miles behind them and, up ahead, long trails of smoke from other pyres. Somehow being a noncombatant hadn't seemed so bad when he'd discussed it with the Tribunal. A worthy alternative, helping those in distress, something he could do with pride. No one had mentioned sitting on an open French road in bright sunlight while half the Luftwaffe took free shots at him.

He hated not so much the thought of dying but of dying disgustingly, like the young officer. Somewhere, back along that long road lined with casualties and crosses, Don had lost the sense of buoyancy that went with being a teenager. His bowels were liquid, his legs had turned to old iron and he was gripping the steering wheel too tightly. He was scared. He was also angry. Maybe his father had been right.

The convoy was stopping. Evening was casting long shadows as they drew up to a crossroads. No signposts, but Merville, their destination, had to be north. From the east a motorcycle approached throwing up a large cloud of dust. Someone was in a hurry. The driver halted, wiped the sweat and embedded flies from his face and told them in a flat Canadian accent that everyone was falling back towards the ports. Merville wouldn't be any damned good, not by the morning.

He also told them of a wounded airman, French, whose parachute had become entangled in trees off the road a couple of miles back. He was injured, but not badly. Couldn't walk, a broken ankle, perhaps. He'd been left propped up against the tree awaiting help. Or the Germans, if they got there first. Yet there had been reports that Goering was threatening to execute captured French pilots in retaliation for what he claimed was the shooting of German pilots while they were still strapped in their parachutes. Ten French for every German, he had promised. So it didn't seem much of an option, leaning against a tree waiting for Harry Hun.

The light would be gone in an hour, but it would only take twenty minutes to reach him, ten in anything light like a jeep. Don spoke a little French. He volunteered to go.

Life is made up of a million insignificant fragments that fall in a manner out of our control and often beyond comprehension. A decision is made, a hand is lifted, a life changed. Don gunned the engine and disappeared.

The trees were easy to find, as the Canadian had promised. They stood in isolated line like so many that seemed to be scattered aimlessly across the French countryside. The Frenchman was propped between the bulging roots of a tall poplar, his face drained grey with pain, his left ankle twisted awkwardly, the canopy of his parachute billowing in the branches high above his head.

'Hello, chum,' Don greeted, reaching for his flask. 'Er . . . *vous avez un problème*?'

'Ah, the English have arrived. At last. With water. But where were your planes?'

'Busy, I expect,' Don muttered, taken aback at the aggression and the Frenchman's very passable English.

'But not busy in France. Or does the RAF only fly in the rain?'

'Look, do you want a lift, or have you got something else planned for this evening?'

The Frenchman gave a Gallic shrug of contempt. 'To the next town. If that is not too much trouble. I shall not need to bother you for long.'

For a while, the pain seemed to silence the Frenchman. Don gave him morphine, bound the injury then helped him onto his one good leg and led him to the jeep. He leaned against the side, breathing heavily from the effort and wiping sweat from his forehead. It was then that they heard the noise—a terrifying mixture of roaring motors and mechanical aggression that within moments seemed to have engulfed them. Both on the road and in the air above them, mighty machines swept past them in the direction of the convoy.

It was a matter only of moments. First the Messerschmitts, then the pounding of five-centimetre guns from panzers as they hurtled along the road. The convoy huddled round the crossroads like a target in a crosswire; Don and the French airman watched as it was overwhelmed and annihilated. Men and ambulances reduced to a million insignificant fragments.

The panzers did not stop. Neither did the armoured units that followed, not until darkness had fallen. When at last they felt they could risk it, Don and his reluctant ally edged quietly out from the trees. The horizon to the east had been turned into a sheet of flame. They drove west.

* * *

Colville rapped cautiously on the bedroom door. It was more than two hours after midnight. He knew Churchill would still be awake.

The sight that greeted him was extraordinary. Churchill was standing beside his bed, naked except for a silk vest, with a fresh cigar in his mouth. Slowly he removed the cigar and stared at Colville through a meandering fog of smoke.

'What is it, Jock?'

It was the first time he had addressed Colville in any manner other than formally, but it was difficult to insist on formality when your trousers were hanging over the back of a chair.

'We've at last managed to get through,' Colville replied. It had been a chaotic day with all the telephone links to France cut. For many hours the government in London hadn't the slightest idea what was happening across the Channel and, as the evening had grown longer, Churchill had grown increasingly depressed. What little news was available contained no crumb of comfort, and the holes in their knowledge had come to be dark pits of gloom.

'And?' Churchill demanded, sensing the younger man's reluctance.

Colville tried, but his throat was parched through want of sleep. It came out as no more than a whisper.

'Abbeville.'

'Oh, my,' Churchill gasped, sitting on the bed. 'Abbeville—Abbeville,' he repeated. 'You realize what that means, Jock? They've reached the Channel. We are cut off. That Bloody Man has sawn our great alliance in two.'

It was worse than that. French resistance had melted like butter, allowing the Germans to pour through the gap so that the BEF was now separated not only from the bulk of the French army but also from its own supplies. Only three Channel ports were left under their control—Boulogne, Calais and Dunkirk at the most northerly tip of France. Abbeville was barely a day's drive away.

The old man had tears in his eye. He seemed to be looking at a photograph of his father that he kept by his beside.

'But we shall fight, Papa, we shall fight,' Colville thought he heard him whisper, before he closed the door behind him.

* * *

'Heard you were half Red Indian, Chips.'

'Oh, at least half, my dear ambassador,' he replied jauntily. 'Bareback is my favourite style.' Channon squeezed his knees and his mount broke into a gentle canter. It was an extraordinary thought: Channon was the most immaculately presented of Englishmen, from his clipped Oxford accent to the carefully folded silk handkerchief in the breast pocket of his riding jacket, yet he had been born in Chicago. As Kennedy had once said unkindly of him, he had given the concept of 'going native' an entirely fresh meaning.

'You'll need more than a goddamned horse to get yourself out of this mess,' the diplomat called after him. 'Wouldn't you say, Rab?'

The three of them were riding through the early morning on Rotten Row, the bridle trail that wound around London's Hyde Park. It was dry, the hooves kicked up dust with every step. Even with its bright May plumage the park looked decidedly gaunt, disfigured by gun batteries and long entrails of trenches that had been ripped hastily from its earth.

'Metaphors about donkeys led by jackasses

tumble through the mind,' Butler responded. 'I've never known such confusion. Winston wants the BEF to strike south and re-establish contact with the French. Gort says that's impossible and insists on a withdrawal to the ports. Meanwhile the French seem incapable of fighting in any direction and do nothing but demand that we send them more planes to destroy.'

'I hear Winston sent Ironside—what do you call him? Chief of the Imperial General Staff? Hell of a monicker,' Kennedy mocked. 'Anyhow, he sends Ironside to France, so my sources tell me. Wants him to talk with Gort, bend him about a bit, try to bring him round. Fat chance. I'm told there was more blood spilled in that room than along the entire Western Front that day. Gort refused point blank and said old Winnie's plans to strike south were madness. Was that the word he used? Yeah, I'm sure of it. Madness.'

'Your sources are, as usual, remarkably well informed. Catching up with the French army is like trying to catch a receding tide. Run as hard and as long as you like, but somehow the French always run faster.'

'And you're left standing up to your neck in—'

'Mud. Precisely.'

'Ironside's pulled a tough one. The French wouldn't talk to him, Gort shouted at him and a German bomb blew him out of his bed when he got back to Calais. Tell me truly, Rab, you think he's gonna be any safer here in London in a couple of weeks' time?'

The Minister didn't answer. He kicked ahead, as though trying to leave behind the awful, unspoken conclusion.

'It's one of those little paradoxes of human nature,' Butler began again as Kennedy caught up with him, 'that while, with every passing hour, Winston becomes more powerless on the field of battle, at home he struggles to establish the pretence of ever-greater authority.'

'Meaning?'

'The new Emergency Powers. In the name of freedom, he is turning himself into a dictator. Unlimited powers. Confiscation of profits. Compulsory direction of labour. And he complains about fascism!'

'Sounds more like communism to me.'

'Why, he could even order Chips down the coal mines.'

'And ruin his manicure? What would be the point?'

'That's the problem, Joe. There is no point, to any of it.'

'At least Hitler knows what he wants. What does Winston want apart from endless war?'

'A place in history.'

'And I understand Herr Hitler intends to give it to him.'

'Winston's so extraordinarily blind. Grabs for himself the powers of the meanest little Nero and pretends that it's all to do with maintaining man's inherent right to emancipation and independence.'

'So long as you're not a dark-bellied Indian.'

'Steady,' Butler cautioned, pulling on the reins. 'I'm not sure that your Indians have done any better than ours.'

'One of 'em sure has,' Kennedy responded, nodding at Chips.

'But for how much longer? What will happen to

us? Everything we hold dear in this country, our property, our freedom, our associations, are all under threat.'

'Yeah, but from who?'

They had slowed to a gentle walk, treading carefully as their thoughts and fears began to find form in the cool morning air.

'It's his nature, grown worse. The stubbornness. The impetuosity. Such comprehensive unreason.'

'The lust for power.'

'That at his will he may do danger with.'

'What?'

'Oh, forgive me, Joe. A little Shakespeare.'

'A little conspiracy.'

'We are simply considering options, Joe.'

'Then consider *all* the options. Your generals can't stand him. Most of his own Government can't stand him. The King can't stand him. His allies can't stand him. For God's sake, Rab, let me in on this great British secret: What use is Winston?'

The silence screamed out.

'To lose a war for one man's vanity is a misfortune,' Kennedy continued, 'but to lose an empire is madness.'

'Madness,' Butler repeated.

'So consider the options. You want peace. It can come in two forms. One that's agreed with the Germans, or one that's dictated by them. You choose.'

'If only I could.'

'What's for damn certain is that you can't let Winston choose! So consider the other option.'

'The other option?'

'The other-than-Winston option.'

'Then we *are* talking conspiracy.'

'We're talking common sense. And common interest. America doesn't want this European war. It doesn't want England crushed, and it sure doesn't want your navy to end up in German hands. It might come to that, Rab. You've got to do something before it's too late. Use whatever influence you have to ensure that the navy is sent to America.'

'In return for what?'

'For us not supporting Winston. And for not helping this country throw itself on the bonfire of one man's ego.'

'But lose our navy?'

'It either goes to your friends or the Germans will send it to the bottom of the Atlantic. Sink it—or save it. Your choice, Rab.'

The Minister considered, his lips working as though about to speak but unable to find the words. For many minutes his horse walked on, reins loose, lacking direction, doing mindless duty.

Chips was trotting back, summoning them for breakfast at the Dorchester, before Butler finally spoke.

'I shall get me to my master Halifax. Have him place his patriotism alongside his loyalty. See which weighs the heavier.'

* * *

*(Tuesday 21 May 1940. William L. Shirer, CBS.)*

*Good evening. This is Cologne, Germany.*

*I followed the German army into Belgium today as far as Brussels, and drove back here during most of the night to the first microphone I could find. There are two or three things I'd like to say . . .*

*So far as we could observe today, the Allied air force has done very little to hamper German communications in the rear. Though we drove for fourteen hours today, along roads choked with columns of troops and supplies, we did not see a single Allied plane. Along the road to Brussels, the Allies had blown up a few bridges—though others remained intact—and dynamited the road in two or three places. But German tanks and trucks were already thundering over it. There are the British night bombings, to be sure, and I experienced one last night. But I saw no traces of any bomb craters in the many roads we took today.*

*I do not pretend to know what damage has been done in western Germany by these night raids, but I motored through the Ruhr yesterday, and the vast network of railroads there, so important for Germany's war effort, was functioning very well, as far as I could see. I saw hundreds of important factories. Not one hit.*

*Tonight I talked to six British prisoners, all that were left of a whole company. They said they were simply overwhelmed by dive-bombers and tanks.*

*'What about your own bombers and tanks?' I asked.*

*'Didn't see any,' they answered.*

* * *

The tyres offered a dignified protest as they drew to a halt on the gravel inner courtyard of the Palace. The King's assistant private secretary, Lascelles, was there to greet him.

'A splendid day, Prime Minister.'

'My dear Alan.'

Lascelles winced. He hated his Christian name and was called 'Tommy' by everyone—well, almost everyone. Lascelles knew the slight was deliberate.

'His Majesty was hoping you wouldn't mind if the audience took place on the terrace—since it is a little later than he was expecting.'

Ah, the sharpened barb of complaint. 'Pray offer my profound apologies to His Majesty for my delayed arrival. The distractions of the Western Front. Again.'

Once more the words carried meaning that most eavesdroppers might not have understood. The two men loathed each other; their dislike was deep and lingering. There had been bad blood between them for many years—in fact since the last war, when Lascelles had accused Churchill, newly returned from the trenches, of using his parliamentary duties as an excuse to 'lay aside the King's uniform the moment it becomes unpleasantly stiff with mud'. Unforgivable, and unforgiven.

They walked in silence.

The King was pacing the terrace, impatient, bent forward, his hands behind his back, a cigarette between his lips. Nearby his wife was seated beneath a parasol protecting a pot of tea.

'Ah, Winston, delighted you're here. Do you mind? I've asked my wife to join us. I thought we might discuss a little family business.'

'Your Majesties,' Churchill greeted them, raising his hat and bowing low.

'Have some tea,' George instructed.

'Don't be silly, dear,' the Queen protested as Churchill took a seat beside them. 'The tea's cold.

Anyway, after the day he's had, Mr Churchill will want something a little stronger than tea.'

'And so, I believe, will we all,' the King agreed. A servant was sent scurrying.

'I'm so grateful, Winston. I know how ferociously occupied your time is. And I don't wish to disturb you unnecessarily. You didn't mind me writing to you about Beaverbrook, did you?'

Ah, more code. The King had written to Churchill expressing his profound reservations about Beaverbrook's proposed appointment and asking Churchill to reconsider. Churchill had ignored him and gone ahead regardless.

'I understand your position, of course,' the King continued. 'The exigencies of office. But I was hoping we might find a compromise on the other matter.'

'The other matter, sir?'

'Bracken. It really is entirely inappropriate—would break all the precedents—to appoint him to the Privy Council; he's not held any major office of state, indeed he hasn't held any office whatsoever. You see the problem, I'm sure.'

The response began with a form of strained growl, as if as much was being stifled as was being said.

'Sir! The reason Mr Bracken has held no office is because he was a man who chose to come with me into the wilderness rather than kowtow to the demands of appeasers and brutish political enforcers. He stayed with me when all others had fled—stuck with his conscience while others sold theirs cheap. Is he now to suffer still further punishment for remaining steadfast? Is loyalty to become a sin? I pray, sir, that at this terrible hour in our fortunes, when the burden of disaster has been thrust fully upon my shoulders, it is not too much to expect a little help!'

The King had been expecting compliance, or at least conciliation. Instead he had got a cavalry charge. It was fortunate that the drinks arrived, providing a pause for both men to regroup.

'You mentioned a family matter, sir,' Churchill began again, anxious to lead the conversation down more fertile paths. It was yet another of his good intentions that was to die a lonely death that day. The King's shoulders stiffened.

'Yes, Prime Minister. I understand you wrote to the Kaiser. Offered him asylum. You asked him to come and live here. Did you not think of consulting me before you wrote to a member of my family?'

'Sir, the hour was pressing. If it were to be done it had to be done then, or not at all.'

'But he's my cousin. Don't I have a say in this?'

'In normal circumstances . . . but you will appreciate, sir, that the circumstances are far from—'

'It's a matter of not just the common courtesies but also the constitutional proprieties of it all. I am head of state. He is—'

'A man who is no longer head of state. And a man whom many regard as no better than a war criminal. It would have been entirely inappropriate if any communication with him had come from you.'

'I understand it was a f-failure. He showed no interest in the . . . p-proposition. Dismissed it out of hand.'

'Yes, it proved to be a terrible idea, but these things happen. And my presumption has protected you and the Crown from any criticism which might erupt from that failure. As for me, sir, my back is broad.'

It sounded like a silly boast from a man whose patience had been rubbed bare. And, under pressure, George's stammer was back. Ridiculous masculine nonsense.

'Gentlemen,' Elizabeth intervened, 'what's done is done. There is nothing to be gained from history.'

Churchill thought there was rather a significant amount to be gained from history, particularly if you happened to be a hereditary monarch, but he appreciated the Queen's effort to pour what he later described to Bracken as 'whisky upon troubled water'. She was no enthusiast for Churchill—he had offended her greatly by his posturing during the abdication crisis—but she was a most practical woman and determined above all to protect her husband. 'Mr Churchill, you will forgive us, I hope, but the strain of recent weeks affects us all.'

'My apologies to you both if I spoke out of turn, ma'am. You know there is no man in the kingdom more loyal to the Crown.'

'Apologies have no place here, Mr Churchill,' the Queen continued, 'and never must between us. If we differ, let it be in private, and for the outside world let us show nothing but one face and one cause.'

Churchill blew his nose. 'That was so beautifully put, ma'am. I feel like Raleigh, ready to cast myself at the feet of his Queen.'

'Thank you,' she smiled, marvelling—and not for the first time—at this outrageous Victorian charmer. 'But there is something else. The children. Friends have said we should consider sending the girls away, perhaps to Canada.'

Tears welled in Churchill's eyes. His reply came slowly, every word weighed.

'That, Your Majesties, would not be possible.'

Once again the King bristled, but Elizabeth reached for his hand to still him. This was not a time for mannish posturing; it was not a joust, nor any form of confrontation—not yet, at least.

'Please try to understand,' Churchill continued, shaking his head. 'You are symbols—in much the same way as the old Kaiser is a symbol. You have no choice in the matter, you were born to it—just as the little princesses have been born to their role. And the task of the Royal Family at this moment is to act as a banner around which others might rally, to provide a beacon of light and resistance that will stretch into the farthest corners of our land. The road that lies ahead of us will be long and arduous, filled with much grief, and it may not be successful. But there is still hope. And on that flame of hope may depend our nation's survival. If you or the little princesses were to leave the country at this point, then that flame would be extinguished and we would lose everything. Me, my life; you, your crown—for they would most surely bring back your brother. And England, our England, that island of Nelson and Shakespeare, of Empire, of decency and brotherhood, would be nothing but a sad and distant dream.' His tears were flowing freely now.

'You are saying I have no say over the fate of my own d-daughters?' George persisted. 'The girls are to stay here—for the sake of appearance?'

'For the chance of deliverance.'

'Sounds like one hell of a gamble, Winston.'
'It is.'
It was now the turn of the King to take the Queen's hand. He stared into her eyes for reassurance before returning to his Prime Minister, the stammer gone.
'I was not born to this job. I inherited it by circumstance and I find its constraints very heavy. Wearing the crown is a duty I don't always enjoy or even understand, but it is a duty I must do. I think I shall need your help, Winston, if I am to do it well.'

# CHAPTER SEVEN

As an alliance, it didn't have much to say for itself. Don had given the Frenchman the last of his morphine. The airman had struggled, muttered and then passed out as they drove onward through the darkness, guided only by moonlight, not knowing which direction might be safe. Don was alarmed at the prospect of running into the advancing Germans, but he was still more afraid of doing nothing and allowing himself to be overwhelmed by the panic and confusion he felt inside. His friends were dead, his unit obliterated, and war for Don was no longer a matter of picking up the pieces but of a struggle for his own survival. He had to do something. So he drove.
When the airman came round almost an hour later and asked where they were, Don had to admit he was totally lost. The Frenchman offered nothing more than a withering look and waved him on.
Towards dawn they came upon a town guarding

the confluence of several waterways. A sign said it was called Aire. On its outskirts they stopped a passing bicyclist, with whom the Frenchman exchanged hurried words before directing Don through a series of back streets until they drew up outside a large house bearing a doctor's plate. Sustained banging on the door woke him, and after a heated exchange in unintelligibly rapid French, the ankle was inspected and more morphine administered, but the doctor decided it was no more than a serious strain and bound it tightly.

As soon as the doctor had finished his work, another forceful discussion took place.

'He docs not want us here,' the Frenchman explained. 'Some German units have been reported nearby. He says the war is coming too close. And it appears he has a weak heart.' There was no disguising the contempt.

'So where do we go?'

'To the war.'

'But your ankle . . .'

'My ankle will heal better in a French bed than in a German prison bunk. Anyway, you saw what happened to your friends. It doesn't look as if the Germans are much interested in taking prisoners.'

It was a point that had not escaped Don.

The Frenchman lit a foul-smelling cigarette while he fought the pain and reassembled his thoughts. 'The doctor says the Germans are in Abbeville, so we cannot move south. We must go north. Forty miles. To Dunkirk, Calais, Boulogne, perhaps. That is where our armies will be, with their backs to the sea. That is where the retreat must stop.' He coughed and winced with the pain. 'No, not Boulogne,' he continued, shaking his head. 'If the Germans are in Abbeville, Boulogne will be their next target. The next step up the coast. So we go to Calais.'

'Don't I get to have an opinion in this?' Don demanded. 'You seem to forget that I drive the jeep.'

'And I give the orders,' the Frenchman spat back. 'I have the higher rank, and you are in France.'

All this was true enough, but Don was beginning to dislike the arrogance that this Frenchman hung around him like a cloak. He had half a mind just to leave the bastard here to the mercies of the Germans.

'Anyway,' the Frenchman continued, 'you are lost. You have no idea where you are. You are as likely to end up heading for Berlin as towards your British friends.'

Which was also true enough. He was way beyond his depth. He was also exhausted, hungry and very frightened: not in much of a position to argue.

'But why Calais?' he persisted.

'Because it is still free!' the Frenchman snapped. He drew deeply on his cigarette and his mood seemed to soften. 'And because I live there. I want to see my family again before I die. Anyway, my brother still owes me money,' he added, anxious not to display weakness. He threw away his cigarette and swivelled himself off the examination table. The doctor rushed forward with a crutch, anxious to get him on his way. The airman hopped on his good leg as gently as possible, then tried a couple of uncomfortable steps towards the door.

'You know Calais, *Monsieur l'Anglais*?'

'Oh, yes,' Don replied. He'd seen it out of his bedroom window almost every day of his life.

'Good. We go.'

Don wondered if, like the Frenchman, there was anyone he would want to see again before he died. As he helped him clamber into the jeep and gunned its engine, setting off with the rising sun on his right hand, he came to the conclusion there was no one. He had no one special in his life, no girlfriend, no loved one, no family at all. Except for his father.

* * *

Ruth Mueller had always had an agreeable relationship with her local butcher, Mr Jarvis. In her eyes he was the embodiment of what an English butcher should be, with a heavily striped and slightly bloodied apron wrapped across a large stomach, above which his customers would always discover a welcoming smile. He wasn't like Watts, the other local butcher. Watts always seemed to want to serve them short and would make up any discrepancy between what was on his scales and what was permitted on the ration by slicing off the smallest piece of meat and hoping it would be enough to make up the weight. You might end up with a chop and three additional grudging scraps, which in Ruth's case often meant scraps of fat. On the last occasion she had complained, and he'd made it clear that not only was she at liberty to buy her meat elsewhere but, in fact, he would rather prefer it. Since then it had always been Mr Jarvis.

Mr Jarvis had been more than fair. He could see from her appearance that Ruth was not well nourished and could tell the reason why from the way she had to scrape through the change in her purse. So when Ruth had asked him for scraps for her cat, offal that didn't fall on ration, he had on several occasions managed to wrap a kidney or a little piece of liver in amongst what he called the kitty bag so that both Ruth and the cat could eat that night. It didn't happen so often that it looked like charity, but frequently enough for it to make a difference. He was a good man, was Mr Jarvis.

His customers, however, had grown less understanding. Nothing to do with the kitty bag; everything to do with the invasion in France. Ever since that morning, a conspicuous silence had fallen upon the other women when Ruth Mueller entered the shop. They would turn and stare at her, but not look her in the eye. Jarvis overcame the discomfort by raising the volume of his own voice to an even higher level than usual, greeting all the women together so that he didn't have to be polite to them one by one.

Yet this morning she had asked for some cat scraps and he had said it wasn't possible, he had none. Even though there was a tray of waste pieces in full view behind him.

The war had come to Pimlico.

* * *

The Frenchman had been right. Boulogne was next.

It came upon them with an awful suddenness for which they were still unprepared, and particularly so for Edward Halifax, dragged yet again from his bed. He found Ironside and other military men, equally bleary-eyed, standing around the old man's desk like schoolboys parading before their headmaster.

'The panzers have turned north,' Churchill announced quietly.

And their weariness was gone. The Germans had a choice. They could have swung south to take on the retreating French and to fall upon Paris. But instead they turned north, to fall upon the British and the Channel ports. Boulogne would be next.

Quietly, privately, they had all prayed that the German panzers would sweep in the other direction, for in spite of their professional composure they knew that once the tide had set it would be impossible to turn. It would sweep the entire British Expeditionary Force away. They all knew that.

Except, it seemed, Churchill.

Halifax looked on with a mixture of admiration and bewilderment. The stubbornness of this man was beyond all reasonable limits. It was as though he were still fighting the battles of an ancient time when a cry of Shakespearean defiance from atop a horse might turn a battle on its end. But panzers were deaf; they didn't listen. They just kept coming.

'Where are the French?' Churchill demanded of his generals.

It was difficult to know. Telephone communication across the Channel had grown so desperate and disrupted that the only way of getting any manner of certainty was to fly someone over from the battlefield in France, by which time the information was already out of date. But they could tell what the French were doing, could smell it in their nostrils in spite of all the diplomatic denials.

'They're falling back on Paris. Defending their own. Leaving the way open for the panzers.'

'But they promised they would be counterattacking north,' Churchill protested. 'Weygand himself promised me.'

'Only if we also counterattacked south to meet up with them. And Gort says he cannot.'

'Oh, rid me of generals who will not fight!'

'He has a Victoria Cross, Prime Minister. I don't think his valour is in question,' Ironside intervened.

'It's not his courage I question but his tactics. He's suffered less than five hundred casualties in the entire campaign, yet he withdraws. If he withdraws north and the French withdraw south, the laws of physics demand that the Germans will win. And when we have our backs to the sea, when our footing is sand and our reinforcements are nothing but the seagulls, what will the good Viscount Gort's tactics dictate then?'

Silence.

'He must advance! He must. We are all agreed that he must?'

You couldn't know with Churchill. He threw these suggestions out at his Chiefs of Staff and it was never clear whether he was stating a fact, issuing an order or seeking their advice. In his memoirs he would insist that he never did anything without their approval. In practice, he carried on until someone spoke up and objected. When they did, he would try to bludgeon and bully them into submission. He was always demanding action, even when the situation screamed out for prudence; he was perverse, it was his nature, like a tortoise trying to enter a hundred-yard dash.

'We are all agreed that he must,' he repeated.

And no one contradicted him.

'The French also insist that we send them several more squadrons of fighters,' a voice ventured.

'Then we must try.'

Yet now there was dissent. The Chief of the Air Staff spoke out. 'If we send them more fighters, what difference will it make to the war in France?'

'It might keep the French fighting,' Churchill snapped.

'That is a possibility, Prime Minister. No more than a possibility. Yet one thing we all know for certain,' the Air Chief continued, taking a step forward like a matador approaching a bull, 'is that if we lose more fighters in France we will ruin any chance we've got of effective resistance when the Germans invade here.'

They all heard it. *When*. Not *if*.

'We can't win this battle in France,' he continued, 'and if we try we could end up losing the entire war.'

The moment of silence that followed seemed to stretch to eternity. With a single phrase their nightmares had ventured into the open. They might lose this war.

Churchill's impatience sprang forward. 'But if we do nothing we might lose the entire British Expeditionary Force.' There was an edge of frustration in his voice; Halifax thought it bordered on desperation. 'We must give the French every encouragement to fight.'

'Yet the French insist it's the British who are not fighting.' The argument was going round in circles.

'So Gort must move south. Better the BEF goes down fighting than be swept onto the sands. And let us promise the French more squadrons. A symbolic gesture of alliance.'

'We must not send them to France,' the Air Chief objected, clearly incensed.

'Then base them in Kent and Sussex,' Churchill growled.

'But that would greatly reduce their flying time over France.'

'Which will greatly reduce their rate of attrition. I thought you would welcome that.'

'What will the French say?' Halifax joined the fray. 'How can we promise them fighters, yet keep them in England?'

'The French High Command is so confused it doesn't even know where its own armies are, let alone the RAF. Let us not confuse them any further. We simply won't tell them.'

It was breathtaking duplicity. If only he could fool the Germans so easily. The British Prime Minister had become little more than a card sharp.

At that moment a phone rang on a desk in one of the far reaches of the room. An admiral strode to pick it up, listened carefully, then held the receiver out at arm's length in some puzzlement.

'They say it's our commander in Boulogne.'

Amidst the chaos of submarine cables that crossed the Channel, a circuit had at last been completed. It wouldn't last for long. Halifax watched in bemused horror as, with surprising energy, Churchill sprang across the room to grab the phone. Moments later he was engaged in a heated discussion about which end of the quay the troops should be fighting from. He barked orders, then listened, but not for long, before he was shouting once more.

'Commander, if there are so many tanks massed in front of you, it should be easy enough to hit a few!'

Then the connection went dead. Boulogne was gone. Churchill was left looking at the phone trying to will it back to life.

The war was being played from hour to hour, without any plan, and every hour it was getting worse. Halifax was decided. This was, indeed, madness. It could not go on.

* * *

*(Thursday 23 May 1940. William L. Shirer, CBS.)*

*Good evening. This is Berlin.*

*I returned here from the front a couple of hours ago after a four-hundred-and-fifty-mile drive from the Belgian border. Berlin, I must say, seems a little quiet after three days of hearing the big guns go off and the heavy bombs exploding . . .*

*Correspondents of the three American press associations and I had quite a time of it making ourselves heard on the telephone with our reports last night because of the noise of British bombs and the German anti-aircraft guns nearby. Actually, the British bombers were aiming for an important military objective about a hundred yards from our hotel. They kept at it all night, and were always warm, so to speak, but not hot. The nearest they hit was about four or five hundred yards from the hotel, and though the bombs jarred us, they did not jar us enough to break any windows . . .*

*During the day, at least on the Belgian front west of Brussels, where we were, the Allies do not do any bombing. And one of the things that impressed me most was the picture of the German army bringing up men, guns and supplies, jamming the roads with them for miles and miles behind the front, without hindrance from the Allied air forces. I'm convinced that the ease with which the German Command has been able to bring up reinforcements and guns and ammunition, and at an unbelievable speed, is one of the reasons for the German success so far.*

*I understand that this is not the case on the other side because of the deadly work of the German air force behind the Allied lines. This state of affairs gives the Germans a tremendous advantage even before the battle starts . . .*

* * *

It was only forty miles, yet they had spent two days trying to get to Calais and still they weren't there. They might never make it.

It was partly the roads, of course, flooded to impassability with refugees. An entire nation seemed to be on the move. Teachers, nuns, bakers and sweeps, bureaucrats who had fled their bureaux and policemen who had long since given up trying to police; they came in lorries, on tractors, in carts, on foot; horses pulled cars and children pushed their own prams until they came together to form vast eddies of humanity that swirled across every route. They had only one thing in common, these refugees, their terror of the advancing Germans. They came from all points and were heading they knew not where, choking every route with their despair.

The refugees were one reason why it seemed to Don that he might not make it. The other reason was the bloody Frenchman.

The sous-lieutenant—Don still hadn't been entrusted with his name—seemed intent on discovering more to complain about with every passing mile. If it wasn't Don's driving it was the despicable nature of the British-built jeep as it coughed and choked its way in low gear through the press of those around them. More than once Don thought about leaving him to fend for himself, or at least handing him over to the next detachment of French troops.

The troops were everywhere, standing around or squatting disconsolately in villages and at crossroads, even sitting in roadside cafés and simply waiting. It was from the soldiers that Don and the Frenchman got their supplies of fuel. It seemed they had plenty to give away. But none was carrying arms.

It was as Don was filling up with more purloined petrol that he saw an artillery unit disconsolately spiking their guns.

'Why are they doing that?'

'Doing what?'

'Destroying their weapons.'

'They appear to have forgotten to give you any weapons at all,' the Frenchman snorted in contempt.

'I'm noncombatant.'

'Like the rest of your countrymen.'

'We all came to France to do our bit.'

'Ah, there speaks a true Englishman. Happy so long as his battles are fought on someone else's ground. Just like the last war.'

'That's enough! My father fought in France. We left millions of dead behind.'

'And your government seems determined not to repeat that experience. Is that why they have refused us planes and sent only four miserable divisions?'

'Ten! We sent ten.'

'Ten? France has more than a hundred. But as we say, the English will always fight to the last Frenchman.'

'I've been driving all day and I don't see too many bloody Frenchmen fighting for anything!' Don retorted.

The words had an extraordinary effect on the airman. His fists clenched. His face, up to that point so stiff with resentment, seemed to melt into a state that mixed revulsion with panic. His lips became twisted; his eyes lashed out in search of some elusive target. He couldn't find it, so instead he grabbed his crutch and began beating it against the bonnet of the jeep with all the might he could muster standing on one leg, until the bonnet was riddled with huge dents and the crutch had been left in many fragments.

When he had finished, tears had washed away every trace of his rage to reveal nothing but dishonour and degradation.

The sous-lieutenant was a Frenchman. This was his country, his soil, he wanted to fight for it but no one else would help, least of all his own countrymen. France was dying. He had been fleeing from the truth as furiously as he could, but he only had one foot—and one man to help him. An unarmed Englishman. The truth had at last caught up with him. The heart of France had all but stopped beating.

The strength remaining in his one leg seemed to fail him and he slumped forward; Don rushed to catch him. He held the sous-lieutenant in his arms until the pain had hidden itself once more.

'Well, Pierre or Pascal or whatever your name is, I think it's about time we got you to Calais.'

* * *

Friday 24 May. Churchill had been in charge for precisely fourteen days. The newspapers that morning were all of a similar mind, but it was the *Evening Standard* that captured the mood most vividly. Its headline was simple: 'PREPARE FOR THE WORST!'

* * *

It had poured with rain for the first time in months. It came like a harbinger of dark times, yet the ground still resisted the cut of the spade. In the moonlight, the gardener bent over his work, digging a hole broad and deep enough to bury a dog, hard against the brick wall that separated the garden from the churchyard. Owls screeched in the moist Essex night. Somewhere close at hand a fox barked sharply and pheasants spluttered their displeasure, but the gardener toiled on, piling shovelfuls of earth to one side.

He was not alone. A cigarette glowed in the darkness from beneath the branches of a nearby tree. The gardener muttered as his spade struck a thin root; he chopped through it and dug deeper.

Eventually he straightened. 'I think it's ready,

sir.'

'Are you sure?'

The gardener climbed into the hole to give an indication of its depth. He had been told there must be no lights, no chance of them being seen. They had waited until almost midnight; the rest of the staff should be abed.

Chips Channon stepped forward. 'Very well, Mortimer. You may proceed.'

Two tin boxes wrapped in oilskin were lowered into the hole. The larger, lower box contained the diaries that Channon had been keeping since he was a young man. He stood in prayer for their safekeeping; he was burying part of himself, and, history would argue, the most important part. A second box was laid on top containing other precious possessions: his watches, Fabergé curios, sentimental items.

Channon picked up a handful of the dry earth and let it trickle over the boxes, which sounded back at him like a muffled drum. 'Until we are reunited,' he whispered.

'God willing, this will all be unnecessary, sir,' the gardener offered, beginning to pile on the rest of the soil.

Channon did not respond. God seemed to have been busy elsewhere these last few weeks, a world away from Essex. For the first time in his life Channon was grateful for his American passport. He suspected he was going to need it.

* * *

'I hope you don't mind a walk in the park, Joe. Nowadays I'm beginning to find my office a little . . .'

—he searched for a word—'claustrophobic.'

'Edward, you've got an office like a palace. Biggest I've seen, outside of Hollywood.'

'Nevertheless . . .'

'Nevertheless it's too close to Downing Street, eh?'

Halifax and Kennedy, the Minister and the Ambassador, stepped out around the lake of St James's Park. Kennedy was enjoying himself; Halifax appeared strained. The bonds that had secured the many strands of his orderly life seemed to be on the point of dissolving. He'd been having difficulty sleeping, even on the nights when the telephone didn't ring.

'You heard that Boulogne's gone?' Kennedy enquired.

'Yes. That was one thing that did manage to filter its way through to me. Joe, it's all such a mess! I scarcely know what to do.' He stopped, took out a handkerchief and wiped the inner lining of his bowler hat. 'Rab suggested I should have a private word with you.'

The American laughed. 'Out here—no eavesdroppers, no evidence.'

Halifax bit back his distaste. Kennedy irritated him: he was so tactless, so new world, so clearly on the make. And yet he was perceptive, could see the fault lines, the growing disloyalties—perhaps because he was himself so congenitally disloyal. Halifax needed him. Whatever was left of the world after this war was finished would undoubtedly be new; it would be gauche, self-serving and overwhelmingly self-centred, no matter whether it was run by Germans or Americans. Halifax had once been Viceroy of India, a ruler of millions, but by this stage his ambition amounted to little more than the hope that, when the fuss had died down, there would be a modest corner of the world that could remain unashamedly traditional, run along lines that emphasized continuity and an old established order. If it meant having to sacrifice much of the Empire and British influence in the world, he could live with that. It was going to happen eventually, with or without the war. Empires came, and empires closed; the British had had a good innings. What did it matter if they retired early, and just a little hurt? He didn't want to fight for world supremacy; he didn't much want to fight at all.

'Joe, forgive me for being blunt. Matters in France are becoming so very difficult—'

'Edward, you call that being blunt? France isn't difficult, it's a flaming disaster.'

'It faces us with a dilemma. You see, there are those who hold that it would be impossible for Britain to fight this war on our own.'

'Yeah, I've talked to a few. More than a few.'

'*If* France were to collapse . . . if that were to happen, America would be our only hope of continuing with the war. So let me put the matter directly. Are there any circumstances in which America will come and help us fight?'

The Ambassador thought for a moment. 'If hell freezes or Alaska floats away. Otherwise, no.'

'You are sure?'

'Edward, I've seen the telegrams that Winston's been sending Roosevelt. Practically down on his knees, begging for help. Saying catastrophe is just around the corner. Answer's still the same.'

'Winston is always going on about America as if

. . . well, as if he expects the cavalry to come riding to our rescue at any moment.'

'So did Custer.'

A pelican screeched from its rock in the middle of the lake. Halifax raised his head, looking anxiously towards Downing Street as if he expected to see Churchill at a window with a raised set of binoculars.

'Then if not war, would America be willing to help us pursue a peace?'

'What sort of peace?'

'Who can tell until we start talking? But an immediate end to the war, some agreement over Europe, the return of a few of Germany's colonies, perhaps. I think in the circumstances we would have to be flexible.'

Kennedy didn't pause before replying. He knew what to expect; he'd been as well briefed by Butler as had Halifax.

'You know we'd help on that, Edward. No one wants this ridiculous war to continue. But I can't see Winston agreeing to it.'

The Foreign Secretary's head bent like a heron staring into a murky pond. 'Let us suppose for a moment that Winston weren't a problem. Could we do that, Joe? Just hypothetically? Where would that leave America?'

'Anxious. But not out of it. Problem is, Edward, you've got Germany and you've got Russia and—hell, who knows what's gonna happen there? What we wouldn't want to see is a peace deal which ends up making either of those two more of a threat.'

'Be a little more specific.'

'Figure it this way. The jig is up for Britain. You talk peace now and you'll get a better deal than you will later on, but even so Hitler will demand you hand over your military. Army's not a problem, that's already as good as gone. Your air force, too. But the navy? Well, that's something else. You know we couldn't be happy if your Royal Navy ended up in Hitler's hands. Hell, in a couple of years' time it could end up in Moscow. Do I make myself clear?'

Halifax winced at the suggestion.

'So the way this particular game goes, Edward, is that we'll give you all the help with a peace that we can, so long as you give us your navy.'

'*Give* it to you?'

'Sell it, loan it, scuttle it—anything so long as it doesn't end up covered in swastikas or the hammer and sickle. And you'll find Hitler a hell of a sight more reasonable about a peace treaty if you don't have a navy. What's the point of playing poker with a man who's clean out of chips?'

'There might be only one problem with that.'

'Which is?'

'Winston.'

'Hell, I thought we were talking hypotheticals.'

'He seemed so remarkably unhypothetical at our last encounter.'

'Then damn the hypotheticals and start talking miracles, Edward. Because that's what you'll need if you're gonna climb out of this hole.'

* * *

Boulogne had gone. They would fall upon Calais next. And back in London they seemed to be either ignorant or indifferent. Or was it incapable?

The young captain had followed his instructions

to the letter. Much to his surprise, they had worked. A bloodied face and a battle-stained tunic was still so unusual in the corridors of Whitehall that it got the bearer past most of the roadblocks before anyone had time to recover from their surprise and ask him what he was up to—until he had reached all the way to the Upper War Room in the Admiralty.

The Chiefs of Staff were gathered with their staff men for the evening conference, but Churchill was late, still at dinner, keeping them all waiting, and their mood was fractious.

'Who the hell are you and what the hell are you doing here, Captain?' one of the Chiefs barked as the young officer appeared in the room. He offered a salute that had lost its starch; the eyes were glazed with fatigue.

'I have just come from Calais, sir.'

'Ah! How's it going?'

'It's not, sir. Not going at all. It's . . .'

Chaos. A total balls-up. An unmitigated bloody fiasco. But he didn't say so. These were the men responsible and a captain couldn't overwhelm the Chiefs of Staff with a frontal assault.

'My commanding officer sent me, sir. He wanted you to know the situation. First hand.' He glanced behind them at the situation map pinned to the wall. It still showed British units in Boulogne.

'Then you'd better give your report, Captain,' one of the Chiefs barked. No one asked him to sit down, even though his knees were trembling with exhaustion.

'Sir, the situation is desperate.'

'Desperate? Get a grip on yourself, Captain, you're clearly very tired. Perhaps you don't realize that we've just sent you reinforcements.'

'Sir, we have been sent many things, but none of them are of much use for reinforcement.'

'We sent you a battalion of tanks only yesterday.'

'Sir, the tanks haven't yet been unloaded.'

'Ridiculous! And inexcusable!' There was an impatient rustling of papers.

'Sir . . .' It was his moment, and he knew it could not be repeated. It was the only chance he would get, perhaps the only chance the entire garrison at Calais would get. But he hadn't slept for three days and he was still deaf in one ear from the blast of a shell that had killed the man standing next to him. The dead man's blood was still on his uniform. His CO had urged caution and self-control, but his control was slipping away with his every word. How could these men know what they had to do unless they were told the truth?

'It just isn't working. You see, the tanks are loaded in the bottom of the supply ships along with the other heavy vehicles. We need them most but they are the last things to come off. I know that's according to regulations but . . . Above them are packed all the artillery guns and machine-guns. They're packed according to regulations, too, in thick mineral jelly for a sea voyage, even though it's only Calais. And on top of that is loaded the fuel for the tanks, once again all done according to regulations. But the fuel comes in four-gallon cans. It's taking hours to shift them. The mineral jelly's taking more hours to clean from each gun. Then we discovered that they've been shipped without any ammunition. Half the parts are missing. The whole dock area is under constant bombardment, there is no electrical supply for the cranes so the stevedores are refusing to work and—'

'Enough! Pull yourself together, man.'

'Sir, with respect, it's impossible to hold off a German advance with guns that have no ammunition and tanks that are sitting at the bottom of a supply ship!'

He'd lost it. Everyone knew it, including the captain himself. And it was the only chance he would have.

'Captain, you are clearly overwrought. You can get some rest now.'

'*Sir—*'

'Leave, Captain!'

It had all fallen apart, and it was his fault. He had never known such shame.

At that moment the door opened. Churchill bustled in, followed by cigar smoke and Brendan Bracken.

'Ah! What have we here?' the Prime Minister exclaimed, eyeing the dishevelled state of the captain. 'A warrior, by the look of you. Good to have one around at last.'

'The captain was just on his way out.'

'Mr Churchill, I was bringing messages from my commanding officer.'

'And you must take a message back to your commanding officer that it's his responsibility to sort matters out, not to come complaining here,' an encrusted military voice interjected, growling in warning. 'Tell him to make proper use of the reinforcements we've sent.'

'The reinforcements have arrived?' Churchill enquired. 'Excellent.'

'We sent another battalion of infantry yesterday,' the voice added. 'Queen Victoria's Rifles.' He decided to omit any reference to the tanks. Just in case.

Oh, but what did it matter? The captain was going back to Calais and he was going to die. He turned angrily. 'You've sent a motorcycle unit. Without any bloody motorcycles!'

A hush fell across the room. They each waited for the other to reprimand this overwrought officer, or at least to contradict him, but no one did.

'Can this it true?' Churchill eventually asked.

'Sir,' the captain began, about to throw away his reputation, after which throwing away his life would seem so much simpler. 'The First Battalion, Queen Victoria's Rifles, is a territorial unit, not regular army. They are a motorcycle reconnaissance unit. The QVR arrived in Calais yesterday without their motorcycles or any wireless equipment. Many of the men are armed with nothing but revolvers.' He couldn't stop now. 'I regret to inform you, gentlemen, that the QVR are having the greatest difficulties with these revolvers. They don't seem to be very good at stopping panzers.'

Military brows in every part of the room turned purple with indignation, but so did Churchill's. He crushed his cigar in his fist—something that Bracken had never seen before in all his years with the old man. The flakes of tobacco rained about him like discarded reputations.

'Somebody—*one of you*—tell me that this is not true.'

No one spoke.

Churchill turned to the young officer. 'Captain, who is your commanding officer?'

'Brigadier Nicholson, sir.'

'And what does he need?'

The captain recited a short list of requirements, the first of which was to establish a chain of command that bypassed most of the War Office. Nicholson had said that might give them a fighting chance . . .

'Agreed. Anything else?'

'Your prayers.'

'Captain, rest assured. And rest yourself. You look as if you have had an unusually long day.'

'With permission, sir, I'd rather return directly to Calais. To brief Brigadier Nicholson. I think I can be of more use there than in a bed in London.'

'Then fly, and fight. Go with our prayers, and our thanks.'

The captain saluted, more sharply this time, and was gone.

It took a moment for Churchill to compose himself. A rage was upon him that demanded to be cast upon these useless men, but it would be better dealt with at another time. He turned his back on the military. 'Brendan, that young officer reminds me of someone,' Churchill muttered.

'Who?'

'Me, of course.'

At last he turned to the others. 'Who was that remarkable young man?'

No one knew. And they never did find out, not even after the battle for Calais had finished.

# CHAPTER EIGHT

The librarian glanced up from her reading of the *Evening Standard* and looked across to the far side of the reading room. She was worried by what she had just read, and her concern flowed into irritation at the woman who had spent all morning in the archives section, reading old copies of *The Times*.

For some while after her appearance in the community, the librarian had tried to treat Ruth Mueller as just another refugee, one of the many that had flooded into London in the last few years. But Mrs Mueller was different, so unlike the rest. There was not a trace of Jewishness in her make-up and she didn't mix with the others, keeping herself very much to herself. On one occasion another refugee had muttered at her in Yiddish and she had shaken her head violently and almost run out of the room. She offered no clues as to her background, but it was clear she was neither Pole nor Czech, which left little doubt. The librarian came to the same conclusion as the women in the butcher's shop: Ruth Mueller was German, or Austrian. Either way, what was she doing here in London? How was it right that she was living off others, when the war started by her own kind meant there wasn't enough to go round even for Londoners? And why was she asking so many questions about Winston Churchill?

She was sitting there now, going through old newspapers with meticulous care, searching for every reference to him—even his father.

And she called herself Mrs Mueller, but if that were so, where was her husband?

Everyone leads a double life nowadays, the librarian thought. She herself had several lives—not only in the library but as a market gardener on her father's allotment and as a Red Cross volunteer three nights a week. But what sort of double life did Mrs Mueller lead?

Nothing about this woman seemed to add up. In a time when walls had ears and careless talk cost lives, strangers were not only a matter of curiosity but also of concern. There was all sorts of talk about fifth columnists who masqueraded as civilians but who fought for the enemy, even tales about German soldiers dressed up as nuns or policemen. You couldn't trust anyone in these times, and there was something very odd about Mrs Mueller, the librarian decided. Somebody should do something about it.

* * *

In the time they took to rcach Calais they saw not a single German soldier. They crept along through a strange no man's land of war. The Germans had already passed through it but had neither stopped nor yet returned, while French troops mostly sat around and waited indolently for when they did. On all sides, refugees swirled backwards and forwards like fish in a narrowing net.

The sous-lieutenant's first name was neither Pierre nor Pascal, but Claude. Claude Dubuis. As they drove, the Frenchman began to fill in a few more of the gaps: his earlier life as a junior customs official at Calais, which had given him his good command of English; his family—a widowed mother, his younger sister (he'd lied about having a brother), a jealous stepfather and an ageless story of male rivalries that had ended with Claude leaving home for a new life in the military. He was lean, a long-distance runner, he explained: 'They thought I would fit comfortably into a cockpit.' So they had put him in the air service, *l'armée de l'air*.

'And you found a new family,' Don concluded quietly.

In response, Claude stared bitterly at the groups of idle soldiers and spat.

They were not many miles from Calais. As they came nearer and he began to recognize familiar landmarks, Claude grew increasingly agitated and insisted they drive on through the failing light. As the day faded, they found themselves passing a wayside field in which a large number of small fires were flickering—refugees, several hundred of them, and most with nothing for protection but the clothes they wore. At the sight of military uniforms, several began to complain and gesticulate. They were not welcome. From the darkness came a priest, young, weary, his soutane stained with dirt, who led them aside and explained that the refugees had only that afternoon tried to force their way into Calais but had been turned back from one of the bridges.

'By the Germans?'

'*Non*, by the English. At gunpoint. They say it is too dangerous.'

'We are going to Calais,' Claude responded defiantly.

'It will be dangerous for you, too,' the priest responded sadly. He led Don and the hobbling

Frenchman to a bank of thick trees at the end of the field, and from its far side they could see it all. It was a clear, warm night and the view stretched before them for miles. They had no difficulty in seeing Calais in the darkness. The town was burning at every point, the battlements of its old walls outlined in cruel detail against the orange and yellow flames that ate at every part. Explosions echoed through the night as its arteries burst; the town seemed to be crying in pain. An ancient church steeple had been almost eaten by fire. Even as they watched, it fell, crashing to the ground and sending up a plume of smoke and violent ash. It was like watching the sacking of a medieval fortress. Calais was being burned alive.

In the distance, beyond the fires, they thought they could see dark shadows on the sea, and the beams of searchlights weaving angry patterns in the sky. The coast of Dover.

Home.

'These people wanted to walk into that?' Don uttered in horror.

'They think they can get boats. Sail to England,' the priest explained. 'They have nowhere else to go.'

'The English army's done them a favour,' Don added.

'They do not think so. Many of them are Jews.'

The priest pointed to other fires, nearer at hand, which seemed to form a cordon around the city. 'The Germans,' he said.

'Their signal fires,' Claude added.

'Signals to what?' Don asked.

'To their bombers, so the bombs fall on the British and not on themselves.'

As they watched, a petrol dump inside the town exploded, sending a fist of swirling fire thrusting to the sky.

'So what do we do now?' Don muttered.

'We go home, of course.'

It was an insane suggestion. They would have to run two military cordons with nothing more for cover than a clapped-out jeep, but home was on the other side for both of them. They had to try.

They overcame the German cordon with surprising ease. The Wehrmacht wasn't expecting to be rushed from behind, and even victors have to sleep. But as they crashed their way towards the walls of Calais, a shot rang out from in front of them and they heard the vile sound of a bullet ripping the air only inches above their heads.

'Don't shoot! English!' Don shouted.

'*Ne tirez pas!*' Claude added in support.

And they were through. But the most difficult part was yet to come.

With a rising sense of urgency they sought out Claude's home, in the suburb of Calais-Saint-Pierre. With every corner, Don could feel his companion's mixture of excitement and rising dread. 'It still stands!' the Frenchman exclaimed as they turned into the final street.

But they found Claude's home abandoned, its windows gaping like empty eye-sockets and its door badly boarded. The family Dubuis had fled, evidently in a considerable hurry. But at least they had been able to flee.

'You want to go in?' Don asked.

The Frenchman shook his head. 'No. There is no point. We should never have come to this place.' Then he fell silent and would say nothing more.

* * *

It was Channon's fault. He'd issued what he called a 'prodigious papal bull' that permitted no dissent. They were to dine, and dine lavishly. Colville had protested that he had neither the time nor, in truth, the funds, but Channon had told him to stop being ridiculous. 'Chips's treat,' he kept singing, leading him by the arm through St James's to the door of Wiltons, the famed seafood and game restaurant in King Street. Standing in the entrance waiting to greet them was Mrs Bessie Leal, the establishment's formidable proprietor. Chips placed his cloak on her arm and a kiss on her cheek, and she conducted them to a booth in the most prominent part of the restaurant. Butler was waiting for them.

'Ah, dear Jock, hotfoot from the front line,' the Minister greeted. 'You look as if you need a drink.'

He poured. A Krug Private Cuvée. Something hidden deep in Colville's memory bank suggested that this was expensive; the taste confirmed it. Everything was excessively good: the smoked salmon, the Scottish lobsters, none of it falling foul of the ration. The price took care of that. The steak, kidney and oyster pie, too, washed down by a prodigious Haut-Brion claret.

'Chips, what are we celebrating?' Colville ventured, confused.

'Celebrating?'

'I don't wish to appear ungrateful, but I've just watched two weeks' wages tipped down our throats and we've scarcely started.'

'My dear Jock, inside a couple of weeks every

penny we have might well be worthless. Money will be fit only for throwing at urchins and lighting fires, so I thought we'd enjoy it while we still may.'

'And I hear our Prime Minister is scarcely stinting himself,' Butler added.

It was true. War had not disrupted Churchill's legendary dinners. They were as important to him as oxygen—indeed, perhaps more so. Oxygen enabled him to survive, while dinner enabled him to live, and the stain-encrusted lapels of his suit bore witness to the fact that the old man lived well.

'How is our dear leader?' Butler continued. 'I fear he's overworking. Trying to do not only his job but everybody else's job, too. Would you believe that the Foreign Office received a long note from him yesterday instructing us about the poor punctuation and grammar in some of our recent despatches? War rages across France and yet he finds time to manoeuvre commas around the page. Extraordinary. Or perhaps it's his sense of humour.'

'Forgive me, but it's been a difficult day and I'm not sure my own sense of humour is up to all this.'

'No, it's you who must forgive me, Jock.' Butler laid a hand on the sleeve of his young companion in a gesture of apology and affection. 'As you say, these are hard times. And if I seem light-hearted, it's only because at times I daren't think about what's happening to us. All my fears are taking form. We should never have started with this wretched war, and why are we still fighting it? Explain it to me. For Czechoslovakia? It's gone! For Poland? Gone, too, and good riddance! For France, when it won't even fight for itself? Or is it that we are fighting for no better reason than

Winston's overweening pride?' Butler gripped Colville's arm more tightly, in warning. 'He doesn't get on with his Ministers; he is coming to be loathed by his generals. The French are in despair at his hollow lectures, and the Americans simply ignore him. I even hear reports that Roosevelt, far from admiring him, has always regarded him as totally second-rate. It's a conclusion that seems to be almost unanimous.' The fingers were now digging fiercely, even painfully, into Colville's arm. 'Jock, we are a great nation. We cannot allow one man to ruin it!'

Colville had never known Rab quite so venomous. It was said he had a mean streak, that he was the only man in the kingdom who could stretch a partridge to six, but he seemed intent on carving Churchill even thinner.

It was impossible to deny the faults in the old man. He was so mercurial. A dozen daft ideas came with his morning rashers, but hidden in amongst them was occasionally a shaft of pure brilliance. Abusive, excessive, impossible, but the next moment in tears of remorse and affection. In truth, Colville didn't know what to make of the man.

Yet if Colville were to exchange his cheap blue suit for a uniform and fight at the sharp end, as he planned, who would he want guarding his back? Not Joe Kennedy, for sure, not even in broad daylight. And, in truth, probably not Rab either. He was so adept at seeing every side of a question that it made you giddy trying to tag along with his intellectual dances. Men like Chamberlain were reasonable and reliable, but so clearly out of time and place. And perhaps that was the answer. This was not a time and place for reason but for excess in everything—in commitment, in courage, in blind faith, in unquenchable and bloody-minded stubbornness. And it was impossible to imagine Winston guarding his back, for he would never be behind him but way out in front, leading the charge himself, demanding that you follow.

As he struggled with these thoughts, Colville found Butler holding up his index finger, bidding them to silence. From the neighbouring booth floated a familiar voice.

'He's rotten, totally rotten,' the voice insisted, 'the greatest menace this country's ever had. Why, the entire Empire could be sacrificed on the altar to his egomania.'

The look of exquisite delight that played around Butler's lips gave Colville no doubt that this intervention was entirely fortuitous. Words such as 'monstrous obstinacy' and 'monumental wrong-headedness' spilled across the wooden partition. 'In just two weeks we've lost Holland and most of Belgium, the French have all but given up and we've got a million men trapped in Flanders. That man's as dangerous as Caligula,' the voice concluded. 'Should have his throat cut.'

There was a scraping of a chair. An immensely tall figure passed by, then paused. It took a step back.

'Oh, God,' Colville screamed inside.

It was Sir John Reith, formerly the Director-General of the BBC, in which post he had been both respected and feared in equal degree. More recently and until two weeks ago he had been a member of the Cabinet as the Minister of Information. He towered over the table, his dark eyebrows knitted together in their habitual scowl, the sniper's scar on his cheek more vivid than ever.

Even Churchill would admit that the circumstances around Reith's sacking had been unfortunate. The two men had loathed each other for years. When he became Prime Minister, Churchill's immediate instinct was to have him out. Unfortunately, during that first chaotic weekend, no one at 10 Downing Street knew of Sir John's whereabouts, so there had been no softening word, no exchange of courtesies, simply a formal letter of dismissal from the Cabinet sent to wait for him at his club. It was barely excusable in the dire circumstances of upheaval and war, but to Reith it was deliberate insult. He had found little consolation when as an afterthought he was given the consolation post of Minister of Transport. It didn't carry Cabinet rank. It was like asking a duke to eat in the kitchen.

Reith was a Scotsman, built of granite with a subtlety to match, and given to outbursts of extreme emotion and irrationality. Two dark and furious eyes now glared at Colville.

'How can you work for that man?' Reith demanded.

With that, he strode off.

Butler was struggling hard to contain his mirth. Chips hurriedly ordered another bottle of the claret to celebrate.

'He's quite mad,' Colville breathed, shocked.

'Of course he is,' Butler agreed, 'but the relevant thing, Jock, is not that madmen like Reith should hold such opinions about Winston, but that he should feel sufficiently comfortable to voice them in public. Turning tides, that sort of thing.'

Colville swallowed another glass to quell his unease. How could he still work for Churchill? You didn't need to be a madman like Reith to ask the question. Why, even the King's mother, Queen Mary, had written to Colville's own mother, one of her ladies-in-waiting, asking exactly the same thing.

Some time later he stumbled out into St James's, confused, disorientated, and not simply through the drink.

* * *

He didn't seem to notice her intrusion. Perhaps he didn't hear: a gramophone was playing, scratching out some comic opera. He was sitting in a dark corner before the portrait, half-heartedly conducting the orchestra with a tumbler, gently weeping.

*But if patriotic sentiment is wanted,*
*I've patriotic banners cut and dried;*
*For where'er our country's banner may be planted,*
*All other local banners are defied!*
*Our warriors, in serried ranks assembled,*
*Never quail—or they conceal it if they do—*
*And I shouldn't be surprised if nations trembled*
*Before the mighty troops, the troops of Titipu!*

He looked up, not bothering to hide his tears. His tie was askew, his thin, faded red hair adrift.

'*The Mikado*. Gilbert and Sullivan. Very English. You wouldn't understand.'

He waved her to a chair and continued a melancholy humming.

'Victorian, you know. So much *simpler*, those

times. You fought, you lost, you won . . . But mostly you won. And there was always the next time.' He mumbled along to the record for a moment in a voice sodden with alcohol and remorse.

'My father took me and my brother Jack once. To the Dolly Cart. Oh, an evening to remember. They all turned their heads to look at us in our box and whispered behind their programmes. Jack and I were so proud. I talk about my father a lot, don't I?'

She didn't bother to answer.

'I feel so lost. What would *he* have done?' Churchill rose and stood as close as he could to the portrait, looking up. 'What would you do, Papa? I want to strike south, to get our army to fight. But they won't.' For a moment his memories seemed to have taken him to another place; the glass waved in his hand as he mumbled in poor tune: '"Our warriors, in serried ranks assembled, Never quail—or they conceal it if they do . . ."' Suddenly he stopped and began to sob. 'Damn you, Gilbert. And damn you, Sullivan!'

It was like watching a great ship breaking up on rocks. Soon there would be only fragments and a fading echo.

'I decided to sack my leading general today. Not up to the job. None of them are, but I can't sack them all.' More tears. 'But withdraw? Sneak away like a thief in the night?' He jabbed a finger at the portrait. 'He never showed weakness. He went into exile rather than bow low, even to the King.'

Ah, that old Aylesford nonsense. She'd read about it only that afternoon. Seventy years ago; she'd gone back that far. And so had he. If his father wouldn't bow it was only because dead wood didn't bend, it simply broke. And it wasn't the King but the Prince of Wales, long before he came to the throne.

'But I am not as he was,' the son whispered mournfully.

'I agree,' she offered, deciding it was time for her to play a part.

*And if you call for a song of the sea,*
*We'll heave the capstan round,*
*With a yeo heave ho, for the wind is free,*
*Her anchor's a-trip and her helm's a-lee,*
*Hurrah for the homeward bound!*
*Hurrah for the homeward bound . . .*
*the homeward bound . . .*
*the homeward bound . . .*
*the homeward bound . . .*
*the homeward . . .*

The record was stuck, mocking him. He snatched the needle away to silence it.

'Has it come to that?' she continued. 'The entire British army dragged back across the sea?'

'Oh, if only that were possible! If only we could bring them back. I'm told we might gather in a tenth of their number—thirty-five, maybe forty thousand. But no more. And if they will not fight, the British army will be smashed. Our young men will die in vast numbers within sight of the white cliffs of England, of their home.'

'So what will you do?'

'Wait. That's all we can do.'

'For what?'

He turned on her. 'For *him*. That Man! Bloody Hitler! Wait for him to choose. To decide whether he wants to be in Paris first, or in London. Either way, I can only pray they will have shot me before that moment comes.'

'Who?' she pressed, puzzled.

'Hah! There is no shortage of volunteers; they flock like starlings in autumn. Any number of my Cabinet. Half the General Staff. Perhaps the general I decided to fire today, or the Member of Parliament I had arrested this afternoon.'

'What had he done?'

'Done? Nothing, absolutely nothing.' His arm flailed the air, stretching for his argument. 'Not yet, at least. But he would have, I know it. He has suspicious friends. He hates me. They all hate me. They are polishing their muskets even now and arguing who will have the honour of the first shot.'

She was irritated with this outpouring of self-pity. It was as if the great ship had already broken apart and there was nothing left but the wailing of those who claimed it wasn't their fault.

'So you think you will be alone when they put you up against the wall?'

'Perhaps not. But I shall be the first!' It sounded almost like a mournful boast.

'All dictators perish with such delusions.'

'What?'

'When you are gone, do you think the world will remember you as a martyr for freedom? A man who died fighting for liberty like your Admiral Nelson? Mr Churchill, let me tell you something. You are no Nelson, you are nothing but another in a long line of autocrats, a man whose first instinct in office has been to grab for himself all sorts of powers over others—even to imprison them for doing nothing. To force them to do exactly what he wants.'

'In the service of a higher cause.'

'Straight out of *Mein Kampf*. At least Hitler had the decency to get himself elected before he turned himself into a tyrant.'

'That is a disgraceful—'

'And you say you will be first up against the wall,' she continued, cutting straight across him. 'But I don't think so. Do you know who will make it first? The Jews and the other refugees—the ones you have been rounding up under your Emergency Powers. Oh, you argue it is only for troublemakers like Mosley and the others, but what about the thousands of people you have arrested for no greater crime than fleeing from Hitler?'

He was stretching for the argument once more, less confidently, his whisky slopping over the side of his glass. 'It is so very difficult with these enemy aliens,' he protested, 'some may be fifth columnists, quislings, enemy agents, all sorts of undesirables.'

'In Germany they call us *Untermenschen.* But tell me: what is our crime? We are people who fled in fear from Hitler. Now you send round your police to lock us up.'

'Only the men. As a precautionary measure,' he insisted, beginning to splutter and sound feeble.

So, he didn't think that women could be troublemakers?

'They disappear overnight, and no one asks questions . . .' she whispered, remembering.

'It is not like that,' he insisted.

'You're putting so many of us in camps that Hitler won't even have to go looking for us when he gets here. Don't you see? You have done his job for him.'

'Is that what they will think of me?'

Oh, this pathetic man! Her tone was contemptuous. 'They will think of you much as they did your father, except less kindly. He did less harm.'

Churchill clutched his chest. Never had he been lashed so cruelly, or hurt so deeply, by a woman.

She was pointing at the portrait like a prosecutor in accusation. 'Look at your father. He told you to know your enemy. The trouble with you, Mr Churchill, is you have no idea who your enemy is. You stand there like a spoilt child blaming the rest of the world for your miseries. Half the young men of this country are fighting flame-throwers while you hide here in the dark, fighting ghosts.'

He gasped as if he had been slapped in the face.

'And while we are discussing your father, let us get the record straight. He didn't march proudly off into exile. He was banished. Thrown out. Is that the path you want to follow, Mr Churchill?'

'What would you have me do?' His anger was returning.

'Don't you dare ask me how to fight your wretched war. I know nothing about war. But I do know men, Mr Churchill. So stop wallowing. Stand up, even if it's only to be put up against a wall. Don't let them drag you away as they did your father.' She sprang to her feet to confront him. 'And if you're going to lose, doesn't it matter *how* you lose? Don't you think it matters to those men on the beaches in Calais and Dunkirk? If they're going to die, let it be for something they believe in, and for someone who believes in them.' Tears had sprung to her cheeks now. 'Don't . . . don't let them die in vain, least of all for one man's vanity, like young German boys. Give them something to die for—or better still, give them something to live for!'

They stared at each other through their tears, like parting lovers.

'And if they end up dragging you away, Mr Churchill, put up a struggle. Don't go meekly into the darkness. Shout! Cry! Make a good end of it. For God's sake, don't be like your father.'

'Get out! Get out!' he stormed, stamping across the room until he was leaning on his desk for support. He was breathing heavily, trying to cope with the pain. 'Get out,' he insisted once again, though more quietly. 'I've got a damned war to fight.'

She left, relieved. She had refloated the ship and it was sailing back into the storm.

## CHAPTER NINE

Shortly after four, Bertram Ramsay stepped out onto his balcony and sniffed the damp air of dawn with a naval man's caution. Ramsay hadn't seen his bed the previous night, nor the night before. Not the best way to plan a military campaign, without sleep, but as he had told his staff, sleep was for the righteous and the ready. And they weren't ready.

Be prepared, he had been instructed. Just in case. But be prepared for what?

Vice Admiral Bertram Home Ramsay was a quiet but single-minded individual—too single-minded for some of his superiors in the Royal Navy. A couple of years previously, he'd grown frustrated at some of their archaic methods and had been rash enough to let it show. They'd thrown him out, aged fifty-five, put him on the retired list to make way for an older man.

They'd not found any further use for him until the war had broken out, and then he'd not been given charge of anything more manoeuvrable than a desk buried inside deep tunnels—although, in truth, the desk was not without its powers, and the tunnels were unique.

Ramsay was something of an expert on the Dover Straits, so at the outbreak of hostilities he had been recalled and given the role of Flag Officer Commanding, Dover. The headquarters for this task were located in huge vaulting tunnels: interlocking brick-lined galleries that had been hacked out of the east cliffs by French prisoners during an earlier war against Napoleon. In those days they had been used as underground barracks for thousands of troops, complete with fireplaces, a water well, and a young lady of arguable virtue called Mary Ford, whose name was kept alive in the graffiti left embedded in the soft chalk walls. But war this time around offered no such gentle distractions. There was barely enough time to scribble a short note home. Ramsay and his small team worked constantly, ate occasionally and rarely slept.

Some days earlier they had been instructed to prepare a contingency plan—just in case. The war had been drawing closer; at first the battle front had been spread across several countries, but with every passing day it was being squeezed into a smaller corner of France. There were now only two ports left open to the British army: Calais and

Dunkirk. Ramsay had spent the last few days shuttling anxiously between the maps on his desk and the brick-and-iron-railing balcony that formed the end of his tunnel where it emerged from the cliffs. From that balcony he could see it all. He had watched as Boulogne had disappeared in an evil smudge of shell-bursts and ash that had stained the horizon on what had been a cloudless day. Calais would shortly follow; he could see it with his bare eyes. All night long the flames had fought against the darkness, gaining ground, and first light revealed plumes of foul smoke rising high into the air. Through his binoculars he could see the clock tower on the Hôtel de Ville staring at him through the smoke; automatically, he checked it against his pocket watch. The clock was still running. If only time would slow, run back for just a little, give them a few extra hours to prepare for whatever lay ahead.

But what did lie ahead? No one could tell him. Would the long-awaited advance upon the enemy begin, when they would be expected to ferry across vast quantities of new supplies to help the BEF on its way? Or would it be that other option—retreat, rout—when they would try to salvage as much as they could from the chaos of defeat?

Which would it be, what should they plan for? he had asked. Everything, they had replied. Just in case.

In case of what? They couldn't tell him. But as he looked through his binoculars at the carnage across the water and the first wave of dive-bombers going in for their attack, he knew without any measure of doubt what they were facing.

Disaster.

* * *

Don rubbed his eyes. He was having difficulty believing what he saw.

He had woken to find burnt paper and cinders falling around him like autumn leaves. Down one gutter of the street crept a tide of burning oil, while on the other side rushed water from a broken main. Fires blazed everywhere, smoke filtered out the early sun. A violence had been hurled upon Calais with such compelling force that nothing seemed to have survived intact.

And yet there was the owner of a café, setting out his tables on the pavement as if it were an ordinary day. He was elderly, stooped, the Croix de Guerre dangling from his waistcoat. Crazy, perhaps, but what else did he have to do, how else could he find distraction from what was happening around him? A body lay on the street corner, a civilian, amidst a scattering of rubble. When the café owner had finished laying out his tables he sat down with a bottle of cognac, raised a glass to his dead neighbour, and drank.

A far more extraordinary sight was that of the defenders of Calais. So far as Don could see, they consisted mostly of members of the 1st Searchlight Regiment. The principal task of a Searchlight unit was, as their name implied, to operate large searchlights in the hope of dazzling and blinding any low-flying and dive-bombing aircraft. They had practically no infantry training and were never expected to engage the enemy with anything other than giant torches. Yet here they were, manning positions against panzers, bloodied but not yet beaten.

Then a sight still more impossible. Infantrymen were amongst the Searchlights; at first Don assumed that they were perhaps training the Searchlights in the use of the Bren guns and the Boys anti-tank rifles that were being passed back and forth between them. But no, it was the other way round. It was the infantrymen who were taking instruction, soldiers of the Queen Victoria's Rifles . . .

Don and Claude had no more time to wonder at the extraordinary sights of Calais before the war caught up with them again. A single-engined Fieseler Storch spotter plane flew overhead, leaving a trail of white smoke to indicate the front of the British line. It had barely disappeared before the barrage began. Suddenly it seemed personal. The Stukas appeared to know precisely where Don and Claude were cowering and launched wave after wave upon them. Paving stones were tossed through the air, shards of glass formed themselves into terrifying volleys of missiles, and on all sides fragments of broken buildings tried to reach out and bury them. But this was merely the overture. The panzers picked up the score and began hurling flaming shells that bounced along the street, leaving trails of sparks as they ricocheted along the cobbles. The noise was so intense that it became impossible to speak; even when they tried, the dust filled their lungs and made them choke.

As the smoke and dust cleared, they could find no trace of the café proprietor and barely any trace of his café. On the corner lay the body of a young girl, her skirts blown up above her waist. There was no time to move her; a British soldier knelt and gently pulled her tartan skirt down over her knees.

As he rose from tending the dead girl, the soldier saw Don and Claude. He shouted something that was unintelligible against the roar of the new fires and waved anxiously to them. They shook their heads. He shouted again.

The defence of Calais had been planned around a series of shrinking perimeters. The first had been set at the pinch-points on the roads and bridges beyond the outer walls, with the second perimeter provided by the walls themselves. Now the commanding officer, Brigadier Nicholson, had ordered a further retreat, to positions in and around the medieval Citadel that guarded the western side of the harbour. Nicholson had done this because earlier that day he had received fresh instructions from the War Office. These instructions had been passed down and had filtered through as far as the soldier who was now waving at Don and Claude.

At last his words stumbled through to them. Something about pulling their fingers out. Because they were all going home.

* * *

When Colville walked into Churchill's bedroom a little after nine, the Prime Minister was sitting up in bed wearing a florid red silk dressing gown and surrounded by a shower of papers that had emerged from his Ministerial box. It took only a moment to gauge the old man's mood.

'Tell me, Jock. On whose bloody side Gort is supposed to be fighting?'

'Prime Minister?'

'Calais is under blockade from the Germans and Gort's tanks are less than twenty miles away. So why doesn't he attack? Break through the encirclement? Punch a hole through the panzers from behind and send them limping back home? He keeps complaining that his nine divisions are about to be starved out yet he refuses to send even a couple of brigades to clear his supply lines through the port. What the hell is he doing?'

'He's under pressure along the entire front. It must be difficult to disengage.'

'Damn his difficulties! The Germans seem able to dance around bloody France to their heart's content while our own tanks seem incapable of moving even a few miles.'

'The situation in Belgium is looking very fragile; we've just had a report in from . . .'

He trailed off. Churchill was no longer listening. He was reading a note, and the hand that held it was trembling. It was a copy of a telegram sent to the garrison at Calais a few hours beforehand while Churchill was asleep. It was signed by a junior officer, and informed Nicholson that in spite of the previous instruction permitting him to evacuate his forces, there had been a change of mind. The junior officer reminded Nicholson that technically he was under the orders of the local French general 'who has ordered no repeat no evacuation'. This meant, the telegram continued, that 'you must comply for the sake of Allied solidarity. Your role is therefore to hold on . . .'

To hold on. Without assistance? Against overwhelming numbers of panzers? For the sake of 'Allied solidarity'? Simply so that someone in the War Office could avoid a row with the French?

'Jock, to die for one's country is one thing. But to tell a man he is going to die for his superiors' convenience is an abomination!' Churchill was shouting, attacking the telegram in fury, ripping it to shreds. 'Find out who sent this wretched scrap. Have him strung from the highest tower. I mean it! I will not have this. I will not have this! Do you hear?'

He threw himself out of bed and the entire contents of his Ministerial box cascaded to the floor.

* * *

Yet already it was too late. As Don and Claude made their faltering way back behind the new defensive line, they could see British tanks being set ablaze by their own crews, fuel supplies being put to the flame, truck engines being run without oil until their vital parts had seized. They couldn't know it, but even as they made their way inside the Citadel, an officer was hacking away at the cross-Channel cable that provided the only telephone link between Calais and England. The British army didn't want to leave behind anything that might be of use to the enemy, so they were smashing and destroying as much as possible, because they had been told they were going home. Their new orders hadn't yet made it through.

* * *

Ruth had read the newspapers quickly that morning. She had found little in them to detain her. Boulogne had fallen; the editorials were full of gloom about imminent invasion; and for the first time the names of women had begun to appear in the lists of those killed. But she noted that they were still advertising holidays in Paris with 'special rates for members of the Allied forces'. Oh, the English and their sense of humour.

Yet as she walked around the streets of London, so little seemed to have changed. Breastworks of sandbags had appeared at a few places around Whitehall, manned by soldiers with serious-looking guns, but they offered nothing but smiles and already seemed something of a tourist attraction. Crowds of boys gathered round, hoping for sweets. Londoners had been taking their own precautions, too. Removing pictures from the walls. Storing valuables. Preparing buckets of sand. But the shops in the West End seemed as crowded as ever—almost more so—with people spending money while they still could. They were preparing for invasion as though it were Christmas. Ah, the English!

Ruth wondered what it was like in Berlin. She had listened to one of the American broadcasters on her wireless last night, who had recounted just how normal Berlin seemed. The pavement coffee shops of the Kurfürstendamm were packed with people who seemed to have nothing more on their minds than their ice cream and *ersatz* coffee. Every theatre was open and packed, every lake and woodland outside the city teeming with excited families, the Tiergarten echoing to the sound of children's laughter, so he reported. No air raid since last September.

On the surface London seemed much the same, but Ruth sensed that something here was changing.

The English were stubborn, didn't jump to conclusions, were slow to reveal their emotions. Yet there was a sense, which perhaps a foreigner could pick up more easily, of something going astray. The thrust south had been promised for days but still hadn't happened, and it was beginning to dawn on some that perhaps it never would, while the ridiculous sense of English fair play was leading some to conclude that because they had won the last one, perhaps it was Jerry's turn this time around. There was no obvious despair, but you could hear the rustle of growing doubts. The collective stiff upper lip was freezing solid, and the English marched along looking straight ahead, fearful of what they would find if they glanced to the side. Their belief in themselves was gently rocking.

And the English didn't seem to hate enough. She remembered how in the last war the Germans had been swept up in a tide of hate that had hurled their menfolk onto the barbed wire and at the throats of the enemy. The Germans seemed to have hidden depths to their ability to hate that the English simply didn't possess. Perhaps it was because the English had fought wars over so many centuries and had grown soft and complacent, while the Germans were so new to the game, more enthusiastic.

The Germans were not like these English. The English found bizarre fulfilment in their rose bushes and ridiculous sports, in their ironies and subtleties. The Germans had no subtlety. You could see that in their philosophy, which was full of abstractions and no good at debating the ethics of the torture chamber.

Perhaps that was why no one had stood up to Hitler. Not the Social Democrats, not the Catholics, not nationalists, not the old leaders, not the generals. There had been no civil war against Hitler, no war of any sort until Hitler himself had been ready to start one. And now no one else seemed ready to stand up to him.

Except Churchill.

The preposterous, pretentious, deeply flawed and drunk Winston Churchill.

And Ruth Mueller, of course.

The newspapers that morning had been full of rumours about the invasion. What would it be like if that happened? She had run from them once, and now there was nowhere else to run. She wouldn't get a second chance. That's why she had no choice but to do what she could to stand up to Hitler—even if it also meant standing up to the tantrums of that ridiculous Mr Churchill.

* * *

Ramsay slipped out onto his balcony to check the time. He no longer trusted his watch. The endless days spent locked deep inside the earth combined with the lack of sleep had begun to disorientate him; he needed to get out to make sure whether it was afternoon or the dead of night.

A blast of sunlight and salted breeze slapped him in the face and revived his senses. Beneath him, the three huge quays of the harbour jutted out into the sea, and between them craft of all kinds bustled about their work like bees around a hive. This was his hive and they were his bees, although there were many parts of this increasingly kaleidoscopic operation about which he knew little or nothing. It wasn't lack of interest but rather a matter of delegation; it was the only way to get things done with a small staff. Delegation required both judgement and faith—and as every day had slipped past, it seemed to be requiring more faith than ever.

Across the Channel in Calais, it still continued. The glare of the sun made it more difficult to see with the naked eye, but it was possible even at this distance to hear the barrage of fire that was being laid down upon the town. They had told him to be ready for evacuation, then resupply, after which no one seemed able to tell him what to expect. But he knew what the troops in Calais could expect. Poor bastards.

He sighed, sucked in a breath of sharp salt air, checked his watch. Time to descend once more to his underworld. As he put his pocket watch away, with his usual habit he raised his binoculars to the clock across the water.

His sigh turned to a soft moan of despair. Even through the smoke and glare it was unmistakable. A swastika was fluttering above the Hôtel de Ville.

*   *   *

As they fell back, the defenders of Calais began to leave many of the landmarks behind. The Hôtel de Ville, the theatre, the Gare Centrale, the Hôpital Civil: all were now German. But the docks and the Citadel weren't. The Citadel of Calais was a towering construction of the stoutest walls built almost four hundred years earlier to guard against the English; the sons of England were to find many reasons to be grateful for the diligence of the medieval engineers.

It was a day not of ordered recollections but of images that would embed themselves into the memories of men for as long as they lived. Lace curtains fluttering in the breeze to reveal the snout of a Bren gun; the scorching heat of buildings as they burned around you; the slow realization that you hadn't eaten for two days and might never eat again; English soldiers finding cover behind an upturned Louis-Quatorze table while a Frenchman took his shelter behind the bodies of two dead comrades; foxholes being dug with helmets, with no time to dig graves; last rites; last breaths; whispered lies about relief columns; unarmed soldiers waiting their turn for a rifle, waiting for someone to die; images of soldiers drinking champagne—not because they wanted to be drunk but because there was no water and their thirst was irresistible, and each man willing to exchange a crate of champagne for a handful of bullets.

Yet in the midst of the carnage there were civilians, dousing the flames as their houses burned, scurrying across bullet-racked streets to safer shelter, even opening their shops to hand out food to anxious customers.

Don and Claude witnessed this, and much more. As they stumbled onward, with Claude in ever-increasing pain, they saw an armoured car bearing a white flag stopping on the far side of the Pont Georges Cinq—the German side. A civilian emerged and walked forward. He was an elderly man, bald with a neatly trimmed moustache and hooded, sorrowful eyes.

'*Je suis le Maire de Calais*,' he told the guard

manning the roadblock at the British end. 'My name is André Gershell. I ask you to consider surrendering. For the sake of my people.'

'It is for the sake of your people that we fight.'

The Mayor looked wretched. The English were not to know it, but he had remained behind at the Hôtel de Ville when most of those around him had fled. He wanted to do what he could to save his people and to save the old town around the port, which was being destroyed hour by hour; it wasn't for him to decide when the war that had fallen upon his town should end, but he could remind everyone of the costs of it continuing.

He requested that he be taken to the commanding officer. As he stepped forward, he passed near Don and Claude. Claude had spoken very little since the discovery of abandoned home, but as Gershell passed by he grabbed his sleeve. '*Monsieur le Maire*, excuse me. Do you know anything of my family, les Dubuis?'

But there were so many families. With a sad, exhausted stare, the Mayor shook his head and continued on.

Claude watched him disappear, his shoulders crumpled in despair, his head held low from the weight of exhaustion and shame.

'He is either a saint or a total fool,' he whispered, 'to do the Germans' work for them.'

'Why?' Don asked.

'Because he is a Jew.'

It took only minutes for the Mayor to walk the couple of hundred yards to the Citadel. Brigadier Nicholson met him in the courtyard; their interview was brief. 'If the Germans want Calais,' the mayor was told, 'they will have to fight for it.'

But they had bought themselves a little time. While the surrender talks were going on, a lull had occurred in the fighting. There had been other pauses, too. When the Germans had seen the British destroying their own tanks, they had thought it was all over and had relaxed for a while. They did the same thing when they saw the swastika flying from the Hôtel de Ville, but that was still five hundred murderous yards from the Citadel. Then the German forward positions had been shelled by their own artillery, causing more confusion and delay. No German soldier wanted to die for a battle they thought was all but finished. Moment by moment, the day was being stretched towards dusk.

A British artillery unit had struggled all afternoon to repair one of the guns spiked the previous day by the French. Towards evening they were ready to fire their first shell. There was a mighty explosion and much smoke, and for a moment the gun disappeared from view. When it could be seen once more, the barrel was leaning at a curious angle. Slowly, almost gracefully, the barrel fell to the ground with a hollow clatter and rolled away like a children's toy. A little down the line, soldiers from the Searchlight Regiment raised an ironic cheer, only to be rebuked by their sergeant major. 'It's no laughing matter!' he insisted. He marched over to the artillery men to inspect the damage. When he returned he looked witheringly at his men. 'They're laughin' their heads off, too. Ain't anybody going to take this bleedin' war seriously?'

It was just before last light that Don and Claude arrived at the Hôpital Militaire in the shadow of the Citadel. It had taken them all day to make their way less than a mile, Claude hobbling in great discomfort, Don supporting him. The windows of the hospital had all been blown out; there was shattered glass everywhere and it crunched beneath their boots like puddles of ice as they made their way inside.

It was packed—with pain, tragedy, sorrow, death. In every corner a story of sacrifice was being played out. Men moaned quietly as a priest muttered prayers in the ears of the dying; more wounded arrived as shell bursts continued their relentless shaking of the walls. Flies circled, inspecting every man.

'Can I help you?' a ragged nurse asked Claude.

The Frenchman looked at the sights that confronted him, tears in his eyes, and shook his head. 'No, thank you. I'm not that sick.'

* * *

John Standish Surtees Prendergast Vereker, the Sixth Viscount Gort of Limerick, was not a popular man. Although as Commander-in-Chief of the British Expeditionary Force he occupied one of the most senior positions in the British army, he still had superiors. He also had senior men under his command who thought little of him. Partly this was because of his lack of strategic grip—he always seemed to be counting the leaves instead of cutting a path through the forest, as one of them put it—but largely it was jealousy. He had been promoted over the heads of many able officers because of his friendship with the Secretary of State for War, whom he'd met in a collision on a ski slope. The

Secretary of State had long since gone, shuffled out of the pack, leaving Gort in an exposed position from where he could upset almost everyone. And he had. He had infuriated his Prime Minister, and he'd been the cause of the most bitter recriminations from the French for his failure to advance south. They were still insisting he should do so.

Gort had been over-promoted. He wasn't up to the job—not this job, at least. But there wasn't a man on the planet who was. And Gort was nothing if not brave, fearless in the face of hostile fire. He'd won the Distinguished Service Order with two bars in the First War, and a Military Cross. Oh, and there was that dark brown gunmetal Victoria Cross, too, which he'd won at the very end of the war when others were looking towards home fires and family reunions. They only handed out those things for acts of extraordinary valour, for self-sacrifice and extreme devotion to duty in the presence of the enemy. But in those days the enemy was always in front of him.

His headquarters were in a small and undistinguished chateau at Premesques. He sat alone and in silence at his desk in the drawing room with a map spread out before him. Gort was a guardsman; that meant something. Duty. Obedience. Tradition. But as he'd grown older he'd found there was a higher duty that didn't always fit neatly alongside the other values. It perplexed him.

He paced up and down, fretful, before returning to the study of his map. He spent a long time poring over it. Then, early in the evening, he walked through to the small office next door where sat his Chief of Staff, Henry Pownall. His hand lay on his chest where his medals would hang.

'Henry, I've had a hunch. We can't attack south, it's impossible. And I don't like the smell of what we're getting from the front in Belgium. We need to fall back and reinforce our left.'

'You do realize, sir, that's against all the orders we've had.'

'Yes, I know that. All the same, it's got to be done.'

'The French won't attack on their own.'

'They won't attack at all. That's why it's got to be done.'

Pownall sat quietly for a moment. He didn't disagree with Gort's analysis, but the consequences would be enormous. It would mean the end of the BEF. 'Disobeying a direct order from your superiors *and* the PM. They'll have their pound of flesh for that.'

'Better a British butcher than a German one, Henry.'

* * *

*(Saturday 25 May 1940. William L. Shirer, CBS.)*

*Good evening. This is Berlin.*

*In the opinion of German military circles, the fate of the great Allied army bottled up in Flanders is sealed. The Germans believe that army, containing the flower of the French, British and Belgian forces, cannot now escape . . .*

*Tonight the German Command, in giving us a general picture of the situation as it sees it, stated categorically that the Allies cut off in Flanders and the Artois now have no more possibility of breaking out of their trap. As the High Command stated it, quote: 'The end of the enemy here is imminent'. How many Allied troops are cut off? German generals at the front to whom I put the question earlier in the week said about a million. Well-informed circles in Berlin think it may be a little higher than that. Roughly, they estimate the trapped armies this way: four hundred thousand Belgians, five hundred thousand French, two hundred thousand British . . .*

* * *

Although he didn't suspect it, 'Tiny' Ironside's fate had been sealed since the bruising encounter with the young officer from Calais. The chaos wasn't entirely Ironside's fault, but as Chief of the Imperial General Staff it was his responsibility. That went with the job. Everything was his responsibility, not only Calais but Boulogne, the BEF and the entire buggeration factor in France. Decent man, Churchill thought, even a friend, so far as such things went, but *responsible*.

And he had been invited to join Churchill for dinner. He very much wished he hadn't.

He sat opposite Anthony Eden, the Secretary of State for War, with Churchill at the head of the table. The Prime Minister wasn't speaking. He hadn't said a word all through the soup, which he hadn't finished, and they had to wait until the beef and a third glass of wine had arrived before they were offered anything more than grunts. Then:

'Blackness. Nothing but an interminable trail of sorrows leads to this door—and I suspect you have more sorrows for me, Tiny.'

It was just the three of them, informal, first names, say what you like—after all, *he* would. Yet Ironside chose not to dispute his Prime Minister's gloom.

'Where would you like me to start, Winston?'

'Bloody Belgium.'

'Bloody, indeed.' A sight resetting of the lips, a straightening of the back. 'They've broken through. Either side of Courtrai. The Belgians are in retreat, the Germans driving forward. At some points they are probably less than ten miles from Dunkirk even as we talk.'

Churchill, who had been toying with his beef, now pushed it away untouched. Most unusual. Two anxious, exhausted eyes raised themselves from the table. 'What do you think will happen?'

'The Belgians will collapse. Either they will be swept aside by the panzers, or they will throw in the towel. Probably the latter—my information is that King Leopold has lost the appetite for the fight. Which means it will happen sooner rather than later.'

' "It"? What does *"it"* portend in this context?'

Oh, how the smallest of words could contain as many nightmares as a man could ever dream . . .

' "It" means . . . the end. Defeat. Unless somehow we can keep a foothold at Dunkirk. Fetch back some of the BEF. Live to fight another day, perhaps.' His tone made it clear that he thought this was as likely as stumbling upon moonshine in the middle of the day, yet, even before the echo of his words had died away, two fists were pounding upon the table.

'How is this possible? How can it be that one man, with not a single ally, can force his will upon the whole of Europe when we, with all our leagues and ententes and alliances, have been dragged to the brink of disaster? Austria. Czechoslovakia. Poland. Holland. Norway. The Netherlands. Now Belgium. And next France.' The cutlery jumped afresh with every name in the litany. Suddenly the crashing ceased and he was jabbing a finger.

'You see, Tiny, I sometimes think that there is a streak of defeatism amongst our General Staff, that they simply don't want to fight. They think That Bloody Man is invincible. But they're wrong! He's never been tested. He's a paper Caesar who has never faced the trial of true steel. Never been an English schoolboy.'

Schoolboy? What the hell did that mean? Both Ironside and Eden glanced at Churchill's glass, trying to remember how often it had been raised. The man swept on.

'But now the hour has come. We discover the breaking point, not only of him, but of ourselves. You see, he is deluded. Grossly deluded. About us! Every experience he has suggests that the British will not fight this war. He saw that we entered it—were dragged into it—only with reluctance. Since then we have contested it barely at all. But what if we did? There's the question. What if Old England were to rise up and roar its defiance? What if we were to show him that we are lions and not terrified lambs?'

'But what does this all mean, Winston?' Eden interjected, alarmed by the cascade of romantic outpouring and afraid that the old man was, after all, entirely too old.

Churchill didn't respond immediately, but sat with his head up, like a stag testing the wind. When at last he took up Eden's challenge, his tone was far less hectoring. The words came slowly, dragging great weights after them.

'It means that we in these islands must prepare ourselves to withstand the full force of the Nazi onslaught. To place ourselves at the point where so many others have failed. We must continue the fight. We must bring our army back from Europe—or as much of it as providence will allow—and pray that through defiance we will see through to brighter days.'

'But if we lose Dunkirk . . .'

'We shall lose Dunkirk.' His chin had fallen to his chest and his eyes seemed set on a place far beyond this room. 'No power we possess can prevent it any longer. So what matters is its timing, and that depends upon what we do now. The great Nazi scythe has swept through Europe. We must blunt it, and before it reaches Dunkirk.' He turned to each man separately, his eyes suddenly flooded. 'We must stand and fight at Calais, for if we don't do it there we may not get another chance. There is no other way. It breaks my heart, but there is no other way.' He seemed unable to continue.

'Which way is that, Winston?'

'We must issue new instructions to our forces at Calais. No surrender, no evacuation. They must fight to the end. To the last man and to the very last bullet.'

The flood in his eyes began to cascade down his cheeks.

'What else can we do? If there were another door open just a crack'—he brought his finger and thumb together—'I would leap through it.'

'But to tell those men they must . . .' Ironside

shook his head, unwilling to follow the terrible consequences of the thought. 'What *do* we tell them?'

'Something like this should be said to our brave men of Calais,' Churchill declared. 'That their defence of the town is of the highest importance. That every moment they resist protects the lives of their brother soldiers, and every hour they continue their fight is an hour longer for our country to live in hope. That what they do there, the spirit they show, the evidence they provide of our unflinching British will to survive, may yet turn the course of this war. The eyes of the Empire are upon them, the eyes of history, too, and their exploits in Calais will be written as one of the finest chapters in our nation's long history. We shall owe them and their families a debt of honour. We shall never forget.'

A profound silence hung across the table. For a while neither Eden nor Ironside could speak. Eventually it was Ironside.

'To the last man, and to the last bullet? Never in my life have I had to issue such an order.'

'They must fight on, ever on. Our nation's survival may depend upon it.'

He turned to Eden. There were tears in the other man's eyes, too. 'The King's Rifles are there, my own regiment,' Eden whispered. He had fought in the last war and had watched most of them being slaughtered then, too.

'I know, my dear Anthony. I know.'

It took a while for the three men to compose themselves. Then it was Churchill once more.

'We are agreed?'

A further silence, a silence of conspiracy and of consent.

'I am indebted to you both for your courage in this matter,' Churchill whispered.

Ironside cleared his throat, stretched his arms out in front of him, looked straight ahead. 'There's one other bit of business which must be dealt with. Bloody Belgium—as you put it, Winston. You both realize what it means: Gort got it right. If he'd been advancing south as he was ordered, with the Belgians in collapse, by tomorrow the BEF would be entirely cut off and on the point of being wiped out. Three hundred thousand men. His disobedience has spared us that. As it is, I fear that only a miracle can save us now.' He cleared his throat once more, like a stallion before a fence, then turned to face Churchill. 'Prime Minister'—they all noted the sudden formality—'I've been urging on you and on Lord Gort a strategy that has turned out to be fatally flawed.'

They knew this was only partially true. It was flawed, no question of that, right to the hilt, but it had been Churchill's strategy before anyone's. Ironside was taking onto his shoulders a responsibility that in honesty should lie elsewhere at the table.

'Forgive this little speech, it's scarcely the right time—if only I knew when the right time would come—but we are asking for sacrifices by so many brave men, in part because of my failure to anticipate events.'

'You're not alone in that, Tiny,' Eden interjected.

'No, but I am alone responsible as Chief of the Imperial General Staff. I must accept responsibility for these failures, it's the way things should be done. So I must step aside. Somebody else must take over, somebody who I hope will enjoy better fortune.'

Churchill was startled. Ironside resigning? It had been his intention to push him aside, but not at this dinner table. It was a magnificent gesture.

'Tiny, your dedication and valour is beyond question. You need not reproach yourself. If I invited only those who had been entirely blameless over the last few years, this table would be empty. You're right, I think, though. Time for a fresh approach, perhaps a change of luck. But we shall want you here, in some role of the highest seniority, at the centre of things. I shall want your continuing support—'

'And you will have it.'

'On Calais, too. I need your support on that.'

Ah, was Churchill's enduring friendship being offered only on that condition? But it didn't matter. Ironside smiled grimly. 'Bloody ironic, isn't it? My last act as Chief of the Imperial General Staff will be to sign an order that will forever mark me down as—'

'As a man who knew his duty and who did not flinch from it. That's how it will be seen, Tiny.'

'By God, I hope you're right, Winston. But you have my support, of course.'

'And you, Anthony.'

Eden was beginning to harbour a niggling suspicion about the reasons for his invitation. Was it in his capacity as War Secretary, or as one of the King's Rifles? Was he here to offer advice, or to provide cover from any fire that might erupt after the order was issued? But it scarcely mattered. During the last war he had held a withering opinion of Churchill, but in this war, and on this matter, he thought he was right.

'Of course, Winston.'

Churchill rose. 'Whatever the outcome of this conflict, whenever I recall this night, I shall remember that I spent it with two brave friends.'

Three hours later a minesweeper forced its way into Calais harbour to deliver a message to Brigadier Nicholson. (It could not be sent by wireless because all the code books in Calais had already been burned.) The message read: 'Every hour you continue to exist is of greatest help to BEF. Government has therefore decided you must continue to fight. Have greatest admiration for your splendid stand. Evacuation will not (*repeat* not) take place, and craft required for above purpose are to return to Dover.'

Five hours later, all the destroyers standing off Calais in sight of the garrison had been withdrawn.

Two nights later, in a fit of exhaustion and meanness, Churchill instructed Bracken to put it about that Ironside had been fired. '*Pour encourager* . . .' he muttered, 'before it's all too bloody late.'

## CHAPTER TEN

Sunday 26 May. The air that morning lay heavy with the sweet scent of doom. It was raining once more, grey, overcast, washing hope from the skies and blossom into the running gutters.

It had been ordained a National Day of Prayer. Initially Churchill hadn't objected to the proposal—where was its harm?—yet now the day had dawned and he was required at Westminster Abbey at the side of the King, he had begun to resent the imposition. The day had begun badly and would without any measure of doubt plumb more miserable depths. The news from Belgium was as bad as feared and from France growing worse. Defeatism was spreading across Europe like a medieval plague and had even infected the Cabinet room. That morning, Halifax had shown every sign of the sickness. He'd said it was no longer a matter of securing victory but a matter of survival, of safeguarding Britain's independence and if possible that of France.

As Churchill walked the few hundred yards to the Abbey, along pavements that glistened like dead fish, he knew it might not be long before the whole of Westminster caught the infection. 'No longer a matter of securing victory but of survival?' But what had he told the Commons less than two weeks ago? *You ask, What is our aim? I can answer in one word: Victory—victory at all costs, victory in spite of all terror; victory, however long and hard the road may be; for without victory there is no survival . . .*

In Halifax's dignified way, he was declaring a mutiny. Insisting that they sail a different course. Oh, the words were noble enough, 'safeguarding our independence', but how could our independence be safeguarded if the rest of Europe was awash with tyranny? What would Ruth say? He'd like Halifax to find out one day, lock German refugee and English aristocrat into a windowless room and see how long he lasted.

It was wrong to accuse him of defeatism, though. He was not a coward, just completely muddle-headed, believing that there was a way to talk themselves out of trouble. Just like they'd tried before, at Munich. Just like so many had tried with Hitler. To the academic and diplomatic Halifax it represented the triumph of reason, but to Churchill it seemed like the madness of a sailor, cast adrift and dying of thirst, hoping he could drink the sea dry.

Inside the Abbey the air had grown clammy from the rain and the fog of human breath. The King and Queen arrived, carrying their gas masks, and the service began.

Churchill grew increasingly discontented. Oh, why had they chosen the Abbey, this place of tombs, of royal decay, of the end of dynasties? Everywhere he looked there were memorials, reminders of death and fallen heroes. This was the wrong place on a day such as this.

The chanting of prayers began. *Our Father, who art in heaven, Hallowed be thy name* . . . Churchill didn't care for chanting, which he regarded as little more than a form of mass anaesthesia, and today he didn't care for prayers, either.

*Thy kingdom come. Thy will be done, On earth as it is in heaven.*

But what is Thy will? If he had ever been sure, Churchill would have been a regular churchgoer, but at school he had been beaten for a lapse of concentration in chapel, the swishes being delivered with a little homily about how the cross represented the pronoun 'I' crossed out. He hadn't swallowed it then, and all these years later still thought it bunkum. It's what Ruth had said Hitler was about, the destruction of individual identity. But the struggle to carve out that identity was the very stuff of man's existence!

*Give us this day our daily bread. And forgive us our trespasses, As we forgive those who trespass against us . . .*

He fidgeted on his knees, fumbling with the words. Forgiveness? No, never, not Hitler. Forgiveness might be fine for the Almighty, but Churchill found himself quite incapable of it. He didn't profess to understand the ways of the eternal world, but on this earth there would be no forgiveness. No tea and cream cakes at the Palace with That Man! If God wanted to forgive Hitler when they met face to face, that was His business, and the sooner it was transacted the better.

*And lead us not into temptation, But deliver us from evil. For thine is the kingdom, and the power, and the glory, for ever and ever.*

No, it wouldn't be God who delivered them from evil, not unless they decided to start giving Him a bit of a helping hand. The children of Israel hadn't got anywhere by talking, they'd only escaped from slavery in Egypt by forging their way through a sea of spilled blood—the enemy's blood.

*Amen.*

Churchill would never compare himself to Moses, but his reticence had nothing to do with modesty. Moses had led his people to the Promised Land. So far as Churchill was concerned, his people were already in it. Perhaps it was time to remind them what they were fighting for.

Then Bracken was at his shoulder, whispering. Calling him away. There was a war to fight. Churchill bowed his head in apology to the King and, as unobtrusively as a Prime Minister could, walked solemnly from his stall in the choir to the door. As he passed rows of strained, pleading faces, he turned to Bracken.

'We English spend too damned long on our knees,' he growled. 'Ridiculous way to fight a war.'

* * *

Every man has a right to live in hope, and even in Calais that hope had not died. During the night a brilliantly lit hospital ship had drawn into the harbour to evacuate the wounded. Every man had watched it approach, dock, take on its cargo of woes, then steam away and disappear in the direction of home. The wounded would be in hospital in Dover in a couple of hours; those who stayed behind clung to the hope that more ships would follow and they could all die in England. But in the silence of the night that followed its departure, the word was passed round in whispers.

No evacuation.

As dawn broke, the men of Calais could see the cliffs of their homeland emerging from the sea, and nothing but clear water in between. The ships had gone. For once the British army was true to its word. There would be no evacuation.

Every one of them knew it would be today; they couldn't hold out any longer. Sometime before nightfall, in a few hours' time, they would be dead, or wounded, or prisoners. For many, this was going to be their day to die.

Even so, many would die unarmed. There still weren't enough weapons. In places they fought hand to hand, with grenades, bayonets, fists. The Germans were astonished to discover their positions being bombarded with smoke shells—there was nothing else to use. At every point, the

British and their French comrades were pushed back remorselessly towards the sea, yet still they fought on, and on. The German army reports would later tell in awed tones of the 'most tough and ferocious manner' with which the defenders fought, and praise the 'extreme courage' with which they laid down their lives.

As they retreated, the houses behind them were already blazing. They were forced to walk backwards into a forest of flame and exploding glass. Ash and cinder fell like the last moments of Pompeii. The heat was unbearable, their thirst worse. A cry of 'gas' went up, but it was a false alarm, nothing but the chlorine being burned away in the batteries of British tanks that had fought themselves to destruction. When they fell back to the beaches and the dunes, their guns began to clog with sand; they had to strip and clean them even as the enemy pressed down upon them. But by then the British had fallen back as far as they could. In front of them was death, and behind them nothing but an empty sea. Still they hoped, even in the last hour, that the Royal Navy would come to their salvation.

The last hour came around four in the afternoon, although the thick, choking smoke made it seem more like nightfall. Nicholson's headquarters in the Citadel fell. The bastion built to withstand the English had, in the end, proved to be the Englishmen's last redoubt. After that it was every man for himself.

Don and Claude had clung together during the day. Claude had wanted to fight, but there was nothing to fight with, and there was his leg. Being noncombatants did nothing to keep them from danger. They'd been buried beneath rubble, blown over by explosions, cut by flying glass. A bullet had passed through Don's upper arm as they stumbled from a building that was collapsing about them, and his hair had been singed by flames. What part of them wasn't covered by blood was mired in soot and dust.

Sometime later that afternoon they found themselves amongst the grass tussocks and sand hills east of the docks. They watched as a small unit of riflemen retreated along the beach, pursued by German soldiers. Even as they ran, two more fell, until ahead of them another unit of the Wehrmacht appeared. There was nowhere else to go. The English captain stumbled to a halt, his feet now heavy in the sand. He had begun that day with twice the number of men under his command; surely they had done enough? He dragged himself to attention and told his survivors to lay down their arms.

The soldiers of the Wehrmacht approached cautiously, rifles at the ready. A nervous German officer began gesticulating, ordering the captain to give up his weapons, shouting. The Englishman started to laugh. Carelessly he produced two revolvers, blew sand from the barrels, and handed them across. The German was bewildered. They were both empty.

As Don looked back from the beach he saw every street on fire. Calais had become a furnace, the flames reflected in the water of the docks, the outlines of buildings obliterated by a choking fog of smoke that climbed taller than the Hôtel de Ville and Notre Dame. Three thousand Englishmen and eight hundred brave Frenchmen had been sacrificed here, in full view of the coast of Kent.

'What do you think we should do?' he asked Claude.

'My friend, there is nothing left for me in Calais,' the Frenchman responded. 'Whatever has happened to my family, they are no longer here. So we have two choices. We can stay and keep the captain and his men company, or we can try to escape. To Dunkirk. It is twenty miles that way.' He pointed east along the beach. 'We might live to fight another day.'

'But I'm noncombatant and you've got a buggered leg and nothing to fight with.'

'So, we have half an English soldier and half a French flyer. Between us we might just scrape together one proper fighting man, do you think?'

Don looked at his companion, the sweat-soaked hair, the oozing red eyes, the ragged and scorched uniform, knowing that he looked just as wretched. His arm hurt like hell.

'Twenty miles, you say? Know any short cuts?'

* * *

It was all the fault of that wretched Mrs Parnell. While the men kept their own counsel and carried on, the women—not just Mrs Parnell but seemingly every other mother in the parish—would miss no opportunity of grabbing his sleeve and pouring out their tales of woe. He would pretend to listen patiently, then offer a prayer. They had no idea how all the while he twisted inside until it hurt so much he thought he might split in two.

That's what they did in the Bible, they simply fell down and split. *And falling headlong, he burst asunder in the midst, and all his bowels gushed out.*

He felt his strength waning. 'Not again,' Mrs Parnell had sobbed, and she was right. It was supposed to have been the war to end all wars, that's what they had been promised.

But who had promised? Everyone. They'd all said it. Never again. And yet . . .

There was never a better example in all of Christendom of collective guilt, the sort of thing that sprang out of every page of the Bible. Yet the guilt that in recent days had almost overwhelmed Henry Chichester was altogether more personal. He felt it every time he met a woman who had lost a loved one in the last war or had someone serving in this. That was the sort of pain he couldn't match. He couldn't share with the Mrs Parnells of his world. They came to him for strength yet he had none to give. He felt his guilt so strongly he was no longer able to look them in the eye.

Henry Chichester had lost his way. He was supposed to be a leader, a teacher, but he was nothing more than just another ageing and inadequate man. He was surrounded—almost besieged—by people every waking hour, yet he'd never felt more alone. While they talked to him of their own families, their words screamed at him that he had no one, no wife, no son, nothing more than a fading photograph on the mantelshelf.

Everything was his fault, even Jennie's death. He'd tried to blame the doctors, he'd even blamed his son, but that was the most unkind accusation of all. He and Don should have been able to share Jennie, but they never had. He wouldn't allow that, it hurt too much. And perhaps he was jealous that anyone else, even his own son, should have a claim on her.

It was all his fault.

And if it wasn't his own fault, then it must be God's, but he refused to go any further down that path, terrified of what he might find.

Don. His thoughts kept coming back to Don. His son had made no extraordinary demands, had asked for nothing more than to see things his own way. But a religion built around Commandments seemed to have so little room for such youthful indulgences. 'Thou shalt not' didn't leave much scope for discussion over the roast potatoes.

Henry had never understood his son. When Don had gone off to stay with Henry's sister in Sevenoaks for Registration Day so that he could receive his conscription papers at a different address, the Reverend Chichester had accused him of 'sneaking away'. But that hadn't been the point. What Don had done was to spare his father the embarrassment of his son appearing before a local appeal tribunal in Dover, so that his 'sordid little secret'—oh, another wicked phrase uttered in anger!—would never be known amongst his parishioners. It had taken the father months to work out what the son had realized immediately.

Where was Don? He had no idea. Perhaps over there? He allowed his parishioners to think he was. The Reverend Chichester lifted his eyes to the pillar of fire that was Calais.

*And the sun shone upon the water, and the Moabites saw the water on the other side as red as blood.*

Things were much quieter now, the echoes of the bombing and shelling had faded with the evening light. It was almost too quiet. Suddenly he fell to his knees and began to pray more fervently than he could ever remember. He was afraid. He prayed that Don wasn't over there after all, that every one of his previous prayers and demands should have gone unheeded, that his son would never have to endure what he had endured, or do what he had done, or make so many of the same mistakes. Henry Chichester knew he had failed his son. He shuddered as the holy words mocked him. *Eli, Eli, lama sabachthani?*

Father, Father, why have you forsaken me?

And he fervently wished that Mrs Parnell and all the others might suddenly appear, bringing with them their sorrows and open hearts so that he might share his own with them, before he fell down under the weight of his lonelincss and burst in two.

* * *

It was the third meeting of the War Cabinet that day, Sunday, and still they were no nearer the decision.

'Let us consider the matter from a different perspective . . .'

'From whichever perspective you wish, Prime Minister, but it will not change the basic problem,' Halifax insisted.

The events of the day had unsettled them all. Reynaud the French Prime Minister had flown over—brave but hapless fellow—to explain that his government was irrevocably split. There were those who blamed the British, and some who didn't, those who wanted to fight on, and many who did not, and an overwhelming majority who wanted to open negotiations with the Germans. Reynaud himself would not agree to any peace imposed upon France, but he was in a minority and would probably have to go. 'It may cost me my life,' he explained to Churchill, 'but compared with that of my country it is of little matter.' Indeed a brave fellow, and hapless.

Other happenings across the Channel were equally depressing. There was no news from Calais—their last message, from a lieutenant begging for artillery support, was now several hours old—and Dunkirk was said to be a cauldron of disorder, while barely an hour passed without some political secretary or military aide rushing in to interrupt them with news that Belgian resistance was ever nearer the point of collapse.

Halifax was still talking about the Italian option: getting to Hitler through Mussolini. And the Chiefs of Staff had brought forward an analysis about British options in the event of what they ambiguously termed a 'certain eventuality'. Ironically, that eventuality, of France falling out of the struggle, was looking ever more certain even as the paper was being circulated. The military men concluded that Britain might survive without French support, but only if she could replace it with American. Yet France was no more than twenty miles away, while America was on the other side of the world with its head, as Joe Kennedy had apparently told Beaverbrook, 'stuck firmly up its non-interventionist end'.

The day had begun with rainfall and grown darker with every passing hour. Throughout it, they had argued. Halifax wanted to negotiate, Churchill did not. And neither would give way.

'I believe the events of the day have made the

case for a constructive dialogue all the more persuasive,' Halifax contended once again. 'What will happen if the French fail to continue the fight? We shall be left on our own. Without an army—'

'We shall get our boys back!' Churchill intervened.

'I pray fervently that we shall get some of them back, but how many? Even the most optimistic estimates suggest only thirty-five or forty thousand.' Halifax waved the relevant paper; he seemed to have all the arguments at his fingertips. 'Not enough. Not enough to fight. So I believe we must talk. The French have faced the same dilemma and they, too, seem determined that they should talk.'

Halifax didn't mention that this would happen only over the political corpse of their Prime Minister; he refused to be that cheap.

'The French believe they will get better terms if they talk while they still have an army,' he concluded.

'And I believe we will get the best terms if, while we still have our army, we fight,' Churchill began again, an edge to his voice.

'Even so . . .' Halifax was struggling to retain his emotions. He didn't enjoy such bruising encounters, he was an intellectual, not a street fighter, but he was also a patriot. He had to pursue the point. 'Once France falls, the Germans no longer need to pour their resources into their land armies. They can switch to air power. We will never be able to keep up. Which is why we will get the best deal now, but not if we wait. This whole concept of . . .'—he hesitated while trying to paraphrase the Churchill argument without becoming too acerbic—'the noble struggle to the bitter end . . . . may be the stuff of romantic histories.' Attlee winced; it was a shaft too far, dragging in Churchill's writings. 'But it is not an acceptable argument in conditions of modern warfare when that end will be nothing short of disastrous.'

It was heavy pounding of Winston's position. Those around the table paused to catch their breath, but Halifax wasn't finished yet.

'To fight against overwhelming odds, and to lose, would be to throw away our nation's future.'

'And becoming entangled in the Nazi net would be to achieve precisely that!'

'I was thinking of the lives of our young men,' Halifax responded, anguished. 'We will not be forgiven if we turn the whole of these islands into a landscape like that of Calais.'

This was not a battle between two proud men—although both were. It was a battle of worlds, of Halifax's tradition set against Churchill's radicalism, of one's profound belief in God and the other's equally profound belief in himself, of intellect set against passion, of the power of reason against that of the will, of consensus against commitment, of gradualism against overarching leaps of faith, of trust in the ultimate sanity of man against a view that malevolence and evil lurked in every corner and must be burnt out with fire. They were not enemies, these two men, but they were committed to fighting to the finish of this argument as though they were. They couldn't both win. Perhaps neither would.

'Let us be clear about where we stand. Are you suggesting, Prime Minister, that you would refuse to talk, no matter what the circumstance, no matter how reasonable the terms on offer?'

Well, that was the nub of it. They could circle around the issue like a cardinal around a nun, but in the end it had to be brought out into the open.

'Reason?' Churchill demanded sharply. He had to make it a matter of passion now; logic and moderation would never get him through, for Halifax was the master of both. Churchill had to shift the battle onto a ground that he dominated. 'Since when did reason have any place on the table of Adolf Hitler? If we could talk in reason and reach an understanding, even at the cost of some of our colonies—yes, Gibraltar, Malta, some of our African possessions—I would be willing to consider the proposal, but since when in the entire annals of Nazidom has *reason* become the driving force? Every time reason has been brought before That Man, he has abused it. Every time reason has been offered, he has used it as a sacrificial lamb. He doesn't pursue a policy based on reason but upon brutality and force of arms.'

'I don't necessarily disagree, Prime Minister, but I must press you. Are you saying that there are no circumstances in which you would countenance negotiation?'

Of course he'd never countenance negotiation, even if, like Reynaud, it might cost him his position and his life. But how could he bring these exhausted and careworn men along with him to that sticking place? Ruth had explained with such persuasive passion that peace was not an option, but Ruth wasn't here.

'What I propose,' Churchill began, running from Halifax's thrust, 'is that before all else we bring back our troops. Bring them back as an undefeated army, as many of them as possible, holding their heads up high and their weapons in their hands. Then we shall have the greatest possible strength for whatever policy we wish to pursue.'

'But, Prime Minister, they cannot bring their weapons back, the Chiefs of Staff have made that abundantly clear. Every tank, every truck, every tanker and every artillery piece the BEF possesses will be lost. All we can save is some of our men. And even if we manage to bring back as many as fifty thousand, which we are told we cannot, that will leave nearly a quarter of a million British soldiers as prisoners. I don't feel that's much of a bargaining position.'

'Nevertheless, we must try to bring them back. As many as we can.'

'Of course. Perhaps we should have tried that some days ago instead of persisting in the futile policy of having them push south.'

Oh, it was a cruel card to play. It was like screaming from every rooftop that Churchill's policy of unceasing advance lay in ruins, but the stakes were too high for delicacy.

'We must give our troops a chance,' Churchill began, hoping to seize back the initiative, but Halifax was already there.

'Prime Minister, I suggest that we give peace that chance. Let us talk.'

Halifax would not be denied. Churchill could not refuse to talk, not at this point. Halifax had the facts, while Churchill had little else but his fears and what others saw as dark fantasies. He would have to give some ground or he would lose the entire field.

'But can Hitler be trusted?' Churchill began again, casting around for allies. He turned to Neville Chamberlain, his former Prime Minister and rival—a man who had wanted Halifax to succeed him. It was a measure of the desperation Churchill felt. 'You have had more dealings with That Man than anyone in this room. How far, in the matter of negotiations, do you think that Hitler may be trusted?'

And now Churchill was calling in all the favours and courtesies he had showered upon this failed Man of Munich in the two weeks since he had succeeded him. The handwritten letters, the phone calls, the whispered confidences, the refusal to put to the sword those who had been close to him, the suggestion that he should remain living at Number Ten. Churchill had been assiduous in trying to reach out across the ocean between them in preparation for a moment such as this.

The former Prime Minister was a proud man. He didn't particularly care for Churchill, but it was not Churchill who had humiliated him, cast him from office and made sure that the name of Chamberlain would for ever be linked with failure and unforgivable weakness. That was Hitler's doing.

'Trust him?' The dark eyebrows arched. 'No, never trust him.'

And it was enough for Churchill.

'Gentlemen, the hour grows late and we all have other duties. I believe a sense of this meeting is beginning to emerge. We take the point made so persuasively by the Foreign Secretary that we should not refuse to countenance talks with the Italians'—he nodded at Halifax in grudging appreciation of his excellent fight—'but we should approach any such talks with the greatest of care. Might I ask the Foreign Secretary to prepare a paper setting out the detailed grounds we should consider before making any opening to the Italians?'

Ah, the devil of the detail. Halifax was a master of the bureaucratic game and it wouldn't take him long to respond to such instruction, but it had to be enough for Churchill. The men around the table were all exhausted, content to leave it for another day. It had bought him a little time, just as had those brave men in Calais. But time for what? Churchill didn't know.

* * *

Sunday 26 May. It was 18.57 when the order came through. Vice Admiral Ramsay was hovering over the teleprinter in his underground kingdom, held there by impatience but still more by frustration.

He was a quiet and most methodical man, some said lacking in emotion, even cold, yet he couldn't help snatching at the paper as it squeezed from the Admiralty machine.

*Operation Dynamo is to commence.*

Dynamo. It had been named by one of his junior officers after the room in which they had conducted all the planning deep within the chalk cliffs. During the last war the room had been filled with electrical plant; now it held a long polished table across which they could spread every sort of chart, and a couple of cots where some of them slept. No one would sleep tonight, nor for the nights to come.

The evacuation was to begin.

The plan was simple—it had been put together so hurriedly that there had been no scope for complications. The soldiers of the BEF had formed a pocket—or, more accurately, had been pushed by the advancing panzers into a pocket—for several miles around Dunkirk. There were also many French troops in that pocket. Together they would try to hold the perimeter while Ramsay's boats snatched away as many as possible. As troops were taken off, the perimeter of the pocket could be slowly withdrawn, ever closer to Dunkirk, until . . .

Until they ran out of time.

They should have begun days ago, but until yesterday they'd still been arguing about breaking out to the south, not retreating. Now they had been left with no other option, and no one even knew for certain whether retreat was still an option. The burden of it all was revealed in orders Ramsay had received earlier that day. 'It is imperative,' the Admiralty had instructed, 'for "Dynamo" to be implemented with the greatest vigour, with a view to lifting up to 45,000 of the BEF within two days.' Because after that the enemy was going to spoil the whole show.

Two days! Why, oh why, had they waited so long? A few days earlier they'd had three harbours to work from, but now Boulogne and Calais had gone, leaving Ramsay with nothing but the port of Dunkirk to work with. Dunkirk. An ancient seaport tucked up against the Belgian frontier, ringed with medieval ramparts and hemmed in by sand dunes with their coarse, tufted sea grass. The beaches that stretched either side were long and shallow, and gave little protection from the savage weather that swept up the Channel or down from the North Sea. The dunes often shifted during violent storms and so did the offshore sandbanks. These seas looked evil, and were often more evil than they looked. Over the centuries the treacherous, shifting banks had become a museum of maritime tragedy, filled with the bones of boats that hadn't made it.

For the boats that did make it, Dunkirk had been a haven of safety. But that was last week. This week, Dunkirk had become all but unrecognizable beneath the pounding of enemy bombs. Its once fine harbour had been crippled and choked by sunken shipping, its docks had been rendered unusable by the ferocious heat from the burning oil tanks and waterfront buildings, it had no water supplies, no electricity, and in places the panzers were now less than five miles away. Fire, sea, violence. Dunkirk was being squeezed to death.

Ramsay didn't have enough ships for the job and far too few destroyers. It wasn't much of an armada, but they had to try, otherwise defeat would turn to annihilation.

At 21.16 the first ship, *Mona's Isle*, an Isle of Man packet, sailed out of Dover for that smudge of smoke on the horizon that was Dunkirk.

* * *

*(Sunday 26 May 1940. William L. Shirer, CBS.)*

*Good evening. This is Berlin.*

*Calais has fallen. That great French Channel port, familiar to many Americans who have crossed from London to Paris, fell into German hands today after a hard fight . . .*

*Dunkirk, the last of the three great French Channel ports, apparently is still in the hands of the French, though its harbour works, say the Germans, have been continually bombed from the air by Stukas in the last few days.*

*But Calais was the gateway from France to England, the port through which most of the supplies passed for the British Expeditionary Army in France. Its capture by the Germans practically completes the cutting off of Great Britain from its ally on the continent. Moreover, Calais is only twenty-five miles across the Channel from Dover, on the English coast. The massive, mechanized German army is that close to England tonight—twenty-five miles—the first time, unless I'm mistaken, that a hostile army has been that close to England's shores since the days of Napoleon more than a century ago . . .*

*  *  *

She found him on the bridge, guided by the glow of the cigar. It was desperately late, gone three, with the dark shadows of the clock tower of Big Ben looming against the night sky. A figure she assumed to be Inspector Thompson lurked across the carriageway, otherwise they were alone in the damp river air.

'Thank you for coming,' Churchill said. He was different. Courteous. Without a drink in his hand. She wondered if the two conditions were connected.

'Had to get out,' he continued. 'Couldn't stand the atmosphere inside. Needed to find some free English air.'

The tide was running fast; she could hear it slapping against the granite piers of the bridge and saw tiny water sprites dancing in the moonlight. She said nothing; she'd let him reach his destination by his chosen route.

'Had a friend at Harrow school. Jack Milbanke.' A pause for smoke. 'I didn't have many friends; seem to have had trouble with that all my life. But Jack was special. Two years my senior. Unremarkable in many respects, either at games or lessons. Much like me. Although immaculately dressed, much unlike me. You see, he had a style, a distinction, that set him above the rest, and a maturity that I found utterly exceptional. We were always getting into scrapes, that was our nature, but he was always there to restrain me from going too far, or to haul me out when I did. To save me from myself, he said, the prerequisite of any friend of mine. I used to wonder what he meant by that . . . When my father passed through Harrow, he might come to visit, and he would take both Jack and me to luncheon at the King's Head Hotel. Roast beef and rhubarb, I seem to remember. And how they would talk, Jack and my father, as if they were equals, man to man. Oh, how much I wanted to be part of it, to share what Jack shared with my father, but . . . I was a mere backward schoolboy and every time I tried to enter upon their conversation I was always awkward or foolish. Yet it heartened me to know that my father could share such confidcnces with someone of my age, almost as much as I was saddened that it was not with me. I was able to hope that one day it might be my turn.' He glanced at her. 'You're shivering. Where's your coat?'

'I don't have a coat.'

Churchill fell silent for a moment, as though struggling with a problem of higher algebra, then motioned to Thompson. A moment later, she was wearing the inspector's raincoat. There was the harsh clanging of a bell near at hand; a police car sped out from the gates of New Scotland Yard on the Embankment and disappeared in the direction of St Paul's.

'I remember them building that place,' he muttered abstractedly, gazing towards the dark mass of masonry. 'Used convict labour. Straight out of Dickens. Seems so very long ago.'

His mind was wandering, exhausted. 'You were talking about your father,' she prompted.

'No, not at all, why do you say that? I was talking about Jack Milbanke. The firmest friend I ever had. Got into all sorts of scrapes together, always teetering on the edge of disaster, did I say that? Saved me from a thousand thrashings. Went into the army, the Hussars, and off to South Africa. Won a Victoria Cross for rescuing a colleague under heavy enemy fire. Brave, brave man and gallant friend.'

'What happened to him?'

'I killed him.'

A startled silence. 'I don't understand.'

'Gallipoli. He died leading an attack in that awful battle of Suvla Bay.'

'Ah, your battle.'

'Not mine, not in that sense, but they blamed me for it. Twenty-five years ago and still they haven't forgotten. Or forgiven.'

'They . . . ?'

'The Conservative Party. They have long memories. Blamed me for Jack's death and all the rest. More than forty thousand dead at Gallipoli. It's why they won't trust my judgement, always think I am *unreliable*.' He chewed the word to pieces. 'Actually, they think I'm mad. Like my father.' The cigar flamed once more and then flew in a sad tumbling arc down to the dark water below, where it expired with a sigh. 'That's why I wanted to see you. To find someone who would tell me that I am not going mad.'

'You have many qualities, Mr Churchill, but madness is not amongst them.'

'You may yet change your mind, Frau Mueller.' His tone had grown suddenly taut. 'You see, two things happened this evening. First, it became clear that my War Cabinet wants to open peace talks. I may not be able to prevent it. And then we heard that Calais is abandoned. All evening we've been dropping supplies and ammunition to the garrison there, straight into the arms of the grateful Wehrmacht. You see, the British and French are gone. Nearly four thousand of our bravest young men, captured or killed. By my personal order. And for what? For nothing!' The old Churchill was back, the hunched shoulders, the clenched fists that were now beating upon the cast-iron parapet of the bridge. 'Lord Halifax and his like insist that we make contact with the enemy. The enemy! Why, if that's what was required, all I would need to do is to open my window in the Admiralty and holler.'

'Then you have learnt something since first we met.'

'Jack Milbanke always said I was my own worst enemy. Something else I have learnt. But too late, I fear.'

'Not if you stop the talks.'

'I cannot.'

'You are the most powerful man in the country,' she protested.

'Even so, I am not that powerful. Something called the constitution.'

'We had one of those, too. Hitler got himself elected and then nailed it to the forehead of the nearest Jew.'

'Ours is unwritten. It cannot so easily be discarded.'

'Oh, it will take Hitler less than five minutes once he gets here. But that's the difference, perhaps, between you and him.'

'Ah, at last she finds some means of differentiating me from That Man,' he muttered, matching her scorn.

'He cares more. Has more passion, apparently.'

'No one cares more than I!'

'I don't know you very well, Mr Churchill, but I do know Hitler. He wouldn't be standing in the middle of a misty bridge wringing his hands.'

'And what, pray, would you suggest that I do?'

'Do? Whatever it takes! *He* would. Bend the constitution. Break it if you must. Because it will be no good to you if you don't.'

'Ridiculous.'

She grabbed his sleeve; he could feel she was still trembling. 'It was only a little time after Hitler had come to power. In some ways so much seemed the same. The post was still delivered, the coffee houses still open, the trams still ran along the same tracks. Then red posters began to appear. We found them on every street corner, on every bridge, just like the one we're standing on now. The posters went up alongside all the other everyday things like programmes for the theatre or announcements about a new restaurant. Notices of executions, Mr Churchill. When they first happened we read them with surprise and alarm, even disgust, but they kept appearing and soon, like all the other announcements, they began to be taken for granted, read scarcely at all. Each one became just another notice. You heard of bodies washing up along the shores of the Spee, and so you would find yourself setting out a little later than usual when you took the children for a walk along the river on a Sunday morning, just to give the authorities a little time to make sure that everything was . . . tidy. Or you would hear about yet another of those strange people called Communists—oh, it was astonishing how many of them chose to rant and to rave, and to be shot while trying to escape. But if they were trying to escape, they must have done something wrong, deserved it in some way, or so you thought. And then he started on the Jews and before long you wanted your Jewish friends to—to what? To go sick. To break down. To hit or insult you so they would no longer be your friend; even better to leave and emigrate. Anything to get them out of the way. To relieve you of the responsibility of being their friend. Mr Churchill, I don't know what is happening to the Jews in Germany right now—there are too many of them to put on lists at street corners—but whatever is happening and wherever it is happening, the rest of Germany will be looking elsewhere.'

'What is your point?'

'You talk to me about your rules, but this isn't some quaint English game where you do your best and then go off to your country home for tea and wait for the pendulum to swing back in your direction. That's what you like, isn't it, you English? A little give and take, play the game, all gentlemen together and hooray for the underdog. But you can forget the swing of the pendulum once Hitler is here, because all you will encounter is the swinging of his axe. If you fail, Mr Churchill, you will have far more on your conscience than Jack Milbanke and those who died at Calais. You will have to cope with the death of your country and of reason itself. So don't you dare preach to me about your wretched gentleman's rules. They simply won't apply.'

'You seem to hate him so very much.'

'More than you will ever imagine.'

'Why?'

'How many ways are there to hate someone? I hate him as a German for what he has destroyed. I hate him as a Christian for expropriating my God. I hate him as a neighbour because I will never again feel trusted by those I live with, and I hate him as a schoolteacher for ripping children from my arms and poisoning every value I tried to teach them. I hate him for his red posters, for the fear he has created, for the friends I have lost, for the times I looked the other way, for the guilt I feel because I was part of it.' She pulled the coat more closely around her. 'But above all I hate him because I am a woman and a mother. A woman's love is like an ocean, endless, yet he took that ocean and drained it dry. I hate him for that moment in my life when I looked at those I loved most in the world and realized that I no longer knew them.'

She was shivering violently. Churchill turned in

the direction of Thompson and waved to him. 'You must go home, Frau Mueller. I have kept you too long.'

She could hear the coughing of a car engine as it approached from the end of the bridge. It stopped and Thompson opened the door.

'Don't you dare give up, Mr Churchill.'

'I will do everything I can,' he said, climbing in and lowering the window. A grey dawn was streaking the sky. 'I would happily give my life if that were the price for saving my country—as doubtless would Hitler. But unlike him, I have family. You know what I think of family, Frau Mueller. And I have my only son serving in the armed forces, willing to give up his life in this war.'

'As I have, too,' she whispered, watching the car drive away.

## CHAPTER ELEVEN

Ramsay watched *Mona's Isle* return. A destroyer had guarded her until she had reached the gates of the harbour, and now two tugs guided her through. She was without a rudder and there were gaping holes in several parts of her superstructure. Even from a distance he could see that her decks were crowded with wounded. She was the last of the once-proud ships to limp back that morning; several of the others he had sent would never return. She had been shelled by shore guns and hammered by bullets from half a dozen Messerschmitts. Of the 1420 troops who had embarked upon her from Dunkirk, twenty-three were already dead and sixty wounded. The three-hour trip that Ramsay had planned had taken *Mona's Isle* almost twelve.

Very late the previous night, Ramsay had snatched a moment to write a short note to his wife, Mag. 'I have on at the moment one of the most difficult and hazardous operations ever conceived,' he said, 'and unless *le bon Dieu* is very kind there are certain to be many tragedies attached to it. I hardly dare think about it, or what the day is going to bring.'

As he feared, the day brought its many tragedies. It also brought back a total of 7669 English soldiers from Dunkirk. At that rate it would take Ramsay more than forty days to evacuate the BEF.

* * *

King George could see from the impatient stride and prominent scowl that his Prime Minister had arrived on usual form. And in his usual time.

'Your Majesty, pray forgive my tardiness,' Churchill offered, bowing deeply.

It had become standard practice. The phone call ten minutes before he was supposed to arrive to inform the Palace that he would be half an hour late, then leaving the King to hang upon his own devices for another stretch of time. It would be followed by an audience carried out with as much speed and as little dignity as the King's sister-in-law reputedly displayed in bed. Not that George knew for certain, of course, he could never entirely trust the intelligence reports, but there were so many stories about her; some of them had to be true.

There were stories about Winston, too. About

his temper, about his drinking, his constant interfering, his unpredictability, his . . . well, the word had been used. His madness. George had tried to sail in formation with his Prime Minister. He studied his papers, wrote the letters, offered advice, tried not to be a burden, indeed did everything he could to support. But every time he drew alongside, Churchill took off at full speed again, leaving the King twisting in his turbulent wake.

'May I be allowed to congratulate you on your broadcast, sir?'

'Thank you, Winston. Not without its trials.'

'But if I may say so, it was not without its triumphs, either. It was what the people needed to hear. The words were magnificent. Couldn't say it better myself. That Hitler, unchecked, would mean'—he plucked the words from his memory—' "the overthrow, complete and final, of this Empire and everything for which it stands, and after that, the conquest of the world, too." '

'Yet people don't talk about what I said, only how I said it. That I didn't stutter, didn't falter.' George shook his head. 'So frustrating.'

Churchill cleared his throat. He didn't have time to conduct an elocution lesson. 'The war presses, sir. And far from favourably—'

'Yes,' the King interrupted, determined to make his own point. 'That's one of the things I wanted to see you about. Just had a letter from Leopold. Handwritten. Says it's hopeless.'

'As much as I had feared.' The King of the Belgians was becoming a new nightmare on Churchill's horizon.

'I've written back, counselling him to come here.

He won't hear a word of it. Intends to stay in his own country.'

'That might not be wise.'

'It's what you want me to do. To stay. Not to take my family and flee.'

'The situations are not comparable.'

The King chose not to respond, drawing heavily on his cigarette, examining Churchill through the smoke.

'They are in one respect. Belgian Government's split about what to do. French, too. Dangerous situation. Wouldn't like it to happen here, Winston.'

Ah, so he'd heard. Of course, his friendship with Halifax. They'd probably discussed the whole thing over tea.

'It would put me in a difficult position,' the King continued.

'Personally?'

'Constitutionally.'

Ah, the constitution. Churchill's life was suddenly overflowing with lectures about the bloody constitution.

'Frankly, Winston, we wouldn't be in much of a position either to negotiate or to wage war if my Government were openly divided. Couldn't accept that. Would have to do whatever I could to prevent it.'

Churchill's mind raced around the corners of the King's words to see what lay on the other side. It hit him with a blow sufficient to make his heart flutter. He was being warned. The King wouldn't allow his Government to be split. He would rather change it, change his First Minister. Get rid of Churchill. There wouldn't be many who would object to such a move, and a score of constitutionalists would line up to say he was entirely within his powers to do so.

'I understand, sir.'

'Do you, Winston? We live in times of such *change* and very great *sacrifice*.'

Churchill noted the emphasis, which was entirely unnecessary. He'd already got the point. It was exactly the point that Ruth had made. Play the game, drink your tea, die. Except his colleagues wouldn't even wait for Hitler to get here, they would do the job themselves. Churchill knew that this was a battle he was unlikely to win, not when he was fighting on two fronts. He didn't blame the King, he didn't even particularly blame Halifax, the man was only doing what his conscience dictated. Playing by the rules of a gentleman. But Churchills came from a different mould; they didn't accept the rules. Most people didn't even regard them as gentlemen.

And he hated tea.

* * *

Ruth Mueller sat at the corner table of the café, sipping her cup of hot coffee essence mixed with sweet evaporated milk. It was her lunch. The illustration of red coats and rifles on the bottle of the liquid essence had suggested it was a drink that had got the British Army though the Boer War; Ruth had rather lower expectations. She wanted it only to get her through to her simple evening meal. She tugged self-consciously at her sleeve; the cuff was growing seriously threadbare and her attempts at repair were proving more and more pointless.

She would have to forage amongst the second-hand stalls and church jumble sales to find a replacement. And a smaller size: this one was beginning to hang loosely, she'd lost weight. Not that clothing or even lunch was important in the grand scale of things, but there were standards to maintain. It was important to maintain standards; she remembered what could happen when you didn't.

She had spent all morning in the library across the way reading the communal copy of the newspapers and finishing off the last trickle of translation work that she had been able to get. Since the war began there had been plenty of calls for translators, but every time she applied, it seemed she knew German just a little too well. When it came down to it, the life of a refugee wasn't much of a life at all. She made up her mind to ask Mr Churchill for advice—well, help, really—the next time they met. She'd wanted to do that on the last couple of occasions, but they always seemed to get to arguing and the thought had entirely slipped her mind until it was too late. Next time—if there were a next time—she'd make a special effort not to lose her temper or insist that he lose his.

She'd also made a special effort with the librarian. For days there had been nothing but frost blown across the polished wood counter as though she had a dozen books overdue, and Ruth refused to be dragged down into a pit of mutual ill feeling. Standards, once more. But when she had nodded her head and wished her goodbye, it had been like walking through a winter's gale. At least she had tried.

She could see the librarian even now, arms folded tightly across her bony chest, standing on the steps of the library and staring across the street. Two men had also come into the café and were looking around at the handful of customers. They nudged each other. Were coming towards her. She thought she could sense the librarian smiling.

'Frau Mueller?' The two men had stopped in front of her. 'Ruth Mueller?' They were both wearing raincoats in spite of the weather. More memories. Her heart had stopped.

'We are police detectives from Rochester Row, Frau Mueller. Please come with us.'

'Why?' She tried to sound confident, to believe it was a mistake, but the cup was spilling coffee as she replaced it in the saucer.

'The Emergency Powers Act, Frau Mueller.' He waved a crumpled sheet of official paper at her.

'But what have I done?'

'Done? Done?' The two men looked at each other, puzzled. 'You're German.'

'I am a refugee.'

'A German refugee.'

'What crime have I committed?'

'Apart from being a Jerry? Maybe none. But we'll want to know why you've been asking so many questions. Why you're taking such an interest with all the books and newspapers you've been reading. And where all that foreign stuff you've been writing goes.'

The librarian now had two other women at her side and was gesticulating in the direction of the café.

'You cannot arrest me without a charge.'

'Of course we can. Come on, let's do it quietly.

We don't want a to-do. Disturbing the neighbours and all.'

'This is ridiculous. You cannot arrest me simply because I am a refugee. This is England!'

'And this bit of paper's got your name on it. Come on, Mrs Mueller. Let's have no fuss.' He reached for her.

'A fuss? You think I am going to let you do what Hitler's Gestapo couldn't—without a fuss? Take your hands off me!'

The repair on the cuff had gone again. The policeman renewed his grip and wouldn't be shaken off. She struck out at him, and immediately her other arm was pinned. So she kicked out. The table and what was left of the coffee went flying.

'And it's a breach of the peace, too,' one of them said, lifting her off her feet. She seemed so light, they scarcely had to use any effort.

'Stop! Please stop!' she pleaded. 'I am a friend of the Prime Minister. Please ask his office. Please ask Mr Churchill,' she shouted as they carried her towards the door.

The two detectives began laughing. One waved the piece of paper. 'Winston Churchill? Why, it's him who sent us.'

* * *

They went at it again for the third, fourth—no, fifth time in the last thirty hours. It wasn't simply that one was defeatist and the other intemperate and often irrational, although the Prime Minister frequently ventured far beyond the border that marked off reason from the completely absurd.

Halifax believed that if the French gave up the

fight—and in truth they had barely started it—then the war could not be won on the battlefield. The only alternative was diplomacy and negotiation, which might salvage something from the wreck. It was more difficult to be precise about what Churchill thought. In one moment he would grasp at the prospect of American intervention, in the next he would argue the merits of nations going down in flames in order to rise from the ashes. At times his arguments were little more than oratory swamped in emotional incontinence. And as they argued, face to face across the Cabinet table, their restraint and mutual deference began to be cast aside.

Halifax had done what Churchill had requested and had prepared a paper setting out the conditions on which an approach to the Italians should be considered. But Churchill had no intention of considering it.

'I grow increasingly oppressed by the futility of contemplating any approach to the Italians. Mussolini would treat it with nothing but contempt.'

'But yesterday—'

Churchill held up his hand to stay the inevitable intervention. 'In all my life I have never known a time when British prestige has hung so low in the esteem of Europe. Are we to push it even lower by creeping cap in hand to the Italians? We shall get nothing while we are on our knees, yet if we fight . . . ! If we continue with the struggle for two or three months longer, then our prestige will return and our fortunes may look very different.'

Halifax gave up the struggle to hide his exasperation. 'Two or three months? In two or three weeks France may be gone.'

'Let us not be dragged down with the French.'

'We may have no choice,' Halifax responded, too sharply.

'Then let us not be dragged down *like* the French. How much more broadly will history smile upon us if we go down fighting than if we go down like craven spaniels? How much sooner will our country rise up again?'

'Are you saying that under no circumstances—'

'To walk into negotiations now would be to step upon a slippery slope from which there would be no return and where we would find no salvation. Once upon that slope we could never resist the temptation to slip a little further, and slip a little further still, until we found ourselves in a place where there was no light, no hope and no way back.'

'But while we are talking there is always hope. Of reason, of compromise.'

'As you discovered at Munich?'

Oh, but now it had become bitingly personal.

'We neither wanted nor invited this war,' Halifax reminded them. 'We have done our best. No one else has found a way to win it—'

'Except for Hitler.'

'If the Prime Minister will allow me to finish!' Halifax was beginning to find his task impossible. 'There is no disgrace in having fought and failed. But what every jot of experience from across Europe tells us is that if we continue to fight a hopeless war, it will invite only destruction. The time has come to put aside this mad adventure and allow cool heads to find a different solution. And if we act in combination with the French, our powers will be greatly enhanced. We must negotiate.'

'To throw away our independence would be to throw away all hope! Our independence stands like a glowing beacon of light in the darkness that has fallen across the continent. Hitler will eventually be swept aside, that we must believe, by a great uprising of all those oppressed nations in Europe who retain the desire to be free. Our independence, our continued struggle, feeds their hope and brings that day ever closer. We must fight this to the finish!'

Halifax had come to his sticking point. He had swallowed more than enough of Churchill's blustering and ridiculous romanticism, had suffered too often from having his arguments twisted and discarded by cheap debating tricks. Cabinets were intended for sober reflection, not as a stage for one man's empty theatricality. This was an abuse too far.

'No one, Prime Minister, is suggesting that we throw away our independence! And I resent most bitterly the insinuation that it forms any part of what I propose. It is precisely to preserve our independence that we have to open a dialogue—'

'There is no independence upon that slippery slope—'

'There is no independence in cities that have been turned to cinders and a countryside that has been laid waste. That's what fighting to the finish means.' Halifax was picking up the other man's words and throwing them in his face. Now he spoke in a more measured tone, and very much for the record. 'And I, for my part, doubt that I could ever accept such a view.'

They all understood what he was saying. He

would not follow Churchill down that path.

'I want to be clear about where we stand,' Halifax continued. 'Let's not waste our time with an empty debate about hypothetical proposals. Let me put it as simply as I can. Are you saying, Prime Minister, that you would never consider any peace proposals, at any time?'

It was the same fork with which he had pierced Churchill on the previous day. But this time Churchill was more determined—or perhaps more desperate. He would not give way.

'I would never consent to asking for terms. Oh, there may be some imaginary circumstances in which we might be offered terms, in which case perhaps we should give them consideration, but we could be waiting for a thousand years. And it will never happen if we ask for them.'

'How can you be so . . .' Stupidly stubborn? Suicidal? Stuck in your own little delusion? But Halifax had never honed his tongue as sharply as Churchill, and didn't share his taste for the cruel. 'How can you be so *certain*?'

'Because, Foreign Secretary, until we make it clear that we shall fight on, and on, and on, we shall be given nothing. No peace terms, no alliances, no help from the Americans. Why, why, why do you think that Roosevelt sits back and does nothing? Nothing!' He was banging the table now, bullying. 'Why does he ignore all our requests and offer us nothing but empty words? Why? Because while he and the rest of the world believe we may stop fighting, there is not a reason in paradise for him to lift a finger!' He was breathing heavily, struggling to retain his composure. 'I will go even further. We shall need America in this war if we are to win it. But there is skulduggery afoot, even a little treason.' *Treason?* The restraint had gone. 'For instead of being encouraged to lend us his support, Roosevelt is being offered an irresistible incentive to do nothing, for by doing nothing he stands to gather every sort of windfall. Our navy. Our western possessions. Our influence in half the world. And he gets all this simply by sitting back and waiting for pieces of the British Empire to fall into his hands!'

The two men were glaring at each other across the table, their faces suffused, their eyes locked in passion.

'And do you know who has provided him with that incentive, Foreign Secretary?' At least he had refrained from describing it as treason once again. 'Those amongst us who insist that we talk.'

Argument was one thing, accusation quite another. Halifax forced his chair back from the table, wanting to place as much distance between him and his accuser as possible. If he stood up, he would leave, and no one could vouch for the consequences. The Cabinet was about to be torn in two.

It was at this point that Chamberlain intervened. He had played little part in the discussions; from his perspective he thought himself to be above the general fray. As an elder and former chief of the tribe he was willing to stand back and watch others plough the field, but this quarrel had gone many fields too far. He coughed.

'Prime Minister, I wonder . . .' The voice was so familiar to them all. It had called them to order for so many years and did so again now. Everyone around the table took in the sallow, angular features, the strained eyes. No one knew, not even he, that the cancer that would kill inside six months was already at its work. 'I fear I am not as young as the rest of you. Could we pause for a break? Resume in ten minutes, perhaps?'

He had broken the spell. He couldn't know it, but by disappearing to the bathroom he had also performed arguably the greatest service of his long career.

'Of course. Inconsiderate of me, Neville,' Churchill responded. 'Ten minutes, then. I think I shall take a breath of fresh air in the garden. Perhaps the Foreign Secretary would like to join me.'

* * *

'How the sun always manages to shine upon English disasters, Winston.'

'Comes of playing cricket, Edward. Never did care for the game.'

'I've always rather enjoyed it. Civilizing influence. A game for gentlemen.'

'Precisely.'

They had emerged from the gloom of the Cabinet Room into the heady light of a May afternoon when the walled garden of 10 Downing Street received its quota of full sun. The beds of flowers were an abundance of colour, the trees freshly green, the birds declaring their ownership of every branch and bush. The softest time of year. They began walking slowly.

'Do you remember, Edward? Almost twenty years since first we set against each other. I was in the Colonial Office and you'd been appointed my junior. Didn't want you, wanted someone else. Can't remember who. So I ignored you. For an entire fortnight I refused to meet you. Then you marched straight into my office and told me that you had never wanted to be my under-secretary, that you were ready to resign that very moment, but so long as you remained, you expected to be treated properly. As a gentleman.'

'I remember.'

'I behaved appallingly. I had to apologize to you then, and on many occasions since.'

'Today wasn't the first time you have accused me of high treason.'

'But always, in the end, we have found a way to sit with each other.'

'Not any longer, Winston.'

They walked on, Halifax tall and stooping, Churchill stamping with the impatience of unused energy, both preferring to admire the flowers rather than to catch each other's eye.

'My father resigned, Edward. Got up from that same table, in anger, and walked into misery. He never came back. It was the end of his influence.'

'Forgive me, are we discussing the merits of resignation, or the merits of being a Churchill?'

Churchill halted abruptly. 'That is cruel, Edward.'

'And so is being falsely accused of treason! Winston, if the price of sitting at your table is to be bullied and constantly threatened, then I quit my place with a clear conscience.'

'This is a time for embracing public duty rather than dancing upon a conscience.'

'You cannot serve the public duty by denying your private conscience, Winston. At least, *I* cannot.'

Churchill kicked the turf in anger. 'Why do you attack me so?'

'Because you are so utterly and ridiculously intransigent.'

'Intransigent? You think Hitler got where he is by conciliation and debate?'

'We are not German.'

'No, but in a few weeks we damn well might be!'

Churchill turned away. Passion and invective had failed to win over Halifax in the Cabinet Room and he knew it would prove no more successful in the garden. He had to find a different way. He squinted into the sun.

'Edward, we cannot go on like this. We must find a way of resolving our impasse and without resignation. Like gentlemen.'

'I fear it's too late for that. One of us must go.'

'Neither of us must go, Edward. That we must agree above every other issue. If either of us steps aside in anger it would only hand the pass to Hitler. We must fight this out between ourselves and with our colleagues, but whoever wins the argument, there can be no resignation. His Majesty's Government will continue to fight, or if you prevail it will begin to negotiate. But in either event, our cause is lost if that Government is divided and rent by resignation. Division would be death to both our causes.'

'Yet we cannot carry on as we are.'

'I discussed these matters with the King this morning. He is as determined as I that there should be no division—whatever else happens, our disagreements must remain private and unpublicized. Between gentlemen.'

'Gentlemen,' Halifax countered with emphasis, 'do not accuse each other of treason.'

'Edward, I beg pardon for my excess. I was prompted by fear. You know I hold you as a man of the highest honour and I ask your forgiveness. I also ask your patience for a little while longer. I want you to remain in your seat at the Cabinet table until the evacuation from Dunkirk is complete. In the interests of your own reputation and your own conscience, you cannot quit at the moment of our soldiers' greatest peril. It would appear too selfish, too open to misinterpretation, something even your closest friends would find difficult to forgive.'

It was a telling point. Halifax didn't immediately respond.

'Just a couple of days, Edward. You continue to argue your case, but you do it from inside the Government, not as an outsider, not in the'—his arms waved in the air as though trying to ward off wasps—'futile manner of my father.'

'The evacuation will not change the arguments, Winston. Even if we succeeded in bringing off numbers beyond our wildest dreams—say, fifty thousand troops—they will be beaten troops, in no condition to continue waging your war.'

'Nevertheless . . . a proud country, with an air force and a great navy, and still some sort of army. The best negotiating hand you will ever have, Edward, for if that is what the Cabinet desires, I shall step aside—not resign in public dispute, but step aside and hold my silence in order to allow you to do what you so passionately think is right. And I would pray God's blessing on your labours.'

'You would do that?'

'Edward, I give you my word. As a gentleman. It would be my duty. As I believe it is your duty to stand beside the rest of your colleagues while this operation of evacuation proceeds. Until its end. Tomorrow, the day after at best, we are told.'

Halifax moved onward, his domed head nodding upon his long neck as if the problem was too heavy for his strength to bear. Suddenly he stopped once more. 'What is that?' he asked. He was pointing to an unkempt bale of straw standing on its end in the far corner of the otherwise immaculate garden, looking as though it might have been kicked all the way from Cornwall.

'I call it Fritz. Use it for target practice. Even for a few bayonet thrusts. To keep my hand in. Just in case.'

'Winston, you and your war . . .' Halifax wrung his hands in disbelief.

'We are both men of our convictions.'

'Then let us put those convictions to the test. Inside the Cabinet. I will do as you suggest, even as I pray that we shall find another option to your war. To save us all from dying at German hands.'

Churchill had to be content. He had bought a little more time—through deception and a bald lie, but Halifax would not see that, not yet, blinded as he was by that inherent English weakness which required him to regard his colleague as a gentleman. But this wasn't a tea party; Churchill had no intention of ever passing quietly down Halifax's path of peace. That way, he muttered to himself, he was certain to die at German hands. Why, Ruth Mueller would shoot him herself.

* * *

All day they had stumbled along, Claude leaning ever more heavily upon Don's shoulder as the loose footing in the dunes slowed them to a crawl. They were forced to stop frequently, both to allow Claude's ankle to rest and to keep out of sight of Wehrmacht patrols that combed the beach area looking for stragglers. And Don's wound was worse than he'd thought; it felt as if a hot coal was being forced into his arm. As they had attempted to slip out of Calais, they'd almost been given away by a young dog, a cream-and-chestnut spaniel terrified by the bombing, which had barked and yelped at them incessantly, snapping at their heels. They would gladly have shot it, but they had no weapon, so instead they decided to quieten it by appealing to its better nature. It took some time and a sharp nip on Don's hand for it to emerge, but eventually the dog stopped yelping and came forward slowly with suspicion in its eye. These were men, in uniform; the dog had no reason to trust them. But eventually the bond was made and the dog quietened. Trouble was, it wouldn't leave them. They tried to shoo it away, threw sand at it, even stones, but it was the first game the dog had played in days and he scampered off only to return, and they were too slow to flee.

They had no food. Don was weakening, with shock and straightforward exhaustion. When, towards evening, they came across a farm cottage at the end of a rough track, they had little choice but to seek help. Claude knocked and was greeted by a weather-beaten and frightened woman. When Claude begged for shelter, she shook her head, so he asked instead for food. The woman disappeared inside, but when she returned and looked once again at Don, she began shouting and waving her arms.

'She doesn't like you,' Claude explained. 'You're English.'

'Allies,' Don exclaimed. 'Allies!' and linked his arms together, but it had no effect. The woman gave Claude food, even made a point of giving food to the dog, but she offered Don nothing but abuse. She even produced a broom to wave him away; they noticed there was already a white towel tied to the handle.

They were forced to stagger on, the dog close at their heels, keeping well away from the roads, along endless, anonymous trails through the sand dunes, with Claude pointing the way. He explained they would have to make a wide detour around Gravelines, the port that stood between them and Dunkirk.

'You sure you won't get lost?' Don asked, when at last they could go no further and sat down to share what little food the woman had given to Claude.

'How can we miss Dunkirk?' he explained, pointing with a chewed leg of chicken.

The sight was unmistakable. Still some miles ahead, but even in the fading light they could see it. Wave after wave of sharp-winged dive-bombers in the sky, circling, hovering, then swooping with the urgency of hunting kestrels. Time after time. No opposition, nothing to disturb their intent. They would vanish from sight, only to reappear once more, climbing slowly back to the skies upon clouds of billowing smoke that rose beneath them.

That was Dunkirk.

* * *

The outcome of the great retreat would depend upon many things. Courage, judgement, luck, the weather, and upon finding some way of squeezing enough time out of the situation to enable the ships to be guided in and the troops to be brought out. The importance of every hour could be measured in terms of lives and, in order to stretch the hours as long as he could, Churchill had torn up his rulebook of personal ethics. He had lied. Brazenly, outrageously. While he exhorted others to their duties, he acted like a bankrupt desperately scrabbling for every last penny in the hope of fending off the bailiffs a moment longer. He had lied to Halifax. There would come a time when Halifax would surely realize that. But not just yet.

Churchill had even ridiculed his father's resignation. He remembered the moment all so clearly. He had been only twelve. At school. He had been used to boasting about his father to his friends, handing around his autograph, but in a single moment it all changed. His father had gone. And with the formidable eagerness that only young boys possess, his friends began to taunt and torment him. Winston's response was entirely instinctive. Before he had any information on the matter, he sprang to his father's defence, praising the resignation as an act of great conscience that history would shower with glowing accolades. But history was cruel. It had recorded the event as little more than a fit of pique, a temper tantrum, an act that had come as blessed relief to his colleagues. History had spent its time pouring mud all over his father's reputation.

Not that Randolph had minded too much; he'd gone mad and died. Now, from high on the wall of the study, the dark, protruding eyes stared down at the son, gently mocking.

Colville brought him back to the realities of the moment. 'Apologies for disturbing you, Prime Minister, but it's Frau Mueller. We can't find her anywhere.'

Churchill had asked to see her. She'd become a talisman, someone he could rely on to remind him that his cause was right and that he wasn't going mad like his father. Someone who would at least argue with him rather than conspire behind his back. But now she had gone, too.

'Another drowning rat,' he muttered bitterly, and sipped at his whisky.

Colville continued to hover, agitated.

'If you insist on prancing around like a bloody schoolboy in front of his naked sisters I shall use you for target practice,' the old man barked irritably.

Colville immediately regretted what he was about to do. Churchill wasn't worth it, but . . .

'It's Mr Kennedy.'

'Our American friend.' Churchill snorted. 'Got himself into some truly unpleasant trouble, I trust.'

'Got himself a little drunk.'

'Regrettably I cannot condemn him for that.'

'He invited me round for dinner this evening . . .'

'Tell me.'

'It's . . .'

'I know it may not be a pleasant duty, Mr Colville, but duty it nevertheless is. Anyway, I have a fair idea what that Yankee bastard was going on about. I may as well have it confirmed.'

'He was saying how he'd been proven right all along. That England will soon be gone. The war is as good as lost. That it would all stop if it weren't for you.'

'In that very last matter he may well be right.'

'He told everyone that you don't represent the views of the British people.'

'And that the British fleet should be sent to the other side of the Atlantic,' Churchill growled, interrupting yet again.

'Yes,' Colville stammered. 'How did you know?'

'Because I've read it all before,' Churchill responded wearily.

He glanced towards the buff-coloured box that was sent to him daily by the intelligence services and was reserved for his eyes only. One of its regular features was transcripts of Kennedy's phone calls and copies of his cables to Washington. It really was disgraceful conduct on Churchill's part, to have failed to cancel the taps and intercepts that the British intelligence services had placed on US embassy traffic. He kept reminding himself that he must get round to cancelling them, and he would. As soon as the bloody Americans entered the war. In the meantime, the conduct of the ambassador would be noted and one day used in evidence or blackmail or whatever method was most useful in wiping this man's existence from his life, for while Kennedy was in harness there was about as much chance of persuading Roosevelt to rally round as there was of Hitler taking up holy orders.

His most recent telegram sat in the box, intercepted on its way to Washington earlier that evening. 'Only a miracle can save the BEF from being wiped out,' it began. Bugger the man!

'You said there were others present at these outpourings?'

'Yes, sir. The Japanese ambassador, a couple of journalists, one of the Ministers we sacked, a Minister who perhaps we should have . . .'

'Strange company you keep, Mr Colville.' Churchill's tone was heavy with accusation, and it was too much for the young civil servant.

'That's odd, Mr Churchill, because that's exactly what they said. As have many others. If I'd kept a bottle of decent claret for every time someone had asked me why I was working for you, I'd be sitting on one of the finest cellars in London.'

'Insolence!'

'I must be confused. I thought it was loyalty. And my duty.'

Churchill was taken aback by the rebuke. He was confused: by exhaustion, by events, not yet by alcohol, although that might come later as blessed relief. The protruding eyes of his father stared down at him once more, as though challenging him to follow along the same path, casting aside all advice and friendships and pouring abuse on all who dared question him. But Churchill had had enough. Where was he to find the strength to fight the devils of times past when he couldn't even cope with the devils of today?

He held out his glass. 'Pour me a whisky and soda, very weak, there's a good boy.'

It was as close to an apology as Churchill would allow himself, and Colville accepted it, along with the glass. He returned a few moments later bearing whisky and a manila folder.

'There's more?' Churchill raised his eyes wearily.

'Just arrived, sir. Belgium. The King. He intends to sue for peace. To surrender.'

'Yes, yes, I know all the rumours.'

'These aren't rumours. The surrender meeting has been arranged for two hours' time. The white flag's already flying.'

And Churchill's last energies seemed to drain away. He couldn't open the folder but let it fall at his feet. He slumped in his chair; his voice was no more than a whisper.

'So soon? So soon? It cannot be. I had hoped—believed—at least a little more time.'

As Colville watched, the old man seemed to deflate, to shrink, his resistance crumbling like a dried leaf.

'It is the end,' he gasped.

Belgium. That bloodied field of Oudenarde and Waterloo, of Ypres and Passchendaele, the burial ground of brave men and empires, and now perhaps the British Empire, too. The Belgian army defended the eastern flank of the pocket around Dunkirk—the pocket where the fate of Britain's Empire would be decided. Leopold, the King of the Belgians, loved the British, he'd been educated at Eton, but he loved Belgium more. He hadn't wanted this war, he had tried as hard as any man could to keep his country out of it, yet others had decided to turn it yet again into a dying place. Less than three weeks ago Belgium had been at peace, now there seemed only one way of returning it to that condition. Surrender.

And by the morning there would be a twenty-mile gap in the defences around Dunkirk.

The BEF would surely be swept aside, stabbed in the back as they ran to the sea. Their fate could be measured in hours.

Churchill had no idea how long he remained fixed to his chair. Colville had gone, embarrassed, still hurt, left the old man to his misery. Churchill sat listening to the thumping of his heart—or was it the footsteps of the hangman on his way up the stair? The minutes passed—into hours, perhaps, but he did not stir. He was held by the eyes. He wanted guidance, forgiveness, but there was no pity to be found in them, only scorn for having forsaken his own father and dared to think he was the better man. And as he watched, the portrait began to laugh, to sneer, mocking the child for his failures. I might have thrown away a career, but what does that matter when they will hold you responsible for the ruin of an entire empire? I said you were no good, but you wouldn't listen. You fool, you failure!

Suddenly Churchill was standing before it, trembling in anger, defying his father and all the demeaning memories. 'Damn you! Damn you!' he shouted, hurling his glass at the portrait. The glass shattered, covering the oil in whisky and causing a large tear above the left shoulder.

The rage had gone. He climbed the stairs to bed, with steps as heavy as if he were following the footsteps to Calvary. When he reached the top he stopped and sighed. 'Waste of bloody good whisky,' he muttered, before finding his way to bed.

# CHAPTER TWELVE

Ramsay stretched his aching body across the circular chart table in the Naval Operations Room as he examined the large-scale charts spread upon it. He would have been forgiven by almost everyone if he had simply fallen asleep upon it, but he wouldn't have forgiven himself. He was one of those Englishmen who had personalities like a subterranean pool: dark, unmoving, and of unimaginable depth.

He was searching for a new sea route. The shortest route out of Dunkirk had become impossibly dangerous during daylight. It ran straight past Calais and Gravelines and their coastal guns, which were now firing German shells. To add to the chaos, Stukas and Heinkels had fallen upon the harbour in extraordinary number; they had the target of their dreams and were being offered the prize of a lifetime. Shells and bombs pounded everything below. Ships had been sunk, others forced to turn back to Dover, empty. The port was useless, all but destroyed, the town evacuated and all the British troops sent for safety to the dunes. A gigantic pall of black smoke from burning oil tanks spread across the port and could be seen from fifty miles away. The officer whom Ramsay had sent to Dunkirk to take charge had signalled: 'Port continuously bombed all day and on fire. Embarkation possible only from beaches east of harbour. Send all ships and passenger ships there to anchor.'

The beaches? How the devil was he supposed to

get an army off the beaches? But he had to try. There was almost no time left. The signals traffic from across the sea had grown ever more desperate during the night: 'Evacuation tomorrow night problematical,' one had said; 'Last chance of saving them,' announced another. And the instruction to move to the beaches had caused confusion. In the darkness, some boats assumed that Dunkirk had already fallen into enemy hands, and turned back.

As Ramsay lay spread-eagled across the operations table, he felt despair pressing down upon him. If only he could just lie here, sleep, never wake up, let someone else take this weight from him. It wasn't just the Belgians who had ripped a huge hole in his plans, but now the French. Inconceivably they still thought Dunkirk was being held as a beachhead for reinforcements to pour back into France; no one had bothered to tell them that it was all over, that the British were leaving. Understanding had only crept upon them when they discovered the British destroying all their equipment.

More misunderstanding. Some idiot British artillery officer had misconstrued the order to destroy the equipment and spiked most of the anti-aircraft guns, one of their few weapons of defence. The German bombers flew above, almost unmolested. So grim had it all become that Gort had been given permission to surrender when he judged that 'it was no longer possible to inflict further damage to the enemy'.

The BEF had only hours left to live.

But Ramsay had to find another way. The short route had to be abandoned, at least in daylight; it had become a suicide run and already there were reports from the Dover and Ramsgate docks of trouble, of crews refusing to set sail towards what they knew was a funeral pyre.

He levered himself up from the table, a little at a time, like an exhausted gymnast. 'We'll have to go the long way, the Zuydecoote Pass, round our own bloody minefields.'

'But that route's more than twice as long, sir. Twice as much time.'

'Twice as much bombing time. Still, can't be helped. Give the orders,' he instructed. 'And get me some small boats. For the beaches. We're going to need them.'

* * *

Henry Chichester wasn't sure why he'd been drawn to the docks at Dover. It wasn't just the habit of a man in holy orders to offer help at a time of misery, although there was some of that. There were memories mixed in there, too, memories of troopships of an earlier generation bringing him and millions of others back from the killing grounds of France. The same haggard faces and hollow eyes, the bloodied uniforms, the outstretched and desperate hands. And a new generation of women waiting in their huddles of hope and silent tears. How brazenly their men had marched off! And how despairingly they had crawled and been carried back home. Henry Chichester had brought shrapnel back with him. It had remained buried deep inside and caused pain every time he knelt before his God. It would never let him forget.

He'd found little difficulty in getting into the

docks themselves; the usually smooth and orderly manner of naval operations had been replaced by a sense of struggle and hurry. All eyes were upon the biblical black pillar of fire across the water; the guards had taken one look at his clerical collar and saluted him past. Inside the dock, the ships were berthed two and sometimes three abreast at the quayside as they were stripped of all non-essential equipment and loaded with provisions: water cans, food, medical items. Chichester watched as one large ferry boat had its doors, tables, bunks, counters and benches ripped from their fixing points and hurled onto the quayside in order to make more room within. An extraordinary complexity of new equipment was loaded on the decks: rafts, ladders, lifebuoys. The stench of oil hung across it all. Tugs and supply ships scuttled back and forth across the water, moving grey destroyers and other large ships to a berth on buoys in the middle of the harbour, waiting their turn.

You could tell which ships had already been across. They were the ones with the holes and gashes, with the battered funnels and broken masts, with hands washing away grimly at the stains on the decks.

As he walked around the docks, men of all ranks would stop him, ask for a blessing, try to find comfort in his eyes. But Henry Chichester's eyes were elsewhere, constantly searching, he wasn't sure for what.

In one corner of the harbour, out of sight of the women, a long line of bulging blankets had been laid out in a neat naval line. Just as he remembered from long ago.

Then he knew why he had come. He was searching for his son. And his God.

*    *    *

They had almost been taken by surprise as they prepared to cross the road outside Gravelines that came from the direction of Dunkirk. They were distracted, stiff from their cold night on the sand. Their sprains and wounds were complaining of abuse and their stomachs of hunger. The bloody dog kept barking at them. They'd named it Winston.

They had clawed their way up the side of a steep dune and were standing on its top, surveying their path across the road, when they saw a cloud of dust and sand heading towards them from the east. From deep within the cloud came the unmistakable rattle of tanks. In a moment, the exhaustion that had racked their bodies for days had vanished. For tanks heading out of Dunkirk could mean only one thing: the British or French were making a break out or, even better, announcing an advance. The miracle they had both hoped for had arrived! Don and Claude stood on top of the dune, propping each other up and waving frenziedly as the sandstorm came ever nearer.

For their pains, and their naivety, they were greeted by a heavy machine-gun, which poured bullets into the dune around their feet. They had been trying to wave down a squadron of panzers. They threw themselves into the sand as the tanks thundered past. They both knew they were going to die.

'Why are you here, Englishman?' Claude

shouted above the noise, his head burrowed deep next to Don's.

'My father thinks it's because I'm afraid of getting shot at.'

'He is a fool.'

'For once I agree with you, Frenchie.'

Sand sprayed over them as bullets smashed into the dune above their heads. Don could feel Claude wriggling closer. Then his hand was being squeezed tightly.

'Thank you, Donald Chichester.'

'For what?'

'For trying.'

Another burst of fire; more wriggling as Winston buried himself between the two of them.

Then it was past. The panzers hadn't stopped. They were in a hurry.

The two men picked themselves up and began to shake the sand from their blouses. Winston, his courage restored, began barking and raced after the panzers; Don's wound had split open once more and blood was seeping down his sleeve.

'Tell me something,' Don asked, gritting his teeth against the pain as the other man attempted to realign the crude bandage of torn tablecloth that had been bound around his arm. 'Are spaniels English or French?'

'I don't know. Why?'

Don shook his head in bewilderment, gazing after the dog, whose tail was revolving like a propeller as if to give it added impetus in its insane pursuit. 'Definitely French.'

'And there is one thing I would like to know, Englishman,' Claude responded, riding the insult by tying the bandage so tight that it made Don wince.

'What's that?'

'Why German tanks have decided to turn away from Dunkirk.'

* * *

It was the final day of the affair on the beaches. Churchill knew this when he woke, and nothing he learned from the papers that lay strewn across his bed gave him reason for doubt.

The tide of opinion in the press had turned as savagely as any sea. The previous day's editions had bellowed that the BEF still held almost all of the Channel ports, even Calais, that the Germans had suffered countless casualties and mutinies, and three British RAF aces had 'bagged a hundred'. Yet this morning their readers had woken to discover that none of this was true. Calais had gone, the Belgians had gone, and the French showed every sign of following. By tomorrow the entire BEF might be wiped out, stuck on the sands and heading for captivity.

A sense of betrayal filtered through the wadding of the editorial columns; the British public had been misled, and as always the editors in Fleet Street cast around for someone else to blame. Yet Churchill knew that was the least of his concerns.

As so often, there was a twist within the tortures that were piled upon him. Gort's disobedience and retreat had at least given him some better hope of filling the desperate gash in his defences left by the Belgian surrender. So many soldiers were being crushed inside the Dunkirk pocket that some of them, at least, could be turned towards the breach to build a human barricade that could slow the Germans down for a few hours longer. And they were flooding the low-lying areas around Dunkirk; the water levels were beginning to rise, slowing down the enemy even further. The Germans might have to get their feet wet. But nowhere near as wet as the soldiers of the BEF.

Churchill ate a miserable breakfast. So many twists and turns, so much confusion. He didn't know which way to turn, which enemy to face, or even who his enemy was. The weather forecasts were bad. Storms were passing by Ireland that would ripple through to the beaches, making the surf rise, swamping boats and piling more miseries upon their labours. Yet within that lay perhaps yet another twist, for as the weather grew poorer and the ceiling lower, the Luftwaffe might be held at bay.

But who would keep Edward Halifax at bay?

* * *

It was like taking part in the Charge of the Light Brigade, straight down the barrels of the guns, no chance to turn, pushing past the corpses of those who had fallen before, and doing it on a donkey.

That's how the crew of the old steamer had described their journey of the previous day, and none of them wanted to repeat it. A stoker had walked away from the ship the previous night and stepped straight in front of a bus. An accident of the blackout, the authorities described it, but none of his crewmates believed it. They'd been there with him, in Dunkirk.

Now they had been told to go back.

The captain was pleading with them, but his own voice was still ringing with the terrors of their experience and it lacked conviction. He stood on the gangway, barring their path to shore.

How many times had Henry Chichester witnessed such scenes, when the courage to die had deserted men and they refused to fight, overwhelmed by the extent of the expected sacrifice—or was it simply its futility? He had even watched one of them being led away, as the sun was rising after a sad, aching night, and tied to a stake. Punishment, as decreed by the military code, for those who refused to fight. He was a soldier well known to Chichester. Corporal Collins. A good man, with three children back in Birmingham and a wife he wrote to every week. He had stood before the stake and denied the accusation that he was a coward and afraid to die. He had told his executioners he was refusing to obey orders to kill others because he knew it to be wrong, and all he wanted was to go to God with a clear conscience. As the cusp of the sun had broken through the night, his wish had been granted.

Henry Chichester had been part of that firing squad. It had been one of the reasons why, after the war was over, he had gone in search of God. He wanted to experience those same depths of faith as Corporal Collins, to share his certainty and sense of reconciliation. There had to be some meaning behind the suffering he had seen, and he knew it would take a higher mind to understand it, for no matter how hard he had tried, Henry Chichester could not. So he had taken refuge in his God. And he had prayed every night of the passing years that his rifle had been the one which held the blank bullet.

Yet in spite of all the prayers and the suffering, it was happening again.

The fury he had thrown at his son was not simply anger at his raw presumption in usurping the place of a man like Corporal Collins, but also for resurrecting such tormented memories and reminding Henry Chichester of his doubts. There was also fear—a father's fear for a son who insisted on standing out against a world that would surely crush him as casually as they had crushed the corporal. Which made him wonder. Perhaps, after all, it wasn't a lack of courage on Don's part. Perhaps it was that he had too much of the damned stuff. Henry Chichester didn't know any longer which it was. He should have. He should have known his son better.

He stood at the bottom of the gangway. He didn't know any more whether it was right to send these men, but they would have to go, and it was better that they go with courage. He raised his hands like an ancient prophet, his voice ringing out.

'Wait on the Lord! Be of good courage, and He shall strengthen thine heart. Wait, I say, on the Lord!'

The confrontation at the head of the gangway stopped as they all turned to look at him, startled. Yet as they stared, he was brushed aside by another figure forcing its way up the rickety wooden walkway.

'Thanks for your offer, Reverend, but I think we'll leave it to a rather more orthodox authority for the moment.'

The sergeant in the Military Police swore loudly

at the crew as he thrust a very British barrel at them.

Sullenly, the crewmen drifted back to their stations.

*      *      *

Only Bracken and Colville were left.

When a man's purpose had come to its end, others shrank away. No one would tell him to his face that the game was up; he might only discover the truth when they refused to play any longer and made excuses not to stand beside him in case failure was infectious. Two had stayed with Churchill, and Colville only because it was his paid employment.

Churchill sat in his oak-panelled room in the House of Commons and stared morosely at the telephone on his desk, willing it to ring, even though the only messages it brought were those of danger and despair. He felt utterly alone in the manner that only a man who has spent his entire life surrounded by audiences could feel.

Even Ruth Mueller had fled, vanished, refused to be found. As the men in Churchill's world increasingly turned their backs on him, her irritating presence had sparked him back to life, set him up for the battles ahead, and for the battles he had to fight within. But now she was gone, too.

'They all abandon me,' he muttered.

'Not bloody surprised,' Bracken responded, recognizing the corrosive self-pity in which his friend sometimes bathed, and determined to drag him out of it.

'What? What did you say?'

'I said that I am not bloody surprised,' Bracken repeated, blowing a blue ring of Cuban smoke from the depths of a cracked leather armchair. 'You are so damnably offensive.'

In normal times Churchill would respond to the barb by fighting back; instead, he kept his silence, eyes closed, lost in some other place.

Bracken glanced across at Colville. The old man had a parliamentary statement to make in a few minutes with yet another War Cabinet to follow; it was no time for him to fall off his form. Colville understood the hint and shuffled through the pile of papers in front of him.

'A note from the Treasury, Prime Minister,' he began, 'about your new salary.' It was usually enough to engage his immediate attention, some snippet about his personal funds, but today was not like other days. Silence.

'Hell, Winston, snap out of it,' Bracken demanded, deciding for the direct approach.

An eye, its rims red and sore, prised itself open.

'There seems so much to do, and so little time to do it,' he announced wearily.

'Let us help you,' Bracken insisted.

'I fear no one can help me.'

'That's because you refuse to allow anyone to help!'

Colville sat up in alarm. It had sounded so suspiciously like his own voice.

'You take sides with him—with Bracken?' Churchill barked, rousing himself. 'You think I am—what were the words?—damnably offensive?'

Colville hesitated, trying to judge the distance of the stones across the swamp before he jumped, but he took too long.

'There, Brendan,' Churchill shouted, jabbing his own cigar in Colville's direction, 'exactly what I mean. I pay this man and all I get is sullen disloyalty.'

The insult stung Colville. Why was it only Churchill who was allowed to feel exhausted and be open in his feelings? Why did the rest of the world have to dance in constant attendance on his whims and petulance? He liked to pretend that he was fighting this war on his own, yet he sat there smoking while many of Colville's friends were away in France and might never be coming back. Suddenly Colville had had enough of the old man's temper and tongue.

'You do not pay my salary.'

'I am the *cause* of your salary being paid,' Churchill corrected himself.

'Then I beg to relieve you of that responsibility and be allowed to join the armed forces.'

'You want to desert. Like all the rest.'

Colville sprang to his feet. 'I resent that! I don't want to desert, I want to serve, but you never allow anyone to get close. You never explain, you never tell anyone around you what's going on. You issue orders and expect blind obedience.'

'That is what happens in war.'

'This isn't your private war! Do you know what they are saying about you, Mr Churchill, behind your back? That you are so bent on your war that you'll fight it to the last woman and child. That you intend to go out in such a blaze of glory that all of England will be turned to ash. They're saying that you can't control yourself. That you're no better than Hitler.'

Churchill looked across to Bracken for his

customary reassurance, but his friend seemed engrossed in a detailed examination of the ceiling.

'How dare you!' Churchill began his defence with a bullying growl, but Colville knew the technique all too well.

'I dare, Mr Churchill, because sometime very soon, a week, a month, I may be put up against a wall and shot for no better reason than having served you as loyally as I could. So I have the right. What I don't have is any reason to continue.'

'Then you have my permission to leave.'

'I don't believe I need your permission, sir.' And in as determined a manner as his trembling hands could manage, Colville began to arrange the papers on his desk into a neat pile before putting them into his briefcase.

'What do you intend to do?' Churchill asked.

Colville was too wrapped up in his own unexpected emotions to notice that the old man's voice had lost its aggressive tone. 'I'd like to join the RAF.'

'Why?'

'Because . . . Because . . .' Did it matter why? Even in his calmer moments Colville had difficulty putting his preference into words. 'I came back from Chequers this morning—preparing it for your first visit this weekend. Do you know there's only one telephone in the entire place? In the pantry.'

'We may need the pantry for more than that.'

'And at the station, as I was waiting, a troop train came through. It was crowded with evacuees from Dunkirk. I can tell you, a defeated army is a terrible sight.'

'A defeated British army is the worst sight in the world.'

'And there were a couple of RAF men in uniform on the platform beside me. We all know they're outnumbered, and we also know they've been fighting as hard and dying as bravely as any group of men ever could. But apparently the boys from Dunkirk don't know. They think the RAF has abandoned them.'

'Our pilots are so few, their enemies so many . . .' Churchill began in protestation, but Colville was not to be denied.

'The soldiers jeered. As the train went past, the British army leant out of the window and jeered the RAF. Called them bloody cowards.'

A gasp squeezed from Churchill.

'So we need more flyers,' Colville said, concluding his argument and shoving the last of his papers into his bag. He looked up to discover Churchill drenched in tears.

'The RAF? The army? Is this the world I have created? Then I must be mad.' He was openly sobbing.

Colville felt prodded by guilt. 'You're not mad, you're . . . surrounded by confusion. Much of it of your own making.'

Churchill seemed not to hear, lost in his misery. He appeared very old.

'What do you mean, Jock?' Bracken prodded gently, joining them once more.

'He turns everything to such chaos. He tries to overwhelm everyone with his energy and his ideas, but they just can't cope. Telegrams, orders, written instructions, notes of advice, demands for information: he fires them off like Nelson firing off his cannonballs. There's no priority, no structure to any of it, he just blazes away in the hope that one in ten might hit. Yesterday'—Colville threw up an arm in despair—'yesterday he sent out demands for information about everything from launching a second front in Europe to reusing dinner scraps.'

'What should we do?'

'Get some sort of system, some sort of order. I know I'm a civil servant and it's the sort of thing I would say, but just occasionally the wretched system works. Perhaps he should tell us not only what he wants doing but what he wants doing first. I don't know, stick a few labels on things. "Action This Day" or something. Just so the dinner scraps can be left till tomorrow.'

A huge sob erupted from Churchill. 'Jock, my boy, please forgive me.'

It was the only apology Colville had ever heard him give.

'And stay.'

The outpouring of emotion overwhelmed the young civil servant. He considered the plea—but only long enough to make the point that it was his decision. Feigning reluctance, he laid his case back down on his desk.

'Please, have those labels printed up. And find Ruth Mueller.'

'Why?'

'Because I have found her to be of altogether unexpected use. Rather like you.'

* * *

His staff insisted that Ramsay take some rest. He had slept very little in the past week and not at all during the last two days—or what passed as days in the subterranean kingdom beneath the white cliffs.

The night ahead would be critical, and they would need the vice admiral at his best. Two of his staff accompanied him to his room at the end of the tunnel and stayed until they had seen him lie down on his cot. He was asleep before they had closed the door.

Ramsay and his staff were beginning to pluck some measure of understanding from the chaos of Dunkirk. The previous day's toll had been heavy: two trawlers lost to mines, two drifters and a troopship by bombs, and one minesweeper had been sunk in a collision. Safety from the Luftwaffe and the artillery came only after dark, but then the sea exacted its toll of confusion as the ships tried to find their way without light or navigation aids to the most congested and wreck-strewn port in the world. Then they shifted to the beaches, with its rising surf, which swamped the dinghies and lifeboats that came to pick up men who had been standing for hours in the water waiting for rescue. Time and time again, the small boats were turned over by surf or exhausted men who filled them to their tipping point. It was all taking so long, moving so slowly.

There was a desperate need for more small boats to speed the work and ferry men out to the larger ships waiting offshore. Orders had gone out to strip every ship on the south coast of its lifeboats and to impress every rowing boat and beach vessel that could be found and floated, but they had lost two convoys of small craft as they were towed across the Channel in line astern, cut through in the dark by ships running blind.

Larger ships came as close as they dared to the gently shelving shore, where they were forced to hover, waiting for their human cargoes, making excellent targets for the bombers. That afternoon Ramsay had counted ninety-five aeroplanes above the beaches, almost all of them German.

Too many men, too few boats, total confusion. Ramsay had sent over one of his best captains to act as Senior Naval Officer in order to give some sense to the situation. He was identified by the letters SNO on his helmet, made out of silver foil from a cigarette packet and stuck there with thick pea soup. Everything was makeshift.

Yet when Ramsay was shaken roughly awake in his quarters three hours later, he was told of two shafts of light that had begun to glimmer in the darkness. More small boats were arriving—dinghies, cabin cruisers, motorboats, lifeboats, rowing boats, launches—from as far away as the boatyards on the Thames, dragged from their moorings by naval press gangs with or without their owners' consent.

And just when they thought every part of the harbour at Dunkirk had been made completely impractical for their purposes, someone had suggested that they look at the mole. The mole was nothing more than a narrow wooden breakwater that projected more than three-quarters of a mile into the sea to protect the entrance to the harbour, and bearing at its end a concrete footing on which stood a small lighthouse. In fact there were two of these long structures, but the western one had already been shattered, leaving just the eastern mole which, although it was riddled with gaps, still stood. It was never intended that it should be used for berthing ships—it was far too flimsy, had no means of coping with the ebb and flow of the fifteen-foot tide, and could be split in two by any careless ship or accurate shell, yet it had to be tried. So they filled the holes in the wooden planking with anything to hand—doors, ladders, benches—and a former cross-Channel ferry, the *Queen of the Channel*, was instructed to try to berth alongside. She did so in darkness, and took on 950 men.

On her way back to Dover, a stick of bombs broke the *Queen*'s back and she sank in minutes. And yet—and *yet,* the mole had worked. Ships could tie up against her, so men could be taken from her. It gave the BEF another lifeline—and one so smothered in smoke from the burning buildings that it might take some time for the Germans to catch on, blinded by the destructiveness of their own bombs.

One other morsel greeted Ramsey when he woke. The storm front was receding and the surf falling. They would bring more men home today than yesterday—perhaps double the number. Still a miserable trickle compared to the flood of men that was beginning to wash up along the beaches but, as he stood on his balcony in the fading light, watching his makeshift armada stretching back from that awful pillar of smoke, he felt his tiredness lifting on the evening air. Every homecoming, every ship that made it back through the entrance to the harbour with its cargo of hope, was like an injection of adrenalin straight to his heart.

*   *   *

More dispute. More deliberation. No decision. Yet another War Cabinet.

Halifax warned of the danger of the destruction of Christian civilization; Churchill replied that any country that bowed to Nazism would be neither Christian nor civilized for long. Halifax countered that they would get better terms now, while they still had their aircraft factories operational and unbombed. Churchill growled that anyone who thought the Germans would allow them to keep the aircraft factories open must think Hitler a fool, and That Man may be many things, but he was no fool.

And neither was Halifax. Churchill had hoped that a period of reflection or a sound night's sleep might have softened the other man's arguments, but he would be neither persuaded nor browbeaten. Yet he stuck to the gentleman's agreement. He threatened disasters of many kinds, but he didn't threaten resignation. The Government was united, but only in its determination to disagree.

They were getting nowhere and taking up too much time—more time than Churchill had allowed. He had asked his senior Ministers outside the War Cabinet to meet with him in his room at the House and they were already flocking outside, so he suggested to Halifax and the other 'big beasts' that they should stand down for a short while and reconvene later.

'Time off for Children's Hour,' Halifax muttered as they scooped up their papers.

It was an apt description. These men of the Outer Cabinet, some thirty in number, had responsibility but little authority. Left to their own devices they would have created the most eccentric confusion, for they were of differing parties and conflicting personal loyalties. Many were still Chamberlain's men; some belonged to Attlee's team; only a few owed their position directly to Churchill. He could not command them, he could only try to lead and persuade. He hadn't met with them as a group since he'd appointed them, and now they gathered, ushered to their places around the table by Bracken. The faces were all anxious; some were exhausted. So was Churchill, and they could see it.

'I have asked you here today to share with you some of my thoughts and feelings as we venture upon this most critical hour. You are—how might I put it?—an exceptional collection of men, of many different passions and political persuasions. I tell you frankly that, in the past, some of your passions and much of your politics have scared the senses out of me. Let us hope you will have a similar effect upon Hitler!'

Around the table, the faces of anxiety were softened by wry amusement. The old man may be facing disaster, but he hadn't lost his humour. They would remember that when they got home. But it would need more than one old man's wit if they were going to win.

He could sense their doubt, almost smell it in the heavy male atmosphere as they crowded round the table. He knew these men well, some for fifty years or more. Much of that time had been spent pushing against each other's ideas and conflicting ambitions—and sometimes, he reflected, simply pushing against each other. Like Leo Amery, whose round, expectant face was a picture of concentration as he listened to Churchill's review of the war. They'd first met at Harrow. Churchill had been at the school barely a month, the lowest form of educational life, when he had hurled the diminutive but most eminent Amery into the swimming pool, thinking him to be a much more junior boy. Amery had emerged, irate and intent on retribution. The young Churchill had apologized, 'I'm sorry,' he explained, 'but I mistook you for a Fourth Former. You are so small.' His words seemed to do little to stem the older boy's wrath, so Churchill had added: 'My father, who is a great man, is also small.'

It had cemented a life-long relationship.

Amery understood ambition, and its price. Three weeks ago Chamberlain had offered him any post in the Cabinet in return for his support, yet despite all his dreams and desires, it had been a price too heavy for Amery. There were older memories, too. Amery could recall Churchill's father, and the day of his resignation. Most of the other boys had taunted Churchill, but Amery had come up to him at lunch and shaken his hand, very publicly, not with approval but simply from understanding. He knew the two Churchills always travelled together, even though they were so rarely seen together.

Even now, as Churchill continued with his review, his father was with him once more, sitting amongst the expectant faces around the table. It had happened so often during Winston's political career; he would imagine his father nearby, watching, never quite approving. It had always spurred him onwards, ensured he never relaxed or took anything for granted, but, just this once, he ached for someone to tell him he was right.

'I have thought carefully in these last days

whether it was part of my duty to consider entering into negotiations with That Man,' he was saying. One or two heads were slowly nodding. Perhaps they'd been talking with Halifax. And, as weariness seemed to seep from every bone in his body, he could no longer deny the possibility that they were right. If neither Hitler nor Halifax were the fool, then perhaps it was Churchill himself.

And then he saw Ruth. He ransacked his last store of energy in order to force her image into his mind. She was sitting at the other end of the table, her hair drawn back around her face, with that determined and Germanic jib of hers. She was frowning, scolding him, warning him. Don't bend, don't you dare bend! You are alone because you understand better than any man here. So take them with you. Do it your way. But trust them, and do it together!

'I will not hide from you, gentlemen, that what is happening now in northern France may turn out to be the greatest British military disaster for many centuries. We are straining every nerve and moving every muscle to get back as many of our men as providence will allow. It may be no more than fifty thousand. But I will not negotiate. It is idle to think that we would get better terms from Germany at this moment than if we went on and fought it out. The Germans would demand our fleet—they would call it "disarmament"—and our naval bases and our aircraft factories and much else besides. We should become a slave state, run by some puppet or other who owed allegiance only to Hitler.'

Growls of support were coming from the far corner of the table; was that where Bracken was sitting? Ruth was slapping the table with her palms.

'No! I will not go naked to the negotiating table. Instead, it is my intention that we should fight on, with all our reserves and all our advantages.' His head was up, his jaw set. 'I cannot tell you what the outcome of that great struggle will be. But if, at last, the long story of these islands is to come to an end, it were better it should end not through surrender, but only when we are rolling senseless on the ground.'

There is sometimes a moment within meetings of men when an idea catches fire and takes hold of those present. Such a moment is rarely planned and almost never scripted but comes about through a fusion of great passion and opportunity. It is often inexplicable, even to those who are there and who become part of it. These men around the table were, all of them, afraid and infected by that English talent for compromise, yet there was not a man in the room who at that moment would have hesitated to give his life for his country.

'Whatever happens at Dunkirk,' Churchill told them, 'we shall fight on!'

Then Amery was on his feet, applauding, at his Prime Minister's side, wringing his hand; and others were following, crowding round, slapping his shoulder and swearing solidarity. Churchill had never known a group of politicians to respond so emphatically, yet he seemed oblivious, his face carved from stone, staring down the table to where Ruth was sitting.

For the first time since he had known her, she was smiling.

* * *

Halifax accepted his temporary defeat. The meeting of the Ministers was nothing more than a skirmish in a longer struggle, but news of their reaction was enough to persuade him that this day would not be his. When the War Cabinet reconvened later that evening for the ninth time in three days, he chose not to press his position on the negotiations. Winston, in Halifax's view, talked the most frightful rot. His mind was a jumble of disorder and naïve sentimentality, and he was petulant to the point of puerility. His nonsense tumbled out in front of them, as if from an upturned dustcart, but this time Halifax ignored it. After all, he had made his case and he didn't have to overwhelm Churchill with logic: events would do that.

Tonight would mark the second night of the evacuation, after which they had been told the operation would probably have to be closed down. No more than twenty-five thousand had been brought back—fewer than expected, and not enough. Halifax had only to wait. It was merely a matter of time.

* * *

'Bring me the moon!'

Churchill was standing at the entrance to his Admiralty study, face flushed the colour of claret, waving his arms and shouting, so far as Colville could determine, utter gibberish. It had been less than ten minutes since he'd taken in a huge pile of intelligence reports, enough to keep the old fellow quiet for most of the night, or so he'd thought.

'Prime Minister?'

'Don't you see, Jock?' Churchill exclaimed, waving one of the intelligence folders excitedly, 'The panzers are turning away from Dunkirk.'

Colville was lost, and admitted so.

'They have changed their plans. Heading south. It can mean only one thing. Paris! Guderian and his panzer troops are glory boys, they want the most glittering trophy—and they must have come to the conclusion that it has to be Paris.'

'How, precisely, does that help us?' Colville asked tentatively.

'Because they don't understand the importance of Dunkirk. They think it's all over, no more than fragments to be swept up by the dumb foot soldiers of the Wehrmacht.'

'And the Luftwaffe.'

'Ah, but there's the wonder of it. They have pushed us onto the beaches—and do you know what effects bombs have upon beaches?'

Colville shook his head in confusion.

'Bugger all! They bury themselves in the sand and go pop! Casualties: almost none at all. It gives us a chance, Jock. And the mole Ramsay's using—only a few feet wide. Covered most of the time in a huge cloud of smoke. A desperate target for the bombers. With luck it may survive a little longer. And so might our army.'

The Germans had changed their strategy. Since the first day of the offensive they had based their plan of attack on a concentrated fist of panzers punching huge holes through the Allied armies. It was a strategy that had brought them monumental success and made them masters of most of Europe. They had swept along, sometimes more than forty miles a day; now they were turning back when they were little more than four miles from the docks of Dunkirk. Their minds were already turning to Paris and the huge victory parade they wanted to claim for their Fuehrer.

As for the British, what threat did they pose? They'd already been seen destroying their tanks, spiking their guns, smashing every piece of equipment in their desperate flight to the sea. They had nothing to fight with and nowhere to go. What was left wouldn't amount to much of a battle at all, little more fun than wringing a rabbit's neck. Ah, but to be first in Paris, to march down the Champs-Elysées, to have the capital of the old enemy cowering at their feet—that was a prize to warm old men on a winter's night. No, Dunkirk could be left to the plodding infantry. It was only a matter of time.

The British Expeditionary Force had been reduced to the role of a spectator at these great events. It had no more military significance, its condition was wretched. It would bring no glory to its conquerors. The once mighty army of England had become irrelevant, and Churchill was overjoyed.

'Let them fall upon Paris—why, the French may save us yet. We must go on like gun horses, till we drop, and pray that the wind and tides are with us. We might get another night out of this, Jock, my boy, so send the ships, assemble the charts, give me the seas—bring me the moon!'

# CHAPTER THIRTEEN

But the winds refused to blow for Winston.

In the early hours of the morning the breeze picked up, slowing down the evacuation once more. And although it brought with it a steady drizzle and a low cloud ceiling that kept the aircraft of the Fliegerkorps VIII on the ground all morning, around noon the wind changed and the skies cleared. At two o'clock in the afternoon, orders were issued for FliegerKorps VIII to attack.

Fliegerkorps VIII was no normal Luftwaffe unit. It had been specially strengthened with other units from as far afield as Holland and Düsseldorf in order to provide a spectacular illustration of the might of the Luftwaffe, and two hours after the order was given, the first of four hundred aircraft—Junkers, Dorniers, Messerschmitts and Stukas with the eerie four-tone whistles on the fins of their bombs—arrived above Dunkirk. There was not a single RAF fighter in sight. And what the Luftwaffe pilots found beneath them seemed to have been plucked from their dreams.

The wind had changed and the smoke was blowing inland. Clustered around the mole were a dozen ships, tied up alongside, sometimes two or three deep. Like an antique print of the English fleet gathered at Trafalgar, one of the pilots later told his excited ground crew. The perfect target.

It wasn't necessary to score a direct hit on a ship to cause the most fearful damage. A bomb close astern could throw it out of the water, ripping off its rudder, even breaking its back. Shrapnel caused horrific injuries, both to metal and to men, slashing open fuel tanks and steam lines and flesh. And the men who were lined up on the narrow mole had nowhere to hide, nowhere to go.

One British seaman later recalled being bombed out of three ships and being machine-gunned in the sea, all in less than an hour. The most extraordinary aspect of his story was that he should survive to tell it. Many didn't.

The mole itself was hit in several places. They plugged the gaps with hatches and wooden planking ripped from the ships.

The ships never stopped. They barged each other aside, nudging up against the mole, picking up what they could, trying to make it back home, weaving, many sinking. The bombers pursued them all the way.

Yet still they kept coming.

* * *

'Cheers, Frenchie,' Don muttered, slightly drunk.

'Bottoms up, English,' Claude responded, repeating the greeting he had just been taught.

They sat with their backs against the wall, peering through the open door of an abandoned cottage that Winston had discovered during one of his forays. The dog had also discovered the small cellar that lay beneath.

Don and Claude were far beyond debating the ethics of looting. Their spirits had fallen so low that, if they had stumbled upon a German patrol rather than the cottage, they might have given themselves up. Neither had changed their clothes or washed thoroughly for nearly a fortnight. During that time they had been shot at, shelled, bombed, buried beneath rubble, burnt and scorched, slept rough, hidden in sand, fallen into mud and any other manner of agricultural material. Their hair stood up like straw after the storm. Their eyes were sunken; they hadn't shaved; their uniforms creaked with sweat and soil. Don in particular was in pathetic shape—his wounded arm had bled copiously, drying to a hard, menacing stain that travelled the length of his sleeve.

They found a hand pump at the back. After much coaxing, it spouted out a grey liquid that was far too brackish to drink but which felt like goat's milk over their bodies. They stood in the afternoon sun, naked, allowing their bodies to dry in the breeze and feeling their numbness and exhaustion slowly sneaking away. Their uniform rags went, too, replaced by clothing scavenged from the bedroom—oh, and new socks. Beyond value. They would have looted an entire village for those. Meanwhile, Winston had begun scrabbling away at a wooden hatch set in the floor, which had led them to shelves filled with bottles and tins. Their celebration of the dog's foraging abilities was dampened by the discovery that the tins contained nothing but foie gras, but they were in no state to quibble. Soon they were settled with their backs against the wall, bottles of an excellent *vin de pays* on one side, open cans on the other, feeling better than they had since first they met. Winston, rewarded with his own tin, slept contentedly in the corner.

'What will you do, Frenchman?'

'If we get out of this? Fight. And find my family. They got out of Calais before the bombardment. I know they are fine.' He scooped another finger of the rich paste into his mouth. 'And you, English?'

'I have absolutely no idea.'

'What about your family?'

'I have none—well, almost none. My mother died giving birth to me. My father . . . he's a vicar. In the church, you know?' He made an irreverent sign of the cross in the air. 'All holiness and hypocrisy.'

'No brothers, sisters?'

'One aunt. Spent a lot of time with her as a baby, till I started going to school. My father used to send me away to her when he got fed up with me.'

'Why do you not like your father?'

Don drank. 'He has a rulebook for his life. I didn't fit into it.'

'He hit you?'

'No. Sometimes I wish he had. What he did was worse. Preaching at me all the time. Drove me wild. Can you imagine what it was like, knowing every day of the week, every week of the year, what you had to do?'

And it came tumbling and grumbling forth, the life of a young man growing up with only his father as companion, surrounded by the drudgery of a clerical life from which every spark of surprise had been squeezed.

'Then he discovered I had a voice and I became a performing monkey—communion, evensong, every Sunday. Then it got to be weddings on Saturdays, too. My schoolfriends played football and had a good time; I got to dress up like a choirboy. He wouldn't even let me smoke, said it would ruin the voice. He drove me crazy. Eventually I got big enough to tell him so.'

'What happened?'

'I stopped singing. Refused to sing another note. It was my sixteenth birthday. He was in a foul mood. He just told me to sing my heart out that day. I said no. I was sixteen and I'd do what I liked.'

More drink. His feelings seemed aroused; his arm was beginning to hurt once more. In the corner, Winston stirred distractedly. Don threw him another tin of foie gras.

'You know, Frenchie, I never got a single break, not in all my life. I always had to be the bloody vicar's son.'

'And did he?'

'Did he what?'

'Get a break?'

'From what?'

'From being your father and your mother.'

Don frowned. 'That wasn't my fault. Anyway, he was never much of a parent. At Christmas he had time for everyone, except for me.'

'He is a priest,' Claude offered quietly.

'Even birthdays. He never gave me a single party, not in my entire life. It was almost like he resented me growing up.'

'Did you tell me that your mother died giving birth to you?'

'Yes, but . . .'

'On your birthday.'

For a moment Don was quiet. He hadn't seen it like that before. *Stupid*. Youth can be totally blind. It can also be short of temper.

'Look, I didn't ask to be born. It wasn't my fault!'

'No, and we don't ask to die, either. There are many things in life we don't get to choose.'

'What are you saying?'

'Only this. That I lost my father. I shall regret it all my life.'

The concept was too difficult for Don to struggle with. The alcohol was dragging him down, and he was giving up the fight to remain awake. Absentmindedly he picked up the wine cork and lobbed it in the direction of the dog.

His last memory, before sleep finally captured him, was of Winston, eyes full of reproach, waddling to the door and, with one final glare of indictment, throwing up.

* * *

Colville went in to check on the old man. He was still sitting there, staring into the empty hearth, as he had been half an hour ago.

'I've just been in touch with Dover, sir.'

Churchill seemed to barely to stir.

'They think today's total will be more than forty-five thousand.'

Nothing.

'It's a terrific total for a single day.'

Now he gathered himself. 'But at what cost, Jock? At what terrible cost?'

'In my opinion, sir, better that the entire bloody fleet be sunk than to hand it over to Hitler.'

'Thank you. I needed someone to say that.' He paused. 'Any sign of the Ruth woman?'

'Not a trace. We're still looking.'

Colville turned to go, then changed his mind. 'The front is still holding.'

'Perhaps they are only allowing it to hold to entice our ships into their shooting gallery.'

'So what are you going to do?' Colville demanded, deliberately provocative—he was learning about Churchill's moods. 'Abandon them?'

Churchill acknowledged his gratitude for the intrusion by rising from his gloom and walking purposefully to his desk.

'No, Master Colville, I will not abandon them. I did that at Calais. I don't want to make a bloody habit of it.'

* * *

The gilded figure of Prince Albert of Saxe-Coburg-Gotha looked down upon them from the throne of the memorial that had been erected by his distraught widow, Victoria.

'Damned appropriate,' Kennedy said, inspecting the ornate imperial carvings and friezes, 'a German sitting on top of the remnants of the British Empire. Almost prophetic.'

Butler didn't respond. They were walking through Kensington Gardens, near Kennedy's home, in morning sunshine. Everything appeared so normal. Nurses pushed prams, young boys sailed boats on the pond, elderly men in tightly buttoned jackets read their newspapers on park benches, dogs chased and barked, and on every side lupins and dark mauve pansies competed for attention. The sights and smells of a summer's day made the distant war seem so irrelevant.

'You know,' Kennedy continued, ruminating on the legendary linkage between the royal families of Britain and Germany, 'when historians look back on this war, they're going to talk about it as a ridiculous spat between family who should've known better. Pointless, like Cain and Abel.'

'Should be like Harrods and Selfridges.'

Kennedy grunted in bewilderment.

'You know, flourishing alongside each other,' Butler offered in explanation, 'room enough for all.'

It was clear the ambassador was still lost in the metaphorical jungle, so Butler brought him to the point of their meeting. 'Your phone call sounded urgent.'

'Needed to hear a voice of wisdom, Rab. Everyone else seems in such a damned rush. Winston hasn't returned my calls; Edward's always in such a frantic hurry.'

'The war.'

'A war in which your Government keeps begging for American understanding and help. So why has everyone suddenly gone so damned quiet?'

'The war,' Butler repeated.

'Bad as that?'

'*Wakeful*, *Grafton*, *Grenade*,' Butler responded. 'Remember those names, and pray for them. Three destroyers lost in a single afternoon yesterday. Along with four troopships and eight other vessels. Not to mention six other destroyers badly damaged.'

'Jee-sus.'

'Destruction so great that the Admiralty has withdrawn all its modern destroyers from the Dunkirk operation. Only the old and expendable are left.'

'This evacuation is madness.'

'Soon half our navy will lie at the bottom of the Channel and much of our air force in pieces on the beaches of Dunkirk—in exchange for an army that will consist of little more than flotsam and a truckload of rifles.'

'And all for one man's pride.'

'It can't go on. The front around Dunkirk won't last for ever. The end will be awful, our entire army swept into the sea. Merely a matter of time, a day or two at most. And for Winston perhaps not much longer. Edward is waiting only for the moment.'

'To resign?'

'It probably won't come to that. The mere threat will be enough to bring Winston down. There will be no option but to negotiate.'

'And hand everything over to Hitler,' Kennedy muttered ruefully.

'Not quite. We've prepared a paper at the Foreign Office suggesting the evacuation of our most precious assets—the Crown Jewels, the Coronation Chair, our gold bullion, our securities and precious stones. Perhaps some of our best artistic works, too. Apparently Winston hates the whole concept but . . . maybe what Winston wants doesn't matter so much any more.'

'Evacuation to where?'

'To some other part of the British Empire.'

'Canada would make sense.'

'Indeed it would. With everything being transported in whatever is left of our fleet, of course.'

Ah, the ships . . .

'You could rely on American assistance—my personal assistance, Rab.'

'Yes, I'm sure,' Butler replied, already way ahead of Kennedy and his breathless personal ambitions. But there was a deal to be struck. 'It would also mean evacuating the Royal Family.'

'Now, that could be a problem. Not to Canada. I can't see the American people being happy with a British king beaching up on their continent.'

'But Canada is part of *our* Empire, not yours.'

'Sure, but you know we have a deep interest in anything that goes on there.'

'In which case, if you object, it will probably have to be Australia.'

'Now steady on . . .'

'Come on, Joe. A resting place for a king in exchange for a navy and our entire exchequer, with a few Old Masters thrown in? Seems a fair deal to me.'

'Well, maybe . . .'

'Think about it. In the meantime you must excuse me. Talking of Harrods, Chips has asked me to meet him there to offer advice on Oriental carpets.'

'Chips needs carpets?' Kennedy enquired, a little incredulous.

'Not really, but he is in the embarrassing position of having the devil of a lot of money. He's trying to spend some of it, buying rugs, antiques, whatever takes his fancy, while it still buys anything at all. As you say, the King's head may be filled with Germanic blood—but his head on a shilling may soon be utterly worthless.'

* * *

The two men set off towards evening, their mouths scraped rough from the wine but their spirits restored by the sleep and their fresh clothes—although Don worried about their clothes. What would happen if they ran into Germans? Would they pass as civilians, or be shot at as spies?

The Germans made it easy for them, even in the dark. The Wehrmacht were so confident they hadn't even bothered to douse their lights. But progress was slow: Don and Claude kept to the country lanes rather than the main roads; then, as they drew ever closer to the front line around Dunkirk, they took to the fields, slipping, stumbling, the mud clinging to their boots. The darkness around them was unnaturally still. The familiar noises of the night—the owls, the foxes, the nightjars—all were gone, leaving only the howling of distant dogs and a bellow of pain from an unmilked cow. Winston slunk along beside them, his tail between his legs.

Then the German guns opened up again and they found themselves face-down in a ploughed field of mud. A weird arch of fireflies formed above them as shells and tracer bullets passed overhead, but only Winston complained. It meant that the Wehrmacht now lay behind them.

They walked into the outskirts of a small walled town. Bergues. Four miles from Dunkirk. For centuries, sailors had used its square tower and belfry as navigation guides. The worst was behind them, Claude said.

The armed guard who challenged them was British. He expressed no surprise at their unconventional clothing; military discipline hadn't been much in evidence in this part of the world these last few days. A glance at Don's pay book was enough to satisfy his curiosity. They asked him what they should do. 'Do?' he repeated. He waved wearily towards the curtain of fire that lit the horizon. 'Dunkirk,' he said, as if that were enough explanation.

Bergues was not as Claude remembered it. Every street was choked with vehicles and weapons that had been hastily abandoned, making their progress difficult as they squeezed between the wrecks and past the fingers of flame that snatched at them from every side. The heat was painful; the only buildings that weren't ablaze seemed to be those that had already burnt and had nothing left to offer. As they came to the centre of the old town they came across a caravan of men that meandered along its main road, with French and British soldiers appearing from the shadows on all sides to join it. They saw wounded men being carried on doors or hauled along in wheelbarrows, and dying men being prayed over by priests. The dead were ignored; there were too many of them.

There was no military order, just shadows of men slinking through the night, a human convoy whose shoulders told of defeat, trudging north towards the still brighter flames. Winston grew increasingly agitated; Claude attached a length of rope to his collar to stop him from fleeing.

At the side of the road they passed an unexploded bomb that had buried itself up to its fins in a pile of foul-smelling earth. A curious pig was licking it.

But it was on the far side of the town that they were overtaken by despair.

Bergues was an agricultural town. It produced many things, one of which was industrial alcohol, stored in huge vats. The well-meaning mayor of Bergues, thinking that these vats were a fire risk to his community, had ordered that they should be emptied and the alcohol drained away into surrounding fields. But the fields had already been deliberately flooded as part of the defences, so the alcohol spread far.

Without knowing it, the convoy of men was walking through a lake of highly flammable spirit.

It might have been a stray shell or even a discarded cigarette that did it. Whatever the cause, the effect was appalling. The alcohol ignited in a sheet of flame. Fifty, perhaps sixty men were trapped on a lake of fire, many of them too far from safety to have any chance of being rescued. Men began turning into pillars of fire.

Don and Claude were powerless. Their instincts were paralysed, their senses overwhelmed by sights, and sounds, and terrifying smells they could never have imagined. They did nothing. Some men managed to stumble from the lake, begging for their flames to be doused; others, further away from safety, screamed for mercy as their bodies began to melt. In tears, soldiers slowly began to raise their rifles and answer their prayers.

One of the burning men staggered from the pit of fire until he was standing only a few feet away from Claude and Don, the silhouette of a half-man, ablaze from head to foot like some Tudor martyr. He was swaying, begging them to shoot him.

It was Don who did it. Picked up one of the many abandoned rifles at the side of the road and pulled the trigger until the screaming had stopped.

It was some time before they were able to speak.

'I thought you didn't,' Claude whispered hoarsely.

'I had to. It was the only way.'

'That is strange. That's exactly what I think, when I am doing my job,' Claude sighed.

They resumed trudging, in silence, towards Dunkirk.

* * *

No sleep for Ramsay that night. 'I can hardly keep my eyes open, days and nights roll into one and I have no idea whether it is sun or moon outside,' he scribbled on a note to his wife Mag, before yet another interruption forced him to push it back into his desk drawer. His notes were the only form of contact he'd had with his wife for days, hurriedly scribbled devotions that betrayed desperate tiredness and hinted at the still more desperate nature of the task. In return, she sent him gingerbread and fresh asparagus from their garden.

The onward rush of crisis never ceased. Every day, every hour, brought a new test of stamina and ingenuity. He had never given up hope, not up to now, in spite of deadlines and odds that no man could beat. But they had taken away his best ships, the newest destroyers, every one, and told him to get by on scraps. What could he do? He didn't control weather or tides or cloud bases, let alone the Luftwaffe; now he didn't even control much of a fleet. Not for the first time in his controversial career, he felt betrayed.

He paced up and down his room, his shoes clipping on the rough concrete floor and echoing back from the whitewashed walls, a mug of tea that had grown stone cold in his hand.

For three days the soldiers of the BEF had struggled off the beaches by any means they could, in rowing boats, on launches, on rafts, out to the larger ships standing offshore. It was slow, so desperately slow, with thousands of men standing for hours up to their chests in water while they queued for their turn and were strafed from above. Some even tried to swim, but many of them didn't make it, their breeches and boots filling with water and turning to bags of cement.

The bodies floating in the water only added to the problems, along with the abandoned greatcoats and lengths of rope that swirled back and forth in the surf. They fouled propellers and caught on the oars, slowing things down even further. In this place, even dying didn't help.

Ramsay knew that might be the fate of the entire BEF. There were hundreds of thousands of them, still waiting, only a few miles away, out there in the darkness—ah, so it was night. But on what day? He had no idea how long he had left: hours, another day or so? But however long it was, he knew he could never get them off the beaches like this.

It was time to gamble with his last card.

* * *

*(Thursday 30 May 1940. William L. Shirer, CBS.)*

*Good evening. This is Berlin.*

*The great battle of Flanders, as it will probably go down in history, is rapidly nearing its end, the German High Command stated flatly today.*

*The first few lines from the daily High Command communiqué give the story. I quote: 'The great battle in Flanders and the Artois approaches its end, with the destruction of the English and French armies still fighting there. Since yesterday, the British Expeditionary Force has been in a complete state of dissolution. Leaving behind its entire mass of war matériel, it is fleeing to the sea. By swimming, or on small boats, the enemy is attempting to reach the English ships lying off the shore on which our air force is falling with devastating effect. Over sixty ships have been hit by our bombs, sixteen transports and three warships sunk, and twenty-one merchant ships and ten warships damaged or set on fire.'*

*That's how the German war communiqué today described it.*

*Earlier in the day, a special communiqué of the German High Command told of a great air battle over Dunkirk in which the German air-armada strove to prevent the British from extricating what is left of their expeditionary force by taking them back to England in ships. This gigantic air attack, apparently on a scale never before seen even in this war, took place yesterday afternoon after German reconnaissance planes had discovered a great fleet of English transports approaching the Franco-Belgian coast . . .*

*We do not know how many German planes took part, but there were certainly hundreds of them in the air. The British, too, must have sent hundreds of planes into that battle because the Germans claim to have shot down sixty-eight British planes in this one engagement.*

* * *

Dunkirk. Daylight. A place of dead beasts and dead men, some long dead, their bodies unearthed from old graves by the shelling, others yet to find a grave of any kind. Pieces of people's lives. The bodies of more than thirty convent girls outside a burning church, laid out in a neat line, like a choir. Many troops drunk, sitting at the side of the road as though on holiday, waving bottles, waiting for whatever; others in shops, scrounging, scavenging, looting, shoving loaded fists into their packs; and on every side destroyed trucks, and tanks, and cars, and crying cats, and evil smoke, and tangled trolley lines that spread across the roadways like a gladiator's net, and more bodies that were not in neat lines, and roads blocked by wreckage and rubble, and every soldier's pace marked by the crunching of broken glass, stepping over abandoned rifles and the bodies of those who had dropped them. One British soldier sailed along on roller skates, another carried a parrot in a cage, which made Winston bark.

And fog. Dunkirk was covered in a thick mist that kept the Luftwaffe at bay and the seas calm. Small mercies.

A corporal offered them a sip from his water bottle. Don choked: it was filled with brandy.

'Come far?'

'Calais.'

'Jesus.'

'What do we do?'

'Go to the beaches. Best chance, mate.'

'I'd like a new uniform.'

'Plenty around. Just pick up whatever you want. Don't mind the stains.'

'You too, Claude?' Don asked.

He nodded. 'Why not? I think we are fighting on the same side now, English.'

'He's French?' the corporal enquired.

'Yes.'

'Most of the French are over that way.' He waved vaguely.

'We're together.'

'But he's French.'

'Nevertheless, we've come this far . . .'

'Look, you don't understand. You're English and it's'—the corporal's eyebrows arched and he winked slyly—'you know, first things first. On the boats.'

'You mean English only?'

'Froggies have got their own boats. Over there.' He waved vaguely once more.

'Aren't we on the same side?'

'Are we ever?'

'This time, I think.'

'Please yourself. Your funeral.' The corporal rebuttoned his breast pocket; something was hanging from it, glittering. Don remembered the looting.

'Anyway, I'm off,' the corporal announced. 'Best of British.'

So they searched out uniforms and struggled eastward, to the beaches.

Nothing could prepare them for the sense of violation that hit them as they crested the final dune. They sank to their knees, knowing that everything they had dared, and seen, and risked, had been worthless.

The beach was broad and endless, and infested with men. All about them were the abandoned remnants of the vehicles that had carried them there—cars, buses, tanks, bicycles, lorries, ambulances, and horse-drawn carts—stuck in the sand and smoking, while the sea as far as they could see was littered with the bones of boats that would never take them off.

It was all so desperate. A line of trucks had been driven far out into the shallow water, one behind the other, to form a jetty across which soldiers clambered and alongside which small boats nudged as they tried to pick them up. One steamer had deliberately rammed the beach, its engines still running to keep it straight, while soldiers used it as a bridge to the smaller boats that hovered at its stern. Improvisation. Hopelessness. Men swimming, disappearing; rafts being lashed together, then breaking apart; boats being rowed out to sea with nothing but scraps of wood and rifle butts. In the mist, a mile or so offshore, larger vessels waited, and waited, for this chaos to deliver up to them some form of catch.

'What's the point? Tell me, Claude: what's been the bloody point?' Don shouted in despair.

Whatever organization there was on the beaches seemed to be aimed at forming the men into long lines, swirling like sand snakes across the beach, doubling back on themselves time and again until the head of the snake had thrust itself into the sea. There it waited until it was almost submerged. But for what? It seemed so slow, so pointless. Even as they watched, two riderless horses charged along the beach, splitting the snakes to pieces. If two nervous horses could achieve that, what might a squadron of Me-109s do?

Don and Claude sat in the sand, their last remaining energies smothered by dejection.

Don felt shamed at being part of anything that could be reduced to the sort of rabble he saw in front of him, and along with the shame came a violent surge of anger at the lies he had been told about the war. But he also now knew that he, too, had told lies about this war. Memories began crowding in upon his thoughts—the girl on horseback, the young officer in the farmhouse, the blazing, pleading soldier—experiences that had ripped apart the stark moral certainties he had taken before the Tribunal. And it made him wonder if it had ever been truly a matter of conscience, or had his moralizing been little more than malice, intended for no higher purpose than to get back at his father? Don was a young man who had painted for himself a picture of life filled with vivid colours and decisive brush strokes, but it bore no resemblance to anything he had seen in the last few days. He gasped. Had it been only days?

Beside him, Claude slept, but Don couldn't settle. He lay struggling with his emotions, feeling insignificant, until the afternoon sun began to evaporate the mist that was hanging above the sea. As it did so, he saw the horizon filled with a mass of tiny black dots. They drew closer, and slowly began to take shape and meaning. Small boats of every description. Fishing smacks. Drifters. Trawlers. Scows. Cement-carriers. Cabin cruisers. Motor launches. Sailing barges. Cockleboats from Leigh-on-Sea and barges from the River Thames. Even grain-hoppers and mud-dredgers. An armada of little ships.

Don didn't know it, but he was watching Bertram Ramsay playing the last card in his pack.

* * *

Operation Dynamo was supposed to be a state secret. Some hope. Thousands of people were watching it from the clifftops above Dover, and many more had heard whispers. Word got around.

The loudest of those whispers came from the men who ran the Small Vessels Pool at the Ministry of Shipping. Ramsay had demanded small boats and it was their job to obtain them. Every yacht club and boatyard on the south and east coasts got a call. Did they have any self-propelled pleasure craft stout enough for the Channel? Anything from about twenty-odd feet in length? Ah, good, how many? Ready for sea? Then how soon could they be ready? Could they sail on four hours' notice?

They were interested in boats, not excuses. It didn't matter whether owners were away or fees had not been paid; if they floated, they were commandeered.

Individual owners were telephoned, almost apologetically, in the English way. 'It's for the boys in France,' they were told confidentially. 'They may need to borrow your boat. They might need to borrow you, too. No experience in the Channel? Doesn't matter, old chap. No charts, no compass? And the old girl needs a lick of paint? Not a problem. By the way, do you have any friends who enjoy a bit of a sail?'

So they gathered, at Tilbury, at Sheerness, and at Ramsgate. Hundreds of little boats. They came, some with polished brass, others dressed in mud and rust, with names like *Grace Darling*, *Girl Nancy* and *Auntie Gus*, manned by whoever was available. Some of the crews were professional seamen, fishermen, lifeboatmen, naval reserve, familiar with the ways of the sea, but many were civilians, simply weekend sailors who came expecting little more than a lap around the harbour. Many of them had no idea they were going off to war.

Ramsay's requirements were simple. He had ships with a large capacity that could wait offshore, and he had more than three hundred thousand troops waiting on the shore. What he needed was something in between, boats that were small enough to get to the beaches and fast enough to get off again in as short a time as possible, a sort of nautical taxi service. Because, up to now, it had been a complete shambles.

In Dunkirk it was every man for himself, and every boat. The rules of evacuation were made up as they went along, but often it seemed there were no rules at all. Many of the little boats were swamped, as too many men tried to board or the surf got too high. Some were damaged by collisions or shells or bombs, others simply broke down and were abandoned. In spite of the efforts of the beach marshals there was little order on the beaches; soldiers tried to clamber aboard weighed down with everything from dogs to crates of NAAFI cigarettes and other forms of looted booty, even a live goose.

It was never going to be pretty. All that Ramsay could do was to throw as many boats as possible at the long miles of beaches, and hope that they might make a difference. Because, at the present rate of evacuation, the BEF was doomed.

* * *

Viscount Gort sat in a hard, upright chair, looking out through billowing lace curtains to the sea beyond. On the broad stretch of beach between him and the sea he could see tens of thousands of men, and he knew that hundreds of thousands lay a little further to the west. But to Viscount Gort, this was the loneliest place on earth.

Gort knew he would be blamed for the defeat of the BEF. Arguably, he had given the British army its only chance of survival by defying the stupidity of those politicians and desk-warriors who had given the order to launch the drive south, but such delicacies were for historians. For today and for all who lived through it, he was the man who had led the BEF to its ruination. He was its commander, and it was upon his shoulders that the responsibility would fall. He didn't know yet how heavy that burden would be; he would have to wait and see. So that is what he did. He waited. In his headquarters in a seaside villa near La Panne, some eight miles east of Dunkirk.

With every passing hour they brought him more complaints, honed to razor sharpness on the desks in Whitehall. The latest was that the army wasn't where the boats were. He could scarcely believe the pettiness of it. He had marched them back from the jaws of hell, through conditions where most other armies would simply have surrendered, and now the navy couldn't get its bloody boats to them. Well, he was damned if he was going to ask his men to march one more mile. They'd done enough. The navy could come to them. It was nothing but sheer ineptitude on their part. That's what he'd told London, and in precisely those terms. Ineptitude.

So they demanded still more. Now it was that the boats should take a larger number of Frenchmen. More political nonsense. How many times had he told them that every Frenchman put in a boat meant one more Englishman left behind?

The French had the whole of France to creep back into, so why had they squashed into Dunkirk? He'd even had to offer the French an equal share of the eastern mole, and all they'd done was protest that the mole was a French mole and what business did he have in offering them anything that was already theirs. To hell with it. If they were so keen on their wretched mole, why hadn't they expended a little more effort in defending it?

God, it was such a mess. Everything he'd worked for in his life lay in ruins. He didn't know what would pain him more, other men's condemnation or their pity. As events battered him ever more mercilessly, he clung to the instincts that had made him what he was: a brave soldier. He was going to get his men back—or as many men as he could. And while that happened, he was going to show them that he, at least, had not deserted them. He was going to stay right where he was, do his duty as best he knew how, until they were all on board. Then he would be the last Englishman home.

* * *

The beach marshals in charge of the evacuation weren't having any of it. 'No French. French have their own ships,' Don and Claude were told, but no one could tell them where. It wasn't anyone's job to know. And it wasn't the job of the English to evacuate any but their own.

'And no bloody dogs.'

That decided it for them. There was an armada out there, but they wouldn't be allowed to use it, not together. They had to find their own boat.

Boats, boats, everywhere they looked there were

boats. Many of them were upturned and semi-submerged—and more with each passing hour as the wind came in from the sea and the surf began to rise. Some had been riddled with bullet holes or smashed in collisions, others simply capsized and abandoned. It became clear to them why so many had been abandoned when they tried righting one of the waterlogged boats. It couldn't be done. Claude's ankle was still weak, Don's arm useless, and it wasn't long before they were soaked and dejected from their repeated forays into the sea. Every time they tried, they were knocked down, either by the waves or by the boat they were trying to catch, and every time they hauled themselves back up the beach they used up a little more of their strength. Turning over a capsized boat, even a small one, was simply beyond them. But they had to continue trying; there was no other way.

It was the surf that came to their aid in the end, washing close to shore an upturned lifeboat that had probably done duty on an excursion ship. It was small enough for them to turn upright, although it took several attempts. Then they had to bale it out and drag their prize painfully to the shore. Claude had twisted his ankle once more with the effort, but tried to disguise the fact until he collapsed as soon as the lifeboat grounded on the sand.

Winston fussed around them, trying to lick their faces. They were both in desperate need of a rest. They lay panting on the beach, coughing up salt water.

'I preferred the wine,' Claude gasped, choking.

'We should get some help. I can't row, and anyway we've got nothing to row with,' Don spluttered in reply. 'The boat might take six or eight.'

'Ten, I hope,' they heard a voice reply.

They looked up to see a captain of a Guards unit standing over them.

'What do you mean?' Claude demanded, heaving himself up. He saw that there were other soldiers standing behind the captain, all still in full combat gear, expressionless, clean-shaven, and armed.

'I'm afraid I'm going to have to requisition this boat,' the captain explained.

'No, sir, you're not. This is our boat. Find your own.'

'I think we have,' the captain offered, dryly.

'You bloody can't!' Don snapped.

'You don't understand. I already have.'

'But why?'

'Why? Because I outrank you. Because you are French, and you'—he examined Don's borrowed uniform: catering corps—'are some sort of cook. We are Guards, and I'm afraid His Majesty needs us rather more than he needs you right now. So you can regard this as a direct order.'

'Gone deaf, sir,' Don muttered, shaking his head, 'must've got water in the ear. Anyway, you don't have any paddles.'

'Oh, but we do.'

The guardsmen behind the captain indicated the butts of their rifles, then slowly turned them so the muzzles were pointing directly at Don and Claude. Winston began growling.

'Seems I have all the arguments on my side,' the captain said. 'We are also ten, you are two, and I think the boat will just about manage ten out to the ships.' He looked at Don. 'We could try to squeeze one more Englishman in, if you'd like,' he added.

'Go to hell.'

'Dover first, I think.'

Don struggled to his feet, trying to stand as tall as he could and to hide the tremor in his legs and voice. 'You'll have to get rid of me first.'

'Don't be a fool.'

'Better than being a coward. Sir.'

'Then first, I think—just to show intent—we'll get rid of that awful yapping mongrel.' The captain had a revolver in his hand. He was pointing it straight at Winston, but suddenly Don was in his way.

'No! You have the bloody boat. I'll keep the dog.'

And that was the end of it. Soon the guards were gone, paddling slowly out to sea, the captain in the prow, beating time with the butt of his revolver.

'He's my dog, Englishman,' Claude muttered, as they watched the guards drift away. 'I kill you before I let you have him.'

'When we get back to Dover, Frenchie, there's a wonderful pub called the George and Dragon. I'll take you there for a pint. Then I'll play you at darts to see who keeps Winston.'

'Darts? What is darts?'

'A sort of flying game.'

'Then I accept the challenge, on condition that I don't have to drink any of your English beer.'

They continued to watch the backs of the guards as the boat disappeared across the water. Don and the Frenchman were too exhausted to move, even when the Luftwaffe returned, transforming the beaches once more into a cauldron of noise and disorder. The German pilots were back with their commander's encouragement still ringing in their ears, determined to make up for time lost to the mists. Out above the sea, a Heinkel dropped a string of bombs. They tumbled out of the bomb bay, then caught the air and began to swoop, one by one, almost gracefully, to the sea below, where they sent up great spouts of water. One spout of water seemed darker than the rest. It was the bomb that hit the guards' boat full on, and by the time the volcanic sea had finally settled, there was nothing to be seen but a few stray pieces of wreckage.

'Now I know there is a God,' Claude whispered.

# CHAPTER FOURTEEN

Churchill watched events unfolding with an extraordinary lack of grace. His fate and that of the war effort was being decided through happenings over which he had no control. He could do nothing but wait—and he was desperately unpractised in the art of patience.

So when he heard the news of Gort's decision to stay, his immediate response was to jump to his feet in exasperation. The effect, as Colville was later to admit, was frankly awe-inspiring, since he was in his bath at the time.

'Useless! Useless!' the old man roared, rising like Poseidon, casting the waters aside and flooding the floor. 'What bloody good will it do us if our most senior military commander sits on his rump waiting for the Boche to arrive? Isn't it enough that they've won the battle without handing them a trophy to drag back through the streets of Berlin?'

'I think he feels it is his duty.'

'This isn't the *Titanic*! He will come home!'

Colville, who was still uncertain about the wisdom of briefing a Prime Minister in the bath, held out a towel and a loaf of comfort. 'But Ramsay's worked miracles. The numbers he's getting back are rising every day.'

Churchill scrabbled around under his armpit. 'But how many of them are French, Jock?'

As they both knew, no more than a few thousand Frenchmen had been brought back, a trickle compared to the English stream.

'Why does it matter so?' Colville pressed.

'Where were you this afternoon when their Prime Minister telephoned to suggest that the British were running back home and leaving his men to carry the can? At lunch, I suppose. And Monsieur Reynaud is a brave man, so much better than those terrible defeatists who surround him.'

'If you remember, Prime Minister, you sent me to get a fresh supply of your cigars from St James's. I didn't have time for lunch.'

Churchill cast aside both towel and complaint. 'Jock, you must understand, it matters so very much that we are not seen to be fighting just for England. France will fall soon, I fear—sooner, if they feel we are betraying them—and then we shall be alone. But we cannot win this war on our own, Jock. So even after France falls, we must hope that it will rise up again, along with all the other oppressed nations of Europe, until Hitler and his hordes have been swept into hell. We're not fighting for ourselves in this war but for the whole of humanity. If we lose, it will be the end of everything—not just of England but of civilization, of history itself. That is why we must go on to the end, no matter what it takes, and never give in. Never, never, never!'

'So,' Colville began, anxious as ever to bring the old man's romanticism to its point, 'you want more Frenchmen lifted from the beaches.'

But the emotion had taken him, carrying him beyond the point of caution. 'No, not just more. I want an equal number. From now on we must march arm-in-arm with any man who wishes to continue the fight.' He clasped his hands together in front of him. 'One Englishman, one Frenchman. Together. *Bras-dessus, bras-dessous!*'

It was a ridiculous suggestion. They might have only another day at most for the evacuation. Anyway, it would all be over by the time new instructions were sent, so Colville decided not to argue. The bathwater was seeping through the welts of his shoes, and in the morning the old man would be more modestly dressed and, hopefully, more moderately inclined. His sudden passion for the French was confusing—after all, this was the man who had sent squadrons of phantom fighters to their aid and who had danced a jig for joy when the panzers turned away from Dunkirk and towards Paris.

Colville made a mental note. No more briefings in the bath. Next time he would wait for the water—and the old man's passions—to cool.

But, as he was to discover, Churchill meant almost every word.

* * *

Henry Chichester had become a welcome figure around the port of Dover in recent days. In a town overflowing with uniforms of every colour and condition, the simplicity of his clerical collar stood out. Dover heaved with people, and with pain, and he wandered slowly though it all, giving comfort where he could. As they stumbled from their ships or passed him on stretchers, gaunt-eyed men reached out to touch him and looked to him for leadership; they couldn't know that Henry Chichester was so riddled with doubt that he no longer knew in which direction he was heading.

A cancer began to spread through the port. Those who were about to leave for Dunkirk saw the condition of those who were returning, and despaired. Many had been pulled not just from the beaches but from burning wrecks or oil-choked waters. With every day of the ordeal in and around Dunkirk, the conditions had grown worse and the chances of any ship coming back unscathed grown smaller. There had been another great raid from the air—the Luftwaffe claimed thirty-one British ships sunk in a single day. Many others had only just made it back to port, listing, sinking. Some returned with gaping holes in their sides stuffed with mattresses, others with superstructures almost burnt to the deck, but an ever larger number were not coming back at all.

Mutiny was not a term that the port authorities chose to use, but it was becoming noticeable that there was a growing reluctance amongst many civilian crews to sail back towards the inferno. Engines began mysteriously to break down, vessels began to run aground, filters became blocked, valves somehow twisted, bodies grew sick. Even lifeboatmen who had risked their lives to save others on countless occasions began to draw back; facing death was one thing, facing Dunkirk entirely another.

Ramsay had no time to parley or to prevaricate. He sent armed guards and naval crews aboard to stiffen resolve. His time was running out. The ships had to sail, even at the point of a line of bayonets.

On all sides, Henry Chichester's presence was welcomed: by those sailors struck feeble by fear, and by officers who hoped that his words would achieve what a brandished revolver might not. But it was getting more difficult.

An Isle of Man packet steamer wasn't sailing. Trouble on board. Angry voices drifting across the dock; a confrontation on the gangway between crewmen trying to clamber down and a harassed young naval sub-lieutenant standing in their way, backed by a squad of rifles. He tried to reason, but the beaches had no reason, so he tried to threaten, but they all said they would rather die in England than die over there.

Henry Chichester stood at the bottom of the gangway and raised his voice. 'Hear, O Israel, ye approach this day unto battle against your enemies: let not your hearts faint, fear not, and do not tremble, neither be ye terrified because of them; for the Lord your God *is* he that goeth with you, to fight for you against your enemies, to save you.'

They all looked towards him. It was a grime-smeared young stoker who found his voice first.

'What good is God?' he demanded angrily. 'He ain't coming with us. And neither are you.'

It wasn't the first time his faith had been questioned, but he no longer had any glib answers.

What good is God? Henry Chichester no longer knew. He couldn't answer for the Almighty any longer, but only for one man.

'I shall come with you,' he replied, and began to force his path up the gangway.

'Sir, you can't,' the young officer objected, uncertain. 'Do you know how to sail?'

'I can set an anchor and coil a rope as well as any man,' he replied. 'Anyway, have you got a better way of getting this ship to sail?'

The officer was still struggling to find an answer as Henry Chichester pushed his way past.

* * *

They tried to escape from the beach again, this time in the company of others. One of them was the corporal they had encountered in Dunkirk. He seemed to have fattened up; he was bulging: his pockets, his back pack, even the pack intended for his gas mask. When Don asked what he was carrying, he got nothing but another crafty wink in reply.

Together they found a boat, the sort of thing that might be used for an occasional hour on the Serpentine. This time the corporal made no objection as Claude was helped on board—Winston, too, standing in the prow like a mascot. They began paddling, with pieces of timber scavenged from the beach, out towards the boats a mile or so offshore.

They had gone no further than a couple of hundred yards when the skies opened above them and another torrent of death began to fall. The Luftwaffe was back. There was more artillery today, too; the Germans and their guns were pushing closer, their aim growing more accurate. As the bombs and bullets turned the sea to a maelstrom, they dug in their paddles and prayed they were too tiny a morsel for the great Luftwaffe, but a Messerschmitt caught them with a blast across the middle that cut their small craft clean in two.

They were thrown into the water. Claude reached out for Don—his ankle was less of a problem in the water—and helped him cling to a fragment of the boat that was still floating. Nearby the corporal was desperately unloading handfuls of jewellery and watches from his pockets onto a door that someone had tried to use as a raft, but the weight of his packs was dragging him down. He began to struggle with the packs, trying to slip them off, but the sea was winning. Then there was nothing but a fist, still clenched around some trinket, slipping beneath the water. That was the last they saw of him.

With Winston leading the way, they swam slowly and with great difficulty back to the shore. Their uniforms and boots were like anchors, pulling them back. They had been on the beaches for almost forty-eight hours. They had got nowhere.

* * *

As he climbed from his car, Churchill was startled to hear the sound of small-arms fire coming from behind the Palace, but Lascelles, who was waiting to meet him, showed no sign of alarm—although there was nothing unusual in that, Churchill thought. Lascelles was an earthworm. Slice him in two and he would simply carry on wriggling.

He found the King on his lawn. His wife was beside him in a floral print dress that was blowing gently in the breeze, and in her outstretched hand she was holding a revolver. It was aimed at a target some thirty paces away, pinned to which was a large photograph of Hitler. The gun barked. The Fuehrer continued to stare back at her.

'Ah, Winston!' the King greeted. 'I'm teaching the Queen to shoot. Never know—just in case.'

'I hope it will not come to that, sir,' Churchill offered, bowing.

'Yes, but war's a f-funny old business.' He lit a cigarette and led his Prime Minister a little distance away from the impromptu firing range. 'I believe the evacuation is almost over.'

Churchill nodded.

'Remarkable how long we've managed to stretch it.'

'There are still many troops trapped inside the pocket, sir, French as well as British. But we shall do our best.'

'And then what? After the evacuation?'

'In France—capitulation, I fear.'

'Sad. Great country but . . . there seems to be something rotten right at their core. Perhaps it's their habit of changing their system of government—king, emperor, republic, backwards and forwards. Tried them all many times and still don't seem happy. So try a Fuehrer this time and see if it works any better, eh?'

Churchill nodded. He had never rated the King's political acumen very highly, but he seemed to have a point that might even be profound.

'And here—what do you think will happen here,

Winston?'

'That's why I have asked to see you, sir. After the evacuation we shall have to consider the possibility of invasion.'

'Papers are full of it. Can't hide from such things.' Another explosion punctuated their walk. 'Squeeze gently!' the King called across to his Queen. 'Like a puppy's ear.'

'Sir, a few days ago we exchanged words about the position of you and your family. I may have appeared a little abrupt.'

'I prefer plain speaking, Winston. You know, Mr Chamberlain was always so courteous. Talked to me at great length and never told me a thing.'

'I shall always try to deal with you plainly, sir. The other day I said you must stay.'

'Emphatic about it, you were.'

'But there are other powerful voices who think differently. You have seen the paper put forward by the Foreign Office?'

'That the Queen and I should be moved away to some far-flung corner of the island or even sent abroad with all the royal baubles? Of course I have. Discussed it with Halifax.'

Churchill knew it; that was the real reason why he'd come. He couldn't fight on every front, not against the King as well as Halifax and Hitler. He'd struggled with every grain of resolution he possessed to do what he thought was right, but it wasn't enough; he had to give a little, build bridges, stop railing against the entire world. There were times when he had to bend, or risk being broken. And in the matter of the King, it was more important to ensure that the Monarch kept on fighting than to go down arguing about what part of the globe he should fight from. The King against him in combination with Halifax was altogether too powerful. Compromise. Why did he find it so difficult? Nevertheless . . .

'The time may be drawing closer, sir, when we should think about such options.'

'But the other day you said . . .'

'Yes, sir. But the situation has changed and grown ever more perilous. It will be our turn next to face the full force of the Nazi onslaught, and who can say how events will proceed? We must remain confident, determined—but we cannot allow you to fall into the hands of Hitler, not like King Leopold. Of all the disasters that chase me through my dreams, that is the worst. You and your family would disappear, your brother brought back. There would be nothing left to fight for, no flag, no great emblem around which we could rally.'

George exhaled a steady stream of blue smoke. 'You needn't worry, Winston. That will not happen.'

'I, too, have confidence that we shall resist the invasion, but . . .'

The King dropped the stub of his cigarette on the path they were following and ground it out with his toe. 'No, you don't understand. I have discussed it with the Queen. We are agreed. We will not be taken by Hitler. Not alive. That's why we are p-polishing up our skills.' He took a new cigarette from his silver case. 'But neither will we flee. If I run, why should any man stand and fight? As you put it, there would be no flag around which we could rally. Why, it would leave us like France. And we are not like France! No, while there are men willing to defend this realm, I and my family will be staying with them. Right here.' The cigarette began to glow; he drew the new nicotine down deep. 'There—I seem to have made a speech.'

Churchill's thoughts were flooded with admiration at this man—a man whom he had underestimated. There was a simplicity and lack of sophistry in him that was so unlike Halifax. Churchill was glad he had come. He was no longer fighting the war entirely on his own.

Suddenly, another explosion: this time the Fuehrer jumped and fell to pieces. 'Bravo, my dear! A couple more like you and we'll have the whole German army on the run!'

George turned once more to his Prime Minister. 'So we're not going, and neither are the baubles. Let's put them away somewhere safe. Bury them in caves and cellars, wherever you think best. But none must go. I want everyone to understand. We're going to beat them!'

* * *

The *Maid of Manx* was a nautical sheep. She had been built, like so many others, to spend her life meandering in dreary style around the seas of Europe. Her life, like that of any sheep, was intended to be unremarkable and her death to go unmarked. She was a passenger vessel, not a sleek warrior, and she had no chance of getting close to the Dunkirk shore. So she had to sit, and wait, for her human cargo to be ferried to her by the smaller boats. Like all sheep, the *Maid* depended for her survival on being part of a larger flock, hoping that the wolves that snarled and circled would select some other victim, but while she sat, and waited, she made an excellent target.

The wolves pounced while she was still several miles out. Henry Chichester stood in the prow, trying to pretend he had no fear, while the deck hands were unanimous that they weren't going to make it. He felt guilty: he was the reason why they were here, he'd shamed them into coming. And beside the guilt he felt fear—not of dying, he'd faced that many times in the last war, but of dying alone. Without family, and without faith. He knew why he'd come on board. It was his way of challenging God to keep him safe, to prove beyond further doubt that the whole of Henry Chichester's life hadn't been an exercise in futility. He had placed himself in the hands of the Almighty. *Be strong and courageous, be not afraid nor dismayed for the king of Assyria, nor for all the multitude that is with him, for there be more with us than with him. With him is an arm of flesh, but with us is the Lord our God to help us, and to fight our battles . . .*

But the multitude of the King of Assyria, in the grey tunics of the German Wehrmacht, was moving closer. The defensive perimeter around Dunkirk was growing narrower, the guns drawing closer, and their fire becoming more destructive. The Luftwaffe, too, had a point to make. It had promised the Fuehrer that the British presence in Dunkirk would be eliminated within days. They had already held out for a week.

The savagery of the attack was greater than anything the *Maid of Manx* had endured in earlier days. The wolves hadn't selected her as a special target, they were sinking their teeth into every vessel afloat, from destroyer to the least significant dinghy. The *Maid* had already had much of her metal bent by the time she got to her berth, but she made it through and was waiting offshore when the serious stuff struck—bombs or artillery shells, it was impossible to tell which in the mayhem of explosions and water spouts. As the vicar cowered, the bridge disappeared in a tangle of blackened metal and, moments later, a hole appeared aft through which a huge column of fire and steam began erupting. The boiler room had gone. A tin helmet, turned red like a poker in the heat, rolled crazily along the deck on its rim. There was no sign of the deck hands who moments before had been standing nearby. Then the *Maid* broke her back and the Reverend Chichester was hurled into the sea.

*    *    *

*(Sunday 2 June 1940. William L. Shirer, CBS.)*

*This is Berlin.*

*Those British Tommies at Dunkirk are still fighting against the advancing German steamroller like bulldogs.*

*The German High Command is our authority for this in its daily communiqué which has just been given out in Berlin. Here is its account of yesterday's operations:*

*'In hard fighting, the strip of coast on both sides of Dunkirk, which yesterday was also stubbornly defended by the British, was further narrowed. Nieuwpoort and the coast to the north-east are in German hands, Adinkerke and Ghyvelde, six and a quarter miles east of Dunkirk, have been taken.' Six and a quarter miles. That's getting very close.*

*But again, in the air, the great German air-armada continued all day yesterday, the communiqué declares, to harass the British in their attempts to evacuate the British Expeditionary Force. It makes grim reading.*

*'Altogether, four warships and eleven transports with a total tonnage of fifty-four thousand tons were sunk by our bombers. Fourteen warships, including two cruisers, two light cruisers, an anti-aircraft cruiser, six destroyers and two torpedo boats, as well as thirty-eight transports with a total tonnage of one hundred and sixty thousand, were damaged by bombs. Numberless small boats, tugs, rafts were capsized and troop concentrations along the beach successfully attacked with bombs . . .'*

*In three weeks, Hitler's steamroller army has overrun Holland, Belgium and northern France, pushed past the western extension of the Maginot Line on a front two hundred miles wide, and liquidated three of France's best armies and most of the British Expeditionary Corps.*

*How do Germans at home feel about the tremendous victory? As a whole, the German people, I think you can say, are feeling pretty elated. For one thing, they believe they cannot now lose the war—hence the nightmare of another defeat, which their leaders have told them would be worse than Versailles, is removed. That makes them feel good.*

*They also believe that the decisive battle has been won and that the war will certainly be over by the end of the summer. That also makes them feel good. Many Germans I've talked to have an idea that a sort of united Europe—under German leadership, to be sure—will come out of the war.*

*And that will be a good thing. They say it will ensure a long period of peace and probably of prosperity.*

*  *  *

Ramsay watched as yet another desperate and listing vessel dragged herself back between the breakwaters at Dover and knew that his task was almost over. Daylight had become death for Operation Dynamo. There was no point in sending over more ships while the sun was up, for the balance between those saved from the beaches and those sacrificed in the effort was tilting too heavily against them. The German guns had come too close.

There was trouble even in the harbour below—too many crew members going sick or AWOL, anything but going back to that sink of destruction. He could no longer blame them. To order them back during daylight would break the heart of an operation that, in spite of all its difficulties, had been carved from English oak. Yet night in June lasted no more than a handful of hours. His timetable had been cut to fragments. There had to come a point where Dynamo was brought to its close, and that point was almost upon them.

During the morning he had signalled his fleet. One last effort. 'The final evacuation is staged for tonight,' he told them 'and the nation looks to the navy to see this through.' Throughout Dover and the other ports involved, his signal sent a shiver of pride, and also of profound fear.

One last effort.

They would all go at once, descend *en masse*,

take off the remaining men and be back home by morning before Jerry had even noticed. That's what they told themselves. Almost every man in Dover had made plans to spend the next day drinking himself to oblivion. Meanwhile, they waited.

But for Ramsay there was no rest. If daylight meant death for some, it might provide a lifeline for the hundreds of wounded in Dunkirk. They had been left behind rather than take up space that could be filled by fighting men, but now their chance had come: to be lifted off on hospital ships in daylight so broad there could be no opportunity for confusion or mistake.

Ramsay was a cautious man; he took no chances. He arranged for a signal to be sent in clear, from Dunkirk, one that the Germans would be certain to overhear. 'Wounded situation acute. Hospital ship should enter during the day. Geneva Convention will be honourably observed. It is felt that the enemy will refrain from attack.'

The signal was a British guarantee that they would not use the hospital boats to take off anyone other than seriously wounded, and an expression of hope that the Germans would reciprocate. There was only one way to find out if they would.

Early that afternoon, a hospital ship set out from Dover. Painted brilliant white, with a huge and unmistakable red cross upon it. Visibility was excellent. Long before it arrived in Dunkirk, a dozen German planes appeared above it, bombing and machine-gunning the unarmed ship until it was forced back to port.

Yet there remained the possibility that the attack had been a mistake, that the Germans might reassess, might reconsider. The fate of the desperately wounded depended on it. So Ramsay sent another hospital ship, the *Paris*. He watched from his balcony, sipping tea, as she was also attacked. Out of control, she fired distress rockets, which attracted the attentions of still more Luftwaffe planes. Nurses and medical orderlies were machine-gunned even as they clambered into lifeboats. Then the *Paris* keeled over and joined the other wrecks Ramsay had left at the bottom of the Channel. The wounded wouldn't make it, and he knew there would be many more of them before the night was over.

He wasn't an emotionally extravagant man, driven to wild gestures. He withdrew inside his warren to the desk from which he would command the rest of the operation. He lit a candle for the men who had yet to die for Dynamo and placed it in his saucer. It was a twelve-hour candle. It would be more than enough.

* * *

They were the most terrible hours that anyone had spent on the beaches. They were hours in which there was no navy, no help, and when hope itself seemed to have died. The sands and sea were strewn with wreckage, and those that were left behind began to feel they were of no more significance than the debris in thc surf. The previous day there had been the fleet, now there was nothing but rumour, and ill feeling.

Henry Chichester had only narrowly survived his ordeal and he was still confused as he blundered along the beach, unable either to offer help or to accept it from those who offered it to him. He stumbled upon French troops getting drunk and cursing every Englishman, while English troops returned the spite in full measure, and raced motorcycles along the beach or waged large sums of money on which of the beachfront properties would next be hit by a German shell. Some hid their faces in fear, while others came to Chichester as a man in a clerical collar and asked for courage. But to all this, he was oblivious, shaking his head in confusion, which they took to be rejection. In their anger they sneered, mocked him, called him a coward.

It was Sunday. A day when men prayed for their souls. They begged him to help them but he could do nothing and hid away in the dunes, so they fell back on their own resources. They built an altar on the beach from discarded ammunition boxes and put a rough wooden cross upon it. Two small candles were placed in jam jars on either side. A captain began to lead them in prayers; he did his best but it was a desultory affair—his grasp was uncertain and his lack of inspiration echoed through the ranks in front of him. Yet they were determined. They persevered, right up to the time that a flight of Me-109s swept along the beach and forced them to run for cover.

When the planes had gone, the men began to drift back to their makeshift altar. They had nowhere else to go, and their need was greater than their fear.

They tried a hymn, but the words foundered after the first verse and faded on the afternoon breeze. And then the Messerschmitts returned.

The men scattered like withered leaves in

winter.

The attack also blew away the bewilderment and shock that had cluttered up Henry Chichester's mind. He woke from his confusion to find himself looking out at men in despair. They were in pain, they needed his help, and he knew about pain. He couldn't turn his back on them. The German pilots were turning for a third run, and as they approached once again he stepped out into their path and doggedly began to rebuild the altar, no hurry, like a cricket player waiting for the wicket to dry. Bullets spattered past him on either side, but he didn't flinch. He piled the ammunition boxes back on top of each other and tenderly replaced the cross. Another man crept forward and retrieved the candles from the sand. As the growl of engines died into the distance, the Reverend Chichester found his voice carrying far across the beach.

'Lord, make us warriors for Thy peace. Give us courage in the face of danger and compassion in victory, so that we may build a better world.'

Victory? It was about as likely as virgin birth but it was a welcome thought. A few hesitant souls began to return.

'Sin is around us and with us, but all shall be well,' he declared. 'And all shall be well and all manner of things shall be well.' Others began to join in.

'Our Father, which art in heaven . . .'

Henry Chichester had no Bible, no book of prayer to guide him, nothing but a crude altar and his—he might have said his faith, but that he no longer had. He had nothing but himself.

'Give us this day our daily bread, O Lord. For we know that the bread we shall taste tomorrow, whether it be back home with our loved ones, or with you, shall be the sweetest of our lives.'

The words began to stir those around him. Curiosity caught them—who was this man who had his own version of the Lord's Prayer?

'Give us the strength to deal with our sins, as we ask for the strength to deal with the sins of others.'

'Amen,' one of his new congregation muttered loudly, one eye on the sky, grateful that he wasn't being asked to struggle with the concept of forgiving other people's trespasses while he was still chewing on the exhaust fumes of a Messerschmitt.

'And lead us not into a time of trial—for we are not as strong as you—but deliver us from the grip of evil and those who carry evil in their souls.'

The prayer had begun to carry new meaning for Henry Chichester. It wasn't what he'd been taught, but for the first time he was expressing it rather than repeating it, digging deep for something inside rather than reading off a page. If the words were of any importance, they had to be relevant here, in the midst of carnage, and not just during the rituals of his safe, comfortable pulpit.

'For thine is the kingdom, the power and the glory, for ever and ever. Amen.'

A chorus of amens rose from those around him. They looked towards him, expecting more.

'Can we take Communion?' one of them asked.

'But how can we? I don't have . . .' He stopped himself and the flow of excuses he was about to pour upon their hopes. 'Wine, does anyone have some wine?'

'Cognac, father? Will that do?' A soldier thrust his water bottle forward.

'I think the Lord might understand—rather better than your sergeant major.'

'But, vicar, my sergeant major thinks he is the Lord.'

'The Lord is in us all, even a sergeant major. Even in you, Private. So what about bread, then? Biscuits? I'd settle for a couple of bars of chocolate, even. Yes, better still, chocolate. And while we let it melt, let its sweetness remind us of why we're here. For God, and for our families back home.'

It wasn't intended, and it wasn't taken, as light-heartedness. They understood what he was up to, trying to banish their dread, to open up the mysteries of the ceremony so that they could come to it with open hearts and not simply in fear. They didn't need the ritual, and suddenly Henry Chichester realized he didn't need it, either. As he blessed the cognac and a few bars of chocolate, more men began to gather round and kneel in the sand, strangers who didn't know him but knew only his words. As they showed their belief in him, Henry Chichester began to discover a new faith in himself.

None of them moved away, even after he had finished with Communion. There had to be some final word before they parted. He suggested a hymn. So they sang 'Jerusalem', drenched with the imagery of England. Those who didn't know the words sang the tune. Deep, proud male voices raised in celebration of their homeland across the sea.

No one expected them to be able to carry the hymn for the second verse, but as the melody faded into the sound of the rolling surf, another voice—a robust, distinctive tenor—picked it up.

'Bring me my bow of burning gold! Bring me my arrows of desire! Bring me my spear! O clouds, unfold! Bring me my chariot of fire!'

For a moment, Chichester was perplexed. He knew that voice, though it had grown stronger and more precise since the last time he had heard it.

'I will not cease from mental fight, Nor shall my sword sleep in my hand . . .'

The Reverend Chichester's own fine baritone wrapped itself around the other and the two voices reached out across the sand. It would be remembered by many men who were present as the moment when, for just a few beats, the madness stood aside and they thought of something other than defeat.

'Till we have built Jerusalem,' they sang, 'In England's green and pleasant land.'

As they finished, Claude turned to Don from the top of their nearby dune. 'So, that is your father. You know, it would be helpful if he walked on water, too.'

*        *        *

The room was dark. He was at the open window, looking out across Horse Guards with only the glowing tip of his cigar to disturb the blackout.

'The last night, Jock. Ramsay says the sailors can't take any more. Beyond all human endurance.'

'They've been working without rest for days. I don't know how they've handled it.'

'With belief that what they are doing is right. There is no other way. Otherwise war is nothing but barbarism.'

'The Germans raided Paris today for the first time.'

'And the panzers will not be far behind. You know, I got down on my knees to pray that their eyes would turn away from Dunkirk.'

'I've never imagined you as a pillar of the church.'

'No, but after this I might agree to become a flying buttress.'

He brooded for a while, listening to the sounds of a city at sleep.

'What happened,' he asked, 'in Paris?'

'The French were taken by surprise. Their pilots were all at lunch. Only four machines even got off the ground. Four out of forty.'

'We can no longer rely on the French. Soon we shall be on our own.'

'Thank heavens we've got so many of our soldiers back. And thank God for our poor sailors.'

'Tonight, we are all sailors.'

* * *

Love like rotting fruit. Sweetness that springs from a stone.

Don knew his father was a different man. At first he hadn't wanted to believe it, to recognize the character who had so captured the imaginations of the men on the beach and shaken the cobwebs from their souls, but in the end he'd been no more able to deny it than had his father. Henry Chichester was reborn in that hour upon the sands, and the scars of his previous life fell from him like rags.

And Henry knew his son had changed, too. He

could see it in the eyes—eyes that were so much like Jennie's.

For the first time that either of them could remember, Don and his father were able to look back on their lives without feeling like Orpheus and ruining everything. Through the rest of the evening and into the night, they talked—mostly about Jennie. Don hadn't realized, he'd lost track of days and dates, but it was his birthday. They had twenty years to make up, and Henry began at the very beginning, with stories of Jennie. How they had first met, when Jennie was a nurse who had healed so many of his wounds after he'd come back from France. Why he had been so attracted to her: the passion and stubborn intensity that she had passed on to Don, and the freckled nose. How they had both wanted to build something new and fresh in a world devastated by war, and how deeply he had come to love her in the two short years they had together.

Jennie had kept them apart all these years; now, as the colours of the evening slipped beneath the horizon, her memory brought the two people she had both lived and died for back together.

The armada returned that night. In spite of everything, the boats came back. Destroyers, minesweepers, drifters, skoots and many more, searching for more survivors. All four of them made it onto a tugboat: Henry, Don, Claude and Winston. It seemed almost insultingly simple after the struggles of the previous days; there were many fewer to take off now, so many others had already gone. They clambered out along one of the provost jetties built from trucks and gratings and onto a tug that already held a hundred others.

It was not to be a night of great sacrifice in numbers of ships, not in comparison with earlier times. The Germans still fired their guns and sent over their planes, but it was a quarter-moon and the enemy's instinct to kill lost its way in the darkness. There were still mines, of course, and fear of torpedoes, but, for most, the night went well.

They left behind them a harbour filled with dead ships and dead men. As Henry and Don looked back they could see the cruelly twisted ruins of Dunkirk standing out against the flames that were destroying it, while the oil-covered water glittered like tinsel.

Ahead of them lay England, although they could see none of it—no lights, no features, nothing but black night through which they would have to find their way home, and that was no easy task, for the escape routes through the shallows off Dunkirk and the minefields that surrounded them were narrow and busy with a confusion of other ships.

They never saw the armed patrol boat in the sea-lane ahead of them. Unfortunate, of course, nobody's fault, the sort of thing that happens when you play blind man's bluff. They hit it amidships, holing the engine room, and it heeled over and began to sink immediately. The boat was on submarine patrol, hopefully with a relatively small crew, and the skipper of the tug circled the spot in the hope of picking up survivors.

What the skipper could not know was that the patrol boat was laden with depth charges. They were not switched to 'safe' but set for use. The result was that, when the drowning vessel reached the appointed depth, it exploded with terrible effect.

The circling tug was lifted clean out of the water, thrown up on a mushroom of raging angry water, its screws thrashing helplessly in the air. It came down in a position from which there was no chance of recovering.

Don had time only for a glance, an arm outstretched in concern, and in farewell.

Other ships gathered to sift through the pieces, searching for those who had survived. They found a spaniel, barking for attention in the choppy water. When they hauled him in they discovered a rope leading from his collar, and the end of the rope was bound round Claude's wrist. He was still breathing.

Not everybody died that night.

## CHAPTER FIFTEEN

The sharp rapping at the front door drew Channon from his breakfast. He was still in his dressing gown, and irritated. Breakfast was almost the only part of his day that offered him any sort of rest—even sleep was a struggle nowadays—and eggs tasted terrible cold.

It was the American ambassador. He was working his mouth around a wad of gum. Channon mumbled in insincere greeting. When all was said and done, he didn't much care for the uncouth Kennedy, and an Englishman—even of the adoptive variety like Channon—had the right to decide with whom he was going to share his breakfast. He was debating with himself whether he would have to invite the man in when Kennedy's impatience got the better of him.

'I don't understand it, Chips. Nobody returns my calls, my meetings get cancelled. Churchill runs away like a rabbit. Halifax hides. Even Rab cancels our breakfast this morning at the last minute. What the hell's wrong with this goddamned country?'

'Times are a little difficult, Joe,' Channon replied edgily, brushing a crumb of toast from his silk lapel.

'It's more than that. I feel everyone drawing back, like I'm carrying a big bad smell around with me. You smell anything, Chips?'

He could detect nothing but his dying breakfast. 'We have just unearthed a spy in the middle of your code room, Joe,' he suggested wearily. 'I suspect it's simply that people are being a little . . . cautious.'

'Over breakfast?'

'Rab has had a difficult couple of days. You've seen the editorials.'

'It's been a long weekend,' the ambassador muttered. He'd been to Beaverbrook's. 'I'm a bit behind.'

'There's a campaign going on in the press. Like rabid foxes. Attacking all the appeasers: Rab, Neville Chamberlain, Halifax. They're calling them the Guilty Men. Saying they are responsible for every sin in Christendom, from the surrender of Belgium to the shortage of good claret. Everything's *their* fault, apparently. And the ordinary people are so dull, so easily led. They've begun bombarding them with letters. Nasty, brutal outpourings of malice, bundles of the stuff. Arriving every morning. That's probably why Rab had to cry off, he has to open them all himself, poor fellow.'

'Sticks and stones,' Kennedy muttered dismissively, poking at his gum.

'Some people are even trying to pretend that Dunkirk has been an achievement. And in some ways I suppose it has. We hoped to bring thirty, maybe forty thousand back. If you count all the French, we got off nearly three hundred and fifty thousand.'

'Christ, you ought to be getting good at it; you've had enough practice. Norway, Belgium, France. Evacuation's turning into a major British industry.'

Kennedy had a point. He also had a condescending tone that was making Channon begin to feel intensely English.

'Chips, Dunkirk was a disaster, you know that.'

'Could have been worse.'

'Worse? How? You lost everything. Half a fleet, more than nine hundred planes, two and a half thousand guns—and every single one of your vehicles. Right now the BEF couldn't rustle up much more than a pedal cycle. And for what? All in exchange for bringing home an army that's been beaten to crap.'

'Yes, Joe,' Channon responded tartly, 'but you do insist on telling people so.'

'A turkey can't pretend it's a parrot just because it's Christmas,' Kennedy protested, extracting his gum and fixing it to the back of Channon's railings.

'Nevertheless, we still demand a say in deciding at which end we're going to be stuffed!'

'Chips, face it. The jig's up.'

'You may be right. But the jig—as you put it—isn't up until someone finds a way of persuading our Mr Churchill.'

*     *     *

Churchill was preparing a speech when he looked up to find her standing by the door. Inspector Thompson was at her shoulder, dwarfing Ruth Mueller, for she seemed to have shrunk. The eyes were set in dark saucers, her skin stretched across the high cheekbones. One of her lips had been recently split and he could see a horrible bruise on her cheek. Her whole body seemed to be vibrating, like a mirage on a heat-soaked day.

But she was no mirage. She began talking in a low voice that hissed like an adder, words of German that Churchill could not understand but which burnt with acid.

He rose from his chair. 'Your words are wasted, Frau Mueller. I do not understand German, neither do I propose to learn it. Ever.'

Her eyes flared in defiance.

As Churchill came from behind his desk, he realized it hadn't been his imagination; she was trembling. 'What has happened to you?'

'I have been enjoying your hospitality. In one of your concentration camps.'

'Frau Mueller, we don't have such things.'

'Really? Then what would you call a camp surrounded by barbed wire, which you then fill with people who have been arrested without charge and with no trial?'

'I don't—'

'If they were in Germany you would call them concentration camps. So why do you shrink from calling them that simply because they are here in England?'

'There must have been some mistake.'

'That's what I kept telling your Gestapo—I beg your pardon—your brave British policemen.'

Her quiet malice was far more cutting than the wild temper he remembered.

'Perhaps you would like to explain what has happened,' he offered, showing her to a chair. She perched on the edge of the seat, as if she were uncomfortable in his presence.

'In Germany, Mr Churchill, they are called the Nuremberg Laws. You call them Emergency Powers. It amounts to the same thing. Except it took Hitler years to introduce them and you did it inside two weeks.'

Churchill was taken aback. 'But that is for enemy aliens, to be put where they can pose no threat.'

'And I am an enemy alien. You said you wanted to know your enemy, Mr Churchill. And here I am. You have conquered me. Congratulations.'

He looked at her uniform—the same threadbare suit, except more crumpled than ever. One of the seams on the shoulder had begun to unravel. 'What has happened to you?'

'They took me, like the Gestapo tried to do. While I was eating. No explanation. Threw me into the back of a car and straight into a prison cell. Then it was a prison train and a prison boat to the Isle of Man. Hundreds of us; all the children, too. Put out of the way, where we won't disturb your fine English wives while they sip tea and pass around the sandwiches.'

'But there are exemptions—why didn't you telephone? Tell them that you knew me? I don't understand.'

'I told them I knew you. And what did they do? They laughed, said I was insane. Or a spy.'

'And they . . . did that to you?' he asked, staring in embarrassment at the bruise on her face. 'I give you my word I shall find them and—'

'Oh, no.' She waved down his bluster. 'I was given this inside the camp. You have no imagination, you English. One camp for the men, one for the women—you hadn't even thought about what you would do with the children. Everyone locked up together, a boiling pot of Nazis, Jews, Communists, musicians, artists—and animals. Perhaps the English think it is not possible for women to behave like beasts, let alone to be Nazis, but I assure you, it is. The Nazis run the place, of course, when the guards' backs are turned. They assumed I was one of them. When they found out I wasn't . . .'

She shrugged; it made her wince. Suddenly he suspected that beneath the crumpled suit lay other wounds.

'Mr Churchill, I gave up everything I had in life because I refused to become a Nazi. I turned my back on everyone I have ever loved, even my family. And to be told that, in spite of it all, I am as worthless as a Nazi, fills me with a bitterness that you cannot begin to comprehend.'

'But I have been searching for you for days, I had no idea . . .'

Her split lip stretched in an awkward, mocking smile. 'In Germany, too, they say the same thing. What has happened to all those who have disappeared? No one has any idea.'

'I am filled with remorse. This is not what I intended.'

'Locked up in camps, not because of anything we have done but because of what we were born. That should sound familiar to you. It's what you claim to be fighting.'

'There is a difference. I am not like Hitler.'

'You can look very much the same from behind barbed wire.'

'We did not want this war, yet we have to fight it. We must show ourselves as determined as any tyrant, but that does not make us tyrants. Yes, we fight fire with fire, Frau Mueller, but afterwards we shall douse the flames—with our tears, if necessary. You may not see so much difference in what we do, but search for it and you will find the difference in our hearts, and in what we hope for.'

She glared back in defiance, but this time in silence.

'In the past, Frau Mueller, you have always brought me inspiration. I have come to regard you as a friend. I am filled with pain at the humiliation I have caused and I beg you to believe that it was unwitting. I, too, was once a prisoner, during the war in South Africa. I know the sense of degradation it brings. Sadly I am no wizard Merlin. I cannot promise you that I can wave my hand and put right all the wrongs that have been done. But given time, I will try.' He sighed with great passion. 'Given time . . . You have heard of the disaster at Dunkirk?'

'They told us nothing in prison.'

'We have come close to suffering the greatest military defeat in our long history. Our losses in matériel have been enormous. We gave the best we had to our army, the first fruits of every factory in the land, and all that is now gone. How long we shall be able to continue the fight, I do not know.'

'You must carry on. You must!'

'We shall try. But the panzers may roll upon our beaches at any time, and we have nothing to fight them with but stones and our bare hands. There is a tightrope that stretches between survival and extinction, and at Dunkirk we slipped and almost fell. Our army has struggled back, leaving their dead on the other side. I do not know whether I shall ever be able to convince them to hold their heads up high once more and stare the enemy in the eye.'

'While a soldier lives, he can fight.'

'A soldier fights not just with weapons but with his heart. I fear the heart of the British army lies broken on a foreign beach.'

She stared at him intently for a moment before replying. 'They said you were mad. I think they were right.'

'What?'

She rose from her chair. 'Come with me. I shall show you where the heart of your army lies. Call Gruppenfuehrer Thompson outside,' she instructed. 'Tell him we need your car.'

'But where are we going?'

'To the place I have just come from.'

'The Isle of Man?' he spluttered, incredulous.

'No. Victoria Station. It will take only ten minutes. And I think you owe me ten minutes.'

He could not deny her. So, a little later, he found himself being ushered towards a wall of steam and the signs of commotion that were spilling across several crowded platforms.

At the windows of every train Churchill could see the men of the BEF. They were in transit, on their way from Dover to their many different destinations. Their hollowed cheeks told of exhaustion, their stubbled faces of days of despair, and all about their uniforms they carried the marks of their terrible failure. They had limped back home with bowed heads and broken muskets, expecting to receive nothing but condemnation. They had failed. Yet as the trains drew in to their platforms, they found themselves surrounded not by a fog of disapproval but by men waving their hats and women their handkerchiefs. As they leant from the windows it seemed that half of England wanted to shake their hands. The tea bars and sweet stands that stood beside the platforms were swamped by people trying to buy whatever they could to thrust at the men on the trains—tea, coffee, chocolate, oranges—until the stalls were stripped bare and there was nothing left to buy. Young girls reached up to kiss hollow cheeks and stubbled chins, and in their eyes Churchill could see nothing but pride.

Then they saw him. 'It's Churchill. It's Winston bloody Churchill!' he heard one of the soldiers cry, waving so frantically that it seemed he might fall from his train. Others began to rush towards Churchill, the soldiers cheered from their windows, and on all sides a cry went up—'Speech! Speech!'—but he couldn't. He was choking with emotion. Soon he was lost from sight in the middle of the crowd. All most of them could see was his hat, placed upon his cane and held high above their heads, waving in salute.

Eventually Thompson succeeded in dragging him away. Churchill made no attempt to hide his tears.

'So, Frau Mueller, what do you think now, eh?' he mumbled between profound sobs.

Her lips were sore but her eyes said it all. They smiled. 'I think all you English are mad.'

*   *   *

They found Churchill in the garden of Downing Street, rehearsing a speech. His head was down in concentration as he walked, script in hand, his arms waving like a conductor bringing in the full passion of the strings. He did not notice their intrusion for some time and they dared not disturb him. Eventually he looked up.

'Ah, Edward—Rab! My warriors from the Foreign Office. Thank you for answering my summons. I trust you don't object to the informal setting—in fact, it's probably essential. A quiet word with you both, without note-takers and eavesdroppers.' He linked arms with them both, guiding them around the garden as though they were his oldest friends. 'It's about our dear friend Joe. I thought I had better warn you. He won't be with us for much longer.'

'I'd heard nothing,' Halifax said, sounding a trifle affronted that he hadn't been the first to learn of any change.

'No, neither has Joe. Neither has President Roosevelt, for that matter.' Churchill was toying with them, and enjoying it. 'But I have a strong suspicion that the President will come round to my way of thinking as soon as he hears.'

Halifax couldn't resist the bait. 'Hears what?'

'Seems Joe's begun hunting with a new pack of hounds. Got himself involved with a woman, a

Clare Booth Luce. I suspect he's going to discover there's a heavy price to pay for his infidelity.'

'Husband on the warpath?'

'No, completely oblivious, poor chap. Or perhaps he is fortunate in his blindness—I find it difficult to take a strong stand on such questions. It has the advantage of enabling me to keep rather more of my Ministers in office than might otherwise be the case. But the lady in the middle of this matter is an extremely wealthy and influential woman, who is also a prime supporter of Mr Roosevelt's most powerful opponent in his re-election campaign later this year.'

'Ah.'

'Joe is apparently planning to come out against Roosevelt at a time most damaging to the President. I think we should stop him, don't you? Inform the President.'

'Interfere in American politics?'

'I look upon it more as saving the alliance.'

'They are not our allies.'

'Not yet, Edward, but I'm allowed to dream. So I thought I should warn you both, since you are Joe's main points of contact with this Government, that you should not confide in him too strongly. He is a man of not only loose morals but also loose lips. The seepage of information from his embassy has not ceased simply because we have apprehended Mr Tyler Kent. Joe is a man who has, I believe, limited prospects as his country's ambassador. To put no finer point on it, he is on his way out. Don't tie yourselves too tightly to him.'

Both Halifax and Butler knew this was more than an exchange of diplomatic guidance, it was personal. They were being warned off.

'How do we know all this?' Halifax enquired, anxious to learn of the source. Both he and Butler were desperately ransacking their memories for details of their own manifold indiscretions with Kennedy. Oh, the muttered disloyalties. The haggling over those bloody ships. Was all that known to Churchill, too?

'Let us simply say,' Churchill responded, 'that Joe is outspoken even at the best of moments, and even more so when drunk or climbing into someone else's bed.' He would give them no more. He wasn't going to let them know that Kennedy's phone was tapped and his cables read; he much preferred that they should be left to sweat in uncertainty.

'On another matter,' he said, deflecting them along a different path. 'This press nonsense about Guilty Men.'

'It has been tedious,' Halifax acknowledged, his understatement unable to disguise the hurt. The letters had been so cruel—and so many of them.

'I share your pain. It is nothing less than outrageous. Guilty Men, indeed! Heavens, if I were left surrounded only by those with whom I had agreed over the years, I should be the most lonely Prime Minister in all the annals of England's history. So I want you both to know that I have taken every step in my power to make it clear that I will not bow to their pressure to force you from government. You are most trusted colleagues. I have told everyone so. I hope that meets with your approval.'

'Thank you, Winston.'

And with that the trap was sprung. For Halifax was caught between shame and silence. If he resigned now, as he had threatened, it would look as if he'd been forced out by the press campaign. It would be an acknowledgement of his guilt—and, perhaps, his inappropriate relationship with the discredited Kennedy. Yet if he were to remain in government, as a gentleman he would have to do so on terms acceptable to Churchill. Which meant his silence.

'I hope I can ensure that it will stop,' Churchill continued. 'There is so much for us still to do—together!'

Of course he would ensure that it would stop. He'd started the whole bloody thing, through Bracken and Max Beaverbrook. One word, a snap of his fingers, and it would vanish like a morning mist.

The two visitors began to leave. He held them back. 'A moment's guidance from you both,' he requested. He consulted his script. 'Would you use a phrase like "we shall fight them on the beaches"? Is that appropriate? Fighting them on the beaches? If it came to that?'

'Why, yes, of course,' Halifax concurred. What else could he say? He knew Churchill had won their private battle. Butler knew it, too. They would fight, not talk.

And Churchill thought to himself what an aching pity it was, and would always be, that these two guilty men had not fought at Munich, while peace still had a chance.

'Thank you. But now I must prepare. This morning the soldiers of the BEF asked me for a speech. So I intend to bloody well give 'em one!'

*   *   *

Sometimes there is nothing left but words.

Churchill sat on the leather bench beside the Despatch Box, trying to judge the moment like a lover bringing a difficult message. The House of Commons was filled to its capacity, the benches crowded and galleries overflowing. Churchill closed his eyes. He could smell the mixture of fear and expectation that surged around him, could feel it inside himself. This place—this beast—had both borne him high and turned on him with extraordinary savagery; after nearly forty years it still had the capacity to twist his nerves in anticipation.

He opened one eye. Above him he could see journalists with their pencils poised, many peers from the other place—Halifax himself was squeezing into a seat. And Kennedy was in the Diplomatic Gallery, stretching forward for a better view. Damn him—as they all would be damned. But Joe would get there long before the rest.

And Ruth was watching, too. He'd asked her to come, had something he wanted her to hear.

The eye closed again. Time for a last thought, a final flickering of fear. Then he rose.

He cleared his throat. They fell silent.

He had a simple structure. Place deliverance before defeat. Pour honour on those who had given great sacrifice. And leave victims along the way.

He began by talking about disaster, about the German attack that had swept like a sharp scythe through all their plans and sliced almost unopposed through France. Ah, but that was before Calais . . .

'The British Brigadier was given an hour to

surrender. He spurned the offer, and four days of intense street fighting passed before silence reigned over Calais,' he reminded them. He looked around; the House was silent, too. 'Only thirty unwounded survivors were brought off by the navy, and we do not know the fate of their comrades.' His hands gripped the sides of the wooden Despatch Box, his voice muffled with emotion. 'Their sacrifice was not in vain.'

Slowly, he bowed towards Anthony Eden, sitting to his left, in honour of his regiment's sacrifice.

But it wasn't sufficient simply to honour the dead. Someone had to be held responsible for the dreams the dead had taken with them. Churchill needed a scapegoat, someone to blame. A Guilty Man. So all the better that he was foreign. Leopold of Belgium was, he told them, a man who before the war had turned his back on the Allies and who had refused them any assistance. He had hidden away in what proved to be a fatal neutrality. If only Leopold had been wiser, and braver—why, not only might Belgium have been saved but Poland, too! The entire disaster of the last few months might have been avoided! Of all the Guilty Men, he bore the most blame.

'At the last moment, when Belgium was already invaded, King Leopold called upon us to come to his aid'—ah, the sinner come to repentance—'and even at the last moment we came. He and his brave, efficient army guarded our left flank and thus kept open our only line of retreat to the sea.' But they all knew that was not the end of the story. Churchill filled his lungs like a judge about to pronounce the most terrible sentence.

'Suddenly, without prior consultation, with the

least possible notice,' Churchill thundered, 'he surrendered his army and exposed our whole flank and means of retreat!'

It was a devastating indictment. It was also utterly dishonest. Leopold had been telling them for days that his position was hopeless—had even written to the King, who had discussed it with Churchill himself. But leaders sometimes have a need to distract the eye and deflect the truth, to have a target that is set well away from themselves for others to fire at. There are many casualties in war, and Leopold would be one of the earliest and most eminent. He was condemned, and by the time historians had come upon the scene, the body would be rotten beyond resurrection.

Churchill did not enjoy it, yet he felt it had to be done. A victim left at the side of the road as a warning to others. Then he marched on—to Dunkirk.

'The enemy attacked on all sides with great strength and fierceness,' he told them. 'They sowed magnetic mines in the channels and seas; they sent repeated waves of hostile aircraft—sometimes more than a hundred strong in one formation—to cast their bombs upon the single pier that remained, and upon the sand dunes upon which the troops had their eyes for shelter. Their U-boats and their motor launches took their toll of the vast traffic which now began.'

A wife in the Diplomatic Gallery was quietly crying into her handkerchief while her husband sat stiff and resolute, as did every man in the Chamber.

'For four or five days an intense struggle reigned. All their armoured divisions, together with great masses of infantry and artillery, hurled themselves in vain upon the ever-narrowing, ever-contracting appendix within which the British and French armies fought.'

He looked up from his notes. They all knew the story; what mattered was how they would perceive it in the days and months to come. He had to raise their sights. It had been a disaster, certainly, a defeat in some measure, but it was also: 'A miracle of deliverance. Achieved by valour. By perseverance. By perfect discipline. By faultless service, by resource, by skill—by unconquerable fidelity.'

The words came pounding out like a barrage of artillery fire. A tremor began to run along the green leather benches. Many sitting there had found the old man's rhetoric too gaudy, almost glutinous, when he had used it in times of peace, but these were different times. They began to stir in new courage.

'We must be very careful not to assign to this deliverance the attributes of a victory. Wars are not won by evacuations,' he warned them. 'But there was a victory inside this deliverance. It was gained by the air force.' He turned, thumb in waistcoat pocket, towards the small civil servants' gallery behind the Speaker's Chair where Colville sat. Churchill had been tormented by his young assistant's story of how the soldiers returning from Dunkirk had jeered and called the airmen cowards. Englishman set against Englishman. He had to finish that, otherwise they could never win.

'Many of our soldiers coming back have not seen the air force at work. They saw only the German bombers which escaped its protective attack. They underrate its achievements. I have heard much talk of this; that is why I go out of my way to say this. I will tell you about it.' He recounted for them a battle against overwhelming odds, of desperate Luftwaffe attacks, of British heroism, of astounding achievements in the air over France, fighting on even when they had run out of bullets, forcing enemy aircraft into the sea. And the rhetorical flourishes grew ever more extravagant as he paid tribute to the pilots of the RAF.

'The Knights of the Round Table, the Crusaders, all fall back into the distant past as these young men go forth every morn to guard their native land and all that we stand for, holding in their hands these instruments of colossal and shattering power. It might be said of them that: "Every morn brought forth a noble chance, and every chance brought forth a noble knight." They deserve our gratitude.'

Growls of agreement began to swirl through the benches and along the galleries above. The tearful woman had put away her handkerchief.

'Nevertheless, our thankfulness at the escape of our army and so many men, whose loved ones have passed through an agonizing week, must not blind us to the fact that what has happened in France and Belgium is a colossal military disaster.' He had inspired them with tales of valour, but they couldn't run away from the truth—and he would not let them, for otherwise they could never resist what he feared lay ahead.

'We must expect another blow to be struck almost immediately at us. We are told that Herr Hitler has a plan for invading the British Isles.' They all knew it; there was no point in denying it. 'This has often been thought of before. When

Napoleon lay at Boulogne for a year with his flat-bottomed boats and his Grand Army, he was told by someone: "There are bitter weeds in England."' Churchill gazed around the Chamber, tying every one of them in. 'There are certainly a great many more of them since the British Expeditionary Force returned.'

How they embraced these words. The old man was taunting Hitler, defying him with humour. The lady in the gallery clapped her hands in gentle, silent applause.

Churchill's eye ran along the galleries, searching for Ruth. Oh, if only he had a thousand Ruths then victory would be theirs! Yet, with a thousand Ruths, how impossibly peaceless a man's life would become.

'We have found it necessary to take measures of increasing stringency against enemy aliens,' he declared, staring at her; Ruth stared back.

'I know there are a great many people affected by the orders which we have made who are the passionate enemies of Nazi Germany. I am very sorry for them. But we cannot, at the present time and under the present stress, draw all the distinctions which we should like to do.' But trust me, I'm trying, he was saying. 'If parachute landings were attempted and fierce fighting followed, these unfortunate people would be far better out of the way, for their own sakes as well as for ours.'

She shook her head slowly. She understood, but she would never agree. He marched on. And as he did so, he sensed every man and woman in the House marching with him, and behind them many millions more, ready to face the invasion and whatever else lay ahead.

'We are assured that novel methods will be adopted—and when we see the originality of malice and the ingenuity of aggression which our enemy displays, we may certainly prepare ourselves for every kind of novel stratagem and every kind of brutal and treacherous manoeuvre.'

Brutality and treachery. That is what they faced. Yet round him the faces were filled with hope and belief. Belief in him.

'I have, myself, full confidence that if all do their duty, if nothing is neglected, we shall prove ourselves once again able to defend our island home, to ride out the storm of war, and to outlive the menace of tyranny—if necessary for years, and if necessary alone. At any rate, that is what we are going to try to do. That is the resolve of His Majesty's Government—every man of them.' He glanced up to where Halifax was sitting, his body leaning forward, like a great derrick ready for its work. Their eyes met. Stiffly, as though aged in rust, the derrick bowed a little lower. Halifax was nodding his acceptance. But he had to take his Foreign Secretary further—had to take them all further—beyond any shred of ambiguity and obfuscation to a place where only rock-hard certainties prevailed.

'Even though large tracts of Europe and many old and famous states have fallen or may fall into the grip of the Gestapo and all the odious apparatus of Nazi rule, we shall not flag or fail. We shall go on to the end.'

His eyes rose from his triple-spaced script; he no longer needed it. These words came from so deep within Churchill that he had only to close his eyes and they were there. They were the air he breathed, the reason he still lived.

His fist began pounding the Despatch Box with passion, his voice rising. 'We shall fight in France. We shall fight on the seas and oceans. We shall fight with growing confidence and growing strength in the air. We shall defend our island—whatever the cost may be.'

Sometimes there is nothing left but words, but these weren't just words, they were weapons, a great arsenal he had assembled that would do battle when the bullets were all spent.

'We shall fight on the beaches. We shall fight on the landing grounds. We shall fight in the fields and in the streets. We shall fight in the hills. We shall never surrender!'

Defiance. Impetuous, unreasonable, unsophisticated, unflinching defiance, raw and uncomplicated. Like a child kicking a straw boater to pieces.

Several Members were openly in tears as he continued. 'And even if—which I do not for a moment believe—this island or a large part of it were subjugated and starving, then our Empire beyond the seas, armed and guarded by the British fleet, would carry on the struggle, until, in God's good time, the New World, with all its power and might, steps forth to the rescue and the liberation of the Old.'

He knew he and his countrymen could not win this war, not on their own—but so long as Britain and its Empire remained in the war, neither could Hitler. That would have to be enough. The rotten shell of the world Churchill had grown up in was breaking apart, yet from it might fall a seed that, in time, would grow to glorious victory.

*  *  *

When at last the press of people had allowed him to escape and to return to his rooms at the Admiralty, he found her already there, staring up at the portrait, examining the rip in the canvas. She had guessed.

'Like a cancer, this family thing,' she said. 'Clings; you can't get rid of it.'

He came to stand beside her, staring up at the face. 'While I was waiting to begin the speech, I closed my eyes so that I might prepare myself, dig down deep inside. And for the first time in my career, he wasn't there. No longer watching, disapproving.'

'I doubt that he ever truly disapproved.' She pointed at the prominent eyes of the portrait. 'That's not disapproval you can see, it's discomfort—discomfort at the thought that his son would grow up to be so much stronger and more capable than he was. Like all sons you would strip away his sense of immortality. But—don't you understand?—that's precisely what he wanted, to see his own son grow taller than the rest. You are a silly man, Mr Churchill, but then so are you all—all of you—silly men.'

'I hadn't wanted to admit it before, but part of me hates him.'

'Ah, the enemy within.'

'Not any longer, I think.'

'He will always be your father.'

'In truth, not much of one.'

'But that is how he will be remembered, not as a

politician or a statesman, but as a father. Of a great man.'

Churchill looked at her, startled.

'Oh, don't let it go to your head, Mr Churchill,' she smiled, gently mocking, 'Hitler makes speeches, too. But not quite like that one.'

'Thank you.'

A frown crossed her brow. She took a small step back and studied him, as though trying to peer deep inside. 'I'm not sure whether you realize, Mr Churchill, what you have done.'

'Neither am I,' he responded uncertainly, once again finding himself several paces behind her.

'In three and a half weeks, you have beaten Hitler.'

'Beaten him?'

'Oh, he may have won this latest battle but, because of you, he has lost control. You have shown him that unless he is able to defeat you here in these islands, he can never stop this war he has started. There will be no deals, no armistices, no accords, nothing but total victory or his own destruction. You have left him with no other choice. The radio in Berlin talks about the war being over by the end of the summer.' She shook her head. 'His armies might march all the way to the Great Wall of China and it would make no difference. He has lost control of this war. In order to stop it, Hitler will have to go on conquering until there is no one left to conquer, and not even the Almighty has managed that.'

'Do you think he understands all this?'

'Not unless he understands you.'

He took her hand—it seemed so frail, so vulnerable—raised it to his lips and kissed it with great tenderness. 'Then it is my good fortune that you are at my side and not at his. I owe you a debt more profound than I can express.'

'You owe me nothing other than his destruction.'

She picked up her handbag, preparing to leave.

'What will you do?' Churchill asked.

'I shall wait for you to win this war. Then I shall try to find my son and give him a decent burial. He's one of them, you see, a Nazi. Betrayed his father, then he betrayed me.'

'I am so sorry, I never . . .' His voice trailed away in embarrassment. He never knew, because he had never asked.

'Your war will probably be the end of him, Mr Churchill. That is as it must be. But in spite of it all, he is my son. Family. I think you understand.'

She was at the door. 'Something has been bothering me. How did you do it, persuade Herr Halifax to give you his support?'

Churchill's shoulders stiffened in unease. 'He doesn't realize it, but I lied to him,' he growled defiantly. 'Then I threatened him.'

'Just as I thought. Very much like that other bloody man, then.'

A few feet away on the other side of the door, Colville jumped in alarm. He heard something he had never heard before. Winston Churchill was roaring with laughter.

* * *

It had taken Don several days to recover from his ordeal. The water had been so overwhelming, his lungs so weak, his pain so profound.

Their fingertips had brushed, then he was gone.

After a journey of many troubles their lives had been brought together, only to fly past each other once more and disappear into the darkness. Don had fought against it with every remaining crumb of resistance he could gather, had swum and searched and dived beneath the black waters of the Channel until his strength was exhausted, and even then he had carried on, until he no longer knew where the margins of sea and night were joined.

The crew of one of the search ships had discovered Don when they had almost given up hope. He was smothered with the oil through which he had swum, slumped across a hatch cover that had been ripped from one of the wrecks. Fortune had at last thrown in with him; he could so easily have been missed in the profound gloom—as many others had been during previous nights. For several days he lay recovering in a bed at the military hospital in Crookham. It was where he had completed his nursing training, but he didn't recognize it; he could no longer connect with this neat world of calm and order. As the pollution was drained from his body it was replaced with a kaleidoscope of memories that chased each other around his mind, never settling, tormenting him. Every time he turned in his bed, every time he woke, every time he closed his eyes and tried to sleep, he saw his father, but he could not touch him. His body healed, but the pain didn't.

A nurse with dark, understanding eyes telephoned the vicarage, but there was no reply. Neighbours told her the place was empty, had been silent for days. So he asked the military authorities if there had been any sign of a Henry Chichester, but the clerk shook his head; things were so fouled up that even Don wasn't on their evacuation records. It would take weeks to sort out the confusion. There was no sign of his father. Time had run out on their miracle of deliverance from Dunkirk.

When at last he was able to leave the hospital, he had told the nurse, Kathy, that he was going to Dover.

'Why Dover?'

'I have nowhere else to go.'

She had asked to come with him.

'As a nurse?'

'As a friend. I think you will need a friend in Dover.'

They walked from the railway station, up the hill towards St-Ignatius-without-the-Walls. Strangers raised their caps as they saw his uniform and knew from the darkness around his eyes where he had come from.

It was the gentlest time of the year in Dover. The branches hung low with fresh life and a warm breeze carried with it the scent of honeysuckle and salt. But for Don it was a walk through his wasted childhood, and he found his footsteps growing heavier as he dragged behind him the regrets he knew would be with him whenever he thought of his father.

He felt very old, as though much of his life was already past, and what was left to him would be spent looking back. He was glad that Kathy's arm was linked through his in support.

'You had that time with him, on the beach,' she reminded him.

But it wasn't enough, a few moments snatched from a lifetime of neglect.

'Your father would have understood,' she said. 'That's why he was there on the beach. For you.'

'I know,' he replied. 'I as good as killed him.'

'No, that's not true. Your father knew what he was doing. Do you think for one moment that if he had to make that same choice again, he would have decided differently?'

Don didn't reply. He knew she was right, yet it didn't make the regrets disappear or the guilt go away.

'If only I could have told him . . .'

'What? That you were sorry? That you loved him? I think he knew that.'

'But what would I give for the chance to have told him so.'

She squeezed his arm more tightly, not as a nurse, as a friend. They were walking through the churchyard. Someone had been trimming the grass and the air was rich with its sweetness. They passed the old timbered porch—his father's handwritten notices were still hanging there, with their marriage banns and brass-cleaning rosters, just as they had always been, ever since he could remember. The light was beginning to fade, the sea washing gently upon the shore, lying to him, whispering that nothing had changed since last he was here.

They walked around the laurel bush that guarded the gravel path leading to the front door of the vicarage. There was a light on in the kitchen and through the open window came the sound of singing. It was a voice Don thought he recognized, from long ago.

# EPILOGUE

The day after the last troops were evacuated from Dunkirk, the weather changed. Great rollers came crashing up the beaches that would have rendered any further evacuation impossible, but by that time the soldiers of the BEF, along with 123,000 Frenchmen, had already been brought to safety. Winston Churchill had escaped, too.

Four years later almost to the day, Churchill's army was back, clambering up new French beaches alongside their American and Canadian Allies in the extraordinary reinvasion of Europe known as D-Day.

Just as he had done at Dunkirk, Vice Admiral Bertram Ramsay was to play a crucial role in those events on D-Day as Commander-in-Chief of the Allied naval forces. Sadly, he did not live to see the fulfilment of his work. He was killed in an air crash in France shortly before the war's end. He is buried in France, the country he did so much to liberate.

Jock Colville stayed with Churchill, with short absences for service in his beloved RAF. He began as a critic and turned ardent acolyte, but he always kept a sharp eye about him and provided us with a magnificent diary of the events he witnessed at Churchill's side. Chips Channon, too, left a wonderful diary, so rich with beautifully crafted observations on the manners and morals of his time that they more than made up for the total inconsequence of his parliamentary career.

Yet there was a price to be paid for all the mistrust and disagreements that had taken place.

Halifax was a man of immense experience but also of many sides—Channon wrote of 'his high principles, his engaging charm and grand manner—his eel-like qualities and, above all, his sublime treachery which is never deliberate'. And he was not a Churchillian. Five months later, and much against his will, he was shipped off to become Britain's ambassador to the United States. He served in that role throughout the war, and most effectively.

In the same month the American ambassador, Joe Kennedy, was also shipped back home, but there were no new glories awaiting him. Roosevelt knew of his treachery, and as soon as the presidential elections were completed, Kennedy was thrown overboard like scraps from a ship's kitchen.

Rab Butler also remained a controversial figure. Rumours of disloyalty continued to swirl around him, yet Churchill kept him in his Government. Perhaps it wasn't simply a matter of knowing your enemy, but also knowing where he could be found. Many years later, when Butler repeatedly put himself forward as a candidate for the leadership of the Conservative Party, Churchill threw his irresistible weight against him. Revenge was eaten with a long spoon.

Others paid a far heavier price. André Gershell, the brave but forlorn Mayor of Calais, died in a concentration camp, and Brigadier Nicholson, the gallant defender of that town, died in a prisoner-of-war camp, some said of a broken heart.

No one knew precisely how many of the 3800 Allied soldiers involved in the defence of Calais were killed. Many bodies were buried in the rubble and never recovered. There were no casualty returns, no figures for the number of wounded. Those who survived went into captivity for five hopeless years, and came back to find their sacrifice largely forgotten alongside the miracle of Dunkirk.

Blame for the wretched fate of the BEF should have been shared almost universally, yet one man was selected to shoulder the responsibility almost alone—its commander, Viscount Gort. His decision to abandon the thrust south and his insistence that the BEF should fall back on Dunkirk saved not only the British army, it also saved Churchill. But neither the army nor Churchill displayed much gratitude. Gort was never again given a fighting command.

Churchill was not always fair. He was also frequently and abominably rude. A few days after the evacuation of Dunkirk had been completed, his beloved wife Clementine wrote him an extraordinary letter. 'My Darling, I hope you will forgive me if I tell you something I feel you ought to know,' it began. 'There is a danger of you being generally disliked by your colleagues & subordinates because of your rough sarcastic & over-bearing manner . . . My Darling Winston—I must confess that I have noticed a deterioration in your manner; & you are not as kind as you used to be.' It was ferocious criticism from one who loved him so much.

Bad manners—and appalling memory. In his history of the war, Churchill gave his own version of the events of this period. 'Future generations may deem it noteworthy that the supreme question of whether we should fight on alone never found a place upon the War Cabinet agenda,' he wrote. 'It was taken for granted and as a matter of course by these men of all parties in the State, and we were much too busy to waste time upon such unreal, academic issues.'

Churchill, like so many other statesmen, preferred to be remembered in noble words; their actions were rarely as straightforward or so pure.

And Ruth Mueller? She disappeared once more, and this time her whereabouts were not discovered. Pimlico library, where she loved to spend her time, was bombed in the Blitz that began a few weeks later, and there were reports that an unidentified body was found beneath the rubble. It seems probable that it was Ruth.

But the portrait of Lord Randolph Churchill did survive. You can see it for yourself, still with its ripped canvas, in Churchill's studio at his home in Chartwell.

# ACKNOWLEDGEMENTS

I am often asked about the difference between history and drama, as though there is some clear dividing line. There is not. Written history is inevitably only a fragment of any story and can never be complete, and it's surprising how many histories contain desperate errors of omission or simple errors of fact. As I have mentioned in the Epilogue, even Churchill's own version of history could at times be outrageously loose.

Even those histories that are constructed as tightly as possible around 'the facts' still leave room for the sort of speculation about motives and emotions that are such an important component in trying to understand not only what happened, but why something happened.

I'm not trying to pretend that *Never Surrender* is in some way 'the truth'. It is a work of fiction and I have taken all the dramatic liberties required to construct what I hope is an enjoyable read. However, within those constraints I have struggled hard to stay as close as I could to the established events of the time as I understand them. My hope is that this may help readers understand the events of those few tumultuous weeks a little better, and remind them that behind every great event there is usually a man or a woman who is going through some sort of personal crisis. Many readers of *Winston's War* have told me that the novel encouraged them to read more deeply through the histories of that period in order to make up their own minds about the personalities and events. If

*Never Surrender* has the same result, I couldn't be happier.

I suppose this is a convoluted way of getting round to thanking those who have helped me, while at the same time excusing them from any liability for the result. So I shall start by thanking Mrs Joanna Grant Peterkin, the headmistress of St George's School, Ascot, and her staff who so kindly allowed me to trawl through their archives and wander around Churchill's first school. I'm delighted to say that the school has changed beyond recognition since his time, and the happy and welcoming atmosphere the modern visitor encounters bears no resemblance to the harsh Victorian realities of young Winston's day. I am also indebted to two old friends, the Reverend Robert Webb (himself one of my earliest teachers) and the Reverend David Henderson, both of whom gave me much food for thought while I was constructing the character of Henry Chichester. Whatever limited success I've had in depicting his road to salvation is largely due to them. David Jolliffe, who was until recently Director General Army Medical Services, kindly gave me an introduction to the Army Medical Services Museum at Keogh Barracks and also the Royal Logistic Corps Museum at Deepcut, both of which gave of their time and expertise most freely, while Dr Robert Lefever as always has illuminated the darkness surrounding the various medical mysteries I continue to stumble across. I am also grateful to The Random House Group Ltd for permission to reprint extracts from *This Is Berlin* by William L. Shirer, published by Hutchinson/Arrow.

It would perhaps seem strange and even a little

pretentious to offer a full bibliography of the books I have consulted in preparing a novel, but three in particular I found inspirational and commend to anyone wishing to dig a little deeper. The first is *Five Days in London*, written by John Lukacs, who was an old colleague of mine from my days as a doctoral student in America; the second is *Defying Hitler* by Sebastian Haffner. The final book I wish to mention is entitled *Flames of Calais*, written by Airey Neave. The story of the defenders of Calais has been overwhelmed by the events that took place in and around Dunkirk a few days later, and I was spellbound to read Airey's account. He was captured at Calais, escaped from the notorious prisoner-of-war camp at Colditz Castle, was one of the prosecution team at the Nuremberg Trials and eventually became a senior Member of Parliament who masterminded Margaret Thatcher's successful campaign for the leadership of the Conservative Party. That was when I first knew him. I remember an afternoon in early 1979 when I sat with him on a sofa and listened to him talk about his many plans for the future. The following day he was murdered by the IRA. Until I read his book on Calais, I never realized quite what an extraordinary man he was.

And, finally, I must thank the boys—William, Michael, Alexander and Harry. They sat patiently, and usually noiselessly, outside my door during the intensive months spent writing this book. When I heard any sound at all, it was usually their laughter. It made it all worthwhile.

MICHAEL DOBBS
Hanging Langford, July 2003.